THE OBSIDIAN THRONE

THE OBSIDIAN THRONE

ROWAN WRIGHT

All characters in this book are fictional. Any resemblance to persons living or dead, events, or locales is purely coincidental.

Paperback ISBN 978-1-7365735-0-1
Ebook ISBN 978-1-7365735-1-8

Published by Crown & Dagger Press
Rowan K. Wright
rowan.k.wright@gmail.com
instagram.com/authorrowanwright

For my Dad.

I wish you could have seen

this book come into the world.

1

"I'm not so sure about this, Em."

The pig in my arms lets out a little squeal and struggles violently. He'd gone willingly enough when I coaxed him into my car earlier that night, but now he is ready to escape the confines of the backseat. I scratch his bristly chin to calm him down, and he settles his bulk against me, squeezing the air out of my lungs.

"What do you mean?" I ask a bit breathlessly.

Hannah, my best friend and reluctant accomplice, pulls on her braid with the hand that isn't gripping the steering wheel—a nervous habit. "Are you sure this is a good idea?"

I snort. "Are you kidding me? This is a terrible idea."

"Em..."

"Oh, lighten up. I was only joking. This is the best idea I've had in ages."

She groans. "How do I let you talk me into things like this?"

"You're a sucker for my puppy dog eyes. Now, enough talking. Let's get Bacon outside."

Hannah rolls her eyes and shakes her head, but she unbuckles her seatbelt and exits the driver's seat. She shakes her head again when she opens the door to the backseat and sees the pig in all his glutinous glory. Despite her reluctance, Han still helps me maneuver the large black and white pig out of the car and even holds him still while I slip a lead rope around his fat neck.

I glance at my phone. 11:57pm. Time to get going. A large crow lands on a nearby branch and squawks what sounds like a warning.

"Come on, Bacon," I coo, ignoring the bird as it caws once more. "Come on, piggy piggy."

Before he can dash away and drag me down the quiet suburban street, I yank a bag of table scraps out of the front pocket of my black hoodie. Bacon's round snout picks up the scent of the limp lettuce and mushy tomatoes before I can even undo the knot. "That's it, boy. Follow me!"

I navigate backwards down the street, careful not to collide into any of the bumper-to-bumper cars parked along the road. Hannah follows hesitantly, her head constantly whipping to look over her shoulder. There's no one around, of course. This late at night, most of the well-to-do families that fill the cookie-cutter houses are sound asleep in their beds.

After a block, we can hear the music from the party. The melody seeps out of the open windows and into the crisp autumn air, the bass pumping loud enough to be felt in my bones. As we approach the house, I take a sharp left and cut down a narrow alley. I stop just outside of the gate in the tall wooden fence. Bacon trots up to me as I crouch down and attempts to steal the bag of scraps away. He snorts in annoyance, but the music on the other side of the fence is much too loud for anyone but us to hear him.

I pat his round head. "Alright, Bacon. I'm counting on you to make this work. Okay, boy?"

Hannah squats next to me, her fingers plucking at the black knit hat I loaned her. We had dressed for the occasion in all black. We even smeared black paint under our eyes. What's the point of going on a covert mission if you don't look the part?

"I wish you'd quit calling him that," she insists as she leans against the fence.

"It's his name! What else should I call him?"

"I don't know. Pig, maybe?"

I shoot a sideways glance at her as I ruffle Bacon's ears. "How original, Han."

"Well, at least I'm not calling him *something we enjoy eating!*" she hisses.

"I thought about naming him Broccoli, but that just didn't sound right."

Her grimace deepens as my smile grows.

The end of my braid slips out of my own hat as I turn to look at her. I poke my purple ends back into the knitted fabric. "Okay, you remember the plan, right?"

My best friend jumps as a cackle of laughter erupts just behind us. You'd think we were about to pull off an elaborate bank heist instead of a harmless prank. "You mean the plan you came up with twenty minutes ago when you climbed into my window wearing your ninja suit?"

"Yeah, that one."

Hannah sighs. "I open the gate. You let the pig in. I close the gate. We bail."

"Well done, Kemosabe. Let's do this."

I unknot the rope and plant a loud kiss on Bacon's furrowed brow while Hannah stands and fiddles with the latch on the gate.

She finally slides it out of place and wrenches it open. The dark alleyway is instantly flooded with lights. If I thought the music was loud before, I was wrong. As my eyes adjust, I see our classmates and other lowerclassmen lounging around the glowing pool, standing in clusters drinking from red plastic cups and grinding on one another near where a DJ spins out some "sick" beats. The musician rapping over the speakers serenades the crowd with lyrics about big booty hoes.

It doesn't matter to Hannah that we were the only two people in the entire senior class that didn't get invited. She doesn't care that, if not for me, she'd be spending Saturday night binge watching another series on Netflix.

To be honest, I don't really care either. I have never been popular, nor have I ever wanted to be. I'd normally be hours deep in a true crime documentary on a Saturday night. However, I tend to take offense when a person goes out of their way to personally humiliate my best friend and me in front of the whole school.

So, I convinced Hannah to come with me tonight. I snuck into her bedroom and somehow sweet talked her back out into the night and into my car where a large potbelly pig waited for us in the back seat. She's used to my shenanigans by now, so I didn't even have to explain where I got the pig. I convinced her that we would go to Bianca Peterson's house, play my little joke in which we would unleash Bacon into Bianca's yard and make a dash for it, and then go back to her place to watch the season finale of the newest superhero spinoff.

When Bianca sashayed up to our lunch table in the middle of lunch yesterday, the entire cafeteria quieted down. Every eye followed her as she stopped next to us and flashed a chemically brightened smile.

"I'm having a party tomorrow," she announced, loud enough for all of the captive audience to hear. She took two invitations from her designer bag and slid them across the table to us. I stared at mine as if it were cow patty rather than a piece of paper. Hannah, on the other hand, snatched hers up and promised to come in a spill of jumbled 'thank yous' and 'yeses.'

It's only because she lifted up the card that I was able to see the back. In bold letters, the card stated that "Everyone is invited, EXCEPT for pigs!" And below that were two ugly pigs with Hannah's face and my face crudely Photoshopped onto their fat necks.

I ripped the card out of Hannah's hand, but not before the entire cafeteria erupted in laughter.

So, even though I told Hannah I would release Bacon and let him do his damage on his own, in reality, I had a different plan.

The lights and the sudden burst of sound startles Bacon, and he lets out a squeal that cuts through the music better than I could have ever hoped for.

The DJ kills the music with the push of a button, and all eyes swivel to land on me.

Bianca emerges from a crowd of admirers and suck-ups. "Ember?" she asks, disbelief heavy in her voice.

"Hope you don't mind us crashing your party," I reply.

She sneers. "You weren't invited, Ember. Now leave or I will have my father arrest you for trespassing. He's a police officer, you know."

I take a squishy tomato from the pocket of my hoodie and toss it before catching it again. "Really? I thought the invitation said pigs weren't invited?"

It takes a moment for the insult to hit home, just long enough for me to launch the squishy tomato across the yard and into Bianca's shocked face.

I slap Bacon's fat backside, and the shocked crowd audibly gasps. The pig darts forward, his little black eyes glued to the tomato dripping off of Bianca's chin onto the cleavage she miraculously managed to squeeze together with her push up bikini top. Bacon slams into her legs, sending her flying into the pool.

"*Ember!*" Hannah hisses as I whoop and pump my fist in the air. Quickly, I pull down my hoodie to hide the strip of skin that became visible when I jumped. The last thing I need is for my classmates to see my odd birthmark.

Bianca emerges from the pool with an enraged shriek. Black rivers of mascara flow down her cheeks as she screams, "DADDY!"

Jason Paulson's voice interrupts my celebration. "You are so screwed, Ashworth."

I turn to face him and tilt my head to look him in the face. He's Bianca's latest flame, even though everyone knows they cheat on each other every other weekend.

With the hand not curled around a solo cup filled to the brim with some alcoholic concoction, he takes the end of my braid that has escaped once again and twirls it through his fingers. "But I gotta admit, you have balls. Why don't you text me sometime, and we can get together—"

"Not in this lifetime or any other, Paulson."

He shrugs and takes a sip of his drink nonchalantly, as if I didn't just burst his ego. "Whatever. I don't sleep with pigs anyway."

Before he can even see it coming, I ram the palm of my hand into the bottom of his cup. Alcohol and sticky soda shoot into his nostrils and eyes, leaving him gasping and coughing. "Yeah, well, neither do I."

"Ember!" Hannah pleads.

I look at Han and then in the direction of where she's pointing. A bald, middle-aged man wraps a robe around his absurdly hairy beer belly as he stumbles through the French doors.

"She ruined my party!" Bianca whines from where two boys are pulling her from the pool. "Arrest her, Daddy!"

If she calls him 'Daddy' one more time, I might barf. After flipping Jason the bird, I sprint for Hannah and the exit.

"Stop!" Bianca's father commands.

Hannah, two steps ahead of me, actually freezes and raises her arms in the air.

"He didn't say Simon says, Han! Keep going!" I grab her arm and yank her after me down the alley.

"He's a policeman!" she protests.

"And judging by his physique, not nearly as fast as us. Keep running!"

"Hannah...Hannah Banana?"

The streetlights outside lend fleeting rays of light that reveal Hannah's stony face.

I flick on the blinker and turn down her street.

"Han, I'm sorry."

She twists in the front seat to glare at me. "That's it? Sorry?"

"I'm *really* sorry?"

Hannah sighs. "Em, we could have gotten in really big trouble tonight."

I bite my lip and give her my best innocent smile. "But we didn't."

"But we could have. That's the point, Ember. Do you even realize how hard I've worked to get into Stanford? How many hours I've studied and how many scholarship applications I've filled out?"

The security light screwed to Hannah's house flickers to life as I pull into her driveway. I am very aware of how hard my best friend has worked to get into the school of her dreams. From the day I met her, she's told me how it's her dream to go to Stanford. It's where Erick, her brother, is currently going. It's where her father went, and where his father went, and where his father went...

Hannah's family has a hallway in their house that is essentially a shrine to the Ivy League school. Pictures of her family's accomplishments at the school adorned the walls. Framed diplomas and certificates hang on nails strategically placed where the light hits them just so. They even left a section bare for where they will place Hannah's Bachelor's degree. And her Master's. And her PhD.

"Ember, I love you, but I can't risk my future like that again for some petty act of revenge."

"It wasn't petty," I pout.

She sighs again. "Bye, Em. I'll see you at school on Monday."

And with that, she unbuckles herself and exits my car. I watch her type in the security code and duck under the garage door as it lifts. She punches another code in at the kitchen door and the garage door reverses, effectively creating a wall that seems to be made of more than metal between us.

As soon as the security light winks out, the passenger side door opens. Startled, I let out a colorful curse. But it's just Lucien, my ever-vigilant and ever-annoying Guardian. My heart picks up its pace, and I take a deep breath as he slides into the seat beside me. The underlying smell of leather and soap that follows Lucien everywhere fills the small space of my car. I grip the steering wheel so tightly that my knuckles turn white and steel myself for the lecture that's coming in three, two, one...

He opens his mouth to say something, but I stop him with a raised hand. I can barely see him in the dim light of the cloudless night, but I know the scowl he wears at all times is firmly in place and aimed directly at me.

"I really don't want to hear it, Luce."

I throw the Camry into reverse and navigate down the driveway.

Lucien's full lips press into a thin line before he decides he can't keep quiet. "That was rather reckless, Ember."

"It was just a prank!"

"A prank that could have gotten you and Miss Abernathy in trouble."

I shoot him a sour look. "You sound like Hannah. Really, if anyone should be worried, it should be Mr. Peterson. He's the one that's allowing scores of underage minors to drink alcohol on his property."

"Even so...I had to inform your father of your careless actions."

I stomp on the brakes a little harder than I mean to as we pull up to a stop sign. "Lucien! Please tell me you didn't."

"Too late."

With a groan, I lean over the console and punch Lucien's arm several times. "You ass! Dad's going to be pissed."

"Maybe you should think about that the next time you want to go on one of your little adventures," he replies as he smooths the fabric of his shirtsleeve where I assaulted him. Heaven forbid he get a wrinkle.

"Ugh. You're such a stick in the mud."

"It's my duty."

"'*It's my duty*,'" I echo in a mocking tone.

While Hannah lives on the wealthier side of Seattle with Bianca, our house sits in a tidy, little cul-de-sac where young couples with young children come to live mediocre lives. Father thought that a house here would bring about the least suspicion even though he had the connections and the funds to buy a house twice the size of Bianca's.

Lucien continues to try to talk to me as I pull into our driveway and kill the engine, and I continue to ignore him as I get out and sulk up the walkway to shove the key into the lock. I'm about to throw open the door and stomp off to my bedroom to watch cat videos until my eyes bleed when Lucien's hand wraps around my upper arm. Heat floods my face as he pulls me closer to him.

Lucien's dark brows knit together in the shadows of the porch. Subtly, he raises his head and smells the air. Caution permeates each smooth plane of his face as his grip on me tightens. A warning.

"We aren't alone," he tells me in a hushed voice.

I mimic his actions and wrinkle my nose as the familiar smell filters into my nostrils.

Sulfur.

Lucien carefully pushes past me into the foyer. He instructs me to stay on the porch, but I ignore his directions and follow him as he heads down the hall to the kitchen. Silver glints in Lucien's hand. A knife? Where the hell did he get a knife? Before we turn the corner, I hear the bottles and jars of condiments stored in the door of the fridge clink together.

Together, we step into the kitchen, and I flip on the light to reveal a seven-foot-tall demon with his head deep inside our refrigerator.

The demon hits his head on the edge of the freezer door when the light startles him. He straightens to his full height with a low growl and swivels to face us. The snarl on his snout quickly disappears when he spots me standing there with my arms crossed over my chest.

"Balthasar." I don't bother with polite salutations.

"Princess." He bows low. The curved horns protruding from the side of his black head threaten to tangle with the ceiling fan, but he deftly maneuvers around the blades. "His Majesty wishes to see you directly," he informs me in a voice that sounds less like a human and more like glass being crushed under the heel of a boot.

I narrow my eyes at Lucien before turning back to the demon. "It can't wait until morning?"

Balthasar slowly blinks his glowing red eyes. "'Fraid not, Princess."

"Dammit," I mumble. "This is not how I envisioned spending my Saturday night."

Knowing the drill, Balthasar graciously moves aside the rolling kitchen island to reveal the portal symbol carved into the hardwood floor. I step inside the circle without waiting for Lucien to join me. It's his fault I'm in trouble, after all.

I don't waste time once I'm in the portal circle. With a flash, I leave the human world.

I'd really rather not, but my father is expecting me, and it's never wise to keep the Lord of the Underworld waiting.

2

I cough as I come out on the other side of the portal, and my nose wrinkles as the stink of the Underworld burns my nostrils. Sulfur. It's not a smell that one ever truly grows accustomed to. I make a mental note to do a load of laundry when I got back. Over the years, I've learned that not throwing the clothes I wore to the Underworld directly in the washer left them smelling like a demon's backside for weeks.

Balthasar appears next to me without a sound, and we stand quietly next to each other for a few moments on the ledge that overlooks my father's domain.

I suppose most people picture a dark or fiery pit in the ground set to the background music of tortured souls, but they'd be wrong. Of course, I grew up here so I can't picture the Underworld as anything except for the way it is.

In reality, the Underworld actually reminds me of a giant cave that just so happens to house a federal prison. The Pen sprawls below us, every inch visible from our vantage point on the ledge. Built of white stone, the compound rises six stories in the air and spans nearly the entire expanse of the underground cave. The roof of the building stops just inches below the ten foot stalactites dangling from the ceiling. Every decade or so, someone has to go up and chisel off the tips of the cave teeth so they don't get too long.

The denizens of the Underworld are placed in the compound according to their A.C.I.D. score: Aggression, Cooperation, Intelligence, and Deadliness. The ones with the worse scores are sent to the upper levels, while the less dangerous ones are quartered closer to ground level.

And then, if a monster shows particularly good behavior, they can fill out an application to return to the Surface or they can work for my father. Many Underworlders live relatively normal lives up on the Surface. Some, like Nessie and members of the Bigfoot family, just avoid humans while others like vampires and werewolves can blend in among society. The ones that Dad employs down here can have all sorts of jobs. Some act as guards, some as office staff, and some even as janitorial workers. After a couple of centuries, Dad's really got everything perfected. Everyone has their place in the world.

A loud slurp pulls me from my thoughts.

With a raised eyebrow, I look up at my demon companion to see my Chinese takeout box gripped in his clawed hand. I watch as the end of another noodle disappears into his lips.

"I was gonna eat that tomorrow, you know."

Balthasar shakes the contents of the container. "It has mold on it."

"Ugh." I stick out my tongue. "Gross. It's all yours, buddy."

"Thank you, Princess. It is very delicious."

I snort and start down the steps from the ledge. There are more portals down here, but they lead to different parts of the world. Dad's really the only one who knows which one goes where. I went through one on the south side a couple of years ago just to see where it went and ended up in the wilderness of Mongolia. A nomad family just happened to be there when I materialized. Scared the daylights out of them. One man actually fell off his horse. I felt so bad that I just yelled out an apology and went back through the portal.

The stairs lead to the sprawling garden growing behind Dad's house. I say house, but in all truthfulness, it's more of a chateau, and it's the only other building in the Underworld beside the compound. The garden with its black roses and fountains and the house with its tall windows and golden colonnades doesn't exactly compliment the stark white bricks that make up the Pen, but when you're appointed Lord of the Underworld, your house can look like whatever you want.

Let's get one thing straight real quick. The Lord of the Underworld is not Satan, okay? Satan deals with the dead and the damned. My dad handles monsters, creatures, and supernatural beings. Totally different.

Balthasar and I navigate the winding pathways of the garden until we reach the back of the chateau. I make my way up the steps and go inside through a pair of French doors that always seem to be open. As it normally does, the grand entry buzzes with activity. Monsters hustle hither and thither, their arms cradling stacks of papers. Several phones ring at the same time amid the clacking of nails or talons on keyboards. Through a door across the way, several Underworlders sit at computers while others peruse through thick tomes pulled from the bookshelves that line the walls.

"His Majesty is in his office," a voice says in my ear.

I jump and swivel to find Lucien standing just behind me, a smirk upon his smug face. His dark, bottomless eyes shine in the light of the chandelier overhead. The glow from overhead creates a halo of light behind him, highlighting the almost-blue tones of his ink-black hair. My heartbeat suddenly seems too loud.

"Dammit, Luce. How many times have I told you that I hate when you do that?"

"You shouldn't be so easy to sneak up on."

I roll my eyes and stomp off in the direction of Dad's private office.

I suppose I should probably explain Lucien. He is, unfortunately, a rather large part of my life.

After I moved out of Dad's house and into the house on the Surface, Dad assigned a shifter to act as my Guardian. He needed someone who could pose as human for things like parent-teacher conferences and buying groceries.

I kept telling him that I didn't need anyone on the Surface with me. I was ten, for God's sake. I could take care of myself, but he wouldn't hear it. And since he wouldn't listen to me, I made it my job to get rid of the babysitters as quickly as I could.

I'll admit I was a terror as a child. I'd run into traffic, yell colorful expletives in class, purposefully get lost in the store. The Guardians knew that if anything ever happened to me, Dad would punish them. I went through Guardian after Guardian. By the time I was done with them, they all practically beat down Dad's door to resign.

I was fourteen when I stole the car and drove it to a nearby concert. A mage that knows my father well saw me there and reported back to Dad before I could even make it home. That was the last straw. The next day, Dad called me into his office and introduced me to Lucien.

He stood in the corner, quiet as a shadow. I somehow knew just by the look on his clean shaven face that I wouldn't be getting rid of him as easily as the others.

Boy, was I right.

Lucien is stalwart. In the beginning, he almost never let me out of his sight except for when I was in the bathroom or my bedroom. The jerk even had alarms installed on all the windows of the house. Over time, he relaxed a bit, but he never let his guard down. None of my stunts seemed to faze him. When he first started, I was convinced that he didn't have emotions. It took six months for him to even sort of smile. I can count on one hand the number of times I've ever heard him chuckle.

As I've gotten older, I've gotten better at navigating around him. Like tonight, for instance. I managed to sneak out of the house, grab the pig and Hannah, and make it all the way to Bianca's party before he caught up with me. Remember the crow that cawed angrily at me? That was Lucien. *Such* a fun-sucker.

I'm sure he would have shifted and hauled me back to the house had Hannah not been with me. The fool probably thought I wouldn't drag Hannah into my shenanigans.

I used to beg Dad to get rid of him, like we could drop him off at the pound or something, but Dad always gave me the same spiel: "Lucien is your Guardian, Ember. And he will remain your Guardian for as long as I say he will."

To which I always reply, "Uggghhh."

Lucien isn't a demon. I'd probably get along with him better if he was. He isn't a chimera or a vamp or a ghost either. He's not really like anything else down here. I don't quite know where Dad got him. I just know he takes his job very seriously. And that sucks for me. Because he can shift at will into his crow form, he can follow me everywhere—school, the mall, Hannah's house. When his human form is inconvenient or suspicious, he just *poofs* into a crow to stalk me instead.

Hannah noticed that I had a follower years ago. At first she thought it was strange that there was always a crow everywhere we went, but over time, she actually became attached to the feathered git. Despite my protests, Hannah started leaving him little snacks of leftover French fries and bread crusts. She even named him Edgar even though I tried to explain that Poe wrote about a raven, not a crow. When I finally revealed the craziness that is my life to her, she was kind of weirded out by Lucien in bird form. She quickly got over it, though, and she still feeds him French fries, in spite of my complaints.

I can't help but notice the shadow that follows me out of the grand entrance and down the hall. I'm tempted to stop suddenly to see if he'll plow into me, but I decide that would be childish.

Then I do it anyway.

Lucien deftly sidesteps me and takes the two remaining steps to the twelve-foot, oaken door looming before us. He knocks twice before turning the ornate knob and pushing the door open.

I point at his chest as I brush past him. "You've got toothpaste on your vest, by the way."

I'm delighted when he peers down his nose at his immaculate outfit.

"Made you look."

One of my favorite pastimes is insulting his wardrobe. I don't think I've ever seen him wearing something other than crisp white shirts, starched vests and ties, pressed slacks, and shoes shined so well you could check to see if you had any food in your teeth in the reflection. I know Lucien is ancient even though he won't tell me exactly how old. However, he doesn't appear to look a day over twenty. There is nary a wrinkle in his pale face, except for the perpetual line of worry between his eyebrows.

His only response to my little joke is to blink at me. It's a very bird-like response. Sometimes I think he forgets what form he is in. I brush past him into Dad's office.

As I cross over the threshold, I inhale deeply. There are only two places in the Underworld that the evasive stench of sulfur doesn't permeate, and this room is one of them. Instead, it smells like books, most likely due to the twelve-foot-tall bookcases lining the walls behind Dad's monstrous desk. He's behind said desk now, rifling through a stack of papers haphazardly piled before him. Behind his thick black glasses, his eyes look tired. The dark circles that have been there for as long as I can remember appear a bit darker than usual. His dress shirt and suit jacket are wrinkled as well which makes me think he slept in these same clothes.

"Hey, Pops," I say as I half collapse on one of the black, velvety armchairs placed in front of his desk.

Dad looks up for the first time and gives me an exhausted smile. "Hey, kiddo."

"You okay? You look tired."

My father gathers up all of the documents before him and stacks them neatly into one pile. The silver wedding band on his ring finger glints in the light. Even after all these years, he's never taken it off. "I'm fine. Just busy as usual. A unicorn was sighted in the Scotland Highlands yesterday, so we've been doing damage control over there."

On the side table between the chairs rests a bowl of M&Ms. I grab the bowl and balance it on my stomach. "Well, it could always be worse, right? Remember the centaur incident a couple years ago?"

Dad chuckles. "I don't think I could ever forget that."

I toss a couple pieces in the air and attempt to catch them in my mouth. After narrowly missing a yellow M&M, I remind myself to thank the goblin in charge of the kitchens. He knows M&M's are my favorite.

"You're going to get fat, you know," purrs a voice from the corner of the room.

I peek over the side of the chair and groan. "Oh, God. Dad, why is *she* here?"

My father takes a swig from a coffee cup on his desk, makes a face, and spits it back out into the cup. "Ember, don't start... Dare I ask why your hair is purple?"

I blow my violet bangs out of my eye. "I got tired of black. You like?"

"You look ridiculous," chimes the voice in the corner.

"I may look ridiculous, but at least I don't look like a troll."

"Girls," Dad says in his dad-voice. "Enough. I didn't call you here for you to bicker with one another. Em, we'll talk about your hair later, and we'll discuss your punishment for the little prank you pulled tonight. Lucien has informed me of your actions, and I have to say that I'm very disappointed in you."

I crush a red M&M between my fingers and pretend it's Lucien's head.

"Right now, I need to discuss something very important with the both of you. Zilah, come sit down."

Zilah saunters over as I glare at her from the corner of my eye. She settles into the chair beside me with a liquid grace I could never manage. Her ample skirts rustle as she adjusts them around her crossed legs.

Zilah is my twin sister. She also just so happens to be a manipulative, evil bitch.

You might think I'm exaggerating, but I'm not. When we were eleven, she hired a vampire to come to the Surface, kill me, and make it look like an accident.

Imagine his surprise when he got a pencil to the eye after trying to sneak up on me while I was doing homework in my room. That's the number one reason I use old fashioned wooden pencils, by the way. You never know when you might need to stab a vampire in the face. Of course, the current Guardian swooped in after the vampire started screeching and hauled him back down into the Underworld—he thought *I* was the culprit behind my own attack, because that makes a whole lot of sense, and he quit the next day. Upon questioning, Dad found out that Zilah had hired the vamp, but when he confronted her about it, she batted her baby blues at him and said she was only joking.

Only *joking.* And my gullible father actually believed her! And while I'll get grounded for my harmless prank, Zilah tried to kill me and got off with nothing more than a stern talking to.

She was seven the first time she tried to get rid of me. Now we're seventeen, and she's ten times as evil.

We may be twins, but Zilah and I couldn't be more different. She's tall and willowy like Dad, while I'm short and petite like mom was. She got our mother's silver-blonde hair and blue eyes, while I got our father's inky locks and his hazel eyes. She got all the goodies that comes with having a mom that was a vampire, while I seemed to have inherited absolutely nada. I'm all human. Boring, plain, and non-Underworldly human. The tale of how all that worked out is a story for another time.

"Girls, do you know what this winter solstice marks?"

"Four days before Christmas?" I guess.

Zilah sneers. "It marks Father's five hundredth year as ruler of the Underworld, you idiot."

I flick a green candy at her. To my greatest merriment, it strikes her right between the eyes. Zilah doesn't find it nearly as funny, though, and leans forward with a hiss, flashing her pointed canines at me.

"Zilah, calm down! Ember, quit provoking your sister!" Dad commands. He runs his hands through his salt and pepper hair, causing it to stand up on end. With a sigh, he continues, "Zilah is right. This year is my five hundredth year and therefore marks my last year as Lord of the Underworld."

A piece of M&M lodges in the back of my throat when I gasp. My eyes water as I violently hack my lungs out. Zilah rolls her eyes. If I wasn't choking to death, I'd punch her in her pretty face.

"What do you mean, your last year?" I ask when I can breathe again.

"It means it's my last year," he tells me, as if that clears everything up. "That is how it has always been. In order to prevent an abuse of power, the Lord of the Underworld must relinquish the throne to the heir every five centuries."

"Everyone knows that," Zilah disdainfully adds.

Sadly, my brain still hasn't connected the dots. It's been a long night. "So, if you step down, who will be the next ruler?"

Dad's gaze flutters from me to Zilah and back to me. "One of you will take my place."

My face becomes hot as I finally comprehend the magnitude of his words. The way I see it, there are only two possible outcomes. The first is that I, as technically the oldest by mere minutes, would take Dad's place on the Obsidian Throne. That in itself is a laughable idea. I may be his daughter, but the truth is that I have spent almost half my life on the Surface. I just don't belong down here. When I was old enough to go to school, I begged Dad to let me go to school on the Surface. He obliged after I heckled him for nearly four years. He bought our house and came up with the cover story that we still keep today. Dad suggested that I tell everyone that asks that I'm in foster care and that whatever current Guardian was up there with me was my caretaker. So far, it's worked surprisingly well, even though Lucien looks like he's only a few years older than me. I prefer the Surface. I like the sun and the rain, the seasons and the ocean, the people, the food, the normalcy.

And if I become queen, I'll lose all of that. I'd still be able to visit the Surface, of course, but I couldn't stay there for long. I would always have to come back into this pit of monsters. Even worse, Hannah will grow old while I age at a much slower pace. I'll be forced to watch the world go on living without me. The truly sad part, though, is that when Han does die, no one will even care that I'm gone.

The only other outcome is that Zilah will become queen. Just the thought of her on the throne makes me want to throw up the pound of chocolate I just consumed. My father is a good man. He's fair and just. It was his idea to parole out monsters that behaved well, you know. His idea actually reduced the number of incidents on the Surface, and unrest in the Pen is practically nonexistent. The creatures that reside in the Underworld respect him...and fear him just enough to know their place. But if Zilah is the ruler? I can't even begin to imagine the horrors that she will unleash. She is neither fair nor just. Zilah belongs in the Pen herself, on one of the top floors—that's how bad she is. And with the power that comes with the title of queen, I'll be dead before the coronation concludes.

My sister and I bolt up at the same time.

"She can't be queen!" we say together.

Dad comes out from behind his desk as Zilah and I continue to yell at one another. When he reaches us, Dad puts a hand on each of our shoulders and gently forces us back into our seats.

"Let me finish, girls," he orders in his scary, quiet Dad-voice.

We both shut up and cross our arms over our chests.

"Because Ember is the oldest," he continues, "she is rightfully the heir."

Zilah begins to protest, but Dad shushes her. "However, because Ember has spent most of her years on the Surface, Zilah would technically be better suited to rule."

This time I open my mouth to argue, but I shut it after the look Dad shoots me. "Because of this dilemma, I have come up with a solution."

He paces in front of us. "There will be a competition consisting of three Tasks. Whoever completes the Tasks while showing the most courage, intelligence, mercy, and power will become queen."

"Why even bother with a competition?" Zilah asks. "Why don't you just choose your heir right here, right now?"

Dad pauses for a moment and taps a finger on the top of his desk. "I fear I won't make the right decision," he eventually admits. "And I fear that the Huntsmen or the Underworlders would resent me if I chose who would rule over them. The Huntsmen will decide which one of you wins each Task, and they will ultimately choose the new queen. I will have no choice in the matter."

Zilah narrows her eyes before shooting a frosty glare in my direction. I can practically hear the gears turning in her pretty head as she plots my undoing...which gives me an idea.

"But Dad," I say, "what happens to you after the Tasks are over and there's a new queen?" If Zilah does beat me, surely Dad won't let her kill me. He would protect me. Maybe he can even come up to the Surface and live with Lucien and me. It's hard to imagine him in our normal house on our normal street, but I can just barely picture it: Sunday breakfasts consisting of slightly burned pancakes and runny eggs. Us eating and laughing in the dining room. Dad coming to my graduation. Hope blooms in my heart like a flower growing in the middle of a barren plain.

Dad gives me a bittersweet smile. "Well, to be frank, we don't really know. No ruler of the Underworld has ever made it to their five hundredth year. I figure I'll die as soon as the title passes over to one of you, though. I'm over five hundred years old. The only thing keeping me from crumbling into a pile of dust is the immortality of the throne."

The flower that had so quickly blossomed in my chest wilts at his words. "You'll die?" I ask in a small voice. Zilah rolls her eyes at my silly human emotions and picks at one of her stiletto-shaped nails.

"It's past time," Dad says as simply as if he is discussing retirement instead of death. A wishful look washes over his features. "Plus, I miss your mother. Maybe I'll see her on the other side."

My palms are so slick with sweat that they leave behind a smear of wetness as I rub them on my jeans. Dad is still talking, but my heart pounds so loudly in my ears that I hear nothing else. I'm on the verge of a panic attack.

I stand. "I have to go."

Dad calls after me, but I ignore him as I burst through the doors. I have to get to the Surface. I have to breathe fresh air, air that doesn't smell like ten thousand rotten eggs.

Thankfully, Lucien doesn't try to stop me. There's a soft swoosh as his skin and clothes morph into feathers and then he's soaring just over my head as I run toward the exit.

I don't stop sprinting until we reach the ledge that will take us home, and then I have to stop. A wall of black rock holds me up as I try to relieve the fire burning my lungs, and before I know it, the gasps turn into sobs.

Lucien lands on an outcropping of rock a few feet above my shoulder and caws softly.

"Shut up, you stupid bird," I mumble as I wipe tears and snot onto my sleeve.

He caws again, this time a bit resentfully.

"I know you're only trying to make me feel better, but you can't."

Lucien hops up and down and burbles at me.

"You don't understand, Luce. Dad doesn't understand either. I can't do this, but I have to, but I don't want to," I say in a rush. "I'm so confused."

"How delightfully pathetic," a female voice purrs. "You're talking to your bird."

I spin around to find Zilah lounging on the edge of the ledge like there isn't a two hundred foot drop beside her.

"Go away."

She laughs, and it sends chills across my skin. "Ember, Ember, Ember. I don't know how father could even entertain the idea of you being the heir. He must be losing some of his sense in his old age."

I clench my fists. "Don't talk about Dad that way, Zi."

"I can do as I please, Ember. I am the future queen, after all."

Before I can blink, Zilah is standing before me, her face mere inches from mine. It's a vampire trick she perfected years ago. It doesn't scare me anymore, but she can still surprise me sometimes. What does sort of scare me, though, is Zilah's long-fingered hand wrapped around my throat.

A familiar rustling noise alerts me that Lucien has morphed back into his human form. He pushes his way between us, severing Zilah's grasp on me. Although I suspect that he would enjoy shoving her over the edge just as much as I would, Luce can't touch her. She's his princess as much as I am, even if he's my Guardian.

With her heels on, she's tall enough to glare down at me over his shoulder.

"When I am queen, I swear that my first act will be to order your death," she says, voice dangerously quiet. "I'm going to put a hit on your head, Ember. And the Underworlder that manages to kill you first will be rewarded most handsomely."

Before I can even think of a reply, she vanishes. But the echo of her laugh remains behind, chilling me to the core.

See?

I told you she was an evil bitch.

3

"Em, are you sure you're okay?" Hannah asks me for what must be the one hundredth time. "If it's about the pig prank, I told you I'm already over it."

I roll over and shove my face into the pillow. Ever since the meeting with Zilah and Dad three days ago, my stomach has been in anxious knots. I feel like I swallowed a clown, and now he's making balloon animals with my guts. I've played out every possible scenario in my head thousands of times and every outcome is the same—I lose.

The first Task is scheduled to take place in a week, as Lucien likes to remind me on a daily—sometimes hourly—basis. Zilah and I won't know what the Task is until that day, but I already know it's going to be bad. I'll have to wrestle a basilisk or catch a werewolf without being bitten or torn to pieces, or some other nearly impossible Task that has a high possibility of resulting in my gruesome death.

I grumble into the pillow. Hannah pushes my limp body over until I'm on my back, staring up at the popcorn ceiling.

"What was that?"

"I said, my life is over. Call the undertaker. I want to try out my coffin before you put me in it. If it's going to be my eternal resting spot, I don't want to be uncomfortable."

"Ember," Hannah says through gritted teeth. She grabs my shoulders and shakes me. "What is wrong with you! You've been off all week. Please tell me what's bothering you. I'm your best friend. I can help."

I snort. "Fat chance there."

"Em," she growls.

"Okay, okay." Channeling my inner slug, I flop around until I'm somewhat sitting up against the wall adjacent to my bed. Hannah sits across from me, perched on the edge of the mattress, her back as straight as her A's.

I don't exactly remember how Hannah and I became friends. If you were to see a picture of us together, you'd never think we would be best buds. Hannah is nearly six feet tall, so of course I look like a twelve year old when I stand next to her. She always wears her hair in a long, single braid down her back, and she's constantly pushing her thick-framed glasses up her long, thin nose. She likes to wear oddly printed knee-length skirts and turtlenecks, and she gets away with it since we live in Seattle, but I've always wondered where she developed such an eccentric sense of fashion.

Unlike Hannah, my hair usually hangs in a straight curtain past my shoulders. Most of the time it's black like my dad's, but

I have a demon pal who makes small deals. I told him I wanted purple hair, and he told me he wanted a pizza with pineapple and anchovies. Deal struck. Anyway, I can't really harp on Hannah about her eclectic wardrobe considering how mine consists mostly of ripped up skinny jeans and t-shirts you never see because they are under my trusty zip-up hoodie.

The point is, she looks like she lives in a library and I look like the type that spray paints graffiti on prominent legal buildings in the middle of the night. I don't. But that's what I look like. Although, I can't say I haven't been tempted...

But she's been my friend since fifth grade, despite finding out about my other life and my dramatic tendencies, and I love her for that.

She prods my sock-clad foot with a finger, jostling me out of my thoughts. I suck air into my nose in a deep breath and tell her. I don't leave anything out, except for my mass consumption of M&M's which I don't find necessary to the story. When I get to the part where Zilah assaults me on the ledge, Han's lip curls up in disgust and she shakes her head.

"Ugh. Your sister is such a jerk."

"Right?"

"I hate her and I only met her that one time."

"One time's all it takes with her."

"So, what's the first Task?" she asks.

I shrug and busy myself with the fibers of the knee-hole of my jeans. "I don't know. We won't know until that day."

“Hmmm.” She gets up off of the bed and pushes her glasses higher up her nose as she begins to pace across the clean parts of my floor. She deftly steps around piles of clothes and stacks of trash I’ve been meaning to gather all while chewing on her thumbnail.

Knowing this might go on for a while, I slide off my bed until half of my body is draped over the side of the mattress. My eyes lose focus as they drift across the ceiling, and I imagine pushing Zilah off of a cliff, or into the path of a moving train, or into a vat of lava. The longer Hannah paces, the more creative my morbid thoughts become.

“Em!” she says, and I realize she’s been calling me for a while now.

I fall the rest of the way to the floor with a thump. “What?”

“I have an idea. You said that an heir must take your father’s place, correct?”

“Uh-huh.”

“So, that means that your father was the heir five hundred years ago. You mentioned an estranged uncle once, which means that he is technically in third place for the throne, right?”

I sit up straight. “Right...”

“Well, let’s just say that you win the trials—which you will because you rock and Zilah sucks—that means that you will be queen. And as queen, you can bequeath your title to any willing heir, right?”

“Yes...maybe?”

"So, let's find him! I mean, he's got to be better than Zilah. How do we locate his whereabouts?"

I barely hear her as I yank on my Chucks. I stand and grab her hand. "There's only one person that knows that information. To the Batcave, Alfred!"

I've only brought Hannah to the Underworld a handful of times before, and each time she looks around with her mouth open like a child at the zoo. The Underworlders don't particularly like being looked at like that. Some of them don't like humans at all while others like them way too much, but as long as Hannah's with me, they know how to behave. Plus, we won't run into any baddies where we are going. Lucien greets us with a caw as we step through to the Underworld. Hannah waves, but I ignore him and go down the path past Dad's estate and straight to the Pen.

Huge stadium lights illuminate every nook and cranny of the enclosure. These lights were another of Dad's ideas. It's much easier to monitor monsters when you can easily see them. The lights only shut off for a few hours everyday, right when the sun reaches its zenith—most Underworlders are nocturnal, so noon is the best time to cut the lights. I'm not exactly sure how all that works considering they can't see the sun, but Dad knows what he's doing. As we pick our way down the steps, a massive moth the size of a minivan flies in dizzying circles around one such light on the north end.

The Pen, like any prison on the Surface, has several clearances we must go through before we can even get inside the fence that rings the perimeter. The security guards, a chimera named Charles and a witch named Mildred, check us for weapons or any pointy things. They make sure we aren't harboring any supernatural paraphernalia like crucifixes or spell ingredients. Then they take our pictures and make us temporary badges. I technically don't need to do any of this, but when I'm with Han, I jump through all the hoops for her sake.

Once we get through all the checkpoints, Charles uses one of his massive lion paws to hit the button that buzzes us into the courtyard. I take Hannah's hand as we walk into Weirdsville.

Hannah's wide eyes travel to each orange jumpsuit-wearing Underworlder, taking in their strange and sometimes frightening appearances. I know most of the faces here, and they know me. As we walk the straight path that leads to the library, I return several nods and greetings but don't take time to stop and talk to anyone.

"Come on, Han. We can talk to some of them after."

"Ooh, what's that place over there?" She points to the edge of the cavern housing the Underworld. I know what place she's specifically talking about without even looking. Behind a towering chain link fence and warning signs in multiple languages, a large iron door with symbols carved into it sits in the wall.

"There's a cave system in the walls of the cavern," I explain to her. "Dad had it blocked off when we were born. I guess he thought Zilah or I would somehow wander into it when we were kids and fall to our deaths. I mean, my death. I'm sure a hundred foot fall would barely faze Zilah."

"Oh," Han breathes, as if disappointed it wasn't something more sinister. She quickly finds a nearby Underworlder to perk her up, though. "What's *that* thing?"

"That's a kamaitachi."

"It's like a weasel...with sword legs."

"Yep, pretty much. Just be glad his buddies aren't around. They like to ride around in little dust devils and slice up people for kicks. Fun stuff. Now, come on, slowpoke."

The library isn't technically in the Pen but beside it in a long rectangular building, which means we have to bob and weave through quite a few groups of loitering Underworlders. By the time we get to the heavy doors that lead into the library, I have to forcibly tug Hannah along.

"Isadora?" I call out into the stacks.

The doors shut behind us, and we are enveloped in the comfortable silence that resides in all libraries. Rows and rows of wooden bookshelves fill the room, and the sweet smell of old books and dust instantly fills our noses. Welcome to the one other place besides my father's office that doesn't smell like rotten eggs.

Judging by the awestruck look on Hannah's face, we have found her happy place. To the left of the entrance is the front desk, but the chair behind it is empty. Isadora, the librarian, must be somewhere among the shelves.

"Izzy?" I call once more.

"Ember?" a velvety voice coated in a heavy southern accent replies from somewhere deep within the labyrinth of books.

"It's me!" I yell back. "We're up at the front."

"I'll be there inna minute, sweetheart!"

I jump up on the desk and swing my legs while Hannah meanders over to a stack of books balanced precariously in a towering pile on a circular table nearby. A moment later, I hear the tell-tale squeaking of Isadora's book cart, and she emerges from the stacks with a beatific smile gracing her face.

I jump off of the desk and run the rest of the way to Izzy. When I get there, I launch myself into her open arms as she laughs. Her laughter is a low, sweet and soulful sound that fills anyone near enough to hear it with joy. The familiar scent of her flowery perfume—tainted only slightly by the smell of decay—makes the tension in my shoulders melt away.

"Oh, sweet girl, it's been too long!"

"I know." I step back as I guiltily chew on the inside of my cheek. "I'm sorry. I've just been so busy with school."

She bops me on the nose. "I know, honey. Just don't take so long to come see me next time, ya hear?"

I grin. "Yes, ma'am. I brought a friend. Come meet Hannah."

"*The* Hannah?" she asks. "The one I've heard so much about for all these years?"

"The one and only," I say, my smile growing.

"Lead the way, child."

We walk, arm in arm, to where Hannah sits with her nose in a book.

"Hannah, I want you to meet my good friend, Isadora."

Hannah looks up from her book, and her brown eyes instantly widen and her friendly smile somewhat slips from her lips. She recovers quickly and stands, but she looks confused as to what to do.

"Don't fret, sweetheart. I know it's a little disconcertin' meeting me for the first time," Izzy says.

I look from Hannah to Isadora and try to remember the first time I met the librarian. I think I was four. That was around the time I really started getting into books. I couldn't read yet, of course, but I remember loving being read to. I constantly followed Dad around with an armful of my favorite books, asking him to read them to me even though he had read them to me a hundred times before. When he finally couldn't stand it anymore, he brought me here to the library. As soon as I walked in, I was awestruck. I couldn't believe one place could have so many books. And it was here that I met Isadora for the first time, and I think she was glad for the company. She read to me for hours while my parents were busy doing adult stuff.

Not once did it ever bother me that Izzy is a zombie.

Isadora was a young woman living in Louisiana during the 1920's. She worked at a little café that served gumbo on the side of the road, and she saved every single penny she made so that she could buy a car. Her dream was to drive to California to become a "real" actress. She had starred in several commercials and even a few low-budget movies, and she was quickly on her way to becoming the next big thing.

Unfortunately, she never made it.

A rogue zombie bit her on her walk home from work one night, and she turned not long after. One of the HTF found her, but only after she had snacked on a fisherman's brains. I don't blame her for her actions, I never have. Anyone who knows Izzy knows that she would never hurt anyone on purpose. A zombie's urge for flesh is like an addict's need for drugs.

So, that's how Izzy ended up in the Pen. She was quickly granted parole, but she could never return to the Surface. Because the zombie bite technically killed her, Isadora began to decompose on the Surface. By the time she was brought to the Pen, her amber eyes had sunk deep in their sockets, and sections of her black, curly hair had fallen out. Her rich, dark skin developed a green tint and sores covered patches of her flesh.

The good news, though, is that as long as she stays in the Underworld, she won't decompose anymore. Izzy decided to stay instead of being put to rest on the Surface, and Dad put her in charge of the library.

I don't remember being grossed out when I first met her—I had seen much stranger and nastier things by the time I was four. Izzy has always just been Izzy, but I can kind of understand why Hannah is a bit hesitant to touch Izzy's oozing skin. I look down at my hoodie and see a smear of questionable goo.

"Izzy's a zombie," I say, cutting to the chase. "But don't worry, she doesn't bite."

Isadora grins, revealing receding gums over white teeth. "Not anymore, anyway. I just take my burger extra rare."

"It's true. She only eats raw beef and pork now. Sometimes venison and buffalo when the chefs in the kitchen are feeling adventurous," I add.

Hannah's smile finally reaches her eyes. "It's nice to meet you, Isadora."

"Please, child, call me Izzy." My undead friend shakes her head before turning to me. "Now, don't get me wrong, I love visits from you, sweet girl, but why have you decided to come see this old bag o' bones?"

"We need your help."

She nods, sensing my sudden seriousness, and I tell her everything I told Hannah.

"I heard about the Tasks, and pardon me for saying this, but your daddy is being very silly in all this. He knows as well as you and I that Zilah should not be queen."

I stare down at the tips of my shoes. "Well, that's the thing. I know Zilah can't be queen, but I can't be queen either."

Out of the corner of my eye, I see her plant a hand on her hip. "Can't? Or won't?"

I chew on the inside of my mouth. "Both?"

Thankfully, Hannah comes to my rescue. "That's why we need you, Izzy. If Ember wins and becomes queen, wouldn't she be able to bequeath her title to any eligible heir?"

Isadora puckers her lips as she ponders the question. "I believe so."

"That's what I thought," Hannah smugly replies.

"So, you need me to find you an heir?"

Hannah nods a bit too enthusiastically. "Yes!"

"Okay, I can do that. Hannah, would you mind if I spoke to Em alone real quick?"

Hannah obliges, and Izzy takes my arm and walks us toward the front desk.

"Are you sure you want me to do this?" Izzy asks.

"Very sure."

She sighs. "Well, I sincerely hope that you will change your mind. This place could use someone like you."

I scoff. "Right. The last thing this hole needs is me on a throne making decisions. Being an adult."

Izzy looks at me for a long moment, and I wonder what she's thinking. I'm about to ask when she gives me a small shake of her head. The disappointed look in her dark eyes just about cripples me with guilt. Isadora turns and disappears into the stacks without another word.

With my hands thrust deep into the pockets of my jeans, I shuffle over to where Hannah sat back down. I would do almost anything to make Isadora proud of me. I mean, she is the closest thing I've had to a mother since Mom died. But this is the one thing I cannot do. I cannot rule the Underworld. I'm not made for it. I'm just a teenager. I just want to binge watch Netflix and eat copious amounts of potato chips. Is that too much to ask?

Hannah's saying something about how she's surprised Izzy uses the Library of Congress system to shelve books, but I tune her out. Izzy knows me. She knows I'd be no good here. So, why is she being like this? It's times like these that make me think of my mother. I barely remember her. Just snippets. The melody of her laugh. The way her freckles were sprinkled across her cheeks like stars across the galaxy.

What would she say? Would she want me to be queen too? Would she be disappointed in me when I said no?

A massive tome crashes onto the table just inches from where I leaned on my elbow. My teeth rattle together as dust escapes the ancient book like wisps of smoke.

“This is the record of all those that have been kings and queens of the Underworld. It shows the lineages and family trees of each ruler for the past three thousand years,” Izzy explains.

Hannah reaches across the table and strokes the leather binding. “How are there so many if each king or queen rules for five hundred years?”

Izzy grimaces. “The world wasn’t always as safe and peaceful as it is now. More often than not, a ruler would die before their five hundred years were up, and the Throne would be bequeathed to the next heir. And when there was no heir to be had, the Underworld would choose another ruler.”

“Choose?” I ask.

“Yes. In times of need, the Underworld selects the human it deems most suited to run this pit of monsters, and a new lineage begins. Not everyone gets a chance to decide whether or not they wanted to rule, you know,” Isadora says, looking at me.

I’m hit by another wave of guiltiness. The heavy feeling settles into the pit of my stomach, and I’m suddenly really ready to get back to the Surface. I’m going to have to avoid Izzy until she gets over this nonsense about me becoming queen.

“Wait a minute,” Hannah says, pushing up her glasses. “If only a *human* can rule, then why is Zilah even being considered?”

“She’s technically only half-vampire. It’s a weird genetics thing,” I answer with a shake of my head. I slide the thick volume toward me and crack it open. I flip to the last pages, glad to have a reason to change the subject.

"Here we go." I find my name on the second to last page. Ember Elizabeth Ashworth is written in red ink beneath both of my parents' names. My father's name, like mine, is in red ink while my mother's is in black.

Beside my name is Zilah's. I'm tempted to scribble out her name, but a fat lot of good that would do me. Only the Librarian can write in the book, and she can only do it with a special quill. The ink in the quill knows when a person dies, and the ink automatically turns black. If I wrote on the page, the ink would soak into the vellum and disappear. I may not be able to scribble out her name, but perhaps I can change it to just Zi. She hates it when people call her Zi, which is precisely why I try to do it as much as possible.

"The book's almost out of blank pages," Hannah says. "What happens when you get to the end?"

Izzy smiles. "There is no end. The book will add as many pages as it needs."

"You mean, *you* add pages when you need them," Hannah corrects her.

"Nope," I say. "She means the book. It's magic."

Behind her glasses, Hannah's eyes go wide. I laugh. "You are so easy to impress."

"Give me a break," she says. "I didn't even know about magic and monsters until you told me two years ago."

Hannah may be my oldest friend—hell, she's my only friend, who am I kidding?—but I didn't tell her about my freaky family for a very long time. To be honest, I probably never would have if it wasn't for that idiot Benny.

Dad was adamant that I never have guests over to our house. He was afraid we would have a "visitor" from down below and someone would find out about the Underworld. We rarely had visitors, and when we did, it was usually Balthasar. Now, I can understand how bad it would be if Hannah ran into him with his giant, twisting horns and cloven feet, but Dad almost always texts me when Balt's on his way. So, I finally decided to ignore Dad's no guests rule.

Even though Lucien protested, I invited Han over for a slumber party. She arrived on my doorstep with a sleeping bag, a pillow, and her toothbrush. I showed her the house before going down the hall to my room.

"You should be proud of me," I told her with my hand on the doorknob. "I cleaned my room just for you."

Han grinned. "So proud."

I laughed and pushed the door open to discover that it was snowing in my room.

Okay, it wasn't really snowing. But it did take my mind a second to process that the whiteness covering my bed and my floor and everything else was actually the contents of my pillow.

And there was Benny, the scoundrel, bouncing and rolling around in the remnants of my very expensive down feather pillow.

Benny is a gargoyle, one of the stupidest I've ever met, and that's saying a lot considering they're all dumb as...well, dumb as rocks. According to Dad, Benny used to be something fearsome. He was supposedly this big massive piece of stone that guarded some castle in Romania, but he took a tumble during an earthquake and his days of being a big baddie were over. Dad had a stonemason take the biggest chunk of Benny's old body and carve out a new one. The new Benny was about six inches tall. The stonemason gave him a fantastic scowl and some impressive little horns and wings, but the scariness was gone. He'd actually be kind of cute if he wasn't so stupid.

As soon as Benny saw me, he froze. I turned to Hannah with some cockamamie explanation already on my lips. I cleared my throat. "Um. Han, this is my dog, Benny."

Her head turned to look at me before her eyes, almost as if they were stuck on the gargoyle sitting on my bed. "That thing is not a dog."

"Sure he is," I said. "Bad dog, Benny! Down!"

I'd hoped Benny would get the hint and pretend to be a puppy, but that was short-lived.

"Is she eats?" Benny gurgled. "Is she eats?"

That was when Hannah fainted. It was a good thing she was holding her sleeping bag. I think it cushioned the fall. Mostly, anyway.

"No, she is not for you to eat, you useless pebble," I snapped at him. I ran my hands over my face and groaned. "Would it have killed you to be a dog for five minutes?"

Benny panted excitedly. "Is dog eats?"

"Oh, for the love of—Lucien! We have a problem," I called down the hall.

And that's how Hannah learned about the Underworld. She didn't believe me at first, of course. I mean, who would? Oh, by the way, there's an Underworld where the monsters you thought weren't real live, and there just happens to be a portal to it under our kitchen island. It even sounds insane to me and it's my life.

A squelch brings me back to the present. An ear lies on the table just to the right of my hand. "I think you dropped something, Izzy."

"Oh, fiddlesticks." She scoops up the ear and presses it back to her head. "This silly thing just keeps fallin' off. I might need to get it sewn back on. I best be goin' anyway. Hannah, it was so nice to finally meet you."

Hannah's face turns an off shade of green as she waves goodbye and goes back to the book.

Isadora turns to me and playfully chucks me under the chin. "Think about what I said, sweet girl. I'll see you around."

I give her a tight-lipped smile and say goodbye. Izzy grabs her squeaky cart and disappears once more into the stacks.

"Okay," Han says, her voice only a little shaky. She scoots closer to me in order to see the book better. "You said your dad has a brother. Let's start there."

Her long finger traces the line up from my father's name and follows up and across. "Ah! Here he is! Mr. Michael Ashworth. I bet we can Google him and find out where he lives."

"You might want to start with nearby cemeteries, then." My shoulders droop in disappointment. "His name's in black. That means he's dead. He'd be close to five hundred now if he was still kicking."

Han's lips twist to the side. "Well, crap. Okay, time for Plan B. Let's go further back and follow the tree until we find someone that can be the next heir."

It takes us almost an hour of exploring the dead ends of my family tree, but Hannah finally finds him. "Here!" she shouts suddenly. "Max Wu."

I rub my tired eyes. It's past my bedtime. Izzy went up to her rooms on the second story a while ago. Zombies don't sleep, of course, so I don't know what she does up there. I've never thought to ask.

"Max Wu?" I ask. "Are you sure?"

Hannah nods. "Positive. Max is the grandson of your great-great aunt's third cousin. He's the only one suitable to be heir.

All the others are too young, too old, or dead."

A shadow washes over me. I knew he couldn't be far away—he never is, after all. Lucien's always there, watching and waiting for the most inopportune moment to bother me. I swivel in my chair to glare at him, but he's closer than I thought. My heart does a little skip at the sight of his hand on the back of my chair. I cross my arms. "Yes?"

"Time to go," Lucien says. "You both have school in the morning."

I force a cough. "I think school's a no go for tomorrow, Lucy. I fear I've caught a cold."

He looks down his nose at me. His eyes are the deepest brown. Black-brown. "We can run another couple of miles in the morning if you aren't going to go to school."

"No thanks." I stand and push in my chair. Lucien forces me to run a few times a week to keep in shape. You never know when you might come across an Underworlder and have to run for your life, after all. But there was no way in hell I'd run extra miles, even if it did mean missing school. "Let's go, Han. We can creep on Max Wu more tomorrow."

4

"We're home," Lucien says softly.

I blink my eyes open and find that I had inadvertently fallen asleep on his shoulder. He offered to drive Hannah home when I couldn't stop yawning.

I quickly sit up and wipe my mouth to make sure I hadn't drooled all over him. I didn't, thank God.

He kills the engine and we go inside. I make a beeline to my bedroom, not even caring that I still need to shower and change out of my sulfur-infused clothes. I'll regret it tomorrow, but right now I'm just too tired.

I go to open the door, but Lucien's hand stops mine on the handle.

I groan. "Not tonight, Luce. I just want to sleep."

"It's procedure."

I groan even louder. "Forget it," I growl as I stomp off to the living room. I fall onto the couch and tuck my arm under the pillow my face is pressed into.

It's procedure to check my room after we've been out. All because that halfwit Benny somehow snuck through the portal and wound up in my room. Lucien's never found anything in there, but he insists on following Dad's orders.

I'm almost asleep when I feel a blanket drape over me. Lucien slips off my shoes and tucks the end of the blanket under my sock-clad feet.

When I don't feel him anymore, I crack an eye open. From my spot on the couch, I can see him in the kitchen. He doesn't turn on any lights, but the moon is bright enough tonight that his form is clearly visible.

He leans back against the counter and crosses his legs at the ankles. Lucien lets out a sigh, and his shoulders relax. He never lets me see him like this. Relaxed. Calm. Not on high alert. But when he doesn't think I'm looking, I find this other version of him. The version that seems a little more human.

He reaches up and unbuttons the top button of his white dress shirt, his left hand hovering over his heart for just a moment before he pulls his shirt loose from his waistband. He always dresses as if he's halfway ready to go to a black-tie affair. He has an arsenal of black and gray waistcoats in his closet, and he always has one on. Lucien even has his vests and trousers dry cleaned. When he really wants to spice things up, he puts on a suit jacket.

Every year, Lucien takes one personal day. Just one. I have no idea what he does because he never answers the questions I hurl his way upon his return. I have a feeling that Dad has something to do with his once-a-year holiday.

Last year, I seized the opportunity and broke into his room. I just had to see whether or not the dude had any other clothes. I mean, he had to have at least one t-shirt. One pair of jeans. Pajamas. Something.

I cannot express how disappointing that endeavor was. I don't know what I expected really, but his space was more sterile than a hospital room. White blankets on white sheets. No pictures on the walls. No empty soda cans or water bottles lined up on the bedside table like in my room. Nothing. It looked like no one even lived in there, let alone slept in there. Then Lucien got home, and I got busted snooping through his closet. He told Dad, of course, and I was grounded for a week. The real bummer, though, was that all I found in his closet were slacks, waistcoats, and pressed, white, button-down shirts.

When I was officially un-grounded, I went to the mall with Hannah and bought Lucien a pack of dress socks in magnificently gaudy colors. Some were striped while others had polka dots, and one pair even had a pattern of adorable cats on them. I'd left them on his bed the next day with a bow and a note that told him I was sorry for sneaking around in his room. He never said anything about the socks since that day, and I was too embarrassed to bring it up.

Lucien unbuttons his cuffs and rolls up the shirtsleeves to his elbows, revealing muscular forearms. I hate the way he always leaves his sleeves long. I also hate the way he cuts and styles his hair—short on the sides and longer on top, his naturally curly hair meticulously gelled into place. I hate the way his top lip is just a tad bit thinner than his full bottom lip, and I hate the scar that cuts through his left eyebrow. I hate his long, straight nose and his bottomless eyes. I hate how tall he is and the fact that my head only reaches his chest, which makes me feel even more small and petite than usual.

I *hate* him.

But the truth is—the sad, *pathetic*, tragic truth is that I really don't hate him at all.

The truth is something I can't even say, something I can barely fathom. The truth is that I love that stupid git. I love him more than Galileo loved his stars. I love him more than Westley loved Buttercup. I love him more than I've ever loved anything or anyone. Ever.

I love him in a way that constantly shatters my heart, because I know that he will never love me in the same way or even at all.

It happened a couple of years ago. We were sitting on the couch together one rainy Sunday afternoon. I had my laptop on my stomach and my feet in Lucien's lap. I was finishing up an essay for English class, and Lucien was reading a book in a language long dead to this world. Then it just hit me. Why had I never realized how insanely *hot* he was? Why did I ever think his constantly furrowed brow was anything other than endearing? Why did I have the sudden overwhelming urge to see if his lips were really as soft as they looked? These thoughts never even crossed my mind until that moment. Then he looked at me and gave me the barest hint of a smile, and I was a goner.

I'm hopelessly in love with my Guardian, and he has no idea.

And he never will. Because I'll just fall apart right there when he doesn't return the sentiment. And the sad thing is that he won't even know how badly he's hurt me.

Plus, Lucien is an Underworlder. When Dad gave me "the talk" several years back, he was sure to mention that any and all Underworlders are off limits. Just to me, of course. The poor, pathetic human. Zilah can date whoever she pleases since she's half-Underworlder herself. Zilah also doesn't have to have a Guardian.

When I was about eleven, I stormed down to Dad's office and demanded to know why I had to have a Guardian but Zilah didn't. He told me that Zilah was half-vampire and could handle herself. Another con of inheriting all the mortal genes, I guess.

Why, oh why, did I have to fall in love with this infuriating bird-man? It seems to me that there has never been a more ill-fated love.

Our stars are so crossed that even Romeo's and Juliet's stars look at us and say, "Man, you're screwed."

I don't even remember falling asleep on the couch, but a familiar voice alerts me that I've crossed over from consciousness to unconsciousness.

The first time I remember ever dreaming of the Darkness, I was nine. But some small part of me thinks I've always dreamed of him.

It always starts the same.

Ember...

He calls me with a velvety voice heavy with ancientness. I used to be afraid of him, but somehow over the years, I've grown to anticipate his dream visits.

Ember?

The dream is different than any other type of dream I've ever experienced. I'm swimming in a world of pitch black. It's so dark that I can't see my hand in front of my face. I seem to just hover in the air, with no sense of up or down. When I was younger, I would fight it—struggle to right myself and escape the dark. Now, I don't bother.

"I'm here," I say to the nothingness.

I've missed you, Princess.

"You always say that."

The Darkness chuckles, a low rumbling sound that seeps into my every pore. *I don't get many visitors.*

"Let me see you."

Something caresses my cheek. *You know that I cannot do that.*

I sigh. "Just thought I'd ask. Maybe someday you'll change your mind."

Perhaps. There is something you must know.

"Oh? Are you finally going to tell me who you are?"

You will find out in time. Beware the gifts of strangers.

I snort. "Really? That's it? I could have gotten that out of a fortune cookie."

In the dark, I don't see him...but I can feel his smile. *Goodbye, Ember.*

The first Task arrives here before I'm ready. But, let's really be honest here, I'd never be ready for this.

I want to bring Han with me—I need her moral support—but even I have to admit that's a terrible idea. Who knows what this Task will consist of, and I would never do anything to put Hannah's life at risk.

The house is quiet as I get ready. I lace up my lucky Chucks and pull a hoodie over my head. I look at myself in my body-length mirror and blow a wisp of hair out of my eyes. I woke up two days ago to black hair again. My demon pal forgot to mention that our deal was only short term, but I'm not complaining. I got purple hair for two weeks in exchange for a stinky pizza.

I move closer to the mirror until my face fills up my range of vision. My dad used to tell me that I'm the spitting image of my mother, but I've seen the pictures. I can tell you that she was way more beautiful than I can ever hope to be. She was the kind of beautiful that stopped people on the street when she walked by.

My eyes are too big for my face, something I attempt to remedy with thick eyeliner. My lips are perpetually chapped despite the well-used tube of chapstick I keep in my pocket at all times. And the icing on the cake is that I have a spattering of freckles across my cheeks. Dad said Mom had the same freckles, but I seriously doubt they made her look like a twelve-year-old girl scout.

Scowling, I throw my hair up into a ponytail and decide to apply some more eyeliner. I already wasted enough time bemoaning the genes I was dealt. I get a perfect wing tip on my right eye, and I'm making progress on my left eye when Lucien barges in.

"We are going to be late."

He startles me so much that my hand jerks, leaving behind a streak of black from the corner of my eye to my hairline. "Damn it all to hell, Lucien. I'm never going to be able to make them even now."

"Ember. The Task."

"Yes, yes. Give me a minute, will you?"

He shuts the door and I hastily scrub at the wasted eyeliner with a Q-tip. When I'm satisfied I don't look like a complete idiot, I meet Lucien in the kitchen.

He's already moved the island out of the way, and the portal starts to glow faintly. The symbols lining the circle pulse in time with the beat of my heart.

Anxiety about what's to come has been eating away at me, and it's gotten progressively worse over the past few days. There has hardly been a moment when I haven't felt like a twenty pound weight has been on my chest. I don't even think I've eaten a full meal since Monday. I've been too afraid I'd barf it all up.

I kind of want to barf now as I stand at the edge of the portal. Maybe it will be just dry heaves. I don't think the six Tic Tacs I ate today could really produce that much vomit.

I'm still contemplating barfing when Lucien takes my hand. A blush unfurls in my cheeks like a burning flower.

I hate that he can do that to me.

"Ember." Lucien bends to look me in the eyes. He never calls me Em. "You can do this."

"I can?"

"Yes."

"You don't know that."

"Ember."

"Lucien."

"Go through the portal now, or I will drag you through."

I sigh. Leave it to Lucien to kill the moment.

"Fine, you first."

Lucien steps into the circle and disappears. I take a deep breath and consider running far, far away, but I know Lucien would find me and force me to come back. I send up a little prayer to anyone who's listening and go through the portal.

The announcement of the first Task will take place in the Pen. I can't figure out for the life of me why Dad wants to do it there. When he told Lucien and me to meet him in the Pen's courtyard, I asked him why we couldn't just do it in his office. He ignored me and told us not to be late.

Oops.

By the time we get to the courtyard, Lucien has to make a path through the crowd so we can get to where my Dad and Zilah stand on a platform in the middle of the open space.

"Sorry. Excuse me. Hey! Watch it, pal!" I brush past feathers and scales. A minotaur clad in an orange jumpsuit steps to the side after swatting me across the face with his tail.

"Sorry, Princess."

"Yeah, yeah, Jimmy. Just watch that tail, will you?"

"Yes, Princess," he says through his bull lips. Jimmy's an okay dude. Just don't make him angry, and avoid wearing red around him—totally kidding. That whole red thing is just a myth. Jimmy actually told me once that red is one of his favorite colors.

We finally make it through the throng and join my family on stage. Lucien takes up his post behind me, his hands clasped in front of him and his eyes on the inmates.

"I explicitly told you not to be late, Ember," Dad says to me out of the corner of his mouth.

"Father," Zilah says in that infuriatingly slow way where she tends to draw out her words. "Can't you see that she was busy dressing for the occasion?"

I lean past my father's frame and behold Zilah's pageantry in its gaudy glory. She is decked out in an ice blue ball gown that floats to the floor in an ungodly amount of ruffles. Diamonds sparkle across the sheer fabric of her sleeves, making it look like her shoulders are kissed by the stars. And, yes, I did say diamonds. Anyone else might have used rhinestones or crystals, but there is no doubt in my mind that the glimmering gems on Zilah's gown are priceless jewels.

"I didn't know we were attending a tea party, Zi. My memo must have gotten lost in the mail."

"At least I'm dressed like a queen and not like some dirty vagrant."

Dad lifts his arms and clasps each of us by the shoulder. His fingers dig into me, and I bite back my comeback.

"Welcome," Dad says to the sea of monsters dressed in orange before us. "As many of you know, this winter marks the five hundredth year of my reign, which also means that I will be stepping down as King of the Underworld."

Murmurs roll through the gathering like a wave, and I even hear a few shouts.

During his time here, Dad really has reformed the place. From the stories I've heard, the last few kings kind of sucked. Before he built the Pen, the Underworlders used to just run amok around the Underworld, hiding in the cliff caves and eating each other. And the population of the Underworld has multiplied times ten because of Dad. Not only did Dad build the Pen, he also reinstated the Huntsmen, something that hadn't been done in centuries.

Nine men and three women make up the Huntsmen Task Force. Their job is to keep the humans up top safe and to track down and bring back rogue and misbehaving Underworlders. Back during Dad's first year of his reign, he traveled the world to find twelve regular humans to help him whip the Underworld into shape. They were given Affinities, of course—magical qualities that better help them maintain order among the Underworlders—so, they aren't completely human like me, but they used to be.

Sometimes, although it's rare, the Huntsmen will have to kill an Underworlder to protect human life. But thanks to my Dad and the HTF, the good people of Earth don't have to worry about the things that go bump in the night. They're why you don't hear about dragons burning down the countryside or werewolves ripping people to shreds anymore. Monsters have all but faded into fairy tales and legends.

Judging by the discontent radiating out from the crowd, the Underworlders did *not* know Dad is stepping down. And even though all of them are in here because of my dad, I think they will miss him. He treats them well. He treats them like they matter. And all of that, the empire he has built, will crumble under Zilah's rule.

It wouldn't surprise me if she does away with the Pen. Hell, she might even release all of the Underworlders. It would mean chaos and death and destruction on the Surface. I know, deep down, that the majority of the Underworlders standing before me would rather have me than Zilah on the throne. I'm more like our father. They know me, and I know them. I spent most of my weekends and summers down here in the Pen. When Dad got sick of me, he'd send me to Izzy. I loved the library, but I'd often sneak out and into the courtyard. The Underworlders were wary of me at first, but they warmed up, even the grumpiest of them. I'd bring coloring books and crayons, Barbie and her Malibu house, and board games to the courtyard and the Underworlders would play with me. I had to stop playing Texas Hold 'Em with May, though. May's a gamayun, which is pretty much a harpy—but not as ugly—that can see the future. She probably swindled me out of two hundred bucks last summer. The truly tragic part is she used the money to build herself a nest in her cell. All those twenties...now covered in gamayun poop and Lord only knows what else.

Anyway, the point is that I know these monsters. I know their names, their personalities, their stories. Zilah has never taken the time to do any of those things. Zilah treats everyone who's not a vampire like they are lesser, like they are beneath her. But I also know, way deep down, that the true baddies, the ones that weren't allowed out of their cells for the ceremony today, would love for Zilah to become the next queen. They know it will mean their freedom. And that scares the bejeezus out of me.

Dad shushes the crowd with a raised hand. "As tradition dictates, my heir will take my place. And that is where we face a conundrum. Ember, as my oldest, should be the rightful heir."

Several encouraging cries ring out in the courtyard. I stare at the ground as my insides constrict. They think they want me as their queen. But they don't. They shouldn't, anyway. I wish I could tell them how bad of an idea that is.

"However," Dad continues, "Ember has lived most of her life on the Surface. Zilah, while being the younger sister, has lived all of her life here with you."

A little piece of me rejoices that the courtyard is completely silent when Dad mentions Zilah. I don't know why, since I don't want the gig, but it feels good to know I'm liked more than her.

Granted, that's the opinion of a bunch of monsters—but hey, I'll call it a win.

"The law states that should there be two worthy heirs, a competition shall be held. Zilah and Ember will compete against each other in three separate Tasks. Each Task will be increasingly difficult, and the outcome will be judged by the Huntsmen and myself. Whoever demonstrates the most courage, ingenuity, and leadership will take the Obsidian Throne."

The crowd is so quiet that I can hear my own heartbeat.

"And now it's time to announce the first Task." He holds out his right hand before him. The air sparks and ignites into a sphere of blue flame just over the center of his palm. He seems to be able to see something in the flames. He nods and the flame extinguishes without a trace, not even a wisp of smoke. My father's calloused fingers curl into a fist.

I'm about to ask him what that was all about when the sirens go off.

"The HTF has just released ten Underworlders in Seattle," he says over the piercing wails. "Find them."

5

Damn.

I am *not* expecting that.

The crowd goes into a frenzy. The demon guards quickly swoop in and usher everyone back to their cells. A few Underworlders get a little too excited, though. I watch a guard whack a Baba Yaga over the head with his baton because she keeps floating higher and higher in her iron kettle.

My head snaps to the right just in time to see Zilah turn into a swarm of bats and head toward the portal.

Yeah, that's a real thing. I know it sounds silly, a vampire turning into a bat, but it's not so silly when it's your psycho sister and the cloud of leathery wings and sharp teeth are chasing you. Trust me. I know from experience.

It also gives Zi an unfair advantage. I'm going to have to wait for the masses to dissipate before I can leave.

I bounce on my toes, craning my neck over the heads of the Underworlders as I wait for a path to open up. They're moving slower than an elderly person in the canned food aisle at a grocery store. I'm contemplating shoving my way through or body surfing to the gate when I feel someone watching me.

One of the guards, Abba, is completely still amid the rush of bodies around her. When I meet her chartreuse gaze, she jerks her head, gesturing for me to follow her.

I know time is of the essence, but Abba has never said two words to me, and now she wants to talk? I can't help but wonder if she has something up her sleeve that will help me.

I jump off the stage and bob and weave through the Underworlders. Lucien is right behind me, quiet as a shadow. Before I reach her, Abba turns and disappears through the nearest door. I follow her into the first floor hallway.

My curiosity continues to grow as she leads us into an elevator and pushes the button to the fifth floor. I glance at Lucien only to see a scowl on his face. There are some baddies on this floor with some pretty scary A.C.I.D. scores. I have only ever been up this far once, and that was with Dad.

Ever since I was little, Dad has told me that there is no such thing as inherent evil. Even monsters are not inherently evil. All evil is created, either through hate, or jealousy, or revenge, or abuse, or fear, or power.

When I was five, Dad brought me to cell 517 as part of one of his many lessons about the Underworld. Whatever he wanted me to see was in the back of the dark cell, squatting and leaning against the far wall. I remember thinking how it just looked *wrong*. Its limbs were too long. The forearms rested against the ground and its eerily long fingers clawed at the ruts it had carved out of the concrete floor. Its knees almost touched the ceiling, and I realized that if it stood, the monster would be close to ten feet tall. The beast wore an elk skull over its face, obscuring all features beneath it. The deer antlers glinted in the pale light of the cell.

The thing suddenly jerked its head up and stared at the wall inches in front of its face for several seconds. Then, as I watched with wide eyes, it slowly turned to face me. A reflective glint shined in the pits of the deer skull where the monster's eyes should be. My heart pounded in my chest. I grew up with Underworlders. They didn't scare me. But this one...this one was different. It started singing as I watched, its head jerkily tilted to an unnatural angle. Low, baleful tones made the hairs on my arms stand at attention.

Dad told me the Underworlder in the cell was a wendigo. I didn't believe him at first because the thing I had just witnessed was nothing like Ona, a wendigo on the second floor that I regularly played battleship with through the food slot on her cell door.

The first time I met Ona, I was shocked to see how emaciated she was. She only wore a deerskin bikini, allowing me to see every single rib pressed tightly against the skin of her chest. Her limbs were as thin as brittle tree branches in winter. But despite her apparent starvation, her face remained beautiful. I used to smuggle her snacks from the pantry. She would never come out of her cell when I visited, though, no matter how many times I begged her.

I didn't know then that no amount of food would ever satisfy Ona. Dad explained to me outside of cell 517 that a wendigo is a half-beast creature that has an intense craving for human flesh. The more people a wendigo eats, the more powerful he becomes. However, the more he eats, the hungrier he gets. Of course, I was heartbroken when I realized my friend had eaten a person, but Dad told me Ona had no other choice. She was in a blizzard and did what she had to do in order to survive. Kanti, on the other hand, had purposefully murdered and ate humans to increase her powers. She killed seven people before the HTF captured her.

The elevator doors open with a ding, bringing me back to the here and now. I repress a shudder as I remember Kanti's unworldly keening. Thankfully, we take a left instead of right, the opposite direction of Kanti's cell. Although I question my dad's teaching methods, I have to admit that I never forgot his lesson on evil. If anything, it makes me even more wary of where we are heading on this level.

With a couple of quick steps, I catch up to the demon. I clear my throat. "Um...Abba? What's this all about? I kind of have a Task I have to get to."

All demons look similar: shiny, pitch-black skin, horns of some sort, claws or wings or tails. And they all reeked of that godawful stench of sulfur. Abba has horns that sprout from her forehead, curve around her pointy ears, and swirl back out at her jawline, kind of like a ram.

She doesn't answer.

I fall back into step with Lucien.

"Where do you think she's taking us?" I whisper out of the side of my mouth.

"I don't know," Lucien replies. If his brow could become any more furrowed, it would impede his line of sight. It was obvious he wasn't happy about our little detour. "We should not be here. We should be on the Surface already. You should already be tracking down those that escaped."

Abba stops suddenly, preventing me from saying something rather nasty to Lucien.

With one of her curved, three-inch claws, she types a code into a keypad beside the door of cell 588. There's a muted click, signaling the door is now unlocked.

Lucien puts a hand in front of me and pushes me behind him. With his right hand he procures a handgun from the waistband of his trousers.

The door swings open to reveal a short, fat man of Middle Eastern descent. He doesn't look all that scary, with his orange jumpsuit and protruding belly, but he must be something to have been placed on this level. As soon as he sees the gun, the fat, little man resumes his natural state, and I take back my earlier comment.

The compact cell fills with a red-tinged vapor as the djinn rises in the air. His torso grows as his legs disappear into a violent, swirling cyclone of smoke. His jumpsuit rips along the seams, exposing glowing crimson skin over tight muscles. His eyes, moments ago a regular brown, smolder like rubies. He begins speaking a language that sounds sort of like Arabic. His voice is so deep and ancient, it makes my bones hurt and my teeth clench.

Sensing things are about to go sideways, I make a risky move to get things under control.

I skirt around Lucien, sidestepping the hand he puts up to grab me and stop just in front of the threshold.

"You are before your princess and will act as such," I say, proud of myself for actually sounding the part and not like some disillusioned six-year-old. "Revert back to your human state, or my Guardian will be forced to take defensive actions."

The djinn hovers over the ground for a few more minutes. He opens his mouth to say something, but I stop him with a raised hand.

"Human form. Now."

His face twitches in barely suppressed aggravation, but he obeys. The smoke sucks back up into the djinn like someone had pressed rewind, leaving the air clear and calm, as he transforms back to his human form. The only evidence of his tantrum is his shredded jumpsuit.

Hesitantly, Lucien tucks away his gun, but he glares at Abba as he does. "I will inform the king of how you endangered the princess with your careless actions," he growls at her. "Now, leave us."

Abba's top lip lifts up in a hideous sneer, but she says nothing as she spins on her heel and disappears down the hallway. I make a note that she did absolutely nothing when the djinn lost his temper. I'd bet all the savings in my piggy bank that she is Team Zilah.

"What's your name?" I ask the djinn. He crosses his arms over his gut like a frustrated soccer mom at a McDonald's that's taking more than three minutes to push out her ten orders of chicken nuggets. He taps his foot rapidly against the cement floor.

The corners of his mouth curve down in an almost comical grumpy face. His eyes are still red and slit-pupiled. He must still be pissed. "It's Zaahir," he finally spits out. His human voice is nasally. "And I have some pertinent information I thought you'd like to know. I didn't expect to be accosted, though."

"Don't mind him," I tell Zaahir with a wave at the sulking bird-man in question. "Being chronically constipated makes him a little grumpy. What info do you have, and why do I have to have it now? I'm in a bit of a hurry."

"This won't take long, Princess," Zaahir assures me. He points across the hall to cell 589. "Go look in that cell."

The uncomfortable feeling of deja vu washes over me, and my eye twitches. But before I can even move, Lucien strides across the short space and peers into the window slot, saving me from potential years of therapy. "It's empty."

"Well, it shouldn't be," huffs Zaahir. His next words practically drip with sarcasm. "My good friend Khalil is supposed to be in there, but the little weasel somehow escaped during the king's spell."

My eyebrows raise, and I turn to Lucien.

"No one above Level Two should have been released," Luce answers my unspoken question in a quiet voice that gives me the bad kind of shivers.

I face the djinn again. "Why are you telling me this? You should be alerting my dad."

Zaahir rubs his rotund belly. "Two reasons, really. The first being that I want you to win. And the second being that I hate that little jerk.

"I'm guessing that catching a Level Five djinn would give you a better score than your sister, even with her head start," he continues. "And I'm willing to give you Khalil's whereabouts...if I get a little something in return."

"Depends what that little something is." I cross my arms. Knowing how greedy djinn tend to be, I expect him to ask for his freedom. Or at least for a bigger, better cell on a lower level. Maybe even a piece of my royal soul.

Instead he says, "Marshmallows."

"Marshmallows?"

"Yes."

"You want marshmallows," I repeat incredulously.

Zaahir nods and licks his lips. His hand goes from his belly to his black beard, stroking it thoughtfully. "Yes. The jet-puffed ones. The big ones—not the tiny, skimpy ones used for cocoa."

I bite my lip to keep from laughing. "You strike a hard bargain, but it's a deal. Now tell me where Khalil is."

Zaahir rattles off an address in downtown Seattle.

"Thank you, Zaahir. I'll bring you your marshmallows after the first Task is over."

"Princess!" the djinn calls as I turn to go. "You're going to need this."

He picks up something off of his bed. It's circular and appears to be wrapped in a pillow case. "Slap this on Khalil's wrist to trap him. He left it behind on his way out."

I take the object from him and peel back the fabric. Nestled inside is a cuff inscribed with rows and rows of a language I can't read.

"What is it?"

Zaahir smirks, his pupils thinning to the point that they're practically nonexistent. He gives me the heebie jeebies. "Think of it as a way to put the genie back into the bottle."

6

It's raining. Of course it is. What could make this day any better than a bit of running makeup?

Lucien puts the car in park, and I get out. A heavy feeling settles in my stomach as I look up at West Seattle's Children Hospital. Raindrops slap my cheeks and sting my eyes. I'm going to look like a raccoon by the time we make it inside.

"Are you sure this is the right place?" I ask when Lucien falls in step with me up the drive to the hospital's visitor's entrance. The pelting rain seems to have no effect on his immaculate hair.

"This is the address the djinn gave," he solemnly replies.

I clench my teeth until they feel like they'll crack under the pressure.

Like I told you before, djinn are greedy little Underworlders. And they're powerful. They are somewhat elemental, usually fire or air beings, which means they can make themselves invisible at will. They rarely go into their natural state, often only when they feel threatened or are alone. Each one has a human form and some even have an animal form they can transform into whenever they please. The really powerful ones can even cause humans to hallucinate if they maintain skin-to-skin contact. They are strong. Fast. And they live pretty much forever.

The really scary thing about djinn is that they can grant wishes, but it's always for a price. A djinn will grant whatever wish it is that you have, as long as you give them a piece of what they crave most: your soul. Not the whole thing, from what I know. Just enough to sate their appetite. But losing even a piece of your soul completely changes who you are. Many people that make deals with djinn end up killing themselves. All for a wish. And the real kicker is if you aren't super duper specific when you make your wish, the djinn will find some loophole in the terms and conditions and exploit your wish until you wish you were dead.

For example: say you wish for a million bucks. The djinn will make it so, and you'll be happy as a clam for a while. Weeks, months, maybe even years, but then the djinn's trickery will knock you off cloud nine and onto your ass. Maybe a company you've invested in will go under and cast you into poverty overnight. Or maybe the lottery ticket you bought ends up being fraudulent and the feds catch you and you end up spending the rest of your miserable days in prison. Then you're trapped in a cell with an inmate who has a swastika tattooed on his chest for the next thirty years.

That's oddly specific, I know, but it could definitely happen. Especially if a person were to deal with a djinn.

But what's really got my blood boiling now is this djinn's choice of soul food. How dare he come to a place such as this? How dare he prey off parents already mourning the deaths of their sick and injured children? How *dare* he give them hope only to yank it away later?

I'll be honest. I may just kill the little jerk.

We have just walked through the rotating glass doors when a thought hits me. How am I supposed to find this asshole? He's most likely in his human form, which could look like anything. He could be dressed as a visitor or a doctor or a nurse, who knows?

I'm about to ask Lucien when I feel it. I stop mid step and close my eyes.

Lucien's warm hand gently wraps around my upper arm. "Ember? What is it?"

I open my eyes and startle a bit when Lucien's face swims into focus just inches from mine. A silly little piece of me imagines leaning forward, just a little bit, to kiss those slightly asymmetrical lips.

Then I feel it again. The pull. Stronger this time, like there's half a magnet in my belly and its other half is pulling us closer.

"I know where he is," I say.

We start toward the elevator at the back of the room. I push number four as soon as the doors shut. I don't know how I know what floor to go to, but the little tug in my belly assures me we're getting closer.

The doors open and my eyes immediately go to the gently glowing sign posted on the ceiling several feet before us.

ONCOLOGY.

I clench my fist and grit my teeth. That bastard is making deals with cancer patients.

Without waiting for a second more, I follow the feeling in my gut. We trail through several hallways until we reach a corridor ending in a pair of frosted glass doors. I wrench one of them open. My limbs have all started to shake, and I can't tell if it's my internal compass or the fiery rage pulsing through my veins like lava.

I recognize him as soon as I see him. Of course, I've never seen this djinn before, but I know it's him by the way the tingling and the pulling feeling immediately increases to an almost uncomfortable level. There's a current of electricity humming inside my bones, like I could make a light bulb glow, like I could lift my hand and shoot out bolts of lightning and take over the world. The tiny hairs on my arms stand up.

If I wasn't so incensed, I'd actually describe the djinn as swoon-worthy. Handsome. Hot. The kind of attractive that makes girls scribble their names with his in their composition notebooks. He's tall, 6'5" maybe. His skin is bronzed by what I'm sure is thousands of years under the sun, and his long, thick, black hair is twisted into a messy knot at the back of his skull.

The djinn wears light green hospital scrubs, and a mask hangs in front of his throat.

When I first spot him, he's talking to a woman who has clearly seen happier days. Dark circles linger under her red and puffy eyes, and her clothes look like she's slept in them for several nights. She has the air of someone clinging to one last desperate hope. Unfortunately, that hope just happens to be a djinn.

I start down the hallway at a brisk walk. Lucien is calling my name, but I barely hear him. The djinn is so focused on delivering his sales pitch that he doesn't see me until I'm there.

I shove him hard enough to knock him over. Without thinking, I pounce on him and punch his stupid face as hard as I can.

"Ow!" He puts a hand over his smarting cheekbone.

I hit him again with the other fist. Unnecessary? Maybe. But totally worth the bloody knuckles.

He finally realizes who I am as I pull the aqua cuff from my hoodie pocket. His almond-shaped eyes go wide, and his pupils narrow into vertical slits, like a cat's eyes. I notice for the first time that he has a tight necklace—almost like a collar—made of the same stone around his neck. "That's right, you son of a gun," I growl. "Time to go home."

He struggles beneath me, his teeth gritted and bared. My peripherals pick up several tendrils of swirling blue smoke. I have to hurry before he goes full djinn. If that happens, I'll never be able to catch him.

I press my knee into his sternum to knock the air out of his lungs before slapping the cuff against his arm. The two pieces meld together with a satisfying click, and the cuff becomes an uninterrupted piece of blue stone circling the djinn's wrist. "Ha!"

Grinning in triumph, I go to stand up, but Khalil grabs me by the sleeve. His long fingers claw at the fabric of my hoodie, and he jerks me forward.

I expect him to be angry. Or resigned. Maybe even sad or disappointed. Instead, the look in his pale blue-green cat eyes is fear. "You have no idea what you've done."

I open my mouth to ask him what he's talking about when he touches my cheek with one slender finger. The hospital, Lucien, and everything else disappears, and in the time it takes me to blink, I'm transported to a world thousands of miles away.

My eyes flutter as the high sun sears my corneas. Gone is the hospital. Gone is Washington. I kneel on a sea of sand with nothing in either direction as far as the eye can see.

With shaking fingers, I reach a hand down through what should have been Khalil's heart and plunge my fingers into the hot grains of sand. Standing, I attempt to slow my breathing before I truly hyperventilate. My shoes sink into the sand, displacing piles of it that fall in against my ankles and make it hard to get my bearings.

"What the hell?" I ask. "What the *actual* hell?"

The heat of this arid environment has already begun to dry my wet clothes. Sweat begins to form on my forehead and upper lip.

This is a dream, obviously. It has to be.

But how can I feel the sun on my back? The sand between my toes? The sweat dripping down my temples? It has to be a dream, a very lucid dream. There's no other explanation.

"Lucien!"

My voice goes nowhere in this wasteland.

I spin in unsteady circles, straining my eyes to find an oasis or for some hint of civilization. It looks like I'm going to have to Flinstone it out of this hellscape of burning sand and sun. I shout an expletive as loudly as possible.

Does it fix my situation? No.

Does it make me feel better about this crappy situation? You betcha.

I start toward what I'm assuming is the west. After several feet, my right sneaker sinks into a miniature hill of sand. I go to shake the sand out of my shoe and glimpse something half-buried in the golden sand. Crouching down, I dust away the sand to reveal an aqua-colored stone that glimmers in the sunlight.

What is a stone like that doing in a place like this? I pluck it out of the sand. It's small, about the size of a walnut, but it's much heavier than I thought it would be. "What are you?" I wonder aloud.

As if in answer, the desert vanishes around me without warning. The sun extinguishes as if it were nothing more than a candle in the night.

I shove the stone in my pocket and set about stumbling around in the dark, mumbling profanities all the while. After an inordinate amount of time, I find a wall. Well, it's more like I walk into it, but still. Using my fingers, I feel about the cool stone wall, searching for a door or a light switch. But there seems to be nothing but more wall. The musty smell of dead air tells me that I must be in some sort of cave. How do I get myself into these situations?

But the real question is, should I go right or left? I can't even see my hand when I wave it in front of my face. What if I walk in on a slumbering bear or into another wall and break my nose? What if I fall into a pit filled with needle sharp stalactites and become an Ember-kabob? The possibility of death is way too high for my liking.

I growl and decide moving anywhere is better than staying in the same spot. I take off to the right, shuffling forward an inch at a time to avoid any sudden drop offs. After about a hundred yards of scooting along, the cave grows lighter. I hurry now that I can see in front of me, beyond ready to escape this strange dream. The cave abruptly makes a sharp turn, and on the other side is the light source that drew me this way. A small fire burns merrily in the middle of a cavern. A figure on the other side of the fire hunches over something in his hands, the flames before him casting deep shadows over his face. My heart picks up the pace as I look around and realize I have absolutely no weapon to protect myself with should this person be some cannibalistic cave dweller.

I suppose I'm safe as long as I keep the fire between us.

"Hello," I call out, my voice echoing eerily against the close stone quarters. I tentatively approach my side of the fire. As I get closer, I find that the person is a boy who looks to be about my age. "Hello?"

He doesn't look up from whatever he crouches over.

"Hey! Can you hear me, cave boy?" My shout doesn't even phase him. "I guess that answers my question."

I sidle closer to the stranger, and closer, until I'm only about a foot away. The flames continue to cast long shadows over his face, but I recognize the features now that I'm right in front of him.

"It's you!"

It's the djinn. He's skinnier and dirtier than the djinn I just sucker-punched back home, but it's definitely him. His filthy, ragged clothing hangs off of his nearly skeletal frame, and his hair falls into his face in locks matted with only God knows what.

He says something in a different language, and at first I think he's addressing me. But he's not. He's speaking to himself or talking to the item he's holding. His grubby hands turn an aqua-colored object over between the tips of his fingers.

My hands fly to my pockets, but the stone I found in the sand is gone. Khalil must have stolen it from me when I was lost in the dark, that bunghole.

"I don't know what game you're playing at, djinn. But that's my rock. I found it first."

He says something again, and an exuberant smile spreads across his face. I step forward to snatch my stone away from him, but hesitate. Something's not quite right.

It's then that I realize his eyes look different. They aren't the same freakish blue-green cat eyes I looked into at the hospital. These eyes are a light brown made amber by the firelight.

"You're human," I breathe, the realization hitting me in the chest like a sledgehammer. This person is as human as me. If I was confused before now, I'm absolutely mind-boggled now.

I go to touch him, to let him know I'm there, to feel his human body, to see if he is real, but as soon as I brush his shoulder, he fumbles the stone.

It dances across his fingers and dives into the flames with an eruption of glowing ashes.

Desperation washes away the smile that just lit up his features. He says something over and over again before thrusting his hand into the flames.

"You idiot—you're burning yourself!" I yell at him. It's pointless since he obviously can't hear me, but I feel like I still needed to point out how dumb he is for sticking his hand into a fire.

With a groan, Khalil procures the stone from the flames. His skin shines red and blistered all the way up his arm, past his elbow. The fool is lucky he didn't set himself on fire.

He cups the stone in both hands. Khalil breathes a sigh of relief and spends a moment just inhaling and exhaling with his head hung low. Suddenly, his head whips up, his face a mask of puzzlement. He opens his hands where he locked away the stone for us both to discover that the rock is glowing.

"Oh, jeez. What now?" I ask myself.

The light glows brighter with each passing second, illuminating Khalil's face and the dark cave. And it might just be me, but I swear a high-pitched hum comes from the stone cradled in Khalil's palms.

Before either of us can do anything else, the stone explodes. A million shattered pieces hit the walls and us with the sound of tinkling glass. An indigo smoke fills the tiny confines of the cave like someone just set off a gas grenade.

I expect to choke on the smoke, to die a slow and painful death by suffocation, but it doesn't affect me at all. After eddying on the air currents for a few breaths, the smoke begins to revolve in a counter-clockwise movement. As the cave clears, the fog pulls back into a blue stone that now rests on the cave floor.

Don't ask me how it's in one piece again, because I don't know. I nearly got my eye shot out by a shard of that confounded stone when it blew up, and yet, here it is, completely whole again.

When all of the smoke is gone, I find myself alone.

My body moves toward the stone. I don't *want* to move toward the stone, and I certainly don't want to touch it, but some outside force controls my limbs. I'm a marionette puppet despite how hard I fight back.

I clench my teeth and strain against my own muscles, but it's completely useless. My body kneels down and my hand seizes the stone. As soon as it touches my skin, I know I'm in trouble.

The cave disappears as if it never was. And maybe it wasn't. Images begin to flash in front of my eyes. Slow at first, then faster and faster. It doesn't take me long to figure out that what I'm seeing are Khalil's memories.

I see small hands ripping a stale chunk of bread into smaller pieces while hunger claws at my insides. I see a swath of the night sky dusted by millions of stars unhindered by city lights. I see the dark eyes of a young girl before she leans into my embrace as my heart beats against my ribcage with triumph.

I see the same girl lying in a crimson sea on the ground, her throat slit and her eyes seeing nothing. A man holding the knife that stole her life stands over her. Later, I see the people I know to be my mother and father in chains.

I see the cave and the stone and feel an ember of hope glow in the ashes of my broken heart. The hope turns into panic as the flames consume my one chance at redemption. There's pain as I find the stone in the coals, and then an explosion. I see my skin turn blue and feel my body fill with an intoxicating amount of power and magic.

I see the man who killed my beloved cower before me as I eat his dirty soul. I see the frail bodies of my parents in a deep trench. I was too late. Their hands are clasped together, their love outliving their deaths. I see countless faces and taste thousands of souls on my tongue. The greedy, the poor, the angry, the lost, the hopeful, the broken. Centuries pass, the years blurring into each other.

A girl with hair the color of copper with purple magic coursing around her. She traps me, locks me away in a cell. Hundreds of years go by while my surroundings remain unchanged. A chance to escape—a blood pact and an open door. I take it. A boy, his dark skin pallid and his eyes sunken. He wishes for his mother to be happy. I make it so. Another child strikes my face. No—a girl. She's much older than I first thought. There's so much anger in her eyes. She shackles me with a bracelet. She doesn't know. She doesn't know that she's been—

The memories halt abruptly as I'm slammed back into my body. My body. Ember's body. My eyes fly open as I gasp. My lungs burn like I just held my breath for ten minutes. Maybe I did. A ferocious headache pounds in the front of my skull to the beat of my frantic heart as I roll off Khalil and gulp down lungfuls of sweet, yet disgusting, hospital air.

Lucien is suddenly there, his face a mess of worry. His hands hover over different parts of my body, unsure of what exactly is wrong.

"What happened?" he asks.

I attempt to wave him away, but my arm is strangely heavy. So, instead, it just flops against the hospital tile like a dying fish.

Lucien whips out his gun and cocks it, the barrel aimed at the space between Khalil's eyebrows. "What did you do? *What did you do to her*!"

"What do you mean, what did *I* do to *her?* She's the one that attacked me!" Khalil shouts back.

I finally regain some of my composure. "Lucien, put the damn gun away before we get thrown in prison. I'm fine."

He breaks the death glare he aimed at Khalil and searches my face. I have to admit, Lucien's concern on my part is actually quite nice. Who am I kidding, though? The concern practically oozing out of his pores is probably more for his job security than my wellbeing.

"Let's get out of here," I suggest. "Then we'll talk about it."

Lucien helps me to my feet, and my head spins. I feel like I'm stuck on a merry-go-round from hell. "The djinn?" my Guardian asks.

"He comes with us," I answer. "I have a few questions for our little jailbird."

I point at Khalil, who is still sitting in the middle of the hospital hallway. The woman he was speaking to before this whole mind-trip episode is long gone. "Get up. We're taking you back."

He grits his teeth. A sheen of sweat breaks out across his forehead. "No."

And with that he poofs. Seriously, he just vanishes into a puff of smoke. The blue flumes twist into a violent knot in midair. Then, with a loud crack, the smoke collapses into itself and a blue stone falls to the ground. It rolls across the floor to rest at the toe of my shoe.

"Yes, you will." I smirk. I guess Zaahir's cuff really worked.

You'd have thought I learned better than to touch the stone during my little excursion into the djinn's head, but you thought wrong. I push up my sleeves, bend down, and scoop up the glittering stone. As it rolls into my hand, a wisp of smoke escapes from the stone itself. Instead of dispersing in the air like normal smoke would, it floats along the inside of my wrist. My heart jumps into my throat and threatens to leap out of my mouth. The blue mist snakes around my arm. It curves all the way around, creating a circle of smoke just above my pale skin. I hear a tiny *tnk* and watch with apprehension as the smoke solidifies into a thin blue bangle and shimmies down my arm to rest at the top of my wrist, quite similar to the cuff I slapped on to the djinn moments before.

It's exactly the same shade as the rock resting in my open palm. I immediately try to slip the bracelet off, but find that it's too tight to slip over my hand. There's no clasp, no hinge, no way to open the bangle.

I look up at Lucien, unsurprised to find a wry expression clouding his face.

"Uh oh," I say.

With a sigh of exasperation, Lucien leads us out of the hospital.

7

We make it back to the Underworld five minutes before midnight.

We don't meet in my Dad's office like I had imagined we would. Instead we are sent to a room I've only been in a handful of times. The Hall, a massive circular room with thirteen raised seats behind a rich mahogany desk, is essentially a courtroom where Underworlders are given their A.C.I.D. scores based on the atrocities they committed on the Surface and sentenced to the Pen.

The members of the HTF fill those seats now, with the Lord of the Underworld sitting in the middle in the Obsidian Throne. Supposedly, the throne changes to fit each ruler—to match their soul. Dad's is as ornate and kingly as one would expect from a sovereign, with black velvet cushions for the seat and the back. Black thorny vines tangle and twist above his head and behind his shoulders to form the armrests. Two glossy, stone roses carved from obsidian sit at the end of each chair arm. Dad has worn the outer petals smooth with hundreds of years of ruling. As Lucien and I approach, he absentmindedly rubs one of the petals with his left hand.

I briefly wonder how the throne would change if I become queen. Then I remember that I don't want to be queen. *Get it together, Em,* I scold myself.

"Approach the Council," a husky male voice commands. I recognize the thick German accent as Dad's right hand man, the head of the HTF—Armenius. Out of all of the HTF members, Armenius is definitely the most intimidating with his lumberjack beard and his Herculean muscles. All the Underworlders are scared of him, and rightfully so. I'm scared of him too. He's the type of person that tries to joke with you, but the jokes always fall flat, so you don't ever know if he's kidding or if he's being serious. I hate when Dad seats me next to him during our seasonal HTF dinners.

I ascend to the dais positioned in front of the Council's tall seats. A droplet of nervous sweat slides down my spine. Zaahir better be right about Khalil's capture gaining me more points. We had next to no time left after apprehending the djinn, so my Underworlder haul is pretty pathetic.

And so much is riding on this Task. On the way here, I kept trying to reassure myself. Even if I lost this Task, there are still two more. I could still come out on top—I mean, Max could. If we find him, and if we convince him to take this crappy job, that is.

Very aware of the thirteen pairs of eyes examining my every move, I chuck the two squirming pillowcases onto the slate floor before me. I undo the knot of the first pillowcase and unceremoniously dump Benny out. He had escaped the Underworld only to take up a post on the corner of our house. The tiny idiot truly thought he had hidden himself well, but I saw him as soon as we pulled into the driveway. Perched on the gutter like an ugly ass pigeon, Benny stood frozen with his little claws curled up against his stone chest and his mouth open like a shrieking velociraptor.

After grabbing a pillowcase from inside the house, I knocked him off the roof with the neighbor kid's half-flat basketball. It was so easy, I'm about six thousand percent sure I won't even get any credit for his capture and return.

Benny rubs his grotesque head after bouncing off the floor of the Hall. "Ouch. Ouch. Ouch," he mumbles before scurrying up the front of the Council's bench. He skitters across the stately desktop toward the fiery-headed HTF member named Elowen. I'm taken aback for a moment as I realize I saw her in the djinn's flashback. Elowen was the one to capture him all those years ago. I wonder if she knows he was released tonight. She doesn't seem too concerned as Benny creeps up her arm and settles on her shoulder beneath her copper-red curls.

The next Underworlder is a tad bit more formidable. But it's still pitiful. With anxious, trembling fingers, I untie the knot holding the pillowcase shut.

An Ittan-momen shoots out of the sack, hissing as it flies through the air. At the very last second, my hand shoots out and nabs its tail end, preventing it from reaching the Council members. I may have imagined it, but I could have sworn that Nobu cracked a smile. I bet it's not often that he sees an Underworlder from back home.

Before you go researching on Wikipedia, an Ittan-momen is an Underworlder from Japan. It's a sentient roll of cotton that flies through the night and strangles people—think evil roll of toilet paper, and that pretty much sums up an Ittan-momen. Go ahead and look it up if you don't believe me.

It was hiding in my sock drawer. I wanted to change out of my sandy socks—Lucien told me on the way home that I didn't physically go anywhere when I got sucked into Khalil's memories, but that doesn't explain the pile of desert sand I found in both of my shoes—before returning to the Underworld. I pulled open my drawer, and the Ittan-momen sprang at me like someone had booby-trapped my dresser. It wrapped itself around my head several times, blocking my nostrils. It surrendered pretty quickly when I threatened it with a pair of scissors I found lying on my desk, though.

I feel completely inadequate as Armenius waves one of his tree trunk-like arms, gesturing for a guard to come forward to collect the feisty little cotton roll from me. "Do you have anything else, Princess?" His words are a mix of hopefulness and disappointment.

My stomach clenches painfully with the realization that he wanted me to win. I glance at all of the other members of the HTF. Their faces are blank masks, giving away none of their thoughts or feelings, but I can almost feel their dissatisfaction in me like a soul-crushing weight on my shoulders.

I've known all of them since I was a baby. They've all been at Dad's side since the beginning. Some magic has kept them alive for the past five hundred years. I wonder what will happen to them once there's a new ruler on the Obsidian Throne. If Dad dies, will they die too? I push the uncomfortable thought aside.

Dad chose them from all over the world, each one from a different country or region. He explained to me once that he did this so he would have more insight into Underworlders from other places and cultures. Smart, huh? I'd never have thought to do something like that. Another reason why I'm not fit to be queen.

"Yes," I say, but it comes out as more of a croak. I try again. "Yes, I have one more."

As I grab the stone in my pocket, I feel a peculiar sensation against the sensitive skin of my palm. Almost like I had grabbed a live butterfly. I pull it out and study it for a moment, but the blue stone looks exactly the same. It matches the exact color of the bracelet circling my wrist.

I attribute the weird feeling to nerves. Adrenaline. Insanity, maybe.

"Show yourself," I whisper before tossing the stone before the Council.

Before the stone can touch the ground, Khalil explodes from his blue prison with a sound like thunder. Gone is the handsome man in nurse's scrubs. Here is a djinn in his full, terrifying glory.

With an enraged roar, his djinn form grows until he fills the space between me and the Council. He grows so tall that his head scrapes the twenty-foot ceiling. His aqua-colored skin stretches over huge, taut muscles that could, without a doubt, rip my head off of my body. It'd probably be like taking a cap off of a pen for Khalil. But way more bloody. And painful.

Every member of the HTF scrambles to their feet as exclamations in several different languages ring out across the Hall. Panic and helplessness threaten to choke me. I find it hard to breathe. This is definitely not going as I had planned.

Khalil chants in ancient Arabic as his blue-green smoke swirls around him like a tempest. Wind claws at my clothes and tears my hair out of its ponytail holder. The djinn reaches toward the Obsidian Throne, his glowing slit-pupiled eyes focused on the woman who had imprisoned him all those years ago. Purple electricity surges out of Elowen's fingertips toward

Khalil as she stares down the djinn, but her powers have next to no effect on the Underworlder as his massive fingers inch closer to her.

A blue orb slams into the djinn's left eye. The Underworlder roars his fury and turns to find the source. Dad stands tall, his hands glowing with blue flame. "Stand down!" he orders, his voice cutting through the cacophony of chaos and confusion.

My stomach drops to my feet as Khalil turns his attention to my dad, Elowen seemingly forgotten for the moment. Khalil's fingers cross over the desk separating the Council from us. Armenius unsheathes a broadsword from its scabbard strapped to his back and swings it over his head, but the iron blade does nothing to the djinn's aqua skin, despite Armenius' superhuman strength.

The djinn is going to kill my dad.

I step forward. The aqua smoke eddies around my knees, completely obscuring the floor. I have no powers like Elowen or my dad. I don't have brute strength like Armenius. But I do have one thing they don't. I glance at the bracelet surrounding my wrist and then raise my hand to point at the colossal Underworlder before me. "ENOUGH!"

My voice booms in the circular Hall, cutting through Khalil's incessant chanting and the frantic yelling of the HTF. The towering djinn swivels his head to look at me, confusion and agitation etched onto his face.

I raise my chin and square my shoulders. "No more. Return to your human form *now.*"

The howling winds cease blowing like someone had flipped a switch. I feel a pull around my knees and look down to see the smoke flowing back toward the awestruck djinn. As the aqua fog recedes, Khalil's blue skin shifts color until it's once again bronze, and his body shrinks until it's shrouded in the mystical mist. The smoke completely clears within seconds, revealing Khalil on his hands and knees.

I can see him panting from across the room. He hangs his head between his arms, and his unbound hair flows over his shoulders to pool in a dark puddle on the ground beside his hands.

My eyes rove over his broad shoulders and down the line of his strapping back muscles to the round curve of his backside. It takes me a whole hot second to realize that I am indeed seeing his bare bum because he's nude. The only things adorning his naked body are the aqua bracelet and the matching collar.

I avert my gaze as a blush burns in my cheeks. Don't get me wrong, I'm no Sandra Dee. I've had my fair share of boyfriends. Despite being head over heels for that idiot Lucien. I think some part of me hoped that another boy's attention might dampen the unwanted feelings I have for Lucien, but alas. It's all wishful thinking.

I even let one boy get some under the shirt, over the bra action. His name was Micah. We met at a concert, and as it turns out, our preference in music was about the only thing we had in common. Anyway, what I'm trying to say is that I've watched Game of Thrones, but seeing a naked person through a TV is way different than standing across the room from one.

Instead of looking at Khalil's prone form, I turn to the Council. The majority still have their weapons out, half-raised as if they aren't sure whether the danger has passed or not.

Elowen, purple electricity still sizzling and popping along her skin, speaks first. Her thick Scottish accent coats her words like honey. "I know this Underworlder. I captured this djinn almost four hundred years ago. He's a Level Five! Why was he released?"

Dad's dark eyebrows pull down over his eyes. He turns to his right and addresses a short man with a mustache that curls at the ends. Celio has been rocking some sort of facial hair for as long as I can remember, but this style has been my favorite by far. Dad's voice is careful and dangerous as he says, "Celio, explain."

I've never heard my Dad sound like that. He's *seriously* pissed.

"I—I don't know!" Celio stammers. He desperately shuffles through a stack of paper before him. He must not find what he's looking for because he drops the papers and stares at his hands like he had written the answers to a test there only to find it washed away when he wasn't paying attention. He mutters to himself in Italian before saying, "Only

Underworlders from Level One and Two were supposed to be released!"

I have to scrunch up my face to keep the smile from forming on my lips. Celio always reminds me of Mario when he gets flustered and his accent thickens. A slightly hysterical giggle threatens to escape me. I must be losing it.

"Well, clearly something went amiss," Dad snaps. He rubs a hand over his jaw. "We will have to deal with the breach after Zilah presents herself before the Council and the Judgment has been made. We'll have to do inventory to ensure no other Underworlders were released without our knowledge—Ember."

I jump at the sound of my name. My eyes had wandered over to Khalil's prone, naked body once more. He may be an evil son-of-a-gun, but he certainly does have a nice derrière.

"Yes?" I say, voice squeaking.

"Take your djinn into my office and wait there for me. We will discuss today's events then."

My djinn?

"Yessir!" The djinn doesn't look up at me as I approach. I nudge his leg with the toe of my shoe. "Get up."

Surprisingly, he does so without complaint. I keep my eyes directed on the ceiling so they don't accidentally deviate to his no-no area.

"Let's go."

He starts toward the door, his bare feet making next to no sound on the hard floor. Lucien and I follow him closely to make sure he doesn't try to make a break for it. We go down the hallway and take a left, and I direct him into the third room to the right. Dad's dark office floods with light as we enter. Motion sensors—not as Underworldly as torches, but way more efficient.

The djinn, pulling at the collar circling his throat, walks over to a corner of the elaborate Persian rug covering the center of Dad's study and falls to the floor. He folds himself into the lotus position, facing away from us. I watch his back tense up and then relax once, twice, and once again.

The djinn shouts a stream of R-rated curses. He unravels his twisted legs and repositions his body. I hear him inhale deeply and exhale, and then watch as his muscles tense. His open hands, resting on both of his knees, tighten into fists.

The djinn runs his fingers through his hair and pulls, making the tips of his inky black hair sashay in the space between his shoulder blades and butt crack. Khalil heaves a great, big sigh that slowly morphs into what I can only describe as maniacal laughter.

Lucien grabs the throw blanket I bought Dad for Christmas three years ago and tosses it at the man on the floor. Khalil ignores the blanket as it falls into his lap and tumbles over in another fit of hysterics. I stand over him as tears leak from the crinkled corners of his eyes.

I cross my arms. “What’s so funny, djinn?”

His chest heaves up and down. He’s out of breath from laughing so hard. Khalil rolls from his side onto his back. His eyes open, and his pupils rapidly go from circles to slits. Like a cat. They are a peculiar color between green and blue. People don’t have eyes that color.

His body vanishes into a cloud of smoke, but he swiftly reappears. When he materializes, he’s no longer naked and no longer on the floor. Khalil takes two steps toward me, narrowing the distance between us until our faces are inches apart. He wears a dark scarlet, high-collared shirt with gold embroidery and flowing white pants. A white headscarf covers his head and hides his hair.

Khalil’s hand shoots out and grabs my forearm. He examines the band I now wear. “Who told you about this magic?” he asks, gesturing to the bracelets circling our wrists with his free arm.

Lucien takes a step forward.

I make an attempt to jerk away, but it’s useless. “Let’s just say a little bird told me.”

One corner of Khalil’s mouth pulls up in a contemptuous smile. “You are a foolish girl.”

“And you’re a dick.” I pull back my leg and slam my shoe into Khalil’s shin. "That’s for trying to kill my dad.”

The kick does the trick and Khalil instantly releases me. He hisses through his teeth and brings his injured leg up to his chest.

"You'll rue the day we met, Princess. I promise you this," he growls.

"Yeah, yeah. Just sit down and shut the hell up."

His eyes flash with rage, but he acquiesces. Surprisingly.

Lucien comes over to me, his forehead creased in deep thought.

"My, my, my," I tell Lucien under my breath. "For being a big, bad djinn, he certainly listens well."

"Ember—"

"I mean, I told him to stop in the Hall, and he did. Then I told him to sit, and he did! It's like he *has* to obey me," I say, laughing.

"Ember, the bracelet—"

"How crazy would that be, huh?"

"Ember!"

"What!"

The doors to Dad's study fly open, and he strides in with Zilah and several members of the HTF in his wake. Fury paints Dad's usually handsome features into stone. He flings an arm in Khalil's direction and the djinn soars across the room to slam into the far wall. The collision is powerful enough to knock several picture frames to the floor.

"Who released you?" Dad asks calmly, almost quietly. And for some reason, it's way scarier than if he had screamed.

Khlail's hands claw at his throat. An invisible hand squeezes his windpipe and drags him a few more inches up the wall. His eyes just begin to bulge when Dad waves his hand once more. The djinn crumples to the floor and begins to cough.

"Your king asked you a question," Lucien growls.

Khalil looks up. The whites of his eyes are red where capillaries have burst. He sneers. "He is not my master."

I grimace. Wrong answer, dude.

Dad lifts his hand, and his fingers constrict, claw-like. Khalil falls forward as his blood-curdling screams fill the room. Goosebumps crawl up my spine, and I have to look away as Khalil convulses in pain.

My father steps forward and relaxes his hand. I've always known he had power over the Underworlders, but I had no idea the extent of it. Now I understand how he has kept his seat on the Obsidian Throne for so long.

"You will tell me who released you," the king says, his voice quiet yet forceful. "And then you will die."

Khalil's shoulders shake, and at first I think he's sobbing. It's only when he lifts his head that I see his face is split into a triumphant smile. He isn't crying. He's laughing. Again.

"Nothing would please me more than meeting a final death," the djinn states as he pushes himself onto his knees. "But know this, Your Highness: if I die, so does the princess."

Khalil points, and every head turns to look at who he is talking about.

I turn too, but no one is behind me.

"Me?" I ask, my voice a squeak.

"Your daughter is bound to me, and I to her," Khalil continues. "I am under her control."

Father's molten gaze shifts to me. I raise my hands up to show him I have no idea what this lunatic is talking about. My sleeves slip down, and Dad's eyes go from my face to my wrist, where the bracelet rests oh-so-innocently.

Dad has always been an open book. At least to me, anyway. I can read what he is thinking or feeling just from the line of his mouth and the set of his shoulders. So, what I see next may or may not have made me pee my pants a little bit.

He shifts from angry to shocked to horrified to absolutely-freakin-pissed all in the time it takes me to inhale and exhale.

Dad crosses to me and takes my arm. His grip is tight enough to show me he's serious, but still gentle. Even at his angriest, Dad would never hurt me. "What have you done, Ember?"

"I didn't do anything!" I pull my arm free. Why is it that people keep doing that to me? I need to quicken my reflexes or something because it's really starting to annoy me.

He shakes his head. "Why? Why can't you ever do anything right?"

My heart jumps in my throat. His words are a knife to my chest. "Dad—"

"I thought you'd be fine with a Task as simple as this," he says, voice low. "How hard is it to capture a few minor Underworlders? Why must you always make such a mess of things?"

"Excuse me?" My voice jumps several octaves as anger seeps in to replace the hurt. "At least *I* didn't release a Level Five Underworlder. At least *I* caught him and brought him back before he could cause any damage up there. At least *I* could stop him when he almost took out the entire HTF!"

He opens his mouth to retort or chastise me some more, but changes his mind. Dad's lips press into a thin line as he takes a few steps back. He rubs his temples while squeezing his eyes shut. While he regains his composure, I peer around him to find Zilah with her arms crossed over her chest and a smug smile on her mouth. I want to make a rude gesture toward her, but refrain from doing so chiefly because she is standing by Armenius and I don't want him to get the wrong idea.

Dad traverses over to his desk and leans over it, his hands palms-down on the cherry oak wood. He lifts his head and takes in everyone in the room.

"Ember's right," he says. "Which is why I have decided that she has won the first challenge."

"What?" I squawk.

"What!" Zilah shrieks.

"Although she had captured less Underworlders," Dad continues, "Ember did manage to capture a Level Five djinn. She also maintained her composure while the djinn attacked, which most undoubtedly saved the life of several Huntsmen, including me."

"Father!" Zilah exclaims. She crosses her arms and literally stomps her foot like a spoiled child. "That's not fair!"

Dad's expression hardens. It's clear he's not in the mood for his decrees to be questioned. "It has been decided, Zilah. I'll hear no more about it. Now, go and prepare for the next Task. It will take place two months from now."

"But Father—"

"I said, get out!"

The lights flicker in response to his anger. His power courses through the room like electricity. The hair on my arms stands on end.

No one argues with him this time. I duck my head and head to the door with the rest of the crowd.

"Everyone except Ember and the djinn," Dad adds.

My stomach drops. I want to hide behind Lucien, but he exits with the rest with hardly more than a sideward glance in my direction. Zilah stomps out, nose in the air and arms still crossed over her bedazzled chest.

The door shuts behind Armenius as he's the last one to go. I'm still turned away from Dad, and I stand still as stone. Maybe, if I don't move, he won't see me. Like a T-rex.

"Come here, Ember."

So much for that theory.

I go to his desk, but I refuse to look at him. His words really hurt me, even if they were true.

"I thought all the binding jewelry had been destroyed," he begins, voice quiet. "And even if we somehow missed one, all the djinn have been in the Pen for several centuries. Something like this should have never happened."

At 'this,' he gestures to me and Khalil who still sits against the far wall.

Dad continues, "It's old magic, and nearly impossible to break. It can be done, but it will take months of research. Possibly years."

I bite the inside of my cheek and rub a finger along the edge of the desk before me. *Yeah, yeah, yeah. Get to the point,* I think. *Tell me how big of a disappointment I am and let me go, so I can go topside and eat a tub of triple chocolate ice cream and watch some trash TV.*

"Despite what that means, you obviously can't miss school until we figure out a solution. So, Khalil will just have to go to the Surface with you. He'll be enrolled in your school Monday morning. That way you won't miss any of your classes."

My head snaps up. I may have zoned out a bit before, but Dad certainly has my attention now.

"I don't understand. Why do we have to do this?"

Dad sighs. "That bracelet on your wrist that you somehow managed to find and put on means that Khalil is bound to you, and you to him."

"I didn't put it on! A djinn—"

"I don't want to hear it, Ember. I don't care how it happened, but it did and now you will have to deal with the consequences. Khalil will have to be by your side until we figure this out. Depending on the strength of the magic in the binding bracelet, the djinn probably won't be able to be more than a couple dozen feet away from you at all times."

My jaw drops. I glance over my shoulder at the djinn in question. The expression on his face shows me that he's as happy about the arrangement as Dad is. "Well, why can't he just turn into that rock? I can put him in my pocket while I'm at school. Maybe I can let him out when we get home. He can run around the yard a bit or something to stretch his legs."

Dad's already shaking his head before I even finish. "He cannot remain in that form for very long. A few hours perhaps, but then he will revert back to his natural state. However, he may remain in his human form indefinitely."

"Oh my God," I say.

"Indeed. I hope you see how serious this is now, Ember. Old magic shouldn't be trifled with—especially by young, foolish girls."

He cuts me off again as I protest. "Enough. What's done is done. Djinn, come here."

Khalil rises slowly, shakily. His neck is still angry and red from the choking he received earlier. He shambles over to the desk, taking his sweet time.

When he reaches us, Dad addresses him. "Listen to me, djinn, and listen well. If this were any other situation, I would refuse to let you leave this place. However, Ember is too close to finishing school to miss classes due to this predicament. You will go with Ember to the Surface. You will *not* use your magic while there. You will *not* grant wishes. And you will *not* take souls for payment. For all intents and purposes, you will be a normal boy, a foreign exchange student staying at the Ashworth's home. As soon as we come up with a way to unbind you, you'll immediately be called back to the Underworld and imprisoned once again for your crimes."

Khalil reveals no expression except complete and total boredom. I half expect him to fall asleep as Dad speaks.

"Is that understood?"

The djinn gives a barely perceptible nod.

"Very well." Dad drops into the chair behind his desk. "Now get out. I need some peace and quiet. And a strong drink."

I'm still a little in shock by this turn of events, but I don't wait around for Dad to say it again. I take Khalil by the arm and drag him out of the office. Lucien looks perplexed as I burst through the doors and yank Khalil down the hall, mumbling obscenities the whole way home.

8

"No," Lucien says.

"Yes," I reply.

"No."

"That's what he said!"

"There must be another way."

"I wish there was, but there isn't." I take a deep breath before continuing. "Dad said he wants you to go up to the school tomorrow and enroll the djinn. Tell them he's a foreign exchange kid from the Middle East. We'll have to fabricate some records so they don't get suspicious."

Lucien crosses his arms. I mirror him, and we turn from our spot in the doorway to look at the djinn in question.

Khalil reclines against the couch cushions, remote aimed at the TV and flips through channels as quickly as possible. He mentioned on the way up to the Surface about somehow getting a contraband laptop into his cell a few years back. He wouldn't say how he did it, but he binged all of the shows that were downloaded onto it before he got caught and had to give it up. His favorite show he watched was some reality show about a family that was somehow famous although none of them actually did anything. Even though I had never watched it before, I know what show he was talking about. I almost feel sorry for him. Out of all the trash TV to watch on a bootlegged device, he had to watch that one? And he actually likes it? *Blegh.*

"But he's an *Underworlder*," Lucien protests, pulling me out of my thoughts.

"Yes, Sherlock. I'm very aware of that."

"And a Level Five, at that."

"I know, I know." I bite my lip. I really effed up this time. That fat bastard of a djinn is going to get it the next time I make it to the Pen. He tricked me with the bracelet, and I can't believe I actually fell for it. I think I'll buy a bag of marshmallows and just eat it outside his door. Little jerk. I'll stuff my cheeks until I gag, and then I'll just spit them in the trash. Maybe I'll leave one on the rim of his window just to taunt him.

"Ember!"

I shake my head to return from my vengeful daydream. From the look on Lucien's face, he must have called my name several times. "Sorry, what'd you say?"

"Where is the djinn going to sleep?"

"I hadn't thought about that. I guess on the couch until we can figure out something better."

"No. Absolutely not. I don't trust him."

"I'll lock my door. It'll be *fine*, Luce," I add when my Guardian gives me another one of his patented looks of skepticism. "Plus, he can't do anything to me. If I die, he dies, remember?"

"That does not reassure me in the least."

"Yeah, not my best argument. But I'm too tired to care about it now."

I stomp over to where Khalil is watching a rerun of a 90's sitcom. I guess his guilty pleasure wasn't on at the moment. I snatch the remote out of his hand and hit the power button.

"Rude," he says.

"Sit up. We have rules to discuss."

I can't say I'm not pleased when Khalil does as I say. This whole Simon Says game is going to be fun, I can tell.

I stand up straight and narrow my eyes at him. "I don't care if you watch TV all night. Just remember that we have to be at the school before eight. Sleep on the couch. Don't leave this house. And...stay away from sharp objects and firearms."

I throw the remote in his lap. As he picks it up, he asks, "What is DVR?"

"It records shows you want to watch later."

You'd have thought I told him it's the Holy Grail.

"Gods, I love technology," he mutters before pressing play.

"See?" I tell Lucien as I pass by him into my room. "He's all set. Goodnight."

The door shuts before an objection can leave his mouth. I lean against the sturdy wood for a moment. Although my body is exhausted, my mind is still spinning from the events of today. I doubt I'll be able to sleep at all tonight.

I attempt to take a deep, even breath, but it's too late. My chin quivers, and I can't hold it back any longer. My hands clamp over my mouth to muffle my sobs as I slide down the door to the floor.

Dad's words play over and over again in my head. His disappointment set on repeat. Each time I hear those words, the knife in my heart digs in a little deeper, twists a little sharper. I can barely breathe for the pain in my chest. I keep picturing Khalil in his true djinn form. Visions of what would have happened had I not commanded him to stop make me want to vomit. It's been one hell of a day.

The thin bracelet brushes against my cheek as I wipe away the hot tears trailing down my face. Although I know it's useless, I hook one finger inside the bracelet and pull with all my might. I grunt and yank until I'm red in the face and the bangle cuts into my skin. Despite all of that, I don't even put a dent in it. I bend my knees up and rest my head there.

How had I gotten myself into this mess?

And, more importantly, how do I get out of it?

As predicted, I can't go to sleep. I toss and turn and flail about, but nothing I do is comfortable.

A growl emerges from my lips as I turn from my back to my stomach. The only thing that does is make me realize how hungry I am. I can't even remember the last time I ate. A bowl of Cocoa Puffs calls my name from the kitchen.

I slip out of my room, careful not to make any noise. Don't want to wake up the djinn, or worse, alert my helicopter Guardian that I'm leaving the safe zone. After tip-toeing down the hall and pouring the chocolatey goodness into my favorite color-changing bowl, I'm feeling pretty confident that I'll be able to finish my midnight snack in peace.

My confidence is shattered, though, as a shadow fills the doorway just as I bring a spoonful of puffs to my mouth.

"I don't know which one you are, but go away."

The shadow lingers.

"Lucien, I mean it. Just leave me alone, okay?"

He steps into the kitchen, and the light from the moon reveals Lucien in all of his bare-chested glory.

It's a good thing I had finished chewing, because I probably would have choked. "Lucien! My God, put on a shirt!"

I hide my eyes with my hands and wait for him to leave. A fire burns in my cheeks. I've never seen Lucien half-naked before. I mean, I have, but only in my fantasies. Never in real life.

A warm pair of hands circles my wrists, startling me so much that I almost slide off my stool. I expected Lucien to flee the room in mutual embarrassment, not come closer to me. And definitely not close enough to touch me.

"Lucien, what—"

"You were so brave today," he whispers. His words totally catch me off guard. My mouth falls open as he smiles down at me. "I don't think I've ever been more proud of you."

"Wha-what do you mean?"

He raises a hand and rubs the back of his knuckles over my cheek. Goosebumps race across my skin as a shiver shimmies down my spine. "You saved everyone in the Hall tonight—the HTF members, yourself, and your dad. You did so good."

"What are you doing, Luce?" I stand up so quickly that the stool's legs screech against the tile.

He steps even closer. I back up until I bump into the kitchen counter. There's nowhere else for me to go. He's so close. *So close.* All I'd have to do is tilt my head up a bit further and his lips would be on mine.

"Something I should have done a long time ago."

His large hands cup my face, and he closes the gap between us. The planets align, and I'm pretty sure someone is setting off fireworks next door. His soft lips move against mine, and I can't believe that this is finally happening. I've pictured it so many times and so many different ways.

My arms wind around his neck as he lifts me up and sets me on the countertop. I pull him in even closer, my hands snaking into his hair. This is really happening. Oh, my God. This is really happening. My fingers dance over the ridges of his broad shoulders and down his back to his waist. With a sensual sigh, his lips trail along my jawline and to my neck. I close my eyes as a shuddering breath leaves my body.

"Why now?" I manage to ask.

He pulls back. "I thought I was going to lose you today. First in the hospital, then in the Hall. I've never been more scared."

I laugh. "So, all it took was a couple of near-death experiences?"

"I should have done this much sooner," he says with a small smile. "I just didn't know how."

He bends his head again and kisses the pulse just below my jaw. "I love you, Princess. I always have."

The words should have made me explode in ecstasy, considering they're all I've wanted to hear since I realized I was in love with Lucien. Instead, my blood turns to ice, and I push away.

Lucien never calls me that, has *never* called me that. I'm always Ember to him.

I look at him and realize his face isn't right. The scar in his eyebrow is angled the wrong way. His upper lip is too full. His eyes are too light.

"You aren't Lucien."

Fake-Lucien blinks at me, and a smile I've never seen Lucien wear before pulls up the corners of his lips.

"Damn," he says in a voice that's not his. "I went too far, didn't I?"

I squeeze my eyes shut, and when I open them, I'm no longer in the kitchen. I'm in my room. In my bed. And Khalil is standing over me with his hand on my arm.

I jerk away and kick out at him, but the blankets draped over my legs hinder me and the djinn is easily able to step aside.

He cackles. "How sad. And how... *unoriginal.* Could there be a more cliché love story?"

"You son of a—"

"What? You should be thanking me. I've just given you a glimpse of what could be, of what could happen if you would allow me to make it so. All I'd need is just a tiny, little, bitty piece of your soul."

I roll out of bed and tear open the drawer of my nightstand. Inside is a small throwing knife that Lucien insisted I keep after he heard about the vampire incident. I grab it and face the djinn.

"Nuh-uh," he says in a sing-song voice. I want to stab him in the throat as he waggles a finger at me. "None of that, Princess. Remember, if I go down, you go down with me."

"I may not be able to kill you, but I can hurt you all I want."

The djinn rolls his eyes. "Spare me the theatrics. What could you possibly do to hurt me—"

I hurl the knife before he can finish his question. The three-inch blade buries into the meaty part of his thigh. Up to the hilt.

"Quiet," I command as he sinks to the floor. His mouth opens in a soundless scream. "Don't want to wake Lucien. He wouldn't be happy."

I walk over and wrench the knife out. "It's an iron blade if you were wondering. Underworlders tend to dislike this metal more than any other. I guess djinn do too."

Tendrils of blue smoke swirl along his skin. His pupils have reverted back to their djinn state. The cat eyes flash dangerously as he speaks, but no noise comes out.

"What's that?" I ask. "I can't hear you. Human girl got your tongue?"

He goes to move, but I'm faster. The knife's point rests just below his jaw, right where the fake Lucien kissed me minutes earlier.

"I've had enough of your shenanigans," I say to him. "There's no telling how long you and I are stuck together, and I'd prefer it if we could get along. Okay, maybe not *along*, but we at least have to tolerate each other until Dad can break this spell. So, here's what's going to happen: I'm going to put away my knife, and you are going to sit right there while I think. *Comprende*?"

He glares at me, but says nothing.

I wipe the blade on his shirtsleeve before stepping away. Being careful not to turn my back on the Underworlder, I roll my desk chair over to the djinn and find my own spot on the corner of my bed. "Take a seat."

He does so, albeit begrudgingly. A ring of blood stains the white fabric of his pants, but I'm sure he's already healed the wound by now. If it were any other type of metal, he'd have healed almost instantly. Iron takes a little more time to recover from.

"Okay, now where should I start?" I ask, tapping my index finger on my lips. "How about this: don't you *ever* make me hallucinate again, or I swear to God I'll chop your penis off faster than you can say 'Lorena Bobbitt.' Got it?"

He nods.

"Good. Also, you are not allowed to make anyone else hallucinate while you're up here. No one...unless I say it's okay. Bianca could be the exception...ooh, the things we could do—but only if I give you permission!"

Khalil rolls his eyes.

"Oh, and another thing. You are prohibited from shifting into your djinn form while on the Surface. Keep your eyes human. And for the love of all things kosher, do not grant any wishes, don't take any souls, and do *not* do anything to get your stupid self killed. I might be an overly emotional teenage girl with a really weird life, but it's my life and I don't want to die anytime soon. Got it?"

The djinn takes a deep breath and begins talking, but there's still no sound coming out.

"Oops, sorry. You can speak again."

He clears his throat. "I said, I have a request for you, if the princess will allow it."

"Quit calling me Princess. People will look at you funny if you say that on the Surface. What's your request?"

"Would it kill you to say please every once in a while? You're really quite bossy."

"I'm a princess," I tell him. "It's my job to be bossy. Now go."

He rises and goes to the door but stops with his hand on the doorknob. Khalil lifts the arm that his bracelet is on and touches his collar. "You have no idea what it's like," he says, voice tight with emotion.

I don't want to give him the satisfaction of asking him what he's talking about, but curiosity gets the best of me. "What are you going on about now?"

"To be enslaved," Khalil elaborates, voice soft. He doesn't meet my eyes, choosing instead to examine a picture of me and Hannah I have tacked to a corkboard by the door. "For most of my life, I've been someone's slave or in someone's servitude. I refuse to die that way, Ember. I *will* be free. No matter the cost."

Sympathy tugs at my heart strings for a moment. He's right, after all. I have no idea what it's like to be a slave to someone's every beck and call. But then I remember him taking a piece of a terminally ill boy's soul at the hospital and nearly ripping my dad apart in the Hall, and I don't feel so bad anymore.

"Get out...please."

Khalil listens this time. He has to unlock the door before exiting. I relock it as soon as the door clicks shut behind him. Djinns are known to be sly, but this one is proving to be especially cunning. I'm going to have to watch him much more closely from now on.

I glance at the photo Khalil had studied. According to the date I scribbled at the bottom, it's a polaroid from last year. My room is full of them. Dad got me the camera for my fifteenth birthday, and for the longest time I brought it with me everywhere. I had so many pictures that I used to just pin them willy-nilly all over the place. Then Lucien bought me a corkboard to put them on.

A small chuckle bubbles out of me. Lucien told me when he gave it to me that my lack of rhyme or reason gave him a headache. Now all my polaroids are pinned to Lucien's gift. There are at least a dozen pictures of Hannah and me. There's a couple of me and Dad. And there's even one of Lucien. It had been a rare moment when he let his stony mask slip for just a second, allowing a small smile to peek through. He didn't know I was taking the picture until the flash went off, of course—he hates having his picture taken.

It's my favorite of them all.

I touch his picture and then my lips, remembering how real it had felt to kiss Luce in Khalil's hallucination. *Damn him,* I think as I slink back to bed. I'm not even sure which guy I'm cursing as I burrow under my covers. It takes a while, but I eventually fall into a fitful sleep, plagued by dreams of desert storms and a girl lying dead in the sand.

9

"Persia."

Principal Bartkowski scratches his bald head in perplexity. It always amazes me how shiny his head is. A person could be momentarily blinded if they're looking at him and the sunlight hits it just right. I wonder if he actually polishes it at night.

"Persia, huh? For some reason, I was under the impression that Persia no longer exists."

"Common misconception," Khalil says, barely holding back his grin. I roll my eyes. He thinks he's *so* funny.

"Huh," the principal says again. He shrugs and flips through the stack of papers we printed off the internet and forged signatures on. Lucien even managed to procure a fake passport and a phony birth certificate. All in a matter of hours. Impressive, huh?

"Well, everything seems to be in order," Bartkowski says. "I have to apologize for the miscommunication, Mr. Nazari. We would have been much better prepared had we known of your arrival. I don't know why all of the email correspondence went straight into the deleted folder…how strange."

Obviously, there were never any emails, but I allowed Khalil to work a little bit of his magic when he shook hands with Bartkowski. Now the principal thinks Khalil's school has been emailing him the details of his arrival for months.

Bartkowski leans over his desk and pushes the pager button on his office phone. "Susan?"

The chubby, middle-aged secretary who sits directly outside of the principal's office picks up her phone. She's literally ten feet away from us. I'm sure she could hear everything that we said. If I leaned over the arm of my chair, I bet I could even see her bespectacled face watching us through the door. "Yes, sir?"

"Make a copy of Miss Ashworth's class schedule for our new student."

"Yes, sir."

"Thank you, Susan," Mr. Clean, I mean Mr. Bartkowski, says. He releases the intercom button and turns back to the djinn. "You can just follow Miss Ashworth to her classes until we get a hold of your school records. Will that work for you, Mr. Nazari?"

"Of course," Khalil assures him. He practically oozes sincerity. I'd believe it too if I wasn't aware of the douchebaggery within.

Bartkowski stands to usher us out. "Welcome to John Adams High School. I'm sure you will make an excellent addition to our student body."

"Thank you, sir," Khalil replies as he shakes the principal's hand.

The handshake lingers for a second too long. The welcoming smile on the principal's face fades, the corners wavering. I jab an elbow into Khalil's ribs. He smirks and withdraws his hand. Old Barty shakes his head as if he just caught himself lost in thought.

Gritting my teeth, I grab Khalil's sleeve and pull him out of the office as the first bell rings. He takes the schedule Susan the Secretary offers him with a wink—she turns as red as the cherries printed on her dress.

"Don't flirt with the administration," I order as we make our way into the crowded hall. I haven't released my grip on Khalil's cardigan. Yes, you read that right. The djinn could literally wear anything he wanted, and he chose to wear a white button down shirt with a striped tie and a cardigan. He looks like a British schoolboy. A really hot schoolboy, but that's beside the point. He also cut off his hair, which is kind of a shame. It's short now, but he's managed to style it to where it looks purposefully messy. Where he got hair products in my house, I have no idea. Maybe it's magic, maybe it's Maybelline.

"Don't do this. Don't do that," he whines. "I've been imprisoned for hundreds of years. Can't a guy have a little fun?"

"Not your kind of fun," I say over my shoulder. I pull him after me as I weave through the throng of bodies clogging the hall. People keep looking at us. It might be because I keep bumping into anyone too slow to move out of my way, but I know it isn't. They're looking at Khalil. He towers over even the tallest basketball players at John Adams, even while hunched as I yank his arm this way and that way through the halls.

His golden brown skin and freaky eyes don't help disperse the stares either. At least he has his normal pupils on. I can almost feel the female student body swooning as he passes them.

"He has eight cats," Khalil says.

"Huh? Who does?"

"The principal. He has eight cats. Muffins, Mr. Meowerly, Bing Clawsby, Jennifurr, Kitty Poppins, BonBon, Mr. Flufferton, and Admiral Whiskers."

The burst of laughter that escapes me is most unladylike. "Holy hell. That's the best thing I've heard all year."

I turn to him, still laughing. A little smile works its way across Khalil's lips as he realizes that he's the cause of it.

"You're much prettier when you laugh," he says.

My laughter vanishes as quickly as it came. "Ugh! Do not even try your one liners and sweet talk on me, dji—*Khalil.* I don't care how funny or attractive you are, that's never going to happen."

"So, you think I'm attractive?"

I don't think I can roll my eyes any harder. "Of course that's the only thing you heard."

Khalil steps closer and peers down at me. His pupils flicker. "You never know, Princess. More impossible things have happened."

"Well, not this impossible thing. Come on." I pull on his sleeve again, steering us into the classroom. "Mrs. Saldana gives out tardies if you aren't in your seat by the bell."

Everyone else is sitting by the time we make our way inside. I make straight for my desk at the back, one chair behind Hannah who stares me down with eyes the size of basketballs. I can practically hear her think-shouting at me via brainwaves. Instead of sending any brainwaves back, I ignore her and take out my notes. I forgot to text her this morning. With everything else going on, it just totally slipped my mind. Now I'd have to spend my whole lunch break filling her in.

Khalil sinks into the empty desk beside me. He practically lounges in the hard plastic chair, his long legs jutting into the aisle between desks. "What class is this again?"

"Spanish."

"Ah, habla español?"

"No."

"Eso es muy malo. Se dice que el español es el lenguaje del amor."

I roll my eyes. Of course the fool could speak Spanish. I'd never hear the end of it from Dad if a djinn got a higher grade than me.

Hannah finally corners me in the cafeteria. I already grabbed my tray and sat down. Khalil is still in the lunch line, piling his tray with every option the lunch ladies offer him.

"Ember! What's with the lack of communication? I texted you like twenty times last night and this morning."

"I'm sorry," I mumble as I smush my peas. "It's been a rough twenty-four hours to say the least."

She pushes her thick-framed glasses up her nose. "So, what happened? How did the trial go? Who won? Are you okay? And, maybe most importantly, who is *that*?"

She asks the last question with a pointed look in the djinn's direction. He's finally making his way toward us, balancing the mountain of food on his tray with ease. He winks at a table of freshmen girls, causing them to nearly collapse in a fit of shrill giggles.

"Long story short, the trial sucked. I kind of lost but also kind of won. And no, I'm not okay. And *that* is an Underworlder. He's kind of stuck with me for the time being. Don't fall for his charm, he's a bona fide a-hole."

"You wouldn't happen to be talking about me, would you?" Khalil purrs as he takes a seat beside me.

"How'd you know?" I stab the piece of meat the school tries to pass off as Salisbury steak every Monday.

"The look of seething hatred on your face gave you away."

I glare at him. "Maybe that's just my face."

"And here I was thinking you reserved that level of disgust just for me." He jerks his head toward Hannah and flashes his hundred watt smile. "How incredibly rude of me. My name is Khalil, and you must be Hannah?"

I'm a little surprised to see Hannah's dark skin flush. She stutters out a yes and sticks out her hand for a handshake.

"No!" I say, a little too loudly. I slap her hand away before Khalil can make contact with her skin. A group of theater kids sitting at the table next to ours gives us an array of strange looks.

Her light brown eyes are wide behind her lenses, and she tilts her head just a bit, clearly wondering what that was all about.

Khalil shrugs and begins shoveling ungodly amounts of food into his mouth. While he eats enough food for a football team, Han and I huddle close as I give her the long version of the story. Keeping my voice low, I tell her about the trial and the hospital and the djinn and the rock and the desert and the bracelet and Khalil going full djinn in the Hall and the nearly dying and Dad's decree of having the djinn go topside with me. The djinn in question stays silent for the most part. However, he does protest around a mouthful of mashed potatoes when I call him a pompous wet sandwich.

"Ouch!"

"You deserve that. You did try to kill my dad, after all."

He nods and swallows whatever he's chewing. "I'll give you that one."

"Anyway," I continue to Hannah. "That's the detailed version. We're stuck together for who knows how long. Hopefully Dad will come up with a spell or something soon to break the bracelet."

She looks from the djinn to me and back again, her mouth hanging open slightly. "This is *crazy.*"

I scoff. "Uh, yeah. You can say that again."

"So, he can grant wishes?"

"Sure, if you're willing to give up part of your soul only to have your wish go terribly wrong."

Khalil waves his fork at me. "Now, now, now. Don't go giving the girl an inaccurate depiction of my kind."

"Well, it's true. I've never met or heard of a person who was glad to have made a wish with one of your kind."

"People just don't know how to make their wishes. You have to be *specific.*"

"You'd still find a way to twist it up and have it backfire."

"Specificity!"

I face Hannah. "Just don't. Trust me on this one."

"And what, you have magical powers now or something?" Hannah asks, her face filled with awe.

She must be referring to the part of the story where I handed Khalil his ass during the Trial. I shake my head. "Nah. That'd be cool, but I think that was just the bracelet's doing. I'm just your average Joe, Han. No supernatural juice in these veins, unfortunately."

I have a spoonful of questionable apple cobbler in my mouth when I realize how quiet the cafeteria has gotten. The click of Bianca's heels on the linoleum as she saunters across the room is the only sound in the whole place. I'm pretty sure even the lunch ladies pause what they're doing to watch the spectacle unfold. My dessert falls off my spoon and splats onto my plate.

Bianca puts on her plastic smile as she closes in. "Hello," she says to Khalil. I guess she's going to ignore our existence, which is totally fine by me. I go back to my apple cobbler.

"Hello," he replies. He glances at me and raises an eyebrow. I take it he already knows how despicable this sad excuse for a human being is. My expression of seething hatred must have given me away again. I should probably explain why Bianca and I hate each other so much.

The answer? We just do. There are just certain people in the world that don't vibe well together, and that's us. It started as a mutual annoyance for each other when we were younger, and it's progressed to mutual hatred over the years. Any time either one of us can do something to spite the other, we do. I really don't know how I'm going to top Bacon the pig, though...

"I'm Bianca, student body president."

"I'm Khalil, foreign exchange student."

"Welcome to John Adams, we are pleased to have you visiting our school."

She offers her manicured hand to him. I open my mouth to stop the djinn, but then Bianca's icy gaze shifts over to me and her composure cracks just a bit as her lip lifts in disdain. The look lasts less than a second, but that's all it takes for me to realize she plans on taking Khalil from me as revenge for the night of her party. Well, if she wants him so badly, she can have him.

Khalil's hand slides into hers. Her face goes slack for a heartbeat before she shakes her head and blinks back the fuzziness. "Oh, the pleasure's all mine," Khalil insists.

She quickly regains her composure, giving him a smile and a look that seems to promise a little *something-something* in the future, if you know what I mean.

Bianca must see me rolling my eyes, because her gaze shifts to me and goes icy cold again. I knew it was only a matter of time before she turned her malicious intentions my way.

"Oh, sweetie," she exhales, her voice saccharine sweet. "You have something in your teeth."

My face flames even though I know she's lying. The scattered snickers throughout the cafeteria don't help extinguish the heat in my cheeks either.

"Just here," she says, and as she raises her manicured hand to point at her own pearly whites, Bianca somehow "accidentally" knocks over my soft drink. I jump up, but not quite fast enough to escape the river of sticky, carbonated beverage. It waterfalls over the edge of the table to soak into the front pocket of my hoodie.

"Oops! How clumsy of me," she says. The laughter from the audience gets louder. "Here, let me help."

Her fingers find the rim of my tray as she leans toward the napkin dispenser located in the middle of the table. Bianca would have dumped the entire plate of food into my lap had Khalil not stopped it with a steady hand.

And with that same hand, Khalil upturns the tray. Not toward me, but up, flinging my uneaten food against Bianca's white sweater and satin blouse. She jumps back with her arms raised in disbelief as the tray clatters to the ground.

"Oh my," Khalil deadpans. "I'm *so* sorry. I've been working out a bit lately. It must be paying off. "

Across the cafeteria, laughter starts to bubble up. It grows until the sound of it fills the room. Even Hannah—sweet, innocent Hannah who never laughs at anyone's misfortunes—has to cover her mouth to keep from giggling.

A conflicted look flits across the queen bee's face. She has to make a decision right here, right now. She could play it off and forgive the new kid, or she can storm off and kill his reputation before it even exists at John Adams. Bianca takes a deep breath and chooses.

"Don't worry about it," she says between teeth clenched into a forced smile. "Accidents happen."

Hanna offers her a few napkins—she truly is too pure for this world—and Bianca takes them. She dabs at the mess dripping down her once pristine outfit. After realizing it's a lost cause, Bianca turns to go. Her heels lose traction on the wet tiles. She slips and slides, her arms madly pinwheeling as if she can catch the air. Just before she falls, Bianca gains her footing in those outrageous heels, and she straightens back up. My lips pull down in a pout of disappointment. That would have been *too* perfect.

The amused laughter continues as she retreats back to her table of fellow Barbies. I glance out of the corner of my eye at the djinn. He's grinning as he shovels yet more food into his piehole. The boy is a bottomless pit. Han still has her hand over her mouth as if she can't believe what just happened.

Even though I know it was wrong of Khalil to do that to the ice queen, it feels good to finally be on the other end of the laughter.

And because Khalil did it for me...I realize I hate him a little less for it.

10

Surprisingly, the school day continues without any more incidents. I mean, sure, people whispered about us everywhere we went, but that's it. I glared at anyone brave enough to make eye contact, and that seemed to keep people from openly saying anything to me or Khalil.

Something we would have to figure out, though, is the bathroom situation. Seventh period is art which takes place in an outer building. No restrooms. It was no big deal today when I had to go because I just volunteered to show Khalil where the closest bathrooms are. That won't work for us next time considering the closest one was about a fifty yards away in the main building. I'm just going to have to lay off the sodas. Or learn how to hold it until after school.

The final bell rings before I know it, and we are free! No one figured Khalil was anything but a ridiculously hot foreign exchange student! I made it the whole day without strangling the djinn! And Bianca got a big helping of karma pie!

Overall, not too bad of a Monday.

I link arms with Han as we make our way to where Lucien is waiting for us in the parking lot. The djinn strolls along behind us, contentedly munching on a pack of almonds. The dude really can eat.

"Han, I've been thinking."

"Oh, no. That's never a good thing."

"Hardy-har-har. But seriously," I say, keeping my voice low. "I found him—Max, I mean. Through some CIA-level snooping skills, I found out where he lives and what school he goes to. It's in San Francisco. At worst, that's a thirteen hour drive. We could make it a girl's weekend trip. At best, I can convince Balthasar to let us use the portal. We could zip over to San Fran in a matter of minutes."

Hannah purses her lips and pushes her glasses up. "I don't know, Em. I don't think my parents would let me go overnight on a trip that far away."

Deflated, I agree. "You're probably right. Damn. There has to be some way for us to go down there to check him out."

I look around the parking lot as if I can find the answer somewhere there amongst the vehicles of John Adams' students. And then I see it.

I stop so abruptly that Khalil walks into me.

"Hey—you made me drop an almond!"

I ignore him and turn to face Hannah.

"Dude—look!" I direct her gaze to a car parked in the visitor's space. Emblazoned on the car's doors and hood is the crest of a nearby community college. "We can take a college day! Your parents won't care if we go to San Fran because we'll tell them we're going to *Stanford.* Actually, I'm like a thousand percent sure they will love that idea. And," I add as Hannah opens her mouth to protest, "we can really go check out Stanford. That way we won't be lying."

Han beams. "For once, Em, you actually had a really great idea."

I flick her elbow. "What are you talking about, 'for once'? I'm full of great ideas."

Lucien exits our car and goes around to open the doors for us. First mine, then Hannah's. "How did everything go?" he asks, all business as usual.

"Fine, fine. Khalil dumped a tray of questionable steak all over Bianca, so overall, pretty good."

My Guardian bristles. "What do you mean? What happened? Should I alert your father?"

"Lucy, relax," I tell him as I slide into the front passenger seat. "It's fine. We did it. No one knows."

Despite my reassurance, Lucien aims a glare dark enough to kill flowers in Khalil's direction.

"Don't look at me," says the djinn. "It was an accident."

Lucien mumbles something under his breath before getting in the car. Khalil shoots me a wink when Luce isn't looking. I try, but I'm just not quite able to stop the grin from spreading on my lips.

Ember...

I open my eyes to nothingness and groan. "Really? Right now?"

The Darkness has impeccable timing. I was just getting into a dream that involved me, Lucien, and a blanket spread out on the ground under the stars. We hadn't even got to the *really* good part yet.

I squeeze my eyes shut in the hopes that I could slip out of the Darkness' presence and back into the delightful dream I had rather been enjoying. Alas...no luck.

You did not heed my warning.

I think back to the last visit the Darkness paid me. "You were warning me about the bracelet?"

A cool touch tickles the skin on the inside of my wrist where Khalil's bracelet rests. *Yes.*

"An Underworlder gave it to me."

The sand spirit.

I nod. "Yeah, how did you know?"

But who gave it to him?

I fumble around in my thoughts in an effort to recall if Zaahir had said who gave him the bracelet. Either he didn't, or

I couldn't remember. Either way, it's way past time to pay a visit to our fat, little djinn friend.

I sigh. "You're right, I'm sorry. I should have listened."

Do not be sorry, Princess. I wish I could have told you more.

"Why didn't you? A few details could have helped."

The Darkness pauses. *I am trapped here, but sometimes...sometimes the shadows bring me whispers. Sometimes they bring me secrets. Yet many times they bring me nothing. I helped as much as I could.*

Now it's my turn to pause. I chew the skin on my bottom lip, pulling at it until I taste blood. Pity stirs in my heart for him. Over the years, I've come to think of the Darkness as more of a friend than anything, and the sadness in his voice makes my heart squeeze in response.

"Why are you trapped?"

I was imprisoned. Thousands of years ago.

A shiver of foreboding snakes down my spine. "Why?" I whisper.

They feared me.

"Who are you?" It's a question I've asked before, and I receive a different answer each time. When I was younger, he told me he was the boogeyman. He once said he was a lost king of a kingdom long forgotten. One time, he told me there was not a name for what he was. The next time he told me that the earliest name he was ever given was Asbu, and I had laughed.

But when I remembered the dream the next day and typed the name into Google, some links to ancient Sumerian translation pages had popped up. Asbu literally translates to "darkness," so that's what I've taken to calling him. However, that still doesn't answer the question of *who* he is.

I am the one that came before and the one that will remain after.

"That's totally helpful, thanks."

I aim to please.

I smile in the dark. "I want to help you."

I feel him smiling back. *Someday, you will. But we must once more bid farewell, Princess. Your crow is calling you.*

"My crow?"

Until next time, Ember...

"Ember!"

I blink and flinch away from the light. Lucien has a hand on each of my shoulders, and the pain in my neck makes me think he has just shaken me to the point of whiplash.

"Luce? What the—where are we?"

The light fades and I finally see its source. We are in the kitchen, oddly enough, and the portal on the floor glows as if I were about to go through. Or...as if I had just come back.

"Are you all right?" he asks me. His dark eyes scan me for some sign of injury.

I pull back from his grasp. "I'm fine. Why are we in the kitchen?"

He tilts his head in that bird-like way he is prone to doing, and the Darkness' low voice repeats in my mind. *Your crow is calling you.* "You were sleepwalking. If Khalil hadn't woken me up, I think you'd be halfway to the Underworld by now."

"You're not supposed to wake someone up if they're sleepwalking, you know," Khalil chimes in from where he leans against the doorway to the living room. He taps his head. "Bad for the brain."

"Shut up," I growl as I shuffle over to the dining room table. "My head hurts."

"See?" Khalil says. "Told you."

I ignore him as I plant my elbows on the table and put my head in my hands. "Go away, Khalil."

"Fine. I need a few more hours of sleep, anyway. Big history test in the morning. Were the Articles of Confederation signed in 1778 or 1787? I'm not too sure about American history. Now, the history of the Middle East on the other hand..."

I groan and bang my head on the table. I totally forgot. Well, there goes my B average.

"Ember."

I pick my head off the table to find Lucien kneeling before me. The look in his dark eyes makes my stomach drop. "What's wrong?"

He tucks a strand of hair behind my ear. Even the lightest touch of his fingertips on the rim of my ear makes goosebumps race across my arms. Lucien opens his mouth to say something, but ends up shaking his head instead. He stands. "You shouldn't do that again," he tells me. "Sleepwalking can be dangerous, especially if you hurtle head first through the portal."

A flash of anger surges through me. "I'll be sure to remember that when I'm sleeping and can't control what happens to my body."

"Good."

"Fine."

"I would feel better if you would allow me to spend the rest of the night in your room, though. Just in case you try to sleepwalk again."

I must have heard him wrong.

Spend the night.

In my room.

"I'm sorry, *what*?"

"It was actually the djinn's idea," Lucien admits. "Just let me grab my things, and I'll be there in a moment."

"Um, okay?" I'm suddenly glad for the shadows of the night that hide the ferocious blush blooming in my cheeks.

As I follow him into the living room and the hall beyond, Khalil peeks over the back of the couch and waggles his eyebrows at me. Lucien looks at me over his shoulder once more before disappearing into his bedroom, and I give him a fake smile. As soon as he's out of sight, I whirl on the djinn. "What the hell are you playing at?"

"I'm helping you get the guy."

"And why, exactly, are you doing that?"

He shrugs and falls back onto the couch. "You got me out of the Pen. I figure I owe you something for that, and since you won't let me just make him fall in love with you, this is the next best thing, I suppose."

"You suppose?"

He shrugs. "I can quit if you'd prefer. But to be honest, I feel like I've made more progress than you have in years."

I want to hit him, or maybe stab him again...but he's not wrong. I take a step toward my room. "I'm watching you, djinn. No funny business."

He crosses his heart. "I aim to please."

A wave a deja vu crashes over me. That's exactly what the Darkness said to me.

Before this night can get any stranger, I dash over to my bed and sidle in under the covers. I pull them up to my chin and wait for Lucien. *This is it*, I think to myself. *Maybe I'll finally get to see him in his pajamas. Maybe I'll finally witness him sleeping.*

It doesn't take him long.

He comes into my room in exactly the same thing he was wearing in the kitchen. He doesn't even bother bringing a pillow or a blanket. The only thing he carries with him is a book.

Lucien shuts the door and goes straight to my closet to turn on the light inside. "Will it bother you if I leave the light on?"

I shake my head.

"Perfect." He slides down to the floor with a small grunt and cracks open the pages of his book to where he left off. With the hand not holding open the book, he rubs the spot on his chest over his heart. I've caught him doing this movement several times over the years when he doesn't think I'm looking. It made me curious enough that I once asked him why he did it. He told me it was heartburn, but for some reason, I don't believe him.

He peers at me over his novel as I clear my throat. "You're not going to sleep?"

"I don't need much rest."

"Oh."

It's so quiet that I can hear the ticking of my clock on the far wall. "So...whatcha reading?"

"A play."

I prop myself up on an elbow, my fist on my cheek. "A play? Who reads plays?" He ignores me, so I change tactics. "What's it called?"

"The Tempest."

"Interesting. Let me guess—it's about a tempest?"

Luce lets out a low chuckle, unknowingly setting my heart on fire. "Go to sleep, Ember."

"You can get comfortable, you know. I won't mind if you kick off your shoes or something."

He eyes me once more over the top of his book, pausing for what feels like an eternity before he ever so slowly removes his shoes. I hadn't noticed when he sat down, but now there's no mistaking it. He's wearing the socks I bought him. The cat ones.

All this time I had thought he had cast them aside or maybe even thrown them away. I feel like I can fly, like angels are singing the Hallelujah chorus in my brain, like I just won the jackpot. All because of a pair of socks.

"Nice socks."

A small smile plays on his lovely lips. "Thank you. They were a gift from someone special."

Oh, sweet baby Moses in a basket. Did he just say what I think he just said? There's no way I can go to sleep now.

"Are you hot? Cold? Do you want a blanket? I have like six on my bed. You're more than welcome to use one."

He uncrosses his ankles and crosses them again, a lopsided smile pulling up one side of his lips. "I'm fine, Ember. Really. You should get some rest—especially if you have a history test in the morning."

I fall back into my pillows. "I forgot about that."

We lapse into an easy silence, punctuated only by the ticking of the clock and the turning of pages. I close my eyes and try to go to sleep—I really do—but it's hopeless. I can't sleep with him so close, especially with the intimateness of night around us. I know I should just keep my mouth shut, but I have no self control.

"This someone special who has excellent taste in sock-wear...do I know her?"

Lucien drops his book on his lap and actually laughs—a rare sight, to be sure. I turn on my side so I can watch the laughter transform his face. His eyes crinkle at the corners as he runs a hand through his slicked-back hair. He looks almost like a different person with this lightness relaxing his features. I want to pinch myself to make sure I'm not dreaming.

"You're not going to sleep any time soon, are you?"

"Nope. Unless..."

"Unless?"

"I might be able to go to sleep...if you read to me."

He leans forward, dark eyes glinting in the low light. "You won't know what's going on."

"I don't mind. I just like the sound of your voice." I only realize when it's too late that I actually said that last part out loud. My face burns, and I hope it's too dark for him to see.

Luce settles back again. "Fine, if you think it'll help you go to sleep."

"Thank you, Lucy."

"Just know that I don't read aloud often. But...I suppose I can make an exception for someone special with exceptional taste in socks."

He starts to read before I can fully comprehend what he just said, the low melody of his lovely voice filling the quiet between us. I watch him, savoring this moment for as long as I can. But the steady cadence of his voice does its job, and my eyes grow heavier and heavier with each page he turns. I drift off before I'm ready to sleep, awakened only briefly by the feeling of someone brushing my hair back behind my ear.

11

"My dad is going to kill me."

"It's not that bad," Hannah says in an effort to comfort me.

"It's pretty bad. Aren't you failing history too?" Khalil adds, ever so helpful in my time of need.

It's been three weeks since the djinn came to the Surface, and I've only ever wanted to kill him that one time after the hallucination-dream. Actually, we've gotten along relatively well. I finally found someone who loves cheesy horror movies as much as me. We watch one practically every night. So, naturally, it's his fault I didn't study. If we hadn't been up late watching *RoboGator vs Sharkenstein,* I probably would have passed.

"Well, if he doesn't kill me, Lucien will."

At that, all three of us look out of the window of the science classroom to see said future murderer preening his feathers. He catches us watching him and squawks before hopping to another branch.

"It's just one class," Hannah tells me, as if she has any idea what it's like to make a grade below an A plus. "We'll just buckle down and bring it up before the end of the term."

"Cheer up," Khalil says. "It's not the end of the world."

"Easy for you to say," I grumble. "Maybe they could cut me some slack if they knew what goes on beneath their feet."

"Table three," Mr. Wilson calls. "Unless you guys are experts on female anatomy, I suggest you pay attention to the lesson and take some notes."

Hannah lowers her head like a scolded puppy and starts scribbling notes into her composition book.

"I think I would know more about female anatomy than Mr. Wilson," I mutter under my breath to Khalil. He coughs to hide a laugh, earning us another sharp look from the teacher.

The school day mercifully ends not long after anatomy class. Lucien is waiting for us at the school's entrance—not his regular post by the car.

"Uh-oh," Khalil says. "Bird Boy doesn't look too happy."

"That's just his regular expression." But even I have to admit that he looks grumpier than usual.

"Where's Hannah?" Lucien asks as we approach.

"Choir practice. What's wrong?"

He ushers me to the car. "Something's happened. Your father wants you to meet him right away."

"Is it about Spanish?" I ask. "Because if it's about Spanish, he doesn't need to worry. I'll get my grade up. Scout's honor."

Lucien's head whips toward me. "No, actually. But what happened in Spanish?"

"Busted," Khalil sing-songs.

I curse. "Nothing. We planned on going down to visit Zaahir today anyway, so this is actually good timing on Dad's part. Maybe the fat, little djinn knows more than he let on about who, or what, let our djinn out of his cage."

Luce nods. "I've been thinking the same thing."

"Can we stop and get a snack?" Khalil asks. "I'm famished."

"You ate two trays of food for lunch. How can you possibly be hungry?"

He rubs his flat stomach. "I'm a growing boy."

"Ugh. Fine. Whatever. I need to pick up some marshmallows anyway."

Lucien manages to make it all the way to the car before he can't hold it in anymore. "You failed your Spanish test, didn't you?" he asks while opening the passenger side door for me.

I glare at him over the door. Our bodies are so close together, separated only by a few inches of metal and plastic. In the afternoon sun, Lucien's eyes are so dark that I can't see his pupils in his irises. The memory of him reading to me a few nights ago tightens something deep in my core. "I told you—it's fine."

"I guess we'll see what your father has to say about it."

"You don't have to tell him. What he doesn't know won't hurt him."

"Yes, I do."

"No, you don't."

"I'm telling him."

"Tattle-tale," I pout.

The barest hint of a grin pulls at his lips. As small as it is, I feel like I'm witnessing a miracle when I see it and know I'm the one that caused it. Again.

Six gas station burritos, one Big Gulp full of Mountain Dew, and a bag of jumbo-sized marshmallows later, we step through the portal and enter the Underworld.

I know something is seriously wrong as soon as we make the crossing because Elowen is there on the ledge, leaning up against the wall. Her copper-colored hair is tamed into a knot on the top of her head—another hint that she means business. Usually, she lets her wild curls do their own thing. Her purple eyes narrow as she spies who makes up our little crew. It's clear she's still a little piqued that someone had the gall to release her catch.

Speaking of her djinn—as soon as Khalil sees her, he goes djinn. I wave away his vapor. "Dude, chill."

"What is *she* doing here?"

"Will you relax? She's not going to lock you up while we're stuck together."

He simmers down enough to settle in his human form once again. I guess he's still a little resentful about being captured all those decades ago. Talk about awkward.

"Princess," Elowen says with a polite nod in my direction. "I'm here to escort you to the Pen."

"What's wrong? Is my dad okay?"

"He's fine," she assures me in her rolling accent. Her purple eyes dart to Khalil once more. "But there's been a murder."

My stomach drops through the floor. Lucien steps closer and even rests a hand on my lower back. I'm too shocked to even enjoy the way his touch sends electric currents up and down my skin. "Who?"

She pauses. "It might be best to just show you."

Elowen turns and begins down the steps. Khalil, Lucien, and I exchange glances before following her to the Pen. The first thing I notice when we reach the bottom is that there are no Underworlders. They must all be confined to their rooms. I wipe my sweaty hands on my jeans. That is not a good sign. In the seventeen years I've been alive, there has only ever been one other murder in the Underworld.

The most dangerous Underworlders are always locked up in the upper levels, and the ones that could stroll about freely within the fence aren't troublemakers. Plus, Dad always has guards posted, and the guards are always Underworlders who have proved themselves in one way or another over the past five hundred years. Enough so that Dad promoted them to a position of power within the Underworld. There are enough guards that the rest of the inmates rarely get into trouble.

Using a key card pinned to her HTF-issued stab-and-fang-and-claw-proof vest, Elowen lets us through the gates and into the Pen. We continue to follow her silently as she leads us inside and to the elevator. The bad feeling in my gut worsens when she selects the fifth floor button and we ascend.

Khalil leans in. "This can't be good."

"No kidding."

He straightens and takes a ridiculously long slurp of his drink, earning him an evil look from Elowen.

The elevator dings, and the doors open to chaos.

Inside the fifth floor hallway are what appears to be all of the members of the HTF, several guards, Dad, and to my greatest dismay—Zilah. Elowen makes a path through the crowd and guides us to a cell with its door wide open.

I know what we'll find before we reach the cell, but it doesn't make what I see any easier to process when we get there.

The six by eight foot cell—which normally consists of four white walls and a white floor and ceiling—is red. There's blood everywhere. On the walls. On the ceiling. On *everything.* There's so much blood that I can smell the metallic tang of it in the air.

Dad is in the cell with Armenius. They have little plastic booties over their shoes as they crouch down in the middle of the cell and investigate the corpse lying there.

In death, Zaahir seems even shorter and fatter than I remember. He's also missing his head, which is definitely different from the last time I saw him.

"Holy shit."

Dad's head lifts up. "Ah, Ember. I see Lucien got my message."

"What the hell happened in here?"

The Lord of the Underworld puts his hands on his knees and straightens up from his crouch with a soft groan. "It appears that someone or something murdered the djinn, Zaahir."

"It appears that way," I say, still shocked. I squeeze the bag of marshmallows to my chest. What are the chances that he was killed on the same day I planned on coming back to ask questions?

Dad peels off the latex gloves covering his hands. "You mentioned after the first Task that a djinn gave you the cuff you put on Khalil. It was Zaahir, wasn't it?"

I swallow the bile rising up in my throat. "Yeah."

Right then, another member of the HTF named Wilfredo appears in the doorway. "John, I just searched the security footage. I'm afraid to report that it's been tampered with. There's no usable footage for the past ten or so hours."

Dad curses. "Keep the Underworlders on lockdown for the foreseeable future. I want this killer apprehended and dealt with before we let them loose again."

Wil nods and vanishes to do as bidden.

"Ember, I want to talk to you in my office if you have a second."

Zilah is oddly quiet where she stands to the side in a lavender, tea-length dress. Her matching high heels are positioned in one of the only floor tiles not splattered with blood.

"Just me?"

Dad glances at my twin before taking off the set of bloodied plastic booties. He leaves the second, cleaner set on. "Just you," he tells me. "For now."

I can't shake the image of the blood-covered cell as we traverse the Underworld to Dad's office. Besides the grotesque image of the room that keeps popping back into my head, another thought rankles me even more—where in the hell is Zaahir's head?

Dad collapses into the chair behind his desk and pulls the second pair of plastic booties off of his shoes. I guess he wanted to make sure that nothing got on his Italian leather boots. I wouldn't either. Those shoes must have cost a pretty penny.

"Would you like us to wait outside, sir?" Lucien asks from his spot near the door, referring to himself and Khalil.

My father crumples the booties into a ball and tosses it into the trash can. "The djinn can wait outside, but you were with Ember when she talked to Zaahir, Lucien. Maybe you can recall something that she doesn't."

"Yes, sir," Lucien replies.

He holds the door open for the djinn. Khalil pauses for a moment by my side. I think he might say something, but he just takes a deep breath and brushes past me.

Lucien shuts the heavy doors behind Khalil and takes up a post in front of them, his arms crossed over his chest. He glances at me and then gestures with his chin toward the leather chairs in front of Dad's desk.

I go to my preferred chair on the right and sit. The marshmallow bag whistles in protest as I squeeze it to the point of bursting.

Dad looks me over before asking, "Why do you have marshmallows?"

"They were for Zaahir."

His eyebrows raise. "You were planning on speaking to the djinn today? Why?"

I nod. It takes me a moment to find the words. "We were going to ask him about the bracelet. I was going to use the marshmallows as an incentive to answer our questions."

"I should have dealt with him sooner," Dad says, more to himself than to me. He picks at the corner of the desk calendar splayed out before him. Each square of the calendar is filled with dates and times, meetings and hearings. I tried to convince him to get a smartphone so he could use a virtual planner, but he told me he prefers pen and paper. "I should have called him in as soon as the first Task ended. Now we may never know who gave him the bracelet or who let Khalil out."

"What about the security footage?" I ask, thinking of Wil's appearance in the Pen earlier. "Can't Wilfredo pull up the film from the afternoon of the Task?"

Dad's shaking his head before I can even finish my question. "We tried. That day's footage was also tampered with. Now, tell me about what happened the night of the first Task."

I take a deep breath and recount the story to him. Luce fills in some of the finer details that I forgot. Dad writes down Abba's name, and I can't say I feel too bad about the trouble she's about to be in.

Dad asks us a couple questions to clarify a few parts of our story, scribbling down our answers in a leather-bound notebook filled with other notes. For some reason, my gaze lowers to the polished hardwood floor, and I see it—a red stain on the white rubber part of my Chucks. My words fade away as my vision narrows to the bloody smudge on the toe of my shoe.

"Are you all right, Ember?"

I squeeze the bag of marshmallows again, trying to anchor myself to this room and this moment. "I don't know."

Dad comes around the front of his desk and kneels before me. He tugs on the end of my ponytail like he used to do when I was a kid. "Hey."

I tear my eyes away from the bloodstain to see that it's not the Lord of the Underworld addressing me, but my dad. The same dad that taught me how to tie my laces and ride a bike.

He takes my hands in his. His warm, calloused palm wraps around my freezing fingers. "I'm sorry, kiddo. I've been really hard on you lately. I said some stupid stuff last time you came down, and you don't deserve that."

I blink against the burning in my eyes. "No, you were right. I always mess things up."

"I was wrong to say that. You don't *always* mess up, and when you do, you always put things right."

"Well, I can't fix things now that Zaahir's dead, can I?"

"We will get to the bottom of it, kiddo. I promise."

The reason behind the all-consuming guilt I'd been carrying with me since we saw the crime scene abruptly hits me. The bag of jet-puffed marshmallows on my lap suddenly weighs a hundred pounds. "It's my fault he's dead, Dad. If I hadn't taken the bracelet from him, he'd still be alive."

Dad's hazel eyes—so similar to my own—flicker with understanding. "No. Zaahir died because he worked with someone who found him to be a liability. If he hadn't offered you that bracelet to begin with, he'd probably still be here. He made his choices, and you made yours based off of that. You did not kill that djinn, Ember. Okay?"

I nod in agreement, but I still don't quite believe it.

"Someone murdered Zaahir," Dad says, his voice hardening. "And when we find them, they'll pay for their crimes."

I nod again. I probably look like a bobblehead with all the nodding I'm doing today.

"Can I tell you something?"

"What?"

"I'm most likely a bad dad for saying this...but I want you to win."

I can't believe what I'm hearing. "I'm sorry. *What?*"

He has the grace to look sheepish. "I do. If the choice were still up to me, I'd choose you. But it's not. That's why I decided to have the HTF ultimately have the final say."

"You're joking, right?"

"I'm not. You have a way with the Underworlders that your sister does not. She wants the power that comes with the title, and the fact that you *don't* want it makes you all the more suited for the throne."

My cheeks burn with embarrassment, and I give a shaky laugh. "How do you know I don't want the throne?"

He pats my hands and rises. "If you storming out of the Underworld when I broke the news wasn't a clear enough hint, Izzy came and talked to me."

I bite my lip. "Oh."

"She also told me that you were looking for a suitable replacement for your role as heir."

Why, Izzy, why? "About that—"

"I want you to find him," Dad cuts in. "His name is Max Wu, right?"

"Uh..."

"Go find him. Watch him and learn about his life. Then, if you can honestly tell yourself that you can rip him away from his family and his friends, his life on the Surface, his plans and his dreams, his normalcy—if you can do that to him and live with the burden of doing so, please feel free to tell him all about the Underworld."

Dad: one.

Ember: zero.

"Fine, I will." I stand and waggle a finger in my father's direction. "You don't know him, Dad. Maybe he would love to be Lord of the Underworld. I mean, he'll get free housing. He won't have to pay bills. He'll even be semi-immortal."

Dad laughs as he turns to the paperwork stacked on the edge of his desk. "You're going to have to work on your sales pitch if that's the best you've got."

"Duly noted," I say. Surprisingly, his little pep talk perked my spirits up quite a bit. Zaahir is still dead and all, but at least now I feel a little better about it.

I'm almost to the door when Dad calls my name once more.

"Yeah?" I ask over my shoulder. Lucien grabs the handle and cracks the door. My mind is already on the Surface, thinking about what we might do when we get back. Maybe we could order a pizza and get caught up on that one show about the fairytale characters who cross over into the real world. The effects are awful, but the storyline makes up for it.

"I'll see you Thursday?" Dad asks, his voice soft.

Well, so much for feeling good.

"Of course."

"It'll be twelve years this year."

A knot forms in my throat. As if I could forget. "I know."

"Okay. Love you, kiddo."

"Love you too, Dad."

We slip out of the office to find Khalil eating from the bowl of candies in the hallway. He pops the last piece into his mouth. The jerk didn't even save one for me. "Twelve years since what?" he asks. Apparently, he was eavesdropping.

I glare at him. "None of your business. Let's go."

He grins and steps in front of me, blocking my way. "Oh, come on. What is it? Twelve years since you've gotten new shoes? Those are hideous, by the way, and now they've even got blood on them."

"Let it go," Lucien warns under his breath.

"No? Maybe it's been twelve years since the last time your dad let an Underworlder be murdered."

My fists clench, my nails digging into my palms. The fury filling me up makes my fingers tingle. I want to slap that smile off of his face. "If you must know, you raging asshole, it *has* been twelve years since there's been a murder. Which means it's been twelve years since my mom died, okay? Are you happy now?"

Khalil's eyes widen, and he puts his arms up in defense. "Hey, sorry. I didn't know."

I'm not in the mood for his crap, so I snap my fingers and without another word, he transforms into a walnut-sized aqua-colored rock. Mumbling obscenities, I scoop him up and pocket him. Maybe I'll let him out when we get back to the house. Maybe I'll bury him in the backyard so he'll have to dig his way out of the dirt. Maybe I'll flush him down the toilet, who knows? The possibilities are endless.

"Ember," Lucien says, pulling me from my vengeful thoughts. I don't really want to deal with my Guardian either right now, so I don't even slow down. However, he extends a hand and catches me by the arm. And just that simple touch is enough to make me stop and face him.

His touch makes my fury fade away. Lucien tucks a strand of hair behind my ear. My heart jumps as his fingers touch the sensitive skin there. As I stare into his lovely dark eyes, I wonder what he'll do if I kiss him. Because that's what I want to do. I want to kiss him until our lips feel bruised. Until I forget that the anniversary of my mother's death is just days away and a few days after that will be the second Task.

I heave a sigh. I know what he would do. He'd push me away before I even managed to make contact. He'd look at me like I'm crazy, and maybe I am for loving such an oblivious fool.

Lucien seems to play with the words in his mouth. A muscle in his jaw twitches. His hand trails from my upper arm down to my forearm, to my wrist, and finally to my fingers.

I suck in a breath. Just the touch of his skin against mine sends goosebumps racing across my body.

"What is it, Luce?" I ask when I can bear the suspense no longer.

"I just wanted to tell you—"

"You know, I'm honestly surprised you had the guts to do it," Zilah says from the end of the hall, effectively ruining the moment that may or may not have been about to happen.

Lucien pulls away, and the hallway is suddenly ten degrees colder.

I clench my teeth and count to ten. I swear to God, if she so much as looks at me wrong, I'm going to deck her in her pretty face.

I finally turn to face her. "What are you talking about?"

My twin sashays down the hallway toward us. She walks with the grace of a runway model in her four-inch stilettos. She's one of those people who could run an obstacle course in heels and not bat an eye, whereas I am the type of person who can't take two steps in a pair of heels without breaking at least one ankle. Truly. I look like a baby giraffe trying to take its first steps on the deck of a ship in the midst of a hurricane. It isn't pretty.

"Don't play coy, Ember. It doesn't become you. Although, really, does anything?" She laughs to herself and stops a few paces from where Lucien and I stand.

"Zilah, I'm *really* not in the mood right now to deal with your petty bullshit. What do you want?"

"I just find it really convenient," she says, picking at a French-tipped nail.

"Find *what* convenient?"

She brushes back her silver-blonde hair with a haughty flick of her manicured fingers. "That the djinn who just so happened to help you win the first Task is now dead. I mean, I wouldn't go so far as to say he had a good head on his shoulders, but at least he had a head before he helped you."

I gape at her. She has finally lost her mind.

Before I can manage to string the words together for a reply, Lucien steps in front of me and says in a low, dangerous voice, "Are you accusing Ember of killing Zaahir?"

Zilah's eyes rake over Lucien from head to toe, and I want to claw her eyes out when she smirks and says, "Yes, I am. And when Father hears about my theory, he'll have no choice but to remove her as his heir and end this ridiculous competition, so we can all get on with our lives."

She closes the space between us, but Lucien doesn't budge. She watches me over his extended arm as I glare at her from behind my Guardian.

She is entirely too close to Lucien right now. Her boobs are practically pressed up against his chest as she speaks again. "I wouldn't be surprised if Father decides to execute you when he discovers what you've done. Cheating during a Task. Murdering your accomplice. What other rules have you broken lately, Ember?"

My gaze darts to Lucien as if on instinct, betraying the feelings I've been hiding in my heart for so long. Zilah doesn't miss it.

A cruel smile pulls at her lips. "Oh, dear. I may be wrong, but didn't Father expressly forbid you from any relationships with Underworlders? I could have *sworn* that's what he said."

"Shut up, Zi," I bite out through clenched teeth.

"What a shame," she continues in that falsely sweet tone as she faces Lucien, ignoring the fact that I used the nickname she loathes. "You're much too handsome for the likes of my sister."

And with that, she grabs the back of Lucien's head and forces his mouth to hers. I watch in horror, frozen in place and unable to even breathe.

Lucien shoves her away as gently as possible. "Zilah, enough of this. Ember is innocent on all accounts, and I will attest to her innocence should there be any further inquiry."

Zilah laughs in his face. "Go ahead. See if it helps. And I take back my earlier accusation—it's clear that any feelings between you two are completely one-sided."

A sharp pain lances my heart at her words and the truth inside them.

She steps around us and goes to the doors leading to Dad's office. Zilah places one hand on the door handle and uses the other to wipe the smear of lipstick off the corner of her mouth. "I think I'll keep my suspicions to myself for a while longer, Ember. I'm sure you'll slip up sooner or later."

Sick of her voice, I turn on my heel and storm down the hallway. My hands shake as I clench them into fists.

"Oh, and one more thing," she calls after me. I don't bother stopping, but I still hear what she says next. "He tastes as good as he looks, Ember."

She disappears into Dad's office with one last malicious laugh.

12

I've had plenty of awkward moments in my life, but the one that takes the cake is the moment I have to tell the person I love that he has my sister's lipstick on his mouth, all without hinting at the fact that my heart is practically in bits and pieces in my chest.

When I told him, Lucien pulled a handkerchief from his waistcoat pocket and dabbed at his lips.

Then we went into our rooms and promptly ignored each other for the rest of the night.

If that isn't awkward, I don't know what is.

Hours later, I'm scrolling mindlessly along my social media feed when there's a splash and a colorful curse from inside the bathroom.

"Real mature, Princess," Khalil calls out.

I'm so down in the dumps that I can't even grin about the fact that Khalil just materialized in the toilet bowl. I listen to him clamber out of the toilet as I click on a video of a fuzzy panda cub falling out of a tree, but even that fails to lift my spirits.

The djinn emerges from the bathroom dry and in his desert garb. He starts to say some sort of insult but stops himself short when he sees me moping at my desk.

"I really am sorry about earlier, Princess. I honestly didn't know."

"It's fine," I mumble.

"No, I was being—how did you so eloquently put it earlier? Oh, yes. I was being a raging asshole, and I apologize for it."

The corner of my mouth tugs upward.

"I'd like to offer you something as a peace offering, if you'll accept it."

I shut my laptop with a sigh. "For the last time, I'm not giving you a piece of my soul for a—"

He waves his hand impatiently. "No, no. This is something else. Completely free of charge."

I peer into his turquoise eyes to see what mischievous stunt he's up to now. "No catches?"

He crosses his heart. "No catches. On my honor."

I snort at that. "Okay, let's hear it."

Khalil turns my desk chair toward him and folds his long legs into a sitting position on the floor before me. "I'm sure you know that djinn have other talents besides granting wishes."

I nod. Thanks to Dad, I know all about djinn and their magic. Most djinn hail from the Middle East, some in Asia, some in Northern Africa. Pretty much anywhere there's a desert, there's a djinn. According to what Dad taught me from his big book of beasties, djinn can have several forms. They don't like iron and avoid silver as a general rule. Besides granting wishes in exchange for souls, djinn can also see into a person's thoughts and can make people hallucinate as long as they are connected by physical touch. That's pretty much the gist of it, anyway.

"I can do something that most djinn cannot."

"Okay…?" I say, waiting for him to finish. The boy has a flair for the dramatic.

"My kind calls it a memory echo. I have the ability to go into a person's thoughts and find one specific memory to allow that person to experience it again, even if the person can't remember it themselves."

"I'm not following."

He takes a deep breath before explaining it to me again. "I can take you back to your best memory of your mother. It would be like you're living it all over again."

I hesitate for a moment as I go back through the very few memories I have of my mom. "I don't remember much about her," I finally admit.

"That's okay. You were what, five when she passed? Every day you spent with her formed a memory that is somewhere deep in your brain."

I chew on my lip as I contemplate his offer. I'm not really sure I want him rifling through my thoughts and memories considering what he did the last time he was in my head. Plus…there's one more problem.

"Hey," Khalil says. "You can trust me, you know."

"It's not that."

"What then?"

"I'm scared," I whisper after a moment. "What if the memory I have doesn't live up to the picture of her I've built in my head after all these years? What if she isn't how I think I remember her?"

Khalil gives me a sad smile. "May I?"

I nod, and he places his hands under mine. His palms are warm and reassuring. He gently grips my hands. "Just have a little faith, Princess."

He instructs me to close my eyes and to be quiet while he works. It only takes him a minute or so to find the memory where it must have been hidden all this time in the back of my mind.

I open my eyes to a dark bedroom. As my eyes adjust, I realize where I am. I'm in my old room in Dad's estate in the Underworld. And by the sheer number of stuffed animals throughout the room, I can't be more than four.

I roll over and find my mother next to me in the tiny bed.

She's still asleep although I don't know how considering she's on the edge of the mattress. The only light in the room is from the nightlight plugged into the far wall, but even that dim glow is enough to illuminate her beautiful face. Dad is right—I do look like her. I have her freckles and her chin. In the dark, her silver hair looks like the color of snow. I want to reach out and touch her to see if she's real. I want to embrace her and to tell her how much I miss her...but I am powerless in the echo of the memory.

She must feel me watching her because she opens her eyes.

"Emmy?" she says, and I could sob at the sound of her voice. "What's the matter?"

"I had a bad dream," I answer, my voice so much smaller than it is now.

My mother opens her arms, and I scurry to nestle in the warmth of her body. I tuck my head in the crook of her neck. How could I have forgotten that she always smelled like vanilla? I used to tell her she smelled like a cupcake.

"It's all right, sweetheart. It was just a dream."

"A bad dream," I clarify.

"Well, I'm here now. I'll keep the bad dreams away."

"I love you, Mama."

"I love you, Emmy Roo. Go back to sleep."

She presses a kiss to my forehead and then settles into the pillow we now share.

I want to keep my eyes open for a little while longer. I want to hold on to the moment for as long as possible, but my eyelids grow heavier and heavier.

When I open them again, I'm back in my room with Khalil kneeling before me. Tears stream down my cheeks.

The pleased expression on his face crumples. "What's wrong? I thought that was a good memory?"

"It was." I sniff and wipe my nose on my sleeve.

"Then why are you crying?" he asks in exasperation.

"They're bittersweet tears. I hadn't realized how much I had forgotten about her over the years."

"Oh," Khalil mumbles, and he adjusts his turban. "I'm sorry if it upset you. I just wanted to help."

Without thinking, I throw my arms around his neck and squeeze. The turban he just righted topples off and lands on the floor.

"Thank you," I whisper into his ear. "That was the best gift anyone has ever given me."

Khalil freezes, his whole body rigid for a moment. But he quickly relaxes and even puts his arms around me, returning the embrace. He's so warm, and he smells good too—especially for someone who just crawled out of the toilet. I squeeze him tight as I pinpoint the spicy smell of his skin. Cinnamon and something else, maybe sandalwood.

It feels so good to be held by someone that I almost don't hear the unmistakable sound of Lucien clearing his throat from behind me. I peel away from Khalil and wipe my eyes one last time. I turn around to find my Guardian glowering in the doorway.

"Can I speak to you for a moment?" he asks rather tersely.

I sink down into the chair, pulling my legs up under me. "Sure, what's up?"

His dark gaze slides over to Khalil. "Alone?"

Khalil heaves a dramatic sigh before getting to his feet. He grabs his turban and winks at me before heading toward the living room.

As the djinn passes my Guardian, I'm surprised at the amount of tension between the two. It practically makes the air spark. Khalil pauses beside Lucien for the briefest moment, and I'm struck by how different they are. The djinn is several inches taller than Luce, but Luce has more muscle mass. Khalil's skin is dark and warm whereas Lucien's is pale as porcelain. And as for their eyes, my Guardian's are as dark as Khalil's are bright and blue.

The moment of tension seems to last a century. Finally, Khalil brushes by and Lucien closes the door behind him.

"What was all that about?" I ask.

"I could ask you the same thing," he replies, and his voice is odd. I've never heard Lucien use this tone before. It sounds almost...jealous.

"Khalil showed me a memory of my mom as an apology for being a jerk earlier. I gave him a hug afterwards. That's it."

"Oh, so he's *Khalil* now?"

I narrow my eyes at him. "What's wrong with you?"

"You need to keep an eye on him," Lucien says in a low voice as he steps further into my bedroom. "I don't trust him."

"You don't trust anyone," I mutter.

"The second Task is quickly approaching. You should be preparing, not getting cozy with Underworlders."

My fists clench, and I unfurl from the desk chair. "Firstly, how am I supposed to prepare for the Task when I have no idea what it is going to be? And secondly, who I get *cozy* with is none of your business."

He runs a hand through his hair, disheveling the strands that are usually so meticulously gelled into place. "It *is* my business, actually. And I don't think that your father would be very happy to find out that you and the djinn are getting so close."

I throw up my hands in exasperation. "We aren't! It was just a hug."

"A hug can lead to other things." Lucien's eyes narrow.

It's then that I realize we are only inches from each other. Somehow we gravitated toward each other during the conversation, and I didn't even register it. I stare up into his face and lose my train of thought for a second. Even with a scowl, he's devastatingly handsome. I remember that I'm supposed to be mad at him and take a step back. "Why do you even care?"

Lucien lets out a huff of breath. "I am your Guardian. It's my duty—"

"No," I say, cutting him off. "Why do you care about who I'm hugging or cozying up to?"

A muscle in his jaw twitches, but he says nothing.

"Why do you care, Luce?" I ask once more, anger spilling over from my bitter heart into my veins. I had no idea just how bitter I had actually become until I was forced to endure the unfairness of Zilah's stolen kiss this afternoon.

He remains silent. Anger flares up in my chest, bright and burning.

I cross my arms. "I have every right to hug or kiss anyone I damn well please, Lucien. And you can't do anything about it."

"Oh, yeah?" he says between gritted teeth.

"Yeah," I taunt. "Maybe I'll kiss Khalil as soon as you leave. Maybe I'll do more. Maybe I'll push him on the bed and rip off his—"

Lucien cuts me off with a frustrated growl. His hands come up and cup my face as he lowers his forehead to mine. His touch on my skin is nothing but gentle, and the lightest brush of his fingers makes me burn with a yearning for those last few inches between our lips to disappear, for him to crush me against him and sate my soul's forbidden desire. My heart tumbles over in my chest in a never-ending descent as Luce expels a shaky breath. I can sense the same repressed longing in him that I feel deep down in my bones. It's not my imagination, or at least...I don't think it is.

What is *happening* right now? Am I imagining things? Is this still part of Khalil's little dream magic? If so, I am going to seriously injure that idiot when I get out of here.

I pinch myself on the thigh. It smarts enough to make me wince. Nope, not a dream. This is really happening. I'm seconds away from tilting my head up and finishing what Lucien has clearly started. But something holds me back. Perhaps it's the fact that he stopped before anything even really happened.

Before I can throw caution to the wind and end the torture, Lucien shakes his head. He pulls away, and I'm left in the middle of my room with a Lucien-shaped hole in my heart.

"I'm sorry," is all he says before he throws open my bedroom door and disappears down the hall.

Sorry for what? For not kissing me? For almost kissing me? For being rude to me about Khalil? All of the above?

I go to my threshold and watch with a sinking heart as he vanishes into his bedroom. Khalil lounges on the couch with a bowl of popcorn on his stomach. He tosses a kernel into his mouth. "I told you I could make it happen."

It takes me a moment before I understand what he's talking about. "Nothing happened, you dolt."

"Oh, *something* happened." He points a finger in my direction. He scoops up another handful of popcorn. "It's all part of the plan, sweetheart."

I let out a bark of laughter. "You mean your little matchmaking game? Please. And don't call me sweetheart."

"Come on," he says. "Admit it. Whatever I'm doing is working."

I roll my eyes. "You had nothing to do with it."

"Did too."

"Did not, you cocky bastard." I go around the back of the couch and plop down beside the djinn. "Scoot over. Let's watch a movie. I need something to think about besides the fact that I just had my first almost-kiss with Lucien."

I want to pinch myself again. I can't believe those words just left my mouth. I can't believe that actually just happened. Well...almost happened.

Khalil pulls up the trending movies list. "Let's see what we have here," he muses as he scrolls along. "Tell me if anything sticks out to you. We've got a documentary on the Mexican drug cartel, a Hallmark Christmas movie. Oh, what about this one? It's a horror movie about werewolves."

"No," I say, a little too quickly. Khalil gives me a funny look. "Sorry. I just don't like werewolves. Actually, I dislike them most out of all of the Underworlders."

The djinn raises an eyebrow. "Really? Out of all the beasties in the Underworld, your least favorite is the wolfman?"

I nod. "Yep. If it was up to me, they'd all be locked up."

"Any particular reason why?"

I chew on my lip. "I have my reasons. Listen, I don't care what we watch—just not that one, okay?"

Khalil shrugs. "Okay. Hey, what about *Piranhasaurus*? It has half a star."

I let out a breathy laugh, glad that the werewolf conversation has dropped. "Now that I can do."

"Good," Khalil says around a mouthful of popcorn. "I've seen this one before. There's a sexy underwater cave scene. So scandalous—kind of like someone I know."

I knock his leg with my elbow, and the bowl on his stomach topples over.

"Way to go, Princess. You now have popcorn in your cushions."

"Think of it as a midnight snack," I tell him with a chuckle. "You won't even have to get up."

"You are too kind."

Khalil starts the movie. We get to the aforementioned sexy underwater cave scene, and a horrendous blush unfurls in my cheeks. "Um, Khalil?"

"Hm?"

"Not that I care or anything, but what exactly is the next step in your master matchmaking plan?" I ask, adding air quotes around the last part. "I mean, *if* I were to follow it—which I'm not. This is totally a hypothetical question."

"Of course it is." The djinn laughs and pauses the movie. "Well, *hypothetically* speaking, the next step is to do nothing."

"Nothing?" I ask, confused.

He settles back against the couch cushions. "Yep. Nothing. Give Bird Boy some time to process his emotions. You don't want to push him too hard."

"Right, sure. I guess that makes sense."

Using the hand trailing along the back of the couch, Khalil twirls the tips of my ponytail around his finger. "And while you do nothing, we make him insane with jealousy."

I pull my hair out of his grasp. "And how do you propose we do that, oh wise one?"

He presses play again. "Leave that to me, Princess."

After letting the movie roll for a while, I dare to look at the djinn from the corner of my eye. His lush lips curl up at the corners and he chuckles as some poor extra meets a gory death in the mouth of the piranhasaurus. Part of me trusts Khalil. Part of me has even come to consider him a friend. Part of me might even be sad when we find the spell to break the bond between us.

But part of me still wonders...why is he helping me, and what's in it for him?

13

Ember?

"I'm here."

The Darkness strokes the back of my hand with a soft caress. *Your heart is heavy tonight.*

"It's almost that time of year again," I tell him. I don't know how he knows my emotions, but the Darkness always seems to sense what I'm feeling. Even when I was younger, he would know my mood before I could even say anything to give it away.

Ah, yes, he murmurs. *I had almost forgotten. Time seems to elude me in this cage I'm in.*

"Which is where exactly?"

Somewhere far away.

"That's all you're going to give me, huh?"

For now.

I reach out, my fingertips searching for something, anything in the blackness. "Please. Let me help you. No one deserves to be trapped in a place like this."

I do, the Darkness replies. And finally my fingers find something in the nothingness. His hand slips into mine and clasps my fingers in a warm, tender grasp. *Ember, I am not the hero in this story.*

"Then who are you?"

The villain.

A shudder crawls down my spine. Seemingly sensing my unease, the hand in mine tries to pull away, but I grip it tighter, refusing to let go. I'll be the first to admit that the Darkness's words should concern me a bit more, but I've been dreaming of him since I was a kid. He's never once tried anything untoward—if anything, he's warned me at every turn not to trust him. But something in me says there's something more to him than meets the eye. "Maybe you were once, but I don't think you are anymore."

I may not be a villain in your story. Not yet, anyway. But soon a new sovereign will rule on the Obsidian Throne...and if it is you, Princess, then I will become your enemy.

"No," I tell him, as if it's that simple. "I won't let you become that again."

The fingers slip out of mine, but he doesn't pull away completely. His touch whispers along my cheek. *I have been, and always will be, the antagonist. Not even you can change that, Ember.*

"I will, just you wait and see. But please, tell me who you are. I can't help if I don't know who you are."

You would never come back if you knew the truth. No one can love me, not when they know what I am.

"You don't know that."

I do. And while I can't tell you who I am, I can at least show you where I am. Until next time, Princess.

And with that abrupt farewell, the dream dissolves. I expect to wake up in bed considering that's where I fell asleep, but I'm surprised to find myself someplace far, far away from my bedroom.

I stagger as the rotten egg smell of the Underworld assaults my nose and stumble forward only to catch myself on a chain link fence. It takes a moment for my brain to wrap around the fact that this is not another dream and that I am, in fact, somewhere in the Underworld.

When I finally come to my senses, I realize where I am.

I'm several hundred yards away from the Pen, standing outside the fence which serves to prevent curious whippersnappers like me from getting too close to the door on the other side. The lights circling the Pen barely reach out this far, leaving me in shadows. I must have followed the wall to this spot to avoid the guards on duty even though I have no recollection of how I got here. Dad's mansion isn't too far from here—maybe a few hundred feet. The backside is facing me, all windows dark except for one that I'm guessing is Dad's office.

How I managed not to kill myself while I traversed the steep pathway in my sleep is beyond me. Maybe the Darkness had something to do with it. Even from my vantage point across the Underworld, I can still make out the steep drop from the portal's ledge. I swallow the lump that has formed in my throat. Yep. That would definitely have been painful had I taken the wrong step.

Either way, I'm awake now. Here in the Underworld. Standing in front of the door that I haven't thought about since I was a kid.

I can at least show you where I am.

The door that Dad had told me a hundred times to never go near over the years. The door that I thought led to a cave and a nasty death should I ever fall down it. The door that is covered in several different languages and symbols. The door that is the only other place in the Underworld with a fence around it besides the Pen.

The Darkness' voice echoes in my thoughts, and I realize that it was never meant to keep me out—it's meant to keep something in.

The rest of the week goes by in a flash, leaving me next to no time to consider the implications of what might lie behind the door in the Underworld. It's a miracle that I made it back to the Surface and into my bed before Lucien discovered I'm gone. I don't know what my Guardian was up to behind the closed door leading to his bedroom, but Khalil was passed out on the couch when I came back through the portal. The glowing light didn't even phase the djinn as he slept peacefully on the couch. I snuck past him into my room, changed into fresh pajamas, and quickly hid my reeking clothes at the bottom of the hamper in the laundry room before crawling back into my bed.

When I get up the next morning, time seems to double. The seconds and the minutes slip by at alarming speeds. Before I know it, Mom's deathiversary is upon us.

Her deathiversary is the one day every year that Lucien lets me skip school. He even allows me to sleep in. When I finally wake up, the three of us get ready and pile into the car. Lucien and I wear our usual clothes, but Khalil dresses up for the occasion. He comes out of my bathroom dressed head-to-toe in black. He actually looks quite handsome in his black suit jacket and fitted pants—not that I'd ever admit that to him.

Khalil offers his arm to me. "Ready?"

"Ready as I'll ever be, I guess."

He escorts me to the car. Lucien wisely decides to keep his mouth closed when he sees us walking together—although it does please me to see Luce's jaw clench. Mom's gravesite is on the other side of the city, so it takes us nearly an hour to get there. The car ride is quiet but not uncomfortable, giving me a lot of time to think about Mom and the night she died.

Lucien must sense the turmoil swirling around inside of me because he smiles when I happen to glance his way. It is a sad smile, one full of pity and not the least bit flirty, but it's still sweet enough to make my heart go pitter-patter.

Once we arrive, we weave through the headstones until we find hers. Dad is already there, as is Zilah. He stands at the foot of Mom's plot, staring down at the grass and clearly lost in a memory. Dad lifts his head when he finally notices us standing there.

"Hey, kiddo," he says to me with a crooked smile. His eyes are wet. I wonder what he was remembering when we interrupted his thoughts.

"Hey, Pops. Hi, Zi."

Mom's deathiversary is the one day a year my sister and I put aside our grievances and act like civilized people. Even this year with Dad stepping down and the second Task only days away, we behave. For Mom. For Dad.

Zilah opens her arms and we give each other a stiff-limbed embrace. She smells like lavender as her silky, silver-white hair tickles my nose. I know exactly how many hugs I have ever gotten from my sister because this day is the only time we ever extend something remotely resembling familial affection. This year makes twelve awkward hugs. I guess we will have to wait and see who wins the throne to know if there will be a thirteenth. I mean, she might win and off me before we ever even get to Mom's deathiversary again.

I shove my hands in my pockets and make eye contact with Lucien as he keeps watch from a distance. I've invited him several times to join us, but he always politely declines. Likewise, Khalil keeps a respectful distance from us—and Lucien—near the edge of the cemetery while we do our thing.

Dad hands me a bright kitchen towel with honey bees printed on it. Mom loved bees. It's one thing I actually remember about her. Before she died, Dad's mansion was filled with bee decor and paraphernalia. I clench the towel tightly in my fist as I bend down and wipe the grime out of the letters of her name that are carved into the marble.

The stone reads: "CAROLINE ASHWORTH, so dearly loved." Nothing else. No birth or death date. It's hard to swallow past the painful knot in my throat as I run my finger over each letter. Twelve years is a long time, but the pain is still right there under the surface.

While I clean the stone, Zilah plucks any rude weeds and sets out fresh peonies to replace the slightly wilted ones resting in a nearby vase. Dad sends someone to place fresh flowers here once a week, and it's always peonies—Mom's favorite.

Dad pulls a plaid blanket from a basket at his feet and lays it out on the ground. Once our tasks are done, we settle down for lunch as a family.

The clouds that hovered low in the sky all morning have all but faded away by now. The sun peeks out and it's surprisingly nice for late autumn in Seattle. There have been years where we've had to eat our lunch under umbrellas.

We don't talk much as we enjoy our gourmet sandwiches, sliced cheese and apples, and Mom's favorite dessert of triple chocolate cake—all prepared by Dad's brilliant chef. My stomach feels like it will burst by the time I'm done.

When Dad finishes, he wipes his face on a linen napkin before giving us each a kiss on the head. "Girls, I have something to tell you while I have you both together."

"Is it about the Task?" I ask, hoping he's going to give us a hint of what the upcoming Task will entail. Maybe if I know what it is, I'll have a chance to prepare myself.

He nods. "The second Task will consist of a judgment. You will hear testimony from an Underworlder accused of a crime, and you will declare the verdict."

Zilah scoffs and dusts a nonexistent crumb off of her pale pink dress. "That's it?"

I think the exact same thing because the Task Dad just described is way too easy. Here I am losing sleep because I keep thinking we are going to have to slay a dragon or fight to the death in a steel cage. But passing judgment on an Underworlder? Easy-peasy.

"That's it." Dad leans back on his hands and stretches his legs out before him. "But remember: the HTF is not looking for some ruthless ruler that answers every problem with death. We want someone who will look at all sides of the argument, someone who is fair and just."

I watch as Zilah struggles to physically prevent herself from rolling her eyes. Obviously, this information is nowhere near gory and violent enough for her tastes.

We end our family outing the way we always do—with Dad telling us how he met our mother.

I've heard it enough times that I can practically recite it word for word. The story of how my parents met just so happens to be one of my favorite stories of all time, and I look forward to this part of Mom's deathiversary every year.

The year was 1993. Whitney Houston blared from every stereo. Curtain bangs on men were all the rage. Turtle necks and patterns were everywhere. Dad was even rocking a glorious mustache around this time.

It was a beautiful March evening. The sky, dark with thunderclouds and impending nightfall, rumbled as rain began to drizzle over the city. Dad stood under a street lamp and watched as the mist cast a hazy halo around the yellow light above him. It had been years since he went topside. However, considering the troubling circumstances that had been occurring of late, he figured he had better be the one to deliver the news on this dark and stormy night.

As he walked toward the hospital's front entrance, Dad thought about the terrible situation's silver lining. This was the fourth attack in two weeks, but it was the first attack that left behind a survivor. The HTF had dealt with the bodies and the families of the first three victims, but Dad had declared that he would see to the survivor. He had hoped to glean some information from her about the Underworlder who had thus far evaded their clutches.

It was not a common thing for Underworlder attacks to happen so often on the Surface, Dad had made sure of that in the four hundred plus years he had reigned. It was even less common for Underworlder attacks to leave behind corpses. Like a well-oiled machine, the HTF almost always apprehended rogue Underworlders before they could do permanent harm to the human populace. This case, however, was proving to be different.

Dad walked right by the front desk. No one tried to stop him or even said anything to him as he took a left down a side hall toward room 902. Humans often did that, you see. He may not have been invisible outright, but unless he touched or said something to someone, humans usually didn't notice the tall, dark-haired man.

Dad had preferred it that way. The Lord of the Underworld had no desire for friends or even acquaintances, and he certainly never wanted a lover or a family. Friends and family members were nothing more than a weapon that could be turned against him, and Dad would never forgive himself if anything happened to someone he loved because of his position. So, he never allowed anyone to get close enough to him for that hypothetical scenario to play out. Little did he know that that was all about to change.

Dad made his way to the last room at the end of the hall. Posted outside the room was a police officer who ignored Dad until the Lord of the Underworld was just feet away.

The officer was Bernard—an old friend of my Dad's. Bernard was a shifter, meaning he can morph his form into anything or anyone he wants. His favorite body was the one he was wearing that night—a Pacific Islander with shoulders almost as broad as the doorway and geometric patterns tattooed on practically every square inch of available skin, even his face. The shifter stepped aside and allowed Dad access to the hospital room.

Dad gently rapped on the door with his knuckles and entered without waiting for admittance. He always laughs at this part and tells us that he's lucky the woman inside had such bad aim. Before Dad even had a chance to blink, a plastic cafeteria plate whistled through the air and crashed into the wall right beside Dad's head.

The Lord of the Underworld ducked inside and locked eyes with his would-be assailant.

Dad always tells us that it was love at first sight. One glance at her, and he just knew.

As for Mom? Not so much.

The woman who was throwing objects at his prone form stood across the room in a hospital gown and socks, a thick bandage taped to her neck. She had been attacked by a vampire—the same vampire that had recently killed three other people. Dad explained to the woman that she was lucky to be alive and then delivered the dreadful news he had come to the Surface to say.

Vampires are one of the most common Underworlders, which explains why so many mortals know about them and how Hollywood has been able to capitalize on them for the past fifty years. Unfortunately, the reason why they are so common is that it's actually extremely easy to turn someone into a vampire.

Vampires are venomous, sort of like snakes. When they bite someone to drink their blood, the venom contained in their fangs is automatically injected into the bloodstream. Luckily—or maybe *not* so luckily—most victims of vampires don't survive the attack, meaning they don't Turn. They simply die because the venom doesn't have time to take effect.

However, if the vampire's meal doesn't immediately die, the venom stays in the bloodstream for the rest of the victim's life, however long it may be. When death does come, the venom kicks in and the person dies a mortal death and then Turns, effectively beginning their immortal life. There is no cure for vampire venom. If a person is bitten and lives to tell the tale, they will eventually become a vampire.

This was the news that Dad had to relay to the woman. She was in disbelief for quite a while, of course, and the Lord of the Underworld had to return to his realm. Yet...something in him begged him to stay.

Feelings he hadn't felt in centuries stirred in his ancient heart as he looked down upon her. Dad tried to beat it back as he took in her tangled chestnut hair and the smattering of freckles across the bridge of her nose, but he knew he was doomed.

Before he left, Dad asked her name. She told him her name was Caroline.

Although he went back to the Underworld that night, Dad couldn't stop thinking about her. He went back to the Surface several days later and knocked on the door of the bungalow Caroline shared with her roommate. He asked her out for coffee, and the rest was history.

They married the next spring. One of their only surviving wedding pictures is in a shoebox in my closet. Every year after returning home from our cemetery lunch, I take out the photo and try to imagine being there with them.

Their love for each other is so evident on their glowing faces. My mom stood there beaming at my dad in her puffy-sleeved beaded gown, and he smiled right back at her in his baby blue tuxedo. At that moment in time, they thought that their love could conquer every challenge that life threw their way.

If only it had been that easy.

My parents lived ten years in married bliss before my mom became pregnant with twins. She was still mortal at this point in time, but the vampire venom still lurked in her veins, patiently biding its time.

As with most twin births, we came earlier than expected. On the morning of June twenty-first, Mom went into labor. My birth certificate states that I was born at 11:50 p.m.

Minutes later, things began to go downhill. So much so that at 11:56 p.m. Mom died. Her heart stopped due to catastrophic blood loss.

Then, at 12:02 a.m. the next day, Mom Turned and came back as a vampire. Her beautiful chestnut hair faded to silver-white and her brown eyes lightened to a blue-grey. Three minutes later, my sister was born. To the surprise of almost everyone, Zilah was born a vampire. There are less than a dozen born-vampires in existence, and all of them were born to mothers that died during the birthing process. It's more common for the baby to pass during the birth.

That is the not-so-short story of how my parents met and how I was born a human while my sister was born a half-vampire. I often wonder what my life would be like if I had been the second born. Would I have been a vampire? Would I be evil like Zilah? Would we even be having the Tasks right now?

I listen to Dad tell the story as raptly as I had the first time I heard it all those years ago. When he finishes, he gives us both a hug and leaves the cemetery to return to the Underworld. Zilah and I wave at him as he gets into the backseat of a black limo and speeds away. My sister and I part ways without bothering to say goodbye—any semblance of sisterly love between us vanishes as soon as Dad does. I don't know where she goes, and

I don't care. I refuse to be civil to her for a second longer than necessary. I run a hand over Mom's headstone one last time before turning to go. Lucien and I meet up with Khalil at the edge of the graveyard, and the three of us go home.

And just like that—Mom's twelfth deathiversary ends and the second Task is here.

14

"Seriously," Khalil says, "I really think you need one. What says 'judge' more than a powdered wig?"

I glare at him in the mirror as he stands behind me. Someone had placed an ornate body-length mirror in the parlor we currently wait in. I've been in this room maybe once before, and I know it wasn't here before. However, I appreciate the thoughtfulness. It would have been difficult to get ready in Dad's mansion without it. "I am not wearing a powdered wig. I need the HTF to take me seriously, not laugh me off the bench."

He shrugs. "Have it your way then. I will admit that you look stunning in your dress, though."

My cheeks warm as I smooth down the fabric over my waist. I glance to where Lucien is standing by the doors leading into the parlor room and catch him watching me. As soon as our eyes make contact, we both look away. The warmness in my face grows into a burn. "Thanks," I mutter. "But I was going for formal, not stunning."

"Why can't you be both?" the djinn asks.

The dress in question is a black gown with lace sleeves that I borrowed from Izzy. It's a lucky thing that we are close in size and height and that she kept the majority of her dresses from her audition days. While we were digging through her massive closet full of sequins, fringe, and lace, she told me about all of the low-budget movies she starred in when she was human. Many of the dresses were outfits she had completely handmade since she didn't have the funds back then to buy fancy clothes.

I lightly touch the back of my head where Izzy bound all of my hair into an elegant bun on the base of my neck. Despite the entire package of bobby pins and the can of hairspray Izzy used, I'm still paranoid that it will fall out.

Lucien checks his watch for the two hundredth time in five minutes. "It's almost time," he announces, and my bones turn to jelly.

"Easy now," Khalil says, catching me under the arm. If he hadn't been right there to grab me, I probably would have face planted. He leads me over to a plush sitting chair and eases me into it. Lucien watches Khalil assist me in stony silence. In a few minutes, I will open the door and march down to the Hall where a dinner will be served to us and all of the HTF members and their significant others if they have them. Following dinner will be a short intermission...and then the judgment.

I honestly don't know why I'm so nervous. This is most likely the easiest Task of the three, yet here I am being led to a chair like some kind of fragile Victorian-era lady. I focus on my breathing. I need to pull myself together in the next two minutes before anyone else sees me and knows the truth about how ill-qualified I am for this position.

Khalil crouches in front of me. "Hey, just calm down, okay?"

"Easier said than done," I mumble. I try to lick my cracked lips, but my tongue is as dry as sandpaper. I really need some water—or perhaps something a bit stronger than water.

"You got this," he tells me with an awful amount of enthusiasm that I know I don't deserve. He grins at me, his pearly whites flashing in the light from the chandelier above. "We watched all those episodes of Law and Order last night. You're a pro as far as I'm concerned."

I laugh. "Yeah, I don't think that's quite how it works. But I appreciate the pep talk."

Khalil puts his hand on mine. His long fingers practically cover my whole hand. Our eyes meet, and we both seem to notice at the same time that this is a relatively intimate position for us to be in. As if on cue, Lucien appears beside us, casting us in his shadow. Khalil quickly backs away, giving me a wink before he heads back over to the mirror to check his attire—white flowing pants and a turquoise tunic with silver embroidery. His matching slippers are silent on the plush parlor carpet.

Lucien clears his throat, and he extends a hand to me. "It's time."

My Guardian looks dashing as always, but perhaps even more so than usual in his formal wear. He's clothed in a dark tuxedo. He has opted to wear a bowtie for tonight's festivities instead of his usual tie, and I must say...it suits him.

I follow the line of his offered hand up to his dark eyes, and it's in his bottomless gaze that I find my confidence. I take his hand and get to my feet, making sure my skirts cover my beat up, old Chuck Taylors. I purposely asked Izzy for a floor-length dress so that I could wear my sneakers. I'd never make it through the night if I had to do it in heels.

Lucien takes my hand and guides it to the crook of his elbow, and together we exit the parlor. Before we leave the room behind, I glance back at Khalil. He gives me a thumbs up and mouths, *Don't screw up.* I make a face at him, and he chuckles.

Khalil was not invited to the dinner with HTF—something that caused him to say some colorful expletives when we opened the invitation together last week. To be honest though, I can see why the HTF wouldn't want him in attendance. He'll stay here and wait for us to return during the intermission before the second Task.

"He's right, you know."

"Who is?" I ask. Lucien's deep voice makes me jump when he speaks. I'm expecting our short trip to the Hall to be made in solemn silence. Luce isn't well known for motivational speeches, after all.

"The djinn. You do look stunning in that dress."

I take a shaky breath. Although the moment has never been far from my thoughts since our almost kiss, the memory of his face so close to mine floods me with something akin to bubbles. "Thank you," I manage.

"You're welcome."

The giant doors leading to the Hall are only a few feet away now. The low murmuring of multiple conversations going on at once filters through the wood to our ears.

Lucien stops abruptly in the middle of the hallway.

"What's wrong?"

He turns to face me, his eyes searching my face, lingering over my lips. "Nothing. I...I just wanted to say one thing before we go inside."

I give him a moment to say the one thing, but he seems to be struggling to find the right words—something that rarely ever happens to Lucien. I move as close to him as my skirts will allow. "Yes?"

Lucien lets out a breath. "I just wanted to tell you that I have faith in you. Whatever verdict you choose tonight, I know it will be the right one."

"How do you know that?"

He tucks a strand of hair behind my ear. How it escaped the nest of pins is beyond me, but I'm glad it did. Lucien's hand hovers beside my face. After what feels like an eternity and a half, he ever so softly runs the back of his fingers across my cheek. I lean into his touch, savoring the way his hand feels against my skin. I search his eyes, desperate to know what's going on in that head of his. *Kiss me, you idiot,* I think at him, hoping he'll get the message. *Please, just kiss me already.*

Then—almost as if he really did hear my thoughts—Luce tilts his head and leans down toward me. My heart nearly leaps out of my chest as my eyes flutter shut and my lips part. After a couple of never-ending seconds pass, I dare to open my eyes only to see Lucien crouched over his shoe.

It only takes me a moment to register how badly I misconstrued the situation. My entire face fills with heat, and I duck away in an attempt to hide my embarrassment before he can see. *Stupid, stupid, stupid,* I think, mentally kicking myself. There isn't much time before the shame turns into hurt. How many rejections can I take? How many times does he have to show me he's clearly not interested before I get the message? Why can't my heart find someone else to love?

Lucien finishes tying his shoelace and straightens. He refuses to meet my gaze as he adjusts his tux jacket and finishes his previous statement. "Because I know you. I know your heart, and I know that you will make a wonderful queen."

"Lucien—"

"Now all you have to do is convince the HTF of the same thing."

And before I have the chance to tell him he's wrong, that I won't be a good queen, he pushes open the door and leads me into the first half of the second Task.

The massive, U-shaped dining table that we only use for our seasonal 'family dinners' has been moved into the Hall for this special occasion. Porcelain plates with golden rims, crystal wine glasses, and folded linen napkins mark each place setting. There are enough chairs for me, Lucien, Dad, Zilah, all twelve members of the HTF, and the two HTF spouses.

As customary, Lucien and I appear to be the last ones to arrive. Thankfully, though, no one has been seated yet.

The conversations cut off as Lucien gestures for me to enter before him. Dad leaves the group he was talking with and crosses over to me. "You're just in time for dinner, kiddo," he teases before placing a kiss on my cheek. "Hope you're hungry."

I don't know how he expects me to eat before the Task, but I force a smile anyway. I follow him over to where the rest of the party awaits.

"Since everyone is here now, please find a seat. Dinner should be served shortly," Dad calls out to everyone, his voice bouncing off the walls. The HTF members don't waste any time sitting down.

Dad leads me to the head of the table where Zilah already sits. My twin wears a white dress with ribbon-lined ruffles. The color of her gown and the smoky makeup above her icy blue eyes causes her hair look more silvery than usual. Her plush lips are painted a red that would look garish on anyone but her. Dad places himself between us, thank goodness. I settle in the chair to his right and look out at the HTF members, all dressed in their finest.

On the right wing of the table in the first chair, sits Armenius—who looks incredibly uncomfortable in his formal wear. I have no idea how he managed to get his crisp white dress shirt over his bulging muscles, but I'm absolutely certain that if he makes one wrong move, his poor shirt is going to burst at the seams.

Next to him is Nobu, our representative from Japan. He wears a traditional business suit that tastefully covers the tattoos covering every inch of his skin on his arms...and his chest...and his back. I only know about his tattoos because I've seen him practice without a shirt on in the training rooms a time or two. He told me once when he caught me staring that his ink tells the stories of his ancestors.

Then comes Celio, the Italian man who somehow overlooked some specifics of the first Task and allowed Khalil to escape. He chats with Wilfredo who sits beside him. Wil is from Spain, and possibly the youngest of all the HTF members. He has his long, curly hair pulled back tonight which makes him look even younger than usual. I'm guessing he was only twenty or so when he signed on with the HTF. His pretty, young wife sits beside him. She has only been to one other family dinner beside this one, so I haven't had the chance to speak with her for longer than a few minutes. All I know about her is that her name is Esperanza, and she is an artist. Wil holds her hand on top of the table, and his thumb rubs comforting circles over her knuckles as he laughs at something Celio says to him.

Orana and Nalani come next. Orana hails from Australia, and Nalani is a Pacific Islander. The two have always been close. It wasn't until Dad married Mom that they came forward and revealed that they have been romantically involved for centuries. The only reason they didn't spill the beans earlier is because Dad had an unspoken rule that declared that neither him or the HTF members could be in serious relationships due to the violent nature of the job. He had to rescind that order, of course, when he broke his own rule and became involved with Mom.

Shikoba is the last guest on that side. Quiet and regal as always, he watches everyone else while they chat and catch up. His wide mouth tilts up at the corners as Nalani includes him in their conversation. Out of all of the HTF members, Shikoba is the one I know the least about.

Over on the left side of the table, Lucien sits in the first seat. He sips from his water glass and makes polite conversation with Idir and his wife Rashida. Idir might be considered Dad's third in command. You could never tell by the easy smile that graces his swarthy face, but Idir is an exceptional warrior, even more so with his shapeshifting Affinity.

On the other side of Rashida is Rajesh. Raj—bless him—is trying to hold a conversation with Yuli who sits to his left, but he isn't having much luck. Yuli is the human version of Grumpy Cat. In all of the years I've known him, I think I've seen him smile once, and it was still a frown. Yuli prefers his knives and his vodka. It doesn't help that he doesn't speak much English. If Dad needs a dangerous job done, Yuli is the one he calls. Even from several seats away, I can easily make out the three jagged scars running down the left side of his face—a parting gift from a griffin with a particularly nasty temper.

Elowen sits beside him, looking resplendent in a lilac purple pantsuit. She has her red curls unbound again. When she turns her head to say something to the last HTF member on that side of the table, I see a flash of gray perched on her shoulder just under her ear. I narrow my eyes, unsure that I really saw what I think I just saw. But there's no mistaking it when Elowen laughs and shakes her hair over her shoulder. Benny—that sneaky devil—seems to have snuck into our dinner. He clings to her shoulder like some kind of hideous stone parrot. Apparently, Elowen has grown attached to the little git.

The person Elowen chats with is the last member of the HTF, and arguably the most attractive of the lot. And, boy, does he know it. Aislan's pale green eyes flash in his dark face as he chuckles at something Elowen tells him. Ever the flirt, he leans in and whispers something into Elowen's ear. She grins in a way that makes me wonder if there is something more between them than just friendship.

My eyes slide to Lucien, but he's still deep in conversation with Idir. My leg bounces up and down restlessly beneath the table. Why does he have to be so damn complicated? One minute I think he's into me, and the next it's as if I don't exist. He has to know how I feel about him, right? I mean, how can he not after all of these moments we've been sharing lately?

The fool is completely oblivious.

And honestly, I'm over it.

Despite being a three course dinner, it passes by quickly. I manage a bite of each serving before my stomach tangles up into knots, and I have to put down my fork. I'm much too nervous about the Task and far too embarrassed about what happened with Lucien to enjoy the creamy lobster bisque or the savory beef tenderloin with garlic potatoes. I can't even bring myself to take more than one bite of the decadent cheesecake, which really is such a shame. Maybe I can visit the kitchens after the Task and get some of the cheesecake to go.

I try to put on a confident face as Dad stands and all eyes fall on us. "I want to thank all of you for joining us tonight. I consider each of you to be a part of my family, and I am indebted to each one of you for your service over the last four hundred and ninety-nine years."

All of the HTF members look to Dad with the same sense of pride and steadfast devotion. They've all been by him since the beginning. I can only hope that if—and that's a big if—I become queen, I can amass a task force half as loyal as Dad's HTF members.

Dad raises his glass. "A toast. For you all for sticking by my side through thick and thin, and for my girls—one of which will usher us into the future. Cheers."

Every person lifts his or her glass and salutes the Lord of the Underworld. After I take a sip of my water, I happen to catch Lucien watching me over the rim of his own glass. His face gives away nothing of what he is thinking or feeling, and that makes me furious. How could he look at me like that—like nothing almost happened between us?

Dad announces that the intermission has started and that we have fifteen minutes before the start of the second Task. He barely has the words out before I'm scooting my chair back and fleeing the room.

I barge into the parlor room without knocking. Khalil glances up at me from where he reposes on the velvet chaise lounge situated in the middle of the room. "Dinner over already? Did you bring me back something?"

"No."

He sits up at the tone of my voice. "What's wrong?"

I stomp over to where he sits and collapse beside him in a tangle of skirts. He barely has time to move his legs before I settle down on the end of the chair. "I'm an idiot."

"You're just now figuring that out?"

I swat him on the knee half-heartedly.

Khalil scoots closer and drapes an arm across my shoulders and pulls me in close. "I'm sorry. That was a dumb joke. What happened?"

I proceed to tell him about the not-moment I had with Lucien in the hallway. "Why do I keep doing this to myself?" I ask before lowering my face into my hands. I continue, my voice muffled by my palms, "He obviously doesn't see me that way, so why do I even get my hopes up?"

Khalil hesitates before lifting my chin with two fingers. His aquamarine cat eyes are filled not with pity like I'm expecting, but with understanding and another emotion I can't quite place.

"You aren't an idiot," he tells me, smiling. "The heart wants what the heart wants, and it's almost always to the dismay of the poor soul it beats inside of."

He tightens his arm around my shoulders and lets out a long sigh. "Lucien is...an enigma. I'm not even sure he knows what's going on in that head of his. But he'll come around, Princess. You'll see."

"And if he doesn't?" My voice is pitifully small as the words leave my mouth. A single tear leaks out of the corner of my eye.

Khalil slowly raises his hand, almost as if he thinks he might frighten me away if he moves too quickly, and gently brushes the tear away. "If he doesn't, he's a fool. And...perhaps you could open your heart open to another."

My head whips up, and the unfamiliar look in his eyes suddenly makes sense. Does he mean what I think he means?

His hand slides along my jaw, cupping my cheek, while his other arm falls to circle around my waist. I decide not to think at that moment—definitely not about Lucien and how I wish it was him pulling me close. I close my eyes and lean in toward the djinn as he does the same.

Khalil's lips are soft and warm, and he tastes like cinnamon as my mouth opens under his. The kiss is sweet and gentle—the perfect first kiss. And as quickly as it began, it's over. He pulls back with a crooked grin.

We stare at each other for an awkwardly long moment, trying to think of what to say.

Khalil is the first to speak. "That was—"

"It was—I mean, you are—"

A nervous laugh bubbles out of his mouth. "It was *awful*, wasn't it?"

I let out a sigh, relieved that he feels the same. "It was *terrible*."

"Did you, uh, feel anything?"

"Not a thing."

He lets out a groan and falls back against the chaise cushions. "Thank the gods. Me neither."

"It was like kissing my brother," I tell him, grimacing. "I almost feel like I need to brush my teeth or something."

He sits back up and boops me on the nose. "Hey! It wasn't that bad."

We slump against one another as we subside to another fit of laughter. More tears leak from my eyes, but this time it isn't from the same sadness as before. Khalil definitely made me feel better, but my chest still feels tight. What if I'm never able to feel anything for anyone beside Lucien? And what if he never feels the same way about me?

Would I be forced to have my heart broken over and over again? Or—maybe even worse—would I have to settle for someone who doesn't set my soul on fire the way Lucien does?

Khalil bumps me with his shoulder. "Princess, whatever it is that you're thinking right now—stop. I've seen the way our bird man looks at you, okay? Especially when he doesn't think you're paying attention. There is something there between the two of you. I think he just needs time to sort out what he's feeling."

I give him a small smile and rest my head in the crook of his neck and shoulder. "Thank you."

"You're welcome...but, just so I'm clear, what are you thanking me for?"

I wrap my arms around his slim waist and give him a quick hug. "For being a good friend."

He doesn't say anything, but his muscles stiffen under my touch. I glance at the clock on the wall. "Crap! Intermission is almost over."

I rush over to the mirror and brush any stray hairs back into place and dab away any streaks of mascara that may have run during my waterworks. Satisfied, I turn back to Khalil. "How do I look?"

The djinn looks me over from head to toe and he gives me a smile that doesn't quite meet his cat-like eyes. "Like the future queen. Go get 'em, tiger."

I grin and rush out into the hallway, nearly barreling over Lucien in the process.

"What have you been doing?" he asks, taking my arm and pulling me toward the doors that lead to the Hall. "The Task is about to start."

I refuse to look him in the face and instead turn up my nose at him. "I was freshening up." We reach the door, and Lucien turns toward me. He studies me intently for a long moment, long enough that I sigh and finally meet his gaze. *"What?"*

"Your lipstick is smeared."

I don't have time to make up an excuse before the doors are thrown open from the other side and the second Task begins.

15

The Underworlders in the Pen are still confined to their rooms since Zaahir's murderer has yet to be found, but Dad mentioned that he put out a message to all paroled Underworlders to attend the hearings. He wanted an audience for this Task, and I can only imagine why.

The Hall is packed with Underworlders—shifters, vampires, witches, manticores, griffins, gremlins, trolls, banshees, zombies. Practically every monster to ever go bump in the night is here. And as soon as I enter, all of those buzzing conversations cease into a silence loud enough to make my ears ring.

Lucien leads me directly across the Hall to the raised bench at the far end of the room. The dining table has been cleared out to make room for the audience, and the HTF are already in their seats with Dad sitting in the middle at the Obsidian Throne. He nods when he catches my eye and gives me a reassuring smile.

Below the bench on the floor is a mini dais with two black stone chairs. Zilah stands beside her chair, waiting for me. I sigh. I'm late even when I'm on time.

Lucien squeezes the hand that rests on his arm before helping me up the steps to the dais. Once he has delivered me to my position, he melts into the crowd of monsters that rings the room, disappearing into the chaos.

"I hope you're ready for this," Zilah whispers. If another person were to say this, it might come off as encouraging, but when Zilah says it, her words practically drip with condescension. "At least you look presentable for once in your life."

I give her a fake smile. "Thanks, dear sister. And I am."

One side of her red lips lifts in a knowing half-smile. I narrow my eyes at her. Let her underestimate me. I might just surprise her.

Dad stands and clears his throat. His voice is loud and clear enough for even the furthest members of the audience to hear with ease. "Good evening," he says with a broad smile, "and welcome to the second Task. The end of my reign is quickly coming to a close, and soon you will have one of my two daughters ruling you in my stead. Tonight's Task will focus on their ability to assess a situation and deliver fair judgment free of bias and fitting of the crimes committed and confessed."

I chew my lip. I should have this Task in the bag. I mean, really? Zilah fair? Zilah free of bias? Yeah, right.

But then why do I still feel so nervous?

"Because Ember was first to present during the previous Task, Zilah will go first tonight," Dad announces. He tilts his head in our direction and addresses Zi directly. "Choose your door, Zilah, and prepare yourself to judge those you may someday rule."

As he says these words, Dad points toward a set of two doors on the far right side of the room. These rooms are holding rooms, but are very rarely used. When I was little, I liked to hide in them while playing hide-and-seek with any Underworlders I could rope into playing with me.

Now, each door had a painted number on it in gold. Zilah doesn't even hesitate. "I choose door number two," she says, her voice calm and sure. I wish I could sound that confident.

The guard posted by the doors goes to the door on the right and enters a code into the keypad. The door unlocks with a beep, and the guard pulls it wide and vanishes inside. He returns not a moment later with his talons gripping a rope. Despite the large muscles under the guard's scaly skin, he struggles to pull whatever is on the other side of the rope into the Hall.

Finally, the other end of the rope comes into view. The guard readjusts the rope on his shoulder and hauls a massive tank full of green-tinted water into the Hall. Counting the wheels it sits on, the tank is nearly eight feet tall. It's so large that it barely fits out of the holding room. There's not even an inch of clearance between the top of the glass and the door frame. Talk about a tight squeeze.

Water sloshes out over the sides of the tank to splash spectators and floor tiles as the guard tugs the tank forward. With every step he takes to the center of the room, one of the wheels under the tank squeaks in loud protest.

Step. *Squeak.* Step. *Squeak.*

All the way to the middle of the Hall. By the time the guard and the tank reach the center of the Hall, my nerves are frayed to the point of snapping. My eye started twitching around the fifth squeak and has yet to stop. I risk a quick glance over at my rival and see that Zilah is clenching her chair's arms so tightly that her knuckles are white. I'm glad that I'm not the only one a little on edge.

Inside the tank is a siren. She stays in the bottom corner of the tank, but with each slosh of the water out of the top, she jostles back and forth against the glass. Her inky black hair fans out around her head like a dark halo, but two large fins along her hairline where her ears should be ensure that none of her hair clouds her beautiful, terrifying face. I know she is a siren and not a mermaid because she wears a shock collar around her slender throat to keep her from singing and hypnotizing us all. It's not a traditional electrical shock collar, of course, but a collar etched with runes that are linked to Elowen's purple electric magic.

"This siren," Dad reveals, "has been tried and found guilty of luring six sailors of the Republic of Korea Navy to their deaths in her underwater lair. Their bodies were recovered and returned to their families."

The siren slashes her tail through the water. Under the bright lights of the Hall, her purple scales glitter like thousands of gems. She opens her mouth, but Elowen must be prepared for trouble. Before a single note can be sung, a spark of purple electric current rings her neck. The siren curls in on herself in pain and says nothing.

"Zilah," Dad says, his voice grave. "You must choose now whether this Underworlder should be imprisoned and rehabilitated, imprisoned for life, or executed for her crimes against humanity."

Knowing my sister, she will choose execution. The thought of witnessing an execution happen right in front of me turns my stomach. Even though the siren killed all of those sailors, that doesn't mean I want to watch her die. And, knowing Zilah, she'll do it in a terribly violent way. I don't put it past her to overturn the tank and let the siren suffocate on the black stone tiles as we all watch.

Zilah takes her skirts up in her hands and steps down off the dais. Her heels click on the floor as she makes her way over to the tank and peers inside. The siren swims up to her side of the glass and stares back at Zilah. I would have flinched under the scrutiny of the siren's fish-like eyes, but Zilah looks on without an ounce of unease plaguing her features.

"Zilah?" A note of unease tinges Dad's voice as he calls out her name.

"Imprisonment for life," Zilah eventually responds. My jaw drops. It probably would have hit the floor were it not hinged to my skull. "Level Three. No chance for parole."

She taps on the glass with a pointed nail and continues, "The collar stays on as well."

The HTF bend their heads and murmur to one another for a few moments. The crowd does as well. I scan the variety of bodies for Lucien or Khalil and find neither. However, a bright smile and wave catch my attention. Izzy is there in the crowd. She blows me a kiss, and I forget for just one moment what I'm doing and return her smile.

And just like that, Zi's done. She returns to her stone chair with a smug look I want to slap off her face.

After several long moments, Armenius whispers something in Dad's ear. Then Dad straightens and turns to me. "Ember."

I stand and wipe my hands on my dress, hoping my sweaty palms don't leave streaks on the satin.

"The subject of your judgment lies just beyond door number one. Are you ready?"

I nod. Here's hoping my judgment is as easy as Zilah's was. If it is, I totally have this in the bag.

"I'm ready."

The same guard that opened door two for Zilah walks across the Hall and enters another code into the keypad. As soon as he opens it, I know I'm doomed.

From the dark room comes a howl that makes the hair on the back of my neck stand up. The guard leads out a young man with dark, stringy hair that falls forward to obscure his face. His wrists and feet are manacled, and the chain links clink together as he shuffles over to the center of the Hall. I hold my breath as the guard roughly tosses the man down before the steps. As the prisoner falls to his knees before me, he giggles again and mutters something. His eyes flit here and there through the greasy veil of his hair, never stopping long enough to make contact. The clothes that hang off of his skinny frame are filthy and frayed. I can smell him from where I stand several feet away, and my nose wrinkles in disgust. The prisoner clearly hasn't bathed in days, maybe even weeks, and I suspect the dark brown stains caked into his clothes are actually dried blood. He begins to whisper to himself, a constant utterance of words too quiet for me to be able to understand.

"Bryce Dylan Miller, werewolf," Dad says, "was first charged with murder three years ago when he was fifteen. It was his first Shift, so he spent time in the Pen, was considered to be rehabilitated, and was then released back onto the Surface."

Oh, no...

The man before me suddenly lets out a cry and jerks backward, falling flat on his back. The snapping of his bones as they try to shift from human to wolf is audible over his moans. His chest rises and falls as he sucks in ragged breaths. After a moment, Bryce rolls onto his side and convulses before stilling.

The silver manacles around his wrists and ankles are keeping him in his human state, but at a cost. A tendril of smoke unfurls above him and the smell of burning flesh fills the air. Werewolves don't like silver for a good reason. It burns something awful when it comes in contact with their skin, but it's the only way to guarantee they won't Shift.

Miller continues his hushed one-sided conversation as he breathes through the pain.

I just *had* to end up with the door that had a werewolf behind it. My stomach drops all the way to the floor, and I really start to regret eating those few bites at dinner.

"Two weeks ago, he was apprehended by the HTF for the deaths of twelve humans on the Surface."

I whip around and look up at Dad. Twelve murders is unheard of. It just doesn't happen. Not during Dad's reign, anyway. Not with the HTF patrolling the Surface. He nods in my direction, assuring me that I heard him correctly. "The murders took place over a period of three days. We believe that the killings would have continued had the HTF not intervened."

The man in question stops his incessant whispering and looks up. His wide eyes meet mine, and this time they don't dart away. They are fully black—pupil, iris, and everything else. It's like staring into the shadows of a skull. A chill crawls over my limbs.

"I saw the end of everything," he says in a voice hardly loud enough to hear, even though it's deadly silent in the Hall. "I saw the end, and it's darkness. He is coming. He is coming. He is—"

Dad's voice cuts over the werewolf's hoarse warning. "His victims include his roommate, a taxi driver, a vagrant, an elderly woman, a female college student, a recently discharged military veteran, a nurse, a female jogger, a teacher, a bartender, a high school student, and a six-year-old girl walking home from school."

"No!"

Everyone in the room turns to find the source of the outburst, including me.

"I didn't *murder* those people," Bryce declares. His eyes are so wide in his dirty face that I can see the whites all the way around his irises. His eyes are a deep amber. A shudder rolls over me. I could have sworn they were entirely black just moments ago. "I *saved* them. I saw the end, and he is coming. Can't you see? I saved them from him."

The sharp tang of blood in my mouth lets me know I have been chewing on the inside of my cheek a bit too much. I have only seconds to think of what judgment I will pass on this werewolf before Dad asks me to decide.

He is clearly mentally ill. Perhaps he had always been ill or maybe it had been brought on when he was bitten and turned by the werewolf that attacked him. Either way, his sickness had gone on for far too long without help or assistance. I know deep in my heart that this man—this boy—does not deserve to die for the atrocities he committed while in the clutches of whatever disease plagues him.

I know that...but I also know what happened the last time a werewolf this sick was released on the Surface with strict orders to be admitted to an assisted living facility to be diagnosed and treated.

Before being turned into a vampire, my mother worked as a nurse. She was always an advocate for mental health, and that didn't change when she became an Underworlder and married my father. Before her, there was never anyone to fight for the mentally ill Underworlders who might have been wrongly sentenced due to crimes unknowingly committed. She became dedicated to giving them a voice and a second chance.

Dad helped her to open her own care center for Underworlders on the Surface. They staffed it with paroled Underworlders and constructed it to suit every type of possible patient. I won't lie, my mother's cause was needed in the Underworlder community, and she was highly successful in her endeavors. I can't count how many of her patients were cleared after receiving treatment from the Center. There may have been a handful of cases that didn't end the way my mother wished they would—I'm honestly too young to remember—but I can clearly remember the last.

Werewolves are commonly diagnosed with mental illness due to the unpredictability of their condition and the violence of the Shift. Many werewolves become depressed and attempt self harm, especially if they're loners. Wolves in a pack at least have their Alphas and their packmates to support them in the beginning when Shifting is most dangerous. A lone wolf, though, is completely responsible for what happens following a Shift.

It was a lone wolf that killed my mom twelve years ago. A wolf that she had convinced my dad to give a second chance, even after having killed his wife and child during a Shift. A wolf that she had cared for and protected and supposedly treated. He broke into our home in the Underworld and viciously attacked her, after everything she had done for him. By the time Dad and the guards arrived, it was too late

The real kicker, though? I saw it happen.

"Ember?" Dad's voice calls, bringing me back to the present. "It's time to choose whether this Underworlder should be imprisoned and rehabilitated, imprisoned for life, or executed for his crimes against humanity."

My heartbeat thunders in my ears. How does he expect me to decide this boy's fate in a matter of minutes? How can I give a fair ruling considering what happened to me all those years ago?

Amidst the panic in my mind, Lucien's words play back in my head. His confidence in me gives me the strength to open my mouth and say what I know I have to say. "Bryce Dylan

Miller, you are to be executed for the gruesome deaths of twelve humans."

My voice is surprisingly level as I give my sentencing. I can't help but to look back to see what Dad thinks of my verdict. His face is as still as stone, and I can't tell one way or another what's going on in his head.

When I turn forward again, the same guard from before is there with a black box with gold inlay. He opens it and presents to me a gun with a single silver bullet on a velvet cushion.

I take the revolver and the bullet with shaking fingers. It's a Colt .45 with a seven and a half inch stainless steel barrel. Luce is probably making heart eyes at the weapon in my hand from wherever he is in the crowd—Colts are kind of his thing.

It's thanks to Lucien's paranoid diligence over the years that I even know what type of gun this is and how to load it. I know how to shoot too. Every few months, he brings me out to the gun range to keep my skills somewhat sharp. I can't hit the center by any means, but I can at least hit the target most of the time.

I can't miss the bullseye now. I probably can't miss it even if I close my eyes. He's all of ten feet away from me, bound and chained. It'll be a quick, easy death. One silver bullet through the heart. He deserves to die for what he did to those people. That's what I keep telling myself while my fingers open the gate and guide the bullet into the chamber. The guard—Ginger, I suddenly remember, who got the name from the tuft of red hair growing in between his short, stubby horns—sets Bryce back on his knees. The barrel spins in my palm.

"Princess," Bryce says, addressing me for the first time. "You have to understand. I saved them, all of them! You should be thanking me."

"Be quiet," I tell him. My heart is in my throat, choking me. I don't think I have ever loathed an Underworlder as much as I do in this moment. Not even Mom's murderer. At least he was sorry for what he did, as little good as that did.

I raise the gun, click the hammer into place, and aim at Bryce's chest.

My finger finds the trigger.

The world will be safer without him in it. Who knows how many more people he will kill if I let him walk. He killed someone's mom, someone's grandparent, someone's teacher, someone's child. He deserves to die.

Emmy Roo, this world is full of monsters.

I suck in a breath. The memory of my mom's voice trickles up to the surface of my thoughts, making tears spring to my eyes. It's as if she's standing right beside me.

But sometimes the scariest ones live in our own heads.

The revolver wavers in my hand. What am I doing? Suddenly the faces of several Underworlders flash in my mind—Underworlders that Mom helped in her clinic. A banshee. A wraith. A ghost. A vampire. A werewolf. A demon.

She helped them all. And here I am, about to undo everything she ever stood for.

I slip my finger off the trigger.

Bryce looks up as if surprised he isn't dead yet. His dark eyes land on the barrel that still points in his general direction, and I watch his pupils dilate to pinpoints. His amber irises flare gold.

"You would spare me?" He lifts his chained hands toward me in supplication.

"Yes." I'm ashamed of the horrible action I almost made. Mom never would have wanted that. She would have wanted him to get help. For him to be healed, not put down like some sort of rabid animal. How would killing him help those whose lives he stole anyway?

Bryce drops his arms and speaks, his voice octaves lower than before. "You gave me mercy, and now I have to save you too. He told me not to touch you. He *ordered* me to leave you out of it, but I can't now. Not after that kindness."

I know that's his sickness talking. There is no one but himself to blame for what he did. I raise my voice so the crowd can hear me. "We are going to get you help, Bryce. Medicine, doctors, therapists. Whatever it takes."

His face begins to elongate into a more canine shape. Ginger steps in to take hold of his chains once more, but the werewolf swipes him with an arm quickly growing fur where skin should be and long claws where his fingernails were only seconds ago. Someone in the crowd cries out as the guard flies across the room to land against one of the twelve pillars bordering the circular walls.

"I don't need help," Bryce says between wickedly pointed teeth. "But you do, Princess. He told me you are off-limits, but I must save you from the end. I must."

The rags clothing his thin frame tear to pieces as he completes the Shift. Werewolves are nothing like the big cuddly wolves that Hollywood sometimes makes them out to be. Oh, no. Werewolves are quite hideous with great hunched backs and powerful shoulders, long arms and digitigrade-esque hind legs, complete with patches of rough fur over thick gray, brown, or black skin. Definitely not something you'd want to cuddle with. He's easily twice the size he was moments ago. The werewolf wrenches his arms apart, snapping the chains holding his wrists together.

Members of the HTF are yelling behind me. I can hear my name being shouted, but it all seems miles away. Right now, the only thing filling my ears is the guttural growl coming from Bryce's throat. The ounce of humanity he had before the Shift is gone. All that is left is the predatory stare of a wild animal. Black blood drips from his nostrils to splatter on his hairy, skeletal chest.

I know I'm about to die, and I know I should be scared. I should run or scream or fire the damn gun in my hand, but all I can do is stand there as I remember that night.

The window set into the wall on our left shatters, flinging bits of glass to the far ends of the room. Mom pushes me off the bed with her vampire-quick reflexes and turns around just in time to throw up her arms to defend herself. She is strong due to her Underworlder blood, but the wolf is stronger. He takes her forearms in his taloned paws and cracks the bones of her delicate wrists in his vice-like grip. She cries out his name and tries to reason with him.

"Robert, please!"

The only answer he gives is a snarl of rage.

"I know you're in there, Robert. You can beat this! It's me—it's Caroline."

She attempts to reason with him even as he dives for her throat and bites down.

I witness the scene from the other side of the bed. The sheets, white with colorful flowers, are still tangled around my feet. I clench the quilt to my chest as I peer over the edge of the mattress. I want to call out, to help my mother...but fear roots me to the spot. Fear of what the monster might do if it hears or sees me.

Despite what was happening to her, mom's pale blue eyes find mine across the dark room. She reaches out to me and tries to speak. All that leaves her mouth, though, is a line of dark crimson blood that seeps from the corner of her parted lips.

It's only then that I start screaming. And once I start, I can't seem to stop. As soon as I utter a sound, the wolf snaps his head up. Blood drips to the floor like scarlet rain. Scarlet blooms on the plush white carpet like roses.

I scream and scream and scream, so much so that the werewolf drops Mom's limp body to the floor and advances on me. He doesn't get two steps before my bedroom door explodes off its hinges, revealing Dad, Armenius, Idir, and several other HTF members. As I run to safety, the HTF fire round after round of silver bullets into the werewolf's body. It takes a hailstorm of silver before the beast succumbs to his injuries. He falls to the floor beside Mom and Shifts back into his human form. The murderer rolls over, his eyes searching until they land on me.

"I'm sorry," he says before taking one last shaky breath.

Now, here I am, about to suffer the same fate as my mother.

The muscles bunch beneath Bryce's powerful back legs as he gnashes his teeth.

Just as he leaps, a pale hand rips the Colt from my limp fingers. Zilah elbows me back and pulls the trigger.

The bullet hits Bryce right between his lupine eyes, and he falls dead to the floor just inches away from Zilah's satin heels. Someone must switch the sound back on because all of a sudden I'm aware of the madness of the scene. The crowd of Underworlders are yelling and screaming. The HTF is in a tizzy as they scamper down the steps to the bench, some disperse to the audience and some cross over to us. Dad foregoes the steps entirely and springs over the desk to land on the mini dais right beside us. He sweeps us behind him as he ensures that the werewolf is really dead. He doesn't have to do much prodding, though, because the werewolf Shifts back into his human state. Bryce lies on the floor, naked with a hole in his head.

Luce appears at my side and wraps a hand around my upper arm. He has his own gun out now, as if there are more werewolves waiting in the rafters. I want to say something snarky to him about being a little late to the party, but I'm afraid I'll vomit all over his tux and Izzy's dress if I open my mouth at all. The truth of what just happened hits me like a jolt of electricity.

I almost died...all because I tried to do the right thing. Bryce was moments away from ripping out my throat in front of the HTF and Dad, Lucien and Khalil, and the hundred other Underworlds here to watch the spectacle. But I didn't die.

Because my evil twin sister just saved my life.

16

"You can close your mouth now, Ember. You look like a dying fish."

I can't help it. It's been half an hour, and I'm still gaping at her. As soon as Bryce was confirmed to be dead, the Underworlders were ushered out through the main doors while the Zilah and I were escorted through a side door to Dad's office. The HTF and Dad remained in the Hall to deliberate. I really don't know what's taking so long, since Zilah was the clear winner.

Ouch. That hurts to admit.

"Sorry," I say. "It's just that *you* saved *my* life."

She rolls her eyes. "Yes, I know. I was there, remember?"

"But *why*?"

Zilah continues to scrub at her dress with some club soda Dad's secretary found her. She can scrub all she wants, but I seriously doubt Bryce's blood will ever wash out. "Just because, Ember," she says between gritted teeth.

"I thought you hated me."

"I do hate you."

"Well then, why save me? I thought you would enjoy watching me die in such a grotesque way. I mean, I thought the prospect of an Underworlder ripping off my face would make you do a little happy dance."

She scoffs. "Oh, trust me, I would gladly watch a werewolf make a snack out of you—*after* I'm crowned queen."

"What is *that* supposed to mean?"

She stops her furious dress cleaning and stares me dead in the eyes. "When they declare me queen, I want it to be because I beat you fair and square, not because you died some ridiculous mortal death, and I'm crowned by default. I won't be queen because I'm the HTF's second choice."

"Oh..."

She goes back to her bloodstains. "I'll be made queen, and then you can die."

"Here I was thinking you grew a heart overnight."

"I have a heart, Ember. It's cold and black and beats for no one but me."

I drape my legs over the side of the armchair. "You should make Hallmark cards. They could say things like *Eat Shit and Die* and *Hope You Never Get Well.*"

"You seem rather cavalier for someone who nearly had her throat ripped out." Zilah sighs, face distorted with disgust, and drops the now pink rag on the floor with a flick of her hand. At least she got some of it out, although she seems to have made a bigger mess than what she started out with.

"I'm fine," I reply, but that couldn't be further from the truth. Once again, I somehow managed to screw everything up. Once again, Dad will be disappointed in me. I'm terribly tempted to pick up the nearest throw pillow and scream into it until it explodes in a flurry of feathers. Why can't I do anything right?

"Sure." Zilah rolls her eyes and leans against the edge of Dad's desk. "You're fine. Even though you froze worse than that time when you were in fifth grade. What were you in that ludicrous little play you were in—a can of green beans? A corn cob? A stalk of asparagus?"

"I don't remember," I mumble. But I do remember.

I was an eggplant in that godforsaken school performance about the food groups. I had to sing a little ditty about how the first European eggplants actually did look like chicken or goose eggs. But when it was time for me to sing, I panicked. The words that I had been singing nonstop for weeks in preparation for the show suddenly vanished from my head as if they had never even been there.

I stood in the middle of the stage, frozen under the glare of the spotlight, sweating inside the hideous purple contraption my current Guardian helped me make. After several long minutes of suffering, Mrs. Wallace finally came to rescue me.

And by rescue me, I mean remove me from the stage so that everyone could get on with the rest of the play.

Thank God that happened before everyone filmed every instant of their lives and the internet decided an eggplant was synonymous with penis. I can only imagine the memes...

"Whatever it was," Zilah says, "this was even worse. Bryce was seconds away from making werewolf chow out of you, and you just stood there. You even had a gun in your hand, for God's sake."

She eyes me shrewdly, her gray eyes calculating. I wish I had another M&M to fling at her. Or a rock. Anything really.

"So, why didn't you shoot him?"

I look down at my open hands. They feel empty without the sober weight of the revolver resting in them. "I was going to, but then I thought about Mom and I couldn't anymore."

She laughs. "What a time to be sentimental, Ember."

I clench my fists hard enough for my nails to bite into my palms and take a deep breath. "Never mind."

"I guess that answers my question then." She reaches into her ridiculously tiny purse and pulls out a compact. She flicks it open and proceeds to touch up her already flawless makeup. Why even wear makeup when your complexion is as fair and smooth as porcelain?

Don't ask her what she means. It's a trap. Don't do it, Ember! And then I go ahead and I ignore my own advice. "What question might that be?"

She lifts her shoulders as if it's obvious. "We all know you're not suitable for the throne, but I was asking myself whether it's because you're a coward or a simpleton. Now I know it's both."

I give her the one finger salute. "At least I'm not a cold-hearted bitch."

She smiles, the tips of her pointed canines shining in the light. "Oh, Ember. Don't you know? Bitches rule kingdoms."

I narrow my eyes at my twin. How we could have shared a womb but be so different is beyond me. She wasn't always awful. I actually have some memories of us playing together, of us going on a camping trip with Mom. We didn't always loathe each other, so what changed?

"Why do you hate me so much, Zi?" The words are out of my mouth before I can think better of it.

She clicks the compact close. "You seriously don't know?"

"Why would I ask if I knew the answer?"

Zilah pushes off the desk and walks over to me. She towers above me in her heels so much so that I have to tilt my head back to look her in the face. Her pale eyebrows draw together as she glares at me. "I hate you, Ember, because it's *your* fault that Mom is dead. She would still be here if it weren't for you."

Her answer knocks the air out of me, and I fall into my seat. *My* fault? How could she even think that?

Before I can form words to respond, Dad and his not-so-merry band of HTF members waltz through the door. Lucien comes into the room behind them, and a weight I didn't know

I was bearing lifts from my chest. Dad goes to his desk and directs Zilah to the empty armchair next to me. Elowen, Armenius, Nobu, Idir, and Wil spread out behind Dad. The rest of the HTF must be doing damage control.

"Are you okay?" Lucien asks, his voice barely louder than a whisper.

"I'm fine," I assure him, but Luce knows me better than that. He sets a hand on my shoulder and doesn't pull away as I lean my head to the side and rest my cheek on the back of his hand. His warmth steadies and prepares me for the awkwardness and embarrassment that is about to ensue.

Dad takes a deep breath, and his eyes land on me. "Before we begin, I would just like to apologize to you, Ember. It appears that the cuffs securing Bryce were tampered with, which is why he was able to Shift and break free. The guard in charge of overseeing his fetters will be dealt with following this meeting."

From the pitch of Dad's voice, Ginger is in for an ass-kicking. I don't think he'll be seeing the outside of the Pen for a hot minute. I guess the more important question is: who in the hell tampered with the chains and *why*?

"Be that as it may," Dad continues, "the HTF and I have decided that Zilah has won this Task. We agreed that Zilah would have won this round even if Bryce would have remained chained. The ruler of the Underworld cannot eke out judgments lightly. To take back a judgment is to say that you are unsure, and to say that you are unsure is weakness."

I knew it was coming, but the blow still feels like a ghost just drop-kicked me in the stomach. The score is tied now, and I only won the first Task because Khalil decided to go full djinn and tried to kill everyone on the premises. A technicality at best. Now, Zilah has a win under her belt too. The third and final Task will ultimately decide which one of us will replace Dad when he steps down in a month.

And I'll be damned before I let Zilah take the crown.

I don't want to, but if Max Wu doesn't work out and I have to take the throne myself, I will. The Underworld, the Surface, Dad, everyone deserves someone who isn't going to ruin everything that's been accomplished in the last five hundred years.

Plus, I really don't want to die just yet. I refuse to let Zi have me murdered before I have a chance to make out with Lucien.

Speaking of him, he squeezes my shoulder as Dad continues.

"Zilah not only dealt a fair and reasonable sentence to the siren, she also exhibited extreme selflessness and bravery during Ember's judgment."

I snort at that. Zilah is a lot of things, but selfless is not one of them.

Dad swivels to face me. His eyes go from the disgusted expression I'm wearing to Lucien's hand on my shoulder. "What's so funny, Ember?"

It'd be okay if Dad was just angry with me, but the turn of his mouth and the slump of his shoulders reveals a much worse truth. After the talk we had the other day, I think he really believed that I was going to try harder, that I was going to come into my own and beat Zilah.

To be fair...I did try.

I just suck at everything.

"Nothing. Sorry." I hang my head, face burning hot enough to broadcast my shame to everyone in the room.

I dare to glance over at Zilah and immediately wish I hadn't. She's practically radiant with victory.

She looks like that girl you love to hate who just won the plastic crown at the high school prom. I half expect her to start waving at the line of Huntsmen watching us from their posts around the room. But she keeps her hands neatly folded in front of her, subtly obscuring the pink stains marring her dress.

"The next Task will take place on the night of the solstice. Once the winner is declared, I will step down from the throne and the crowning ceremony will take place immediately following that," Dad explains. That means I have a little over three weeks to prepare myself either to be queen or to be killed. Let's all hope it's the former.

"On another note," he adds, "I am greatly concerned with the ominous occurrences happening in the Underworld in the past few weeks. First it was the release of the djinn named Khalil, then the murder of the djinn in the cell across from him. Now a werewolf has gone rogue on the Surface, his shackles tampered with. Someone or something is trying to influence the outcome of the Tasks. Whoever it is will be found, and when I find them..."

He trails off, letting the silence of his unspoken words explain what he has in mind for the person or thing threatening his kingdom.

"I need to speak to the HTF. And Lucien. The rest of you are dismissed."

I look up at Lucien. "Why does he want to talk to you?"

He takes his hand off of my shoulder, leaving it colder than ever before. "I don't know. I'll meet you back at the house. Watch your back."

Zilah turns to go, but pauses beside us on her way out. "Someone is in trouble," she teases Lucien. She bites her lip and winks at him before strutting out of the office.

I glare at her back and imagine setting her on fire. Unfortunately, I don't have any magical powers. But if I did? My sister would be nothing but a pile of ashes in the wind. I still can't believe she had the audacity to blame Mom's murder on me.

A sudden terrible thought claws at my heart. What if Lucien falls for her?

The possibility of it is so slim that it's nearly impossible...but what if? The thought of it alone is enough to make me want to vomit or scream or rip my hair out. Maybe all three.

I push the idea out of my mind and grab Lucien's hand before I can think better of it.

"See you at the house," I tell him and squeeze his hand just once.

And then I skedaddle, grabbing Khalil from the foyer on my way out. As we go home, I make a promise to myself. I'm going to tell Lucien how I feel. Soon. I'm going to open up my heart and let him see all there is to see. And if he doesn't return my feelings...I'll let him go.

Because I can't go on loving someone who doesn't love me.

It'll kill me, and I've got a throne to win.

17

"Not to be rude," Khalil says, "but that could not have gone more wrong. What the hell happened?"

"That is pretty rude."

"The whole thing was a train wreck. If the wreck was on fire. And it plummeted off of a cliff. Into a pit of alligators—"

"Okay, okay!" I rub my temples. "I get the picture. It was a mess, I'll be the first to admit it."

He spins around in my desk chair a couple of times before rummaging around in my desk. Probably for something to snack on. "I'd say 'mess' is a bit of an understatement."

I growl at him as I sort through my dresser for some clothes to change into. I'm going to take a bath to wash the smell of failure off of my skin, and then I'm going to call Hannah to plan out our Max Wu recruitment mission. I'm quickly running out of time to convince him to take my spot to rule over a bunch of scary monsters.

"So, what happened?"

I sigh. Might as well tell him the truth. I give him the rundown of what went through my head from the moment Bryce stepped out of his holding cell. When I finish, Khalil watches me with a funny look on his face as I dig through a pile of clothes on the ground for a clean shirt.

I find one that doesn't smell too bad and straighten up. "Why are you looking at me like that?"

He blinks. "Like what?"

I wave an arm in his general direction. "Like a kid who just got caught with his hand in the cookie jar."

Khalil uses the reference as an excuse to change the topic. "Mmmm. Cookies really do sound good right about now."

He launches out of the chair to land spread eagle on my bed.

"Don't get too comfortable," I say. "Because as soon as I get done scrubbing off the stink of my inadequacy, I'm kicking you out and going to sleep."

The only reply is a soft snore.

I roll my eyes and go shower.

When I emerge from the bathroom in sweats and an oversized t-shirt, the useless djinn is still asleep on my bed. He looks quite comfortable too, lying on his stomach with his arms tucked underneath the pillows. His mouth is slightly open as he snores softly.

"Khalil." I nudge his foot. He doesn't stir. I don't even know if djinn need to sleep. Some Underworlders don't. "Get up. You need to go to the couch."

He rolls over with a grunt. I guess my commands only work if he's conscious.

With an exasperated sigh, I crawl over him and lie down with my back touching the wall. A yawn hits me as I wiggle beneath the covers. "I guess I can call Han in the morning."

I'm too tired to care that there's a boy in my bed. An Underworlder, I mean. Lucien is going to flip his lid when he finds Khalil in my room, let alone my bed. I giggle as I snuggle into my pillow. I actually kind of like that thought.

In the last moments before sleep, I realize that I'm glad Khalil is here. A hollow pit still rests in my chest as anxiety gnaws on my nerves. He wasn't wrong—today was a total fuster cluck. And Zilah's accusation still eats at me even though I know she's full of it.

Despite Khalil's warm body next to mine, I worry that nightmares of Bryce lunging toward me will haunt my sleep. I don't have to worry long, however, because my friend's steady breathing quickly lulls me to sleep.

I jerk awake sometime later. The lingering images of the dream fade from my memory like snow melting on your tongue. I roll over and study the djinn that is surprisingly still in my bed. I wonder where Lucien is and why he didn't drag Khalil out of here as soon as he got home.

In the quiet early morning hours, Khalil looks so peaceful and innocent. I can almost pretend that he's just a regular mortal, like me—that he isn't a monster that takes people's souls as payment for wishes that go wrong for his benefit.

I haven't forgotten where we first met the djinn. I've come to like Khalil, enough so that I now consider him my friend. But that doesn't change the fact that it takes a special kind of bastard to target a children's hospital. Just thinking about it now makes me want to punch his stupid, sleeping face.

He must sense my seething thoughts because he stirs. He gets comfortable again and then reaches out a hand to rest it on my arm. I want to shake him off or kick him out, but I'm still too tired to do anything that requires that much effort. So instead, I close my eyes, and when I open them, I'm no longer in my bed.

I stride down the hallway. The scrubs I stole from the second floor closet feel odd against my skin. I haven't worn physical clothes in so long. At least my costume makes it so that I blend in perfectly with the nurses and doctors that bustle along every corridor.

I continue to follow the call. I heard it as soon as my prison door unlocked and swung open. The call brought me here to this hospital. I have to be getting close now.

After skirting around a nurses' desk, I find the room. I go in without knocking, and the door clicks shut behind me. Inside is a small boy in a hospital bed. Countless tubes snake from him to machines and bags of liquid hanging from stands. A monitor somewhere in the room beeps softly every few seconds.

The boy's head is mostly bald although a few wisps of hair stand out on his pale scalp. As I stop at the foot of his hospital bed, he opens his sunken eyes and smiles at me.

I glance at the woman slumbering with her head down on the side of his bed.

"Don't worry about my mom," the boy tells me. "She's an incredibly deep sleeper."

I nod. "Did you call for me?"

"I was calling for anyone, really."

"Well, you got me. What is your wish?"

The boy resettles himself against his pillows. The smallest movement seems to require too much effort. "It's really that simple?"

"I'll need a piece of your soul, but it'll be so small that you won't even know it's missing."

"That sounds painful."

I shake my head. "Not at all."

"Can't be as bad as a bone marrow transplant, right?"

He closes his eyes as if this conversation has exhausted him, and maybe it has. I'm once again taken aback by the purple shadows ringing his eyes and the pallid tint to his wan skin.

"How old are you, kid?"

"I'll be eleven in two months. If I make it that far, that is."

"Damn."

"Yeah."

"So, let me guess. You want to be healthy again?"

"I've never been healthy," the kid scoffs. "I've had this cancer three times now. I've beaten it twice, but I don't think I can this time around. And to be honest, I'm tired. I'm so tired of being here and being in pain, of being a burden on my mom. And I don't want to wish to be healthy only to have it come back to kill me in a few months or a few years."

I look away at that. He is right. If he had wished for the cancer to be gone, I'm almost certain it would come back later in his life or another sickness would somehow overcome him. Such is the nature of wishes.

"My only wish," the boy continues, "is that my mom will find happiness when I'm gone. She deserves that much and a hundred times more."

He reaches out a frail hand and settles it on his mother's forearm. He doesn't weep or seem bitter that this short life is soon coming to an end. The boy just smiles at her sleeping form and turns back to me. "Can you do that?"

In the thousands of years I have prowled this earth, I have granted countless wishes. Usually, people wish for money or fame or love they cannot obtain by themselves. Some wish to hurt people, for revenge or pettiness or power. Many wish for vain beauty. However, I can count on one hand the number of times a person has made a selfless wish, a wish that benefited them in no way whatsoever.

I lift my hand and call forth my power. After centuries, my magic rises to meet me as easily as the moon rises in the sky every night. It fills me with the same rush that it did that very first time in the cave. My skin lightens to a pale blue-green and vapor fills the small room.

Carefully, I go to the side of the boy's bed where his mother still rests. I place my hand on the back of her neck to see her fears and hopes, her worries and her dreams. As expected, she worries constantly about her son—Benjamin is his name. Even in her sleep, she frets and mourns the eventual passing of her only child.

I release her thoughts and traverse to the other side of the hospital bed.

"You wish for her happiness?"

He nods, his eyelids fluttering shut. "That's all I want."

I place the first two fingers of my left hand on his forehead. "As you wish."

When it's done, the boy sinks deeper into his pillows and drifts off to sleep with a smile lighting up his tiny face. Tomorrow, they will run tests after finding strange results from his labs. They will soon discover the impossible—he is healed. The cancer will be completely gone.

The only thing that could make Benjamin's mother truly happy is for him to be healed. So, that's what I do. Benjamin will never suffer another day in the hospital. I make it so that he will never so much as be ill again, not even a common cold. He will die an old man. For those who are selfless, I make any wish come true. Without consequences.

Just as I step back, the mother wakes up.

"Oh, hi." She wipes the sleep from her eyes. "I'm so sorry. I must have just dozed off for a moment. Is everything okay? Is something wrong?"

I gesture for her to follow me out into the hall so that we won't wake up her son.

She wraps her arms around herself as if she can hold herself together when I deliver the terrible news she's been waiting to hear. Instead I tell her that Benjamin's tests have shown improvements in several areas.

I see a blur of movement out of the corner of my eye, and then something slams into me with the force of a tiny freight train—

I wake up from the memory. Khalil is awake and watching me with his djinn eyes. The slit pupils narrow in his aqua irises as he focuses on me in the dark.

"I'm not as horrible as you might think."

I chew the inside of my cheek. "I'm starting to realize that. But if that's the case, what did you do to end up on Level Five?"

He shrugs. "I have no mercy for the selfish. I've granted many wishes that ended in death or worse."

"Or worse?"

"It's not anything that they didn't deserve. I regret nothing."

I'm silent for a moment. This changes some things, and yet...I've known for a while now that there is more to Khalil than his Level Five label.

Khalil rolls onto his side. "Can I ask you something?"

"What?"

His eyes go back to their more human color and shape. "If you don't want to be queen, why are you trying so hard to win?"

I shrug. "I feel morally obligated to save the world, I guess."

"You really think Zilah would be that bad of a ruler?"

I let out a humorless laugh. "Without a doubt. Just the thought of her on the throne scares the crap out of me. Not only because she'll kill me as soon as she's queen, but I'm afraid about what she'll do with all of that power."

His gaze bores into mine. I don't think I've ever seen him this serious before. "You really believe that?"

"With all my heart."

Khalil nods and turns onto his back. He runs his hands over his face. "Damn. That sucks."

"There's a loophole."

"A loophole?" He cracks an eye open and peers over at me.

"I have a relative—Max Wu. I'm going to try to convince him to take my title if I win. I'm going to go find him."

"You really think that's a good idea?"

I swallow hard. "It's all I've got."

He nods in understanding. "Then what?"

"Then when everything is said and done, I'm going to talk to my dad. I think I can convince him to move you down to Level One or Two."

Khalil beams so brightly that his teeth flash in the early morning moonlight. "You would do that for me?"

"Don't make me regret this, djinn."

He laughs and throws his arms around me, pulling me close in a crushing embrace. I push against him and mutter half-hearted curses. When he finally lets go, he puts his hands behind his head and smiles. "Level Two would be good, but I hear they have cable in the Level One cells."

"Don't get your hopes up too high," I huff as I comb my hair away from my face. "We have to get this bracelet off first. Then we can start thinking about your future living arrangements."

"I'm going to get a DVR." His aqua-green eyes glaze over as he imagines his new cell. "Think of the possibilities, Princess. I'll be able to record everything. Maybe you can come and visit every once in a while, and we can watch cheesy scary movies."

"Khalil?"

"Yes?"

"How did you get out of the Pen?" The question has weighed on me since the first Task, but I didn't have time to question the djinn about it. Plus, I seriously doubt he'd tell me the truth with Lucien around. "I mean, who let you out?"

He goes still. "I don't know, Princess. I wish I did so I could thank them."

Something in his voice makes me think he's lying, but I let it go. For now.

In the memory-dream, he seemed surprised to not see anyone there when his door opened, but something in the back of my head tells me that I'm not seeing the whole picture.

"I also want Netflix," Khalil continues, switching the topic back to his new digs in the Underworld. "Does the Pen have Wi-Fi? If not, your dad really needs to get on that."

I grin at him. "I'll be sure to let him know."

18

Hannah comes over the next day, and we begin planning out our girl's trip/college day/Max Wu recruitment mission. Hannah pulls in a chair from the dining room while I grab us some piping hot pizza bagels, and we get to work.

I crack my knuckles over the keyboard. "Okay, what's first?"

"Instagram. No one our age uses Facebook anymore."

"Found him." I click on the profile handle. "Too easy."

"How do you know it's him?"

"He's my great-grand-third cousin five times removed or something, Han. I can recognize my own relatives, sheesh."

She gives me a look, and I laugh.

"Also, there's only like five Max Wu's out there, and this is the only one who claims to live in San Francisco."

Luckily enough, his profile isn't set to private. I click on the last picture he posted. It's a photo of him and a group of people at the finish line of some sort of marathon. He's sweaty and wearing shorts that are a bit too short for my liking, but at least he has those tights on under them. And even though he apparently just finished running a 5K, he's grinning wide enough for a shallow dimple to appear in his left cheek.

Hannah leans closer to the screen. "He's...cute."

I shrug. "I mean, I guess. I question his choice in running shorts, though."

We scroll down to the next picture. It's one of him before the race. He's crouched next to a young girl in a motorized wheelchair. The caption reads: 'So grateful to run for my best friend Katie! This year, "Run, San Fran" is donating all of its runner's registration fees to the Muscular Dystrophy Association. These donations will help send Katie and kids like her to a summer camp that will allow her to partake in activities like horseback riding and swimming in handicap accessible pools.'

Hannah's big brown eyes get shiny. "Oh, my gosh—he's so sweet."

I think she might actually fall out of her chair as we continue on to the next photo in his feed. This one is a selfie of Max holding his acceptance letter from...wait for it...Stanford.

"Should I just go ahead and make a Max Wu fan page for you right now, or should we do it after dinner?"

She turns the laptop toward her and begins furiously scrolling. I guess I'm going too slow. "Em." Her eyes devour all of the information his Instagram offers on Mr. Wu. "He. Is. Perfect."

Suddenly, my bedroom door flings open so hard that it crashes into the wall behind it. Several polaroids flutter to the floor. Both of us yelp as Khalil saunters in and strikes a pose. "I heard you guys talking about me."

"Dude, what the hell! Why did you kick my door?" I chuck the closest throwable object in his direction—this time, it just so happens to be a pizza bagel.

He catches it and pops it into his mouth with a shrug. "I like to enter a room with presence."

I roll my eyes. "You are so dramatic. And no, you egomaniac, we were not talking about you."

Khalil deflates with a pout and launches himself onto my bed. He seems to be making this a habit, and I don't know if I'm okay with that or not.

He cups his chin in his hands and kicks his feet back and forth like he's a fifth grade girl at a slumber party discussing the latest school gossip. "So, if it's not me, who's Mr. Perfect? And please, gods, do not say Lucien."

I don't even bother responding to that. Even though Luce *is* perfect.

Hannah goes straight back to Max's page. "He volunteers at the local retirement home! There's a video of him dancing with an elderly lady. My ovaries can't take this for much longer."

Khalil's light eyes widen in question. I sigh and begin picking up the pictures Khalil knocked down. "We found Max

Wu's Instagram and are creeping on his page for more information before we track him down this weekend."

Lucien's head peers from behind the door jamb. "Everything okay in here? I heard a noise—"

He cuts off when he spies the djinn lying on my bed. Lucien's dark eyes narrow, and I realize for the first time how tired he looks. Dark circles smudge the pale areas beneath his eyes, and his hair, while still neatly styled, doesn't look as rigid as usual.

When I finally caught up with him after the second Task and peppered him with questions about why Dad wanted to talk to him, he refused to tell me anything except that I was to be extra cautious until the third Task is completed. The two of them are hiding something from me, but getting classified information out of Lucien is like screaming at a wall.

"Everything's fine. Care to join us? We're stalking Max."

"Why are you stalking Max Wu?" Luce hesitantly comes inside my room. I stealthily kick a bra that's lying right there on the floor for all to see under my bed.

"We're going to find him and convince him to take my spot on the Obsidian Throne."

One of his eyebrows curves upward, and I bite my lip. How could one simple eyebrow arch be so damn hot?

"I don't know if that's such a good idea considering all that's happened of late."

Han finally tears away her gaze from the computer screen. She blinks a few times behind her thick lenses as she adjusts to the change in light. "What do you mean? What's happened of late?"

I told Han about the second Task, of course, and how badly it sucked...but I may have left out a few details. Like Zaahir's murder. And Bryce nearly killing me. And Zilah saving me. I gave her the basics, okay? I didn't want to tell her about all of the really horrible stuff because I know she would just worry about me even more than she already does, and I know she's been stressed about school and scholarships and Stanford lately. She doesn't need to add anything to her list of worries right now, especially my problems.

I signal at Lucien to shut up and freeze when Hannah looks back my way. "Nothing's happened," I reassure her. "Luce is just being a Negative Nancy since I lost the last Task. But, hey, I'm not worried! We might be tied now, but there's still one Task left to go."

Hannah's BS radar is notoriously awful, so thankfully, she takes me at my word and goes back to the computer screen. "Let's check out his story," she says as she clicks it.

"Hey, guys!" Max says from the computer. "Just wanted to remind everyone that I'll be at the animal shelter in Greenwood again this weekend. Come by and adopt a dog or a cat. These guys deserve loving homes. Or, if you have the time, stay for a while and help us out. Volunteers are definitely needed."

I bang the top of the desk with my fist. "Well, team. We've found our in."

Khalil laughs. "You're going to go volunteer at a pet shelter and what? Subtly tell Max that he's your long lost relative and you want him to be king of a bunch of monsters?"

"Nope," I reply, looking around at my three companions. "All *four* of us are going to go volunteer at the shelter where I will somehow subtly inform Max of his royal lineage and then ask—and maybe beg—him to step in for me."

"You are the epitome of selflessness, Princess," Khalil drawls from where he continues to lounge on my bed. "Do I really have to participate? I don't like dogs, and they don't like me."

"Yes, and you'll be fine."

"What makes you think Max will want to help you?" Lucien asks from his spot by the closet. He crosses his arms over his chest as I scoop up the last fallen photo. It's actually one of me and Dad. Lucien took it for us. Dad's arm is slung over my shoulder, and we're both making funny faces at the camera. I bite the inside of my cheek. Man, I wish things could go back to the way they were.

"He's a good person. Obviously, he'll want to help me. And..." I struggle to come up with another semi-good reason why this stranger might want to sacrifice everything for me. "I *am* his family. Has to count for something, right?"

"You have to ask your father for permission to travel to San Francisco, especially if you plan on using a portal."

I groan, flopping back onto the couch cushions. "Dad won't care. It's just a short trip."

"It doesn't matter." Lucien crosses his arms over his chest and stares me down. He's not going to budge on this, I can tell. But that doesn't stop me from trying.

"Come on, Lucy," I say with a pout. "It could be our little secret."

"No."

My pout turns into a frown. "You're such an over-protective worry-wart. You'd better lighten up or you'll go prematurely gray."

"You're going to get permission from your father, or you aren't going. That's final."

I might be stubborn, but even I can admit when I've lost. So, the two of us make a quick trip to the Underworld.

For once, Dad isn't in his office. Lucien and I cut through the foyer and up the grand staircase to the second floor. Khalil opted to sit this one out, saying that he wanted to take a nap instead, so I carry his stone in my pocket.

This floor is where Dad's and Zilah's rooms are, and where mine used to be before I moved up top. There's still a bed in there, but I haven't slept in that room since Mom died. Even though Dad had the window and the bloodied carpet replaced, I just couldn't sleep in that bedroom anymore. I would slip out of bed and tiptoe down the hall to Dad's bedroom every night to sleep with him in his massive, four-poster bed. Even though there was close to seven feet of bed for us to sleep in, I always woke up snuggled into his back.

He never kicked me out, though, so I'm guessing he kind of liked it too. I may have lost my mother that night, but my father lost his wife. Although I never saw him cry, I know my dad was broken for a long time after she died. Maybe he still is.

Luce knocks on the dark wood of Dad's suite and goes in first to make sure everything is clear. I don't know what they discussed in their secret meeting the other night, but Lucien's been acting as if he thinks assassins are lurking behind the curtains, waiting for the perfect moment to spring out and kill me dead.

"Come in, come in," Dad says from the sitting room. Dark wood beams cross the ceiling and more ebony wood makes up the wall of shelves across the room. Unlike Dad's study on the first floor, books only take up some of the shelves here. Instead, there are dozens of silver picture frames. Pictures of him and Mom when they were younger. Pictures of the HTF at family dinners. Pictures of Zilah and me when we were kids. I guess I know where I got my love of photography from.

He glances at us over the tops of his reading glasses before going back to the stacks of documents set out before him on the coffee table. His work never seems to end. "What are you two up to?"

I plop down on the tufted leather sofa across from him. "I need to use a portal to San Francisco this weekend."

Dad doesn't bother looking up, and I get the impression that he's only giving me, like, maybe twenty percent of his attention. "And why's that?"

"College day. Hannah and I are going to check out Stanford. Take the tour, maybe do a bit of sightseeing."

At this, he does look at me. A good, long look, actually.

"What?" I ask, squirming. I redirect my gaze to the mantel above the marble fireplace that is situated in the middle of the shelves. Resting there is a sizable painted portrait of our family. Zilah and I couldn't have been more than two. It's the only picture I know of that has all four of us together.

Dad pushes his glasses up to rest in his salt-and-pepper hair and rubs his face as if he's trying to rub away the sleepiness hiding in the fine lines of his wrinkles. He gives me a tired half-smile. "It's nothing. Sometimes I forget you're just a kid."

I want to say, "Exactly! Why do you think I don't want to be queen? Don't you understand that I want to live my life before I dedicate it to keeping the whole world safe from their darkest fears?"

Instead I say, "So, uh, can we?"

"Of course. I'll alert Balthasar so he can escort you to the proper portal. How long will you be there?"

"Just a day," I tell him.

"Are Hannah's parents okay with this?"

"Yes, Dad." For someone who wants me to hold an extreme amount of power, he really does treat me like a child sometimes. "She asked them last night."

He raises his hands with a chuckle. "Just checking, kiddo. Have fun and be safe."

I rise and kiss his scruffy cheek. "Will do. Love you."

"Love you more." Dad flicks his glasses back down and goes back to his papers with a sigh. He stacks them up on the edge of the coffee table, and I go to leave. "Em, one last thing."

"Hmm?"

When I turn back around to see what he wants, I catch him sharing a look with Lucien who stands back by the door. He returns his attention to me. "Make sure Lucien is by your side at all times, okay?"

I nod. "Find anything new about Zaahir or the Task?"

"No, nothing yet. But it's only a matter of time. Bring me back a souvenir, will you?" he asks, and I recognize a dismissal when I hear one.

We exit, and as soon as we reach the ledge where the portal home is, I pin Lucien up against the wall with a righteous pointer finger. "What the hell is going on?"

"I don't know what you're talking about."

"You're an awful liar, Luce. I know you and Dad know something that I don't. Just tell me."

His full lips purse into a line, and he shakes his head. We haven't been this close to each other since the night of the second Task where Lucien decided to tie his shoe at the most inopportune moment. Although I'm still a little piqued at him for that, the temptation to close the distance between us is almost unbearable.

I soften my angry hand and press my palm against his chest, over his heart. "Please tell me?"

His own hands curl into fists. "I can't."

"You mean, you won't." I pull away as anger overtakes the wanting. I spin on my heel to go through the already glowing portal, but Lucien catches my hand and pulls me back.

"I can't, and I won't, Ember. Not because I don't want to, but to keep you safe."

"I'd be a lot safer if you would just tell me what exactly is going on around here."

He squeezes my hand, and for one fleeting moment, I think he will break and reveal the truth. I can see him arguing with himself, but duty comes first. "You're wrong."

"No, *you're* wrong, Luce. And when this—whatever it is—is all over, you'll realize I was right."

19

As it turns out, the other side of the portal to San Francisco just so happens to be in Chinatown. More specifically, a narrow antique shop with newspaper-covered windows and enough dust to make us all sneeze upon arrival.

Lucien converses with a wizened Chinese man who sits behind the counter, and the next thing I know, we are loading up our bags into a taxi and piling in. Hannah and I sit in the middle while the boys sit on the outside. We're so packed into the back seat that the entire length of my body is pressed up against Lucien. If I weren't still fuming about the secrets he refuses to divulge to me, I'd be pretty happy with this arrangement.

Music plays softly in the background as our taxi cab driver escorts us to Stanford. According to the research I did before we took off from Seattle this morning, it will take us about an hour to get there. It's certainly better than a thirteen hour drive, don't get me wrong, but the drive to the university feels like it lasts an eternity since Lucien's bulk is blocking my view out of his window, Khalil passed out as soon as the taxi left the curb, and Hannah has had her face glued to her phone since before we left.

She giggles to herself for what has got to be the sixtieth time today.

"Okay," I say, just loud enough to be heard by us in the backseat. "Who the heck have you been texting all morning, and why are you so giggly?"

It's like she doesn't even hear me.

"Hannah!"

"What? Oh, sorry. Did you say something?"

Like the stealthy ninja that I am, my hand darts out and grabs her phone. "*Who* are you talking to?"

She has the grace to look ashamed. "I'm sorry, Em. It's...uh...no one."

I level a look at her. "Right. No one. Well, I'll just shoot *no one* a text saying how you still sleep with a stuffed rabbit even though you're seventeen."

Her eyes narrow behind her glasses. "You wouldn't."

"I so would. Now, whose number is this?" I scroll through the messages to discover that they go back almost a week. And that Hannah uses entirely too many emojis in her texts.

Her bronze skin reddens. "I'll tell you...but you have to promise not to be mad at me."

I roll my eyes. "Yeah, yeah. Now spill."

She bites her lip. "It's Max."

It takes a whole minute for the words to process in my mind. Hannah has been distracted all week. She barely talked to me at school and hasn't messaged me whatsoever except this morning when she told me she was heading to our house. And it all started after we looked up Max on Instagram.

"What the hell, Han? You've been talking to Max this whole time? Does he know we're coming?"

Han looks everywhere but at me and shrugs. "Maybe?"

"Did you tell him *why* we're coming?" I ask, my voice rising in pitch.

"No, of course not." She pulls her braid over her shoulder and fiddles with the tips of hair. "I'd sound crazy if I told him the truth."

I snort.

"I just told him we're touring Stanford," she continues, "and he offered to come show us around since he's been there a few times."

"Han, this was *not* the plan." I rest my head on the back of the seat and take a deep breath. I had visualized how this meeting will go down in my head a hundred times in the last seven days. I knew exactly how we would approach Max, exactly what I would say, exactly how he would react. And now Han has gone and thrown a wrench in the works.

She grabs my hand. "Em, I'm sorry! Really, I am. I couldn't help it. He's just so cute and so sweet. I didn't even think he would respond to my message, but he did and we just immediately hit it off. We've been texting back and forth constantly since I left your house that night."

I should have seen this one coming. I mean, she was practically salivating over the keyboard when we were spying on him. I peek at Hannah and realize I can't stay mad when she blinks those big, brown eyes at me. "Okay, I'll make a deal with you. If you agree, then I won't be mad at you for completely ruining the plan we all worked so hard on the other day."

"You mean the 'plan' you came up with in five minutes in which you surprise attack Max and then 'wing it' from there?" Lucien chimes in.

"Shut up. No one was asking you." I elbow him in the ribs. If only he knew how many times I played through the scenario in my head.

Hannah purses her lips to keep from smiling and raises her hand. "I do solemnly swear to abide by my terms of the deal, whatever they may be."

"When the time comes for me to tell Max about everything, I want to talk to him alone."

Han gapes at me. "That's it? I promise to agree to any demand you might make, and that's the best you can come up with?"

I shrug. "That's my deal. Take it or leave it."

"I'll take the deal, Howie."

"That's what I thought. Now, let me see those messages. We need to have a talk about appropriate emoji usage."

The breeze off of the San Francisco Bay is cold enough to make me shiver, but at least the scene is stunning. What makes it even better is the fact that there's no one else up here. The December weather must be keeping everyone sane inside where it's warm. Even in my hoodie and jeans, I'm cold. I could stand here and watch the cars coming and going across the Golden Gate Bridge all night long if I didn't think I would freeze to death.

But after the day I've had, I welcome the peace and quiet. If only I could feel my toes.

As if on cue, Lucien appears behind me and drapes his coat over my shoulders. It's a pea coat, of course. Anything else would be below his fashion standards. Either way, it's still warm from his body heat and smells like his detergent.

"Thank you," I say, pulling it tighter around me. I might not be able to hold myself together after I do what I have to do, but perhaps it will be easier if I'm wearing Luce's coat with its silk-lining and too-long sleeves. I bury my nose in the shoulder and inhale, pulling warm air into my frostbitten lungs.

"Where's the djinn?" He joins me by the railing and looks out over the bay as he rests his elbows on the metal bar.

I pat the front pocket of my jeans where Khalil resides in his stone form. "It's a bit too nippy out here for his liking."

"Ah."

He steps closer to me then, his arm brushing against mine. I don't know if he does so because he's cold now without his jacket or for some other reason. The lights of San Francisco twinkle across the bay, and I can't help but wish I was one of those people below on the bridge. A normal person going home to a normal family, oblivious to the terrors of the night.

But you know what they say about wishes.

"I can't do it," I say after a few moments of tense silence.

"I know."

I jerk my head in his direction. "What do you mean, *you know?*"

He blesses me with one of those genuine Lucien smiles I so rarely get to see. "Your father and I both knew you wouldn't be able to do it."

"Gee, thanks for the vote of confidence. Do you realize you have the motivational skills of a potato?"

When we had finally reached the Stanford campus that morning, Max was waiting for us at the base of Hoover Tower just like he said he would be. As we approached, Hannah clung to my sleeve like a cat being threatened with a bath. Lucien and Khalil followed behind us, the latter eating a chili dog as he ambled along. The djinn claimed to have been to the point of collapsing due to starvation when he finally woke up from his nap, so we had the taxi driver stop at a fast food joint so Khalil could quickly find some sustenance.

Anyway, there he was—my only hope, sitting on the ledge of a fountain in the courtyard before the clock tower.

Max had his head bent down as he fiddled with something in his hands, and it wasn't until we reached the steps that led up to the fountain that I realized what he was holding—a single red rose.

I could feel the significance of the moment in my soul. This was it. If Max refused to take my place, I would have to win the Third Task and rule over the Underworld. If I didn't win, Zilah would have me murdered.

I knew my entire life hinged on what would happen next.

He still hadn't seen us at that point. We took the first step up, and I glanced at Hannah. Her eyes were fixed on Max, and there was an expression on her face I've never seen before. I don't think she had taken a breath since we started up the sidewalk to the tower.

My foot was on the second step when Max lifted up his head and spotted us. I watched the scene play out as if it were in slow motion. His eyes immediately found Hannah's, and his face broke out into a breathtaking grin, his dimple showing.

As soon as he smiled, Hannah relaxed. Her grip loosened on my arm. She let go as a radiant smile lit up her face. Some part of me knew then I was letting her go in more ways than just this, and I was powerless to stop it from happening.

The pair had no eyes for anything but each other. The sky could have fallen down around us and I don't think they would have even noticed. I held back as Hannah continued forward, the sinking sensation in my gut making me feel like I was carrying a pound of rocks in my stomach. Max offered her the rose. Han took it and inhaled the scent of the petals as a pretty blush bloomed on her dark skin. The pair eased into the middle of a conversation as seamlessly as if they had known each other all their lives, a conversation I had no part in and never would.

It was then that I knew. A part of me always kind of guessed that I wouldn't be able to ask him to rule in my stead. Like Dad said, I couldn't rip him from his life and live with myself. I just couldn't. And now, seeing Hannah light up like this, I knew without a doubt that I couldn't ask him to help me. I wouldn't take him away from her. She would never forgive me.

So, I let go of the shred of hope that I had been clutching so tight since that night in the library. A gnawing dread of what my future might be took hold deep inside of me as I accepted the bitter truth of the situation. But as Hannah took Max's arm and introduced him to me, the glorious glow of happiness radiating out of her every pore made it almost bearable. Almost.

In the end, I sucked it up. I put on a fake smile when I needed to and said the replies I was expected to say for the rest of the day. First, we toured Stanford with Max as our guide. I still haven't decided if Hannah was even paying attention to the facts Max told us as we walked. I'm pretty sure her mind was elsewhere. When we finished the tour, we all climbed into his Range Rover and explored the city.

Lucien, Khalil, and I were the ultimate third wheel as Max showed us around town. He and Han were too caught up in each other to pay us any mind as we toured the aquarium and the beach. As the sun began to set, we made our way to Battery Spencer. According to Max, this is the best spot in all of San Fran to see the Golden Gate Bridge.

Although...he can't currently confirm that because he and Hannah are currently making out in the parking lot. I didn't really feel like hanging around as they played tonsil hockey, so I trudged up the path to the vantage point. Lucien took flight to scope out the area as soon as we were out of sight of the parking area, and Khalil only made it about fifty yards after that before he decided it was way too much effort and way too cold for him before he shifted back into a rock. I was left alone to enjoy the sunset and shiver in the cold. Until Luce showed up, that is.

"I wish you or Dad would have just told me trying to convince Max was a stupid idea before we came all the way out here for nothing." I sidle a wee bit closer to him in the process. The wind coming off the bay really is frigid. I'd love to give Hannah more time to smooch her new beau, but my teeth are chattering so hard that I'm afraid I might chip a tooth.

Lucien shrugs. "You wouldn't have listened anyway. Plus, today was nice, don't you think?"

His dark eyes reflect the lights from the bridge in the distance as he stares out over the cliff. The wind tousles his curly hair, but he doesn't seem to mind as a small smile pulls at the corners of his mouth.

"I guess it wasn't so bad," I finally manage between spasms of shivering.

Luce chuckles. "Come on. Let's call a cab and go home. It's late and the third Task will be here soon. We must prepare."

I take one last look at the Golden Gate Bridge and all the normal people living their normal lives before turning back to the path. "Don't remind me."

I fumble with Khalil's stone in my pocket for a moment before pulling him out. "Let's go, djinn. Time to break up the love fest and head home."

Blue-green smoke hesitantly trickles out of the rock. I know Khalil must be trying to disobey the command, but ultimately the bond is too powerful. He manifests in front of us swathed in a resplendent white fur coat and matching hat.

Lucien and I hold it together long enough for Khalil to sniff and ask why we're looking at him like that before we burst into laughter.

"Stop laughing at me. It's freezing out here."

"A pimp from the 90's called," I tell him as I wipe the tears out of the corners of my eyes. "He wants his coat back."

"Oh, ha ha."

“Exactly how many polar bears did you murder for this coat?” Lucien adds, sending us both into another fit of laughter.

Khalil aims a rude gesture at us before letting the coat dissolve into mist, revealing the clothes he wore earlier. “Better?”

“Much,” I say. “Now, let’s go home before you decide to build an igloo or something equally ridiculous.”

20

We finally make it back to Seattle a little after midnight. It was a feat to drag Hannah away from Max, but she eventually succumbed to my pleading and pathetic teeth-chattering. Max offered to give us a lift, but we thought it best to call a cab. It would have been a wee bit odd to explain to Max why he was dropping us off at a rinky dink antique shop in Chinatown.

After we went through the portal and arrived back at home, I wanted nothing more than to curl up in bed and pass out, but Khalil was hungry. Again.

"Seatbelt," Lucien tells me as I clamber into the front seat of my car. Khalil and Hannah get in the back.

"What's it going to be? I'm starving," Khalil says from the backseat.

I swivel around. "You just ate an entire party size bag of Cheetos!"

"I have a high metabolism," he informs me as he licks the orange dust off of his fingertips.

"You don't have a metabolism because you aren't human, you buffoon."

"Tell that to my stomach."

"Quit it, both of you," Lucien snaps, all fun and games from earlier gone without a trace. "Ember, you should be focusing on the upcoming Task."

"Luce, chill out. We just got back, and you already reminded me about my impending doom once tonight. I don't need to hear it again."

Lucien pulls into a McDonalds that sits on a quiet street off the busy main road. In the reflection of the door mirror, I spy Hannah staring dreamily out of her window. I look away as I chew my chapped lips.

Why did I have to be the daughter of the Lord of the Underworld? Why couldn't my dad be something normal? Like a dentist. I bet the daughters of dentists never have to battle their siblings for their inheritance.

Hannah doesn't have to deal with this crap. She gets to make out with her crush and not have to worry about her evil sister planning her murder. I cross my arms and pout about the cards life has dealt me.

Lucien rolls down the window just as a burst of static emits from the drive-thru menu. "Welcome to McDonald's. Order when you're ready."

"Hi, uh, yes. Um, I'll take three number ones—Ember, did you want anything?"

I shake my head.

"Hannah? No? Just the three number ones and..." Lucien's eyes dart over to me. "And one extra side of fries, please. Large."

I grin as he pulls the car forward. "Those are going to go straight to your thighs, you know."

"They're worth it."

"I think you've taken one too many handouts from Hannah."

He opens his mouth to retort when a shrill scream cuts through the air. My blood turns to ice. The only time people make a sound like that is when they are in fear for their life.

Silence follows as the four of us freeze.

"What was that?" Hannah asks.

"Whatever it was, it wasn't good," Khalil says.

"Yeah, no kidding, Sherlock." I scoot to the edge of my seat and scan the area.

Lucien pulls his gun from the holster under his arm and clicks off the safety. "Ember, Hannah—stay in the car."

But before he can get out to go investigate, the back door of the McDonalds flies open and an employee stumbles out. She looks over her shoulder, her eyes so wide that I can see the whites all the way around her irises from where we watch in the car. She goes around the side and flees, disappearing from view.

I unclick my seatbelt and slip outside.

"Ember!" Hannah and Lucien call together.

My heartbeat thunders in my chest, pounding out a beat in my ears as I walk in front of the car. Maybe it's just a robbery. Maybe she went to clean the bathroom and found a really disgusting surprise.

Maybe. But knowing my luck? Probably not.

The hair on my arms stands on end and my fingertips tingle like my hands have fallen asleep. That girl wasn't running from anything of this world.

Both Khalil and Lucien join me in front of the car. Thankfully Hannah has enough sense to stay in the vehicle. Luce has left it running, which is probably a good idea in case we need to make a quick getaway.

Over my left shoulder, Lucien looks ready for battle. There's not a hint of fear in his dark eyes.

On my other side, Khalil wears a much different expression. If I had to give it a name, I'd have to say it was curiosity.

I don't even want to know how my face looks. Probably like I'm about to wet my pants.

Inside, there's a bang and a clatter as some kind of metal utensil falls to the floor. I cock my head and strain my ears. There's a sound like something being dragged across the floor, and it's getting louder with each second.

"Vampire?" I guess.

"No," Lucien says with a jerk of his head. "Werewolf, maybe."

Khalil chimes in too. "My money is on a zombie."

Turns out that we are all wrong.

The Underworlder exits the McDonalds, and I almost laugh until I see what it's carrying in its jaws. I have to swallow the bile that rises in my throat as the creature adjusts its grip on the dismembered human arm dangling from its mouth.

"Is that what I think it is?"

Lucien frowns more than he's already frowning, if that's even possible. "I think so."

The chupacabra halts in the beams from the headlights and turns our way, dropping his midnight snack on the pavement.

A chupacabra is an Underworlder native to Central America. They sometimes pop up as far north as Texas, but they mostly stick to rural desert areas of Mexico. Most, like the one in front of us, are the size of a very large dog or a wolf. One might even mistake it for a really ugly, hairless canine suffering from malnutrition. This one was no different. His gray, mottled skin stretches tight over his ribs and pronounced spinal ridge. The chupacabra's large notched ears lie flat against his skull and his knobby tail is tucked between his back legs, signaling to us that the creature is more fearful than anything else.

"Well, he's really far from home." I take a step forward and wave my arms over my head. "Hey, you! Scram! Get out of here!"

"Ember, I don't think that's a good idea," Lucien warns.

"Dude, relax. Chupacabras are super skittish. You just have to scare them off, kind of like a bear."

His lips press into a line. "While that may be true, it's not natural for one to enter a public place such as this. And it's definitely not normal for one to attack a human."

I creep closer to the Underworlder. "It must be really hungry, that's all. Look at the poor thing. He's trembling."

"You are aware that the 'poor thing' you speak of just tore a man's arm off, right?" Khalil asks from behind me.

"See if he's dead, would you?"

Khalil disappears into a cloud of smoke. He's back in a jiff.

"The human is alive, but someone should call 911 pretty soon."

With a pathetic whine, the beast takes a tentative step toward me. His big, black eyes look almost apologetic for what it did inside. And with a face as pitiful as that, I'm almost inclined to forgive him. The chupacabra takes another step, and another, until he's only about a yard away.

I stick out my hand to pet his hairless head. I can't help it. I have a soft spot in my heart for dogs, and a chupacabra is about as close as you can get to a dog in the Underworld—besides werewolves, but those don't count.

The moment I make contact, things take a turn for the worse. The creature flinches away from me as if I slapped him across the muzzle. He yelps and shakes his head, almost like he has water in his ears. When he stills, there is no longer any remorse in his eyes.

It takes me only a moment to know something's very wrong. My heart drops into my stomach. My breath comes fast and shallow as images of my mother the night she died start flashing through my thoughts.

The beast shakes his head once again. A rivulet of black liquid drips from the creature's nose and trickles onto the asphalt. A deep growl, guttural and terrifying, emerges from his throat. My fight or flight response kicks into high gear, with flight winning over fight. I take another step back while the chupacabra's lips pull back to reveal a mouth of pointed yellow teeth. Saliva the color of ink pools and spills over his mandible.

"Easy, boy. Just take it easy."

"Ember, back up. Now," my Guardian commands.

"Working on it," I spit back at him.

But I don't quite work on it fast enough. The chupacabra lunges straight at me, his mouth missing my left arm by mere inches as I leap to the right.

I hit the ground hard and roll. By the time I get to my feet, the beast has spun around. He now stands between me and Lucien and Khalil. Between me and safety.

There isn't much time to think because the beast charges once again, another growl tearing from his throat. And this time, he doesn't miss.

His front paws hit me square in the chest, knocking me flat into my back. Luckily my arms are slightly longer than the chupacabra's neck. I hold him away from me as he snaps his teeth just inches from my face. His breath reeks of blood and rotten flesh. I'd probably vomit if I wasn't so concerned with my face being eaten.

Blobs of the black goo drip from the chupacabra's mouth and land on my cheeks, my forehead, and even my lips. I clamp my mouth shut even though I wanted nothing more than to scream. Distantly, I hear Hannah yelling and pounding on the window of the car. Thank God she stayed inside when my idiot self decided it was a great idea to exit the vehicle.

Although it feels like I'm struggling against the chupacabra for hours, it must be only seconds before Lucien fires a round into the beast's flank.

The Underworlder staggers, which gives me just enough time to shove the beast off me and crawl away.

In my peripheral, Khalil evaporates into a cloud of aqua-colored smoke. One second he's gone, and the next he's here, scooping me in his arms. There's an odd sensation of the floor dropping out from under me as he turns us to mist and transports us to safety. When we materialize, we are safely behind Lucien and his gun.

The bullet only seems to stun the creature, though, because he quickly gathers his wits and turns on his new prey: Lucien.

The chupacabra snarls and launches itself forward.

"Lucien!" I scream, my fingers reaching for him to pull him to safety. But he's too far away from my grasp, and I can't escape Khalil's arms that are locked around me, holding me back.

Another gunshot rips through the night, and this time, the Underworlder falls to the ground, only a foot away from Lucien.

My Guardian fires two more shots into the beast's shuddering body as it flails and thrashes about in the McDonalds drive-thru. Just to be sure, I guess.

His black eyes land on me, and he stills. A change comes over him. Once again, the beast seems to silently apologize. Huge, ragged breaths shake his body as his life comes to an end. And even though he just tried to kill me, I feel a profound sadness that I can't explain.

With one last wretched whine, the beast stills for good as it dies.

Khalil finally releases me, and I approach Lucien. My shaking fingers reach out to touch Luce's arm. "Are you okay?"

He runs a hand through his hair, smoothing it back into place. "I'm fine. Are *you* okay?"

My body is still trembling. Whether it's from adrenaline, the cold, or residual fear, I don't know. All I know is that I'd give just about anything in the world to throw my arms around Lucien's neck and have him hold me as I ugly cry.

Instead, I nod. "Peachy."

The djinn nudges the corpse with the toe of his sneaker. "Well, that was unexpected."

"Indeed," Luce agrees. He holsters his gun and steps away from me. The few feet between us feels like a thousand miles.

"Help me put it in the trunk. We'll call the HTF on the way home. They need to see this."

"I'm not touching that thing," I tell him. "It almost bit my face off."

"Perhaps you should learn from this and start listening to me when I tell you to stay put. Here, grab its back legs."

I make a face and roll up my sleeves. "I blame you, djinn."

"Me?" Khalil asks, bewildered.

"Yes, you. We wouldn't be stuffing a dead chupacabra into the trunk of my car if you didn't *have* to eat something every thirty minutes."

"I see. *This* is the thanks I get for saving your life."

I sigh. "Thanks for saving my life, I guess. Even though it was your fault my life was in danger in the first place."

Khalil makes an exasperated sound as he throws his hands up. He gets back into the car while muttering something in a foreign language under his breath.

Meanwhile, I remind myself to work out more as I struggle to lift the chupacabra. You'd think such a skinny thing wouldn't weigh that much. Together, Lucien and I alternate between carrying and dragging the corpse to the Camry. He pops open the trunk, and we stuff it inside. I grunt as I shove the gangly limbs further into the trunk. I'm quite displeased to see black goo leaking onto the carpet. I'm even more displeased to find that my clothes are also smeared with the stuff. Actually, displeased isn't a strong enough word to describe my feelings.

"I don't think there's enough spray and wash in the world to get this out," I mumble to myself.

"We can get you more clothes."

I stick out my bottom lip in a pout. "But these are my favorite pair of jeans."

Lucien slams the trunk shut. There's a crunch as the lid clamps shut over the chupacabra's tail. I guess I hadn't pushed it in quite far enough.

"Oops. Sorry," I say as I lift and place the now-broken tail inside. "My bad."

Luce sighs.

"He kind of deserved that, though."

"Oh, Ember."

Hannah assaults me with questions as soon as we get back in the car. "Em! Oh, my God. Are you okay? What was that thing? Did it *kill* that person? Why did it attack you? Do we need to call the police? What's that stuff all over you?"

At that, I glance down at my soiled outfit and wrinkle my nose as I smell myself for the first time. I wipe my cheek on my sleeve, nearly gagging at the goo smeared on my shirt. Forget trying to salvage this outfit. The only place these jeans are going is in the trash.

Khalil and I fill her in on what just happened as I dab at the mess on my hoodie with a couple of napkins Luce finds in the console. Han's dark complexion pales when I explain that we will deliver the chupacabra corpse to the Underworld and that the HTF will deal with the one-armed McDonald's employee up here. At her protests, I assure her that he'll be handsomely compensated for his loss tonight. She doesn't look quite convinced, but she stays silent. Lucien puts the Camry in drive and navigates out of the drive-thru lane.

"Wait! We're still getting food, right?" Khalil asks from the backseat.

None of us answer him.

"Right, guys?"

21

You know how in movies the morgue is always this dimly lit place, usually with a flickering light in the corner and a score of quiet, yet creepy instrumental music softly playing in the background?

Well, it's nothing like that.

After we packed the Chupacabra in the trunk, Lucien called the HTF and told them what happened. When we got home, we found Nalani waiting for us. She told us that she would keep an eye on Hannah while Lucien, Khalil, and I went to the Underworld with the chupacabra corpse.

The morgue in the Pen is about the brightest room I've ever set foot in, even though it's in the basement of the Pen, and the Pen is miles below the Surface. Normally, Medusa—yes, *that* Medusa—is blaring 90's grunge music through her desktop computer, but she quickly shut it off when Dad stalked in with a scowl sour enough to curdle milk. He was *not* happy when we told him about the chupacabra incident.

He was so concerned that he didn't even gloat when I told him I decided not to ask Max to go in my stead. Dad simply nodded with a distracted look pinching the edges of his features and continued down the hallway toward the morgue.

Armenius met us just outside the morgue's doors as well. He looks much more comfortable than when I saw him last in his too-tight dress clothes. Tonight, he's wearing a white muscle shirt and black jeans that match the dark leather shoulder holster digging into his gargantuan trapezius muscles. The grips of two ebony handguns peek out at me from under his crossed arms. I'm guessing Dad wants another opinion on the beastie that tried to eat me.

No one beats around the bush once we go inside. Armenius and Lucien drag the chupacabra to the examination table in the middle of the room. As they hoist up the body, I can hear the fluorescent lights buzzing overhead. Once the chupacabra is on the table, everyone backs up to stand in a circle, waiting for Medusa to make the first move.

"Where did you say you found this?" the gorgon lisps, adjusting her sunglasses higher up on the bridge of her nose. I guess one of the reasons Medusa keeps it so bright in here is because she constantly has to wear sunglasses. Dad told her when he hired her that she has to wear them at all times, even when she's alone.

While it's technically safe to look her in the eye as long as she's wearing some sort of eye protection, I still avoid her gaze. Just in case.

"A McDonald's parking lot. Just a few miles from the house," Lucien answers.

Medusa's thin, drawn-on eyebrows rise up into her snakes. We all turn to the Underworlder on the table before us. Armenius grumbles something in German and pokes one of the chupacabra's haunches.

Under these football stadium-worthy lights, I can see every scar and wrinkle and hair on the chupacabra's skin—and trust me, there's a lot. I can also see the puckered bullet wounds in its flank, which means I also have quite the view when Medusa takes the scalpel from one of her snake's mouths and slices the chupacabra open. I can't look away as she makes an incision from the sternum to groin and all of the beast's bloated, swollen organs spill out onto the table.

The tangle of snakes that makes up her hair hiss as the blackened organs settle and the stench hits us like a baseball bat to the face. Her snakes slither and tangle together to form a mask across her nose and mouth. I tuck my chin in my shirt and cover my nose as well, but it hardly does anything to curtail the smell. Even the normally stoic Lucien makes a face.

Dad grimaces. "It's as I thought."

Armenius borrows the scalpel from Medusa and prods what looks to be the small intestine. "Corruption?"

"In its earliest stages." Dad takes the scalpel from Armenius and proceeds to slice what might have been the heart. More black goop oozes out onto the table. I'm glad we decided not to grab more food on the way here.

"What's Corruption?" I ask under my shirt-mask.

Armenius accepts the pair of latex gloves Medusa offers him and slides them onto his meaty hands. "This creature was infected by *übel*—by the essence of evil."

I aim a look of disbelief in his direction. "Armie, come on. You and I both know that evil is not an entity. That was one of the first things Dad ever taught me."

The big man doesn't appear to be listening. He pokes what may have been a kidney, causing it to burst. I yelp and jump back from the table. There's no way I'm getting more of that nastiness on me tonight.

"How peculiar," Armenius murmurs. "The Corruption seems to spread from the inside out. This beastie had it bad. Real bad. But it's exactly like the werewolf."

His voice trails off at the end of the sentence, but I still catch the gist of it. "Hold on a minute—what werewolf?"

Dad and Lucien exchange a quick, nervous look. I narrow my eyes. They're hiding something from me.

"Are you guys talking about Bryce?

Dad shifts from one foot to the other as he lifts his shoulders in a half shrug. "Medusa performed an autopsy on

Bryce after the second Task under my orders. His organs were like this, but not nearly as severe."

I shake my head. Why didn't Lucien tell me this? Could that be the information he's been withholding from me since the second Task? "What's causing this to happen?"

Again, my Guardian and my dad exchange a look.

"Stop hiding stuff from me!" I burst out, voice loud enough in the metal quarters of the morgue to make Medusa's snakes jump in fright. "I'm not a child. I can and *need* to hear what it is that's making the Underworlders go berserk. Especially if I win the Tasks and become the next queen."

"If you win," Armenius adds. I slowly rotate my head to give him a death glare. He shrugs. "Sorry, Princess. The way I see it, you're tied right now with your sister. Anyone could win the throne at this point."

I take a deep breath and tell myself that it would not be wise to attack a seven-foot-tall man with biceps the size of my head. Even so, the idea is tempting.

After regaining my composure, I turn back to Dad and Luce. "Tell me what's going on."

Dad levels a look at me. His hazel eyes, so like my own, have never kept secrets from me. So, why is he now? What's going on that's so bad that he can't even tell me what it is?

"Win the third Task, and we will tell you everything," Dad says after a moment. "If you don't, then it won't be your problem to worry about anymore."

I open my mouth to argue, but he cuts me off. "I need to look further into this. But if this is truly Corruption, it's highly contagious."

He reaches out and lets his hand hover over the body. Without so much as an incantation, his hand erupts in pale blue flame and jumps from his fingers to the chupacabra's corpse. The blue fire spreads over the scarred skin, burning it to ashes without a single wisp of smoke.

Dad looks at each of us in turn as he pulls his arm away from the dancing flames. "Burn any clothes that have come in contact with this beast, and we all must see Katja as soon as possible for a cleansing."

I suppress a groan. I would almost rather have a chupacabra gnaw off my arm than have to go see *her.* I grit my teeth but nod in affirmation. I'll do it, but I certainly won't like it.

Katja is a witch, one of the most powerful in the world. She's also so gorgeous it's stupid. Helen of Troy would have been jealous of Katja. Aphrodite wishes she was Katja. Even the most stunning of Hollywood actresses can't hold a flame to Katja.

Imagine the hottest person you've ever seen. Okay, now multiply their hot factor by eleven. *That's* Katja.

She is the *only* person I have ever seen Lucien flirt with. And on that fact alone, I despise her. Even though she's never been anything but kind and helpful toward me, I still can't stand her. I will purposely walk into a room I have no intention on going into if I see her coming toward me.

Lucien and I say our goodbyes to the others and leave the morgue. I fling open the door so hard that it slams into the wall behind it with a resounding clang. Khalil wasn't invited to our meeting, so he had to remain out here while Lucien and I went inside. He straightens from where he was slumping against the wall, a pout still pulling at his lower lip. Khalil gestures toward the door I just dramatically exited through. "What did that poor door ever do to you?"

I ignore him, fiddling with the bracelet around my wrist. I'm in no mood for Khalil's jokes. Especially not now that we have to go see my least favorite person in the Underworld. It's been a long day, and it's not even close to being over yet. Hot pinpricks sting behind my eyes, and I grit my teeth to prevent any tears from forming.

"Okay then. Find out anything interesting in your little meeting?"

"Nope. Let's go. We have to make a pit stop before we head home, and it's already late."

He falls into step beside me, elbowing me in the shoulder. "What's got your knickers in a twist? Where are we stopping?"

I take a deep breath and mutter the answer with a couple of additional obscenities.

"What was that?"

"I *said* we have to go by Katja's office."

His cat eyes go wide. "Katja the witch? Gods, I haven't seen her in centuries. A man never forgets the first time he sees the lovely Katja. To quote Willy Shakespeare, 'Compare her face with some that I shall show, And I will make thee think thy swan a crow.'"

I clench my fists and look over my shoulder only to see Lucien's lips quirk up just the slightest at Khalil's statement. I clench my fists and pick up the pace. As I turn the corner, I blink up into the light and swipe away the trail of wetness sliding down my cheek so that neither of those two idiots can see my tears.

Katja's office is on the first floor of Dad's chateau in the west wing. A tiny bell jingles as I enter.

I don't bother holding the door for Khalil and Lucien.

"Be right with you!" Katja calls from the back, her voice like birdsong. I take a deep breath and try to let go of my irrational anger. What did it matter if Lucien flirted with Katja? It's not like I have a chance with him anyway.

I inhale again. This place smells like a Bath and Body Works. Honestly, it's impossible to stay mad in a place that smells as good as this.

The boys enter behind me, and I go to look at the shelves lining the far wall and all the oddities stored there to put space between us. Jars and bottles of all sizes, shapes, and colors fill the shelves. Each container has a label with neat, feminine writing detailing its contents. A fat yellow bottle holds some basil in oil while a clear jar stores cinnamon sticks. Beside that one is a bottle with a green tint that contains frog eyes. A purple container on the shelf above that has dried bat wings tucked neatly inside. The witch has quite a variety.

Katja is one of the few Underworlders that has permission to go freely from the Underworld to the Surface. She actually has a shop in New York City where she sells love potions and tells fortunes. From what I've heard, she does pretty well. However, she's strictly regulated by Dad and the HTF. She has to be good enough to keep up profits, but not good enough to draw too much attention to herself and her shop. I'm actually surprised she's down here right now since she spends the majority of her time on the Surface.

"I'm so sorry to make you wait!" the witch says as she enters the room carrying a stack of boxes. Of course, Lucien and Khalil rush forward to help her with her cumbersome load. They practically trip over themselves trying to help her before the other can. I roll my eyes as they each take a parcel and set them down on the front desk. "Goddess, those bottles are heavy!"

Katja is taller than me—but really, who isn't? She brushes her golden hair over her shoulder as she thanks the boys for their help. She's wearing black top with a sheer overlay that tastefully shows off all of her perfect curves underneath, patterned leggings that hug her in all the right places, and some booties with fringe that somehow even make her ankles look attractive.

She finally looks in my direction. "Oh! Princess Ember, what a surprise! You haven't visited the shop in years. My, look how you've grown!"

I stammer, and she cuts me off before I can form a proper response to that statement.

"You are stunning, just like your mother. Did you know that?"

"I—"

"Oh, but what's this all over your clothes?"

Before I can stop her, she reaches out and touches a fingertip to one of the many splatters of chupacabra gunk that landed on me during our little scuffle in the drive-thru.

She withdraws her hand as if I slapped her. Her blue eyes flash black for the quickest moment as a shadow chases over her features. "Corruption."

Great, even the witch knows about Corruption. Am I the only person in the Underworld that doesn't know about this stuff? "Yes, that's why we're here. We need to be cleansed, all three of us."

"Goddess, help us," she whispers in reply. The witch turns and grabs an assortment of bottles from the shelves behind her, hastily shoving them into the crook of her arm.

"All of you, through here." She indicates the doorway with the beaded curtain. "Quickly now. You should have come here directly. I only hope it's not too late."

"Well, that's comforting," I murmur as we're directed through the doorway and down a set of stone steps. I have never been this far into Katja's quarters. Dad let her set up shop in the west wing because you never know when you might need a witch's talents. I had only been into her front room a handful of times in my life, the last time being five or six years ago when I wanted her to make me a potion to make my boobs bigger—she gave me a potion, but it turned out just to be apple cider and sprite, neither of which are known to increase bust size.

The lower room is much dimmer than the front. There aren't windows here, and I suspect that we are actually under the Underworld. The entire room looks like it had been carved out of black, shiny rock. The only light in the room comes from the thousands of candles that flicker along the walls in small jutting shelves and shallow grottos.

In the center of the room is a large pool of steaming, milky-white water. As we hover awkwardly near the wall adjacent to the doorway, Katja pours one liquid after another into the water while chanting a spell under her breath. A cool wind glides through the cave, causing some of the candles to gutter out.

The witch finally finishes preparing the pool and rushes over to us. In one hand she holds a bushel of sage and in the other an incense stick. Using the glowing red end of the incense, she lights the sage and wafts the smoke over all three of us. First me, then Lucien, then Khalil.

She stops in front of the djinn. "You appear to be clean. I will make a potion that you'll have to drink each morning for the next week as a precaution, but you should be fine." She turns to us. "As for you two...you'll need a full cleansing ceremony."

Lucien and I glance at each other, then back at Katja. "Meaning?"

"You'll need to strip off your outer clothes and bathe in the pool as I perform the cleansing spell over you both. Your clothes will be burned, and your soul will be washed clean."

I bark out a short, surprised laugh. "You're insane if you think I'm taking my clothes off in front of these two."

Katja whips her head to stare at me, eyes wide. "This is no time for jokes, Princess. If we don't begin the cleansing process in the next few minutes...I fear we may be too late, especially for you, my dear. You seem to have the worst of it."

"The worst of what?"

Katja chews on her perfectly plump bottom lip. She grabs my hand and thrusts up my sleeve. She says a few words in another language, and I watch in wonder as her hands begin to glow gold against my skin. Her glow seems to spread through my hand and my arm, illuminating me from the inside. The blood drains from my face.

Her golden glow illuminates something dark inside of me. My fingertips appear black as if in the furthest stages of frostbite. They're so black that Katja's glow can't penetrate it. Her grip on my wrist tightens. In the few seconds we stand there together in silence, the blackness visibly grows. I can *feel* it as it crawls inside of me.

"Wh-what is that?"

Her eyes, as blue and pure as the open ocean, hold my stare. "Corruption, or evil in its purest form, and it's spreading fast. Please, do as I say without any more delay."

I swallow and try to shake off the feeling of that blackness moving up my arm. I look up into Lucien's face to see that familiar worried expression furrowing his brows. He nods, and that gives me just enough courage to do what I have to do.

"Khalil, face the wall and do not turn around until I tell you that you can."

"Aw, but Princess—"

"Now!"

He sighs but obeys my command. "Okay, okay."

I turn back to Luce. "Could you, uh, turn around for a second, please?"

He nods and does I ask. As soon as his back is turned, I start ripping off my clothes. I kick off my shoes, pull my hoodie over my head, and toss them in a pile. After I shed my pants, I slip into the cloudy water of the pool. Fortunately, the witch lets me keep my bra and underwear on. Unfortunately, I wasn't planning on getting splattered with evil goop and did not color coordinate.

The water is delightfully warm and opaque and only goes up to my armpits when I stand flat on my feet. I can't even see my hands as I hold them just below the surface. Relief settles over me and my shoulders relax. This won't be so bad then. It's not like Lucien hasn't ever seen me in a bathing suit before. "Okay, I'm in."

Lucien faces the pool, and I feel his dark eyes dance across my bare shoulders. I take a shaky breath and give him the same privacy he bestowed me. The urge to peek behind me as he undresses is almost unbearable. I'm just about to look when I hear him slip into the pool.

The first thing I notice when I face him is the large geometric design tattooed over his heart. I have never seen Lucien shirtless, not in my whole life...except for the time Khalil impersonated him in my dreams, but that doesn't count. To say I'm a bit shocked is an understatement, to say the least.

"You have a *tattoo*?"

He shifts uncomfortably. "It's a long story."

"You should tell me some time."

He looks at me for a long moment, or at least it feels long to me. I could lose myself in those bottomless eyes. "I will," he finally responds. "But let's focus on the cleansing ceremony for right now."

Katja reappears at the pool's edge, this time with a leather-bound book in her hands. She descends down a set of stone steps I hadn't noticed before until she is submerged up to her waist. The milky water laps at her hourglass figure as she gestures us forward. "Come close."

Lucien and I wade through the water. The stone floor is warm beneath my toes, and slick. Luce catches me under my arm when I slip so that my head doesn't sink beneath the pool's surface.

And instead of letting go, his hand slides down my arm to catch my fingers between his. My breath catches in my throat. This...this can't be happening. Can it? I squeeze his hand before he can let go, trapping him in my grip, but he doesn't try to pull away.

Together, we stand before Katja. "You two stand in the sacred *Dwr o' Gwir,* the Waters of Truth. It will cleanse everything from your body that is not of your soul, including the evil that seeks to corrupt you. But in doing so, it will lay you bare. The pool is not called the Waters of Truth for nothing."

"What does that mean, exactly?" I ask with a shiver. Another cool breeze blows through the room and tickles my bare shoulders.

"You will see." The witch says nothing more on the subject and begins the spell. The words that spill from her delicate mouth sound like Welsh or maybe something older, but that's all I know. I have no idea what she's saying, but the wind picks up, so it must be working.

Katja grabs a bowl from the pool's edge, and she fills it with the water from the pool. As her voice rises in volume, she indicates for Lucien to step forward. He does, but he doesn't let go of my hand. Katja pours the water over him. It runs from the crown of his head, plastering his curls to his face to drip off the tip of his nose and the line of his jaw. She repeats the words and pours the water over him two more times.

Then it's my turn.

I can still feel the corruption inside of me, like a spider crawling across the inside of my skin. She fills up the bowl, and I realize with a start that it's actually not a bowl. It's a skull.

She tips the skull over, and I shut my eyes as the water washes over me. Instantly, I feel better. Lighter. Katja scoops up the water and does it again.

I let the water run over my face, over my eyes and my mouth. As I look upward to receive the last cleanse, Lucien squeezes my hand once more. The water rushes over me, and a heaviness lifts from my shoulders that I hadn't noticed until it vanished. When I open my eyes and look at Lucien, I smile. There's an expression on his face that I've never seen before, but I can't quite name it. Then, before I can truly savor his hand in mine, he pulls back. I angle away from him and cross my arms over my chest. I don't know why he even held my hand in the first place, but I almost wish he didn't because now my hand feels more empty than it ever has in my life.

Katja turns the page in her spellbook and says the final lines of the cleansing spell, her voice once again growing louder and faster. The water we stand in begins to glow with that same golden glow Katja used when showing me the Corruption. It brightens until both Lucien and I have to shield our eyes.

On the last word, Katja plunges the skull into the water one last time, and the light winks out with an abruptness that leaves me blind in the sudden dimness. This time when she lifts the bowl out, it's filled with black liquid to the rim.

Very carefully, Katja pours the blackness into a fat, round bottle waiting at the edge. I think all of us release a breath when she puts the stopper in.

Katja blows a wisp of fair hair out of her face. "Thank the Goddess that's through with. You two have no idea how lucky you are. I have towels somewhere in the front office. I'll be right back, and we'll get you guys out of the pool."

As soon as the beautiful witch is out of sight, I sigh. "I wish I was that beautiful. Maybe then you would love me."

It's only in the silence afterwards that I realize I just said my thoughts out loud.

22

I clap my hands over my mouth and face Lucien with wide eyes. "I don't know why I just said that."

Khalil laughs from his post by the wall. "It's the pool, Princess. *Waters of Truth*, remember?"

"Could you give us a moment, Khalil?" I call to him, my voice breaking with nerves and embarrassment. To make matters worse, my face is aflame, and I know I'm about as red as a fire truck. I let my still dripping hair fall forward to hide my utter mortification. I've imagined the moment in which I reveal my love for Lucien at least once a day since that day on the couch several years ago, and let me tell you, never once did I imagine we'd both be nearly naked in a magical pool that forces you to tell the truth.

"I seriously never get to have any fun," the djinn pouts, but then he perks up. "Can I go flirt with Katja?"

"Yeah, whatever." My eyes fixate on Lucien's pale, handsome face. His hair is starting to curl up again as it dries, but his dark locks still hang in his even darker eyes. My insides fill with butterflies desperate to escape.

Khalil doesn't waste a second. Without so much as a backward glance, he vanishes through the door to sweet talk the witch. I finger the bracelet circling my wrist. It's become a nervous habit, something for my fingers to do when I don't know what to say.

With Khalil gone, I turn my thoughts to more important matters. I sink in the water so only my head is visible. On one hand, I want to go beneath the surface of the milky water forever. On the other...this could be my chance to find out the truth. This is the perfect opportunity to finally learn how Lucien feels about me.

All the lingering stares and subtle touches over the last few weeks, just coincidence or something more? Had I imagined everything? Did he feel anything at all for me? I swallow hard around the nervous knot in my throat. All I have to do is open my mouth and ask. It's as easy and as hard as that.

"Ember," Lucien says, breaking my train of thought. "You are beautiful. Please don't ever think that you're not."

I inhale sharply and squeeze my hands into fists. It's now or never.

Deep breath.

Heart racing.

"Lucien, do you have feelings for me?"

The moments between my question and his answer feel like a lifetime.

Finally, his jaw clenches, and he squeezes his eyes shut. Lucien doesn't want to answer, I can see it in the rigid lines of his tense muscles, but finally he does. "Yes."

"What kind of feelings?" I whisper, terrified and exhilarated about what his answer might be.

"The kind that I'm not supposed to have. The kind that makes me think about you all hours of the day and night. The kind that I've struggled with keeping in check, especially since the Tasks started."

My legs feel weak, but somehow I take a step closer to him. "Why do you have to keep your feelings in check?"

He shakes his head as if he doesn't want to tell me, but he opens his mouth and says, "I can't love you, Ember."

My heart soars with elation and breaks into a thousand pieces at exactly the same time. This is it—the answer I've wished on every star for. And yet, it's entwined with the answer that I've dreaded to know since the beginning.

"Even though I shouldn't," he adds, running a hand through his damp curls. "Even though you frustrate me to no end and you seem bent on throwing yourself into danger at every turn, even though you're reckless and childish...I've fallen for you. For your smile. Your kindness. Your silliness. Your courage. Regardless of these feelings, Ember, I cannot allow myself to love you."

Another step forward.

"*Why* can't you, Lucien? If that's how you feel, then why can't you?"

"I'm your Guardian."

"So?"

"It's not proper."

"Forget *proper.*" I close the distance between us. With a shaking hand, I reach up and run my thumb over the sharp plane of his cheekbone. He closes his eyes and shudders beneath my touch.

"Your father has forbidden it."

"I think he'll come around," I tell him, my voice low.

Lucien exhales a shaky breath. "Ember...there's something else you should know."

I rise up on my toes, my hands snaking around his neck and tangling in the hair at the back of his head. "What's that?"

Our mouths are once more only a breath away from one another. His lips part as he exhales, and I lean forward to close the distance one last time. Finally. The moment I've been waiting for so long for.

And then, before my lips can brush against his, Lucien pushes me away.

I stumble backwards, slipping on the slick floor of the pool, and dip into the water with a splash. I manage to keep my head out of the milky white depths, but the moment is gone. The space between us is cold and infinite as the world crashes down around me in a silent crescendo of heartache. I glance down at my chest expecting to see a knife there. The pain is so real that it's hard to breathe.

"I *can't*, Ember. I'm sorry."

"I thought you wanted me?" I ask in a tiny voice. I wrap my arms around myself, suddenly hyper aware of my near-nakedness.

"I do! I do. Ember, please listen to me."

I feel myself shutting down. It took everything in my to put myself out there, and he pushed me away. Despite what he said under the influence of the pool, his actions speak volumes more.

"Ember, please."

I turn away, but his hand catches my arm. Lucien pulls me back to him, taking my hands in his. Tears, hot and shameful, spill over and down my cheeks. He wipes them away and lifts my chin so that I'll look him in the eye. He takes my right hand and presses it to the center of his chest. My palm splays over the intricate tattoo inked over his heart.

"Do you feel that?"

And I do. His heart races under my touch, beating almost as quickly as mine.

"I'm so sorry. I want to forget everything and kiss you until I can't breathe. I want to be with you more than I've ever wanted anything in the thousands of years that I've existed. But we can't. Your father won't allow us to be together...not until you are queen."

And there it is—the traitor known as hope. It stirs in my rapidly beating heart. "Queen?"

He nods, a small smile pulling at his lips. "Yes. Once you've won the last Task and are crowned, we can be together."

"Why do we have to wait? Because I'll do it, Luce. I'll beat Zilah and rule if you're there by my side. I swear I will. I'll do it for us."

He takes a deep breath. Then, ever so slowly, he brings my hands up and kisses my knuckles, one kiss for each hand. "It's not just me," Lucien begins. "Your father forbade any Underworlder to be romantically involved with you."

My brow furrows. "Because of what happened with my mom?"

Lucien shakes his head. "No. He declared this long before your mother passed."

"Then why?"

"The night you were born, a prophecy was made by the Oracle."

"The *who?*" I pride myself on knowing practically every type of Underworlder that has been in the Pen at one time or another, and I've never heard of this Oracle.

"You've never met her. Well...you weren't old enough when she came for you to remember her. She arrived shortly after you and your sister were born. Your mother had already gone through the Turning.

"The Oracle somehow got past all of the guards your father posted and found her way into the room where your mother was recovering and where you two and your father were resting. It was then that she gave the prophecy."

A shiver crawls across my shoulder blades.

"The Oracle spoke and told your parents this: *Two daughters were born to our monarch this night. She who wears the mark of the moon will be queen and bring forth ruin to everything. She will give her heart to one she will rule, and Fate will be cruel. The world will bleed, and the Dark will thus be freed. Two halves must then become whole after paying a terrible toll.* And then she vanished. I don't think she's been seen since."

My hand goes to my stomach, just to the right of my belly button. "The mark of the moon..."

Luce nods. "Your birthmark."

I couldn't see it through the murky water of the pool, but I have looked at the crescent-shaped birthmark on my stomach every day for as long as I could remember. I always thought it was odd, but I never knew it came with a dark prophecy. Lucky me.

"The prophecy is about me, then."

"Yes, and the Oracle is never wrong."

I shake my head. "I don't understand. What does it mean?"

Lucien rubs his thumbs across my fingers. "I wish I knew. Your father took it to mean that you would fall in love with an Underworlder which would somehow cause something terrible to happen. Part of my job is to ensure that you never fall in love with an Underworlder."

He looks down at our hands and lets go with a deep breath. "Like I said, the Oracle is never wrong."

"To hell with the prophecy." I reach out to grab his face. "The Task is in less than a week. What could a few days hurt?"

With the gentlest touch, Lucien takes my hands once more and removes them from his face. "It's only a few more days," he echoes, but in a tone much different than mine. "I'd rather not tempt fate and wait until you're crowned. We've lasted this long. What's a few more hours?"

Knowing that he feels the same way I do? A few days will stretch into eternity. I honestly don't know if I can make it that long. We were so very *close*, and yet still so far. I let out a deep sigh. "I don't want to, but if it'll make you feel better, then fine."

Luce rests his head against mine. "I've been dying to tell you all of this for so long."

"Then why didn't you?"

"I was afraid you wouldn't care for me in return."

I laugh. "Why in the world would you ever think that?"

"Because of what I am."

A tingle goes down my spine, but before I can ask him what exactly that might be, Khalil bursts through the door with a fluffy robe draped over each arm.

"Hope you guys worked everything out," the djinn says, "because I'm starving, and I can hear a plate of pancakes calling my name."

23

Lucien and I agree to keep our plan to ourselves. There were only a few more days until the last Task—how hard could it be right?

After swinging by the house to grab a change of clothes for the two of us, our little trio sets off to get some pancakes. I tried to rouse Hannah to come with us, but she didn't so much as stir when I shook her shoulder. Fortunately, Nalani told us she didn't mind staying a bit longer if we brought her back a breakfast croissant.

By the time we reach the diner, it's that strange time between night and morning when the two blend together, and only the insomniacs and those on the graveyard shift are awake. Lucien slides into the booth on the right, and Khalil drops into the booth on the other side. After a second of hesitation, I sit down next to Luce. I don't fail to notice the pleased expression that crosses his features, and when his hand grazes against mine as we both reach for the menu, I swear a current of electricity courses through my entire body, from my toes to the tips of my hair.

Our waitress, a lady named Ruby with tired eyes but a genuine smile, takes our orders. After looking at the menu, I decide breakfast doesn't sound all that appealing and order a hamburger topped with a fried egg. Luce gets a black coffee. Khalil gets practically everything available on the menu.

"If you are going to eat enough food to fuel a small army, you're going to have to start pitching in," I tell him, rubbing my fingers together.

"Please," he replies with a dismissive wave. "Your father is the Lord of the Underworld, and you're going to be the queen in, like, a week. I know you're loaded, Princess. So, don't give me any of that nonsense about money."

He's not wrong. Shortly after Dad took the throne, he and the HTF did a bust on a dragon that had a penchant for sacrificial maidens. The dragon was escorted down to the Pen, and Dad confiscated the dragon's massive hoard of shiny objects. Dad told me when I was little that the dragon's treasure filled up cavern after cavern in the cave he lived in—piles of gold and gems and other precious stones rose to the ceiling.

So, yeah, we are "loaded" as Khalil put it, but that doesn't mean I want to pay for the djinn's ridiculous snack habits.

Lucien and I share a look. He lifts his brow in an elegant arch, and I bite my lip. Partly to keep from smiling too much and partly because he looks so damn hot when he raises his eyebrows.

Five more days. Five more days.

Under the table, Luce moves his leg just a few inches to the left and rests the length of his thigh against mine. I hardly dare to breathe. How is it possible that the mere touch of his leg against mine is almost my undoing? If I could resist him mostly naked and wet in a mystical pool in a cave, I can resist him in a dimly lit diner with 50's decor. Right?

"Oh, for the love of—" Khalil bangs his fists on the tabletop, making us jump and causing a couple of sleepy truckers to glare in our direction. "I thought you two got everything out of your systems back at the pool!"

I blush and Lucien suddenly becomes very interested in the cars sitting in the parking lot. I duck my head and rip the corner off my napkin. "Um...not quite."

"Well, did you guys do it?"

If I thought the blush was fierce before, I was wrong. "Khalil!" I hiss after peeking over my shoulder to see if anyone heard him. They didn't. We are practically the only ones in the diner except for the truckers snoring into their coffee cups, Ruby, and the cook in the back. I hide the side of my face in my cupped left hand, shielding the diner occupants from the lasers shooting out of my eyes. "That's personal, Khalil. And frankly, none of your damn business."

He shakes his head and tsks as if we have disappointed him. "You didn't. Did you even kiss?"

"You're pushing it, djinn," Lucien grumbles.

"You two are the only people in the world that could be almost naked and still not manage to get it on."

Lucien's fists clench under the table until I reach out and grab one of his hands. The tension leaves his frame as our fingers intertwine.

I take a deep breath and level with the djinn. "We talked. Figured some stuff out. That's all you need to know."

"Pathetic." Khalil crinkles his nose and points at us. "Both of you."

I laugh and look over at Lucien to see him trying and failing to suppress a smile.

"You two have got to stop with the blushing and the smiling and the not-so-sneaky touching, or I'm going to barf."

"Put a cork in it, Khalil."

Thankfully, Ruby arrives with our food. The djinn digs in with a pitcher of syrup in one hand and his fork in the other before Ruby can even let go of his plate. The waitress snatches her hand back as if Khalil might accidentally take a bite out of her in his haste to devour his food. Honestly, she's probably right to be concerned.

"All I'm saying," Khalil says around two cheekfuls of pancakes smothered in blueberry syrup, "is that you guys don't have to tiptoe around me. If you want to make out or whatever, just let me know, and I'll make myself sparse."

With the djinn's blessing, Lucien and I decide to stop denying ourselves every little pleasure. The next day, we sit together on the couch like we have so many times before and watch a romantic comedy. Except this time, Luce drapes his arm over my shoulder and I snuggle into the soft spot between his shoulder and his chest. We fit together like a key into a lock, and it feels so right to be next to him. I have no idea how I managed to go for so long without this. And now that I do know what it's like, I'm never going back.

The next day we hold hands on the way to school, not even trying to hide it from a rather grumpy Khalil who sits in the back seat. I don't know if I have ever been more impatient for the school day to end. As soon as the last bell of the day rings, I grab my bag and rush outside. Lucien is there as he always is, leaning up against the car with his arms crossed over his broad chest. When he sees me coming, his ever present scowl melts into a smile that I know he saves for me. I don't care who sees or what people think as I run to Luce and launch myself into his arms. He grunts as I throw my arms around his neck, clearly not expecting my surprise attack. But he recovers quickly and wraps his arms around me.

"I missed you," he whispers, his lips tickling the sensitive curve of my ear. I shiver as pleasant chills ripple down my arms. We spend the rest of the evening snuggling in my room as I finish up some trig homework. Lucien reads a book that appears to be completely in Russian, his free hand tracing distracting circles on my knee. Needless to say…I do not finish my homework.

The next day, a large crow swoops into the courtyard and lands on our table to join us for lunch. Thankfully, it's chilly and a bit drizzly, so Hannah, Khalil, and I are some of the only ones eating lunch outside. Lucien hops across the picnic table to me and drops a shiny object in the empty slot on my tray.

It's an antique gold ring with a stunning opal stone set in the center. I pick it up with a gasp. The opal catches the light and sparkles a dozen different colors.

Lucien squawks and ruffles his feathers.

"For me?"

He bobs his head as if to say, "Who else?"

I tickle the soft spot on his feathered throat with a wry smile. "And just where did you find this?"

Luce shuffles from foot to foot and shakes his head.

"Keep your secrets then, silly bird. It really is beautiful, though."

"I think I'm going to be sick," Khalil mutters.

Hannah, on the other hand, looks like she's about to applaud. Yesterday, I spilled the beans to her about what happened after the chupacabra incident and revealed the feelings I had been harboring for Lucien all these years.

Hannah told me that she knew I liked him, but she never knew the extent of it. After I told her everything, she hugged me tight and thanked me for bringing her and Max together. I returned her embrace, all animosity about the San Francisco trip forgotten.

I slip the ring on my right ring finger. "It fits!"

Lucien burbles in delight and flutters onto my shoulder. He nibbles at a lock of my hair and butts his head against my cheek before taking off into the sky once more.

"That is so freaking precious!" Hannah whispered-screams.

"I think you mean nausea-inducing," Khalil corrects.

"Don't rain on my parade," I tell him while still marveling at my new ring.

The djinn shakes his head, and stabs at the limp pizza stacked on his tray. I nudge him with my shoulder. "You know, none of this would have happened if not for you. So...thanks."

He scratches his ear and glances at the dark spot in the sky flying in circles over our heads. "Don't mention it, Princess."

I give him a hug before turning back to Han so we can plan our first official double date.

Ember...

It takes me a moment to realize where I am. Just a second ago, I was snuggled up beside Lucien in my bed as he read, and now I'm here in a void of nothingness.

I've missed you.

"It has been a while," I agree. "What have you been up to?"

I'm sorry about the werewolf, the Darkness says, completely ignoring the question poised toward him. *I know you aren't fond of them.*

"Heard about that little incident, did you? And that's a polite way to put it."

You acted bravely.

"Are you kidding me? I froze and nearly got myself eaten. That's not exactly what I would call brave."

You might not call it bravery, but you didn't pull the trigger. Not because you were afraid, but because you were unafraid. You tried to save him.

"Yeah, well, a whole lot of good that did. He still died."

Not because of you.

I blink a few times, thinking back to that day. "Actually, it kind of was. He kept saying that he had to save me, that he saw the end of everything."

The words of a crazed man, nothing more.

"Maybe, but still..."

The next Task is in two days. Are you ready to become queen?

"You sound confident in my ability to beat Zilah." I laugh, the sound more bitter than humorous. "What if I don't win?"

Something in the dark touches my right hand, glides between my fingers with little more than a whisper of shadows. *You have so much more to fight for now, yes?*

I narrow my eyes and search in the nothingness for a hint of the Darkness. "How do you know about that?"

I know many things, Ember.

"Oh, yeah? Like what?"

I know of the prophecy that keeps you from whom you love most.

My eyes widen. "You do know things. Do you think it will come true?"

The Oracle is never wrong.

My stomach drops, but resolve hardens in my bones. "I don't see how me kissing Lucien can bring about destruction or ruin or whatever it is that she said. It's just a kiss. I've had feelings for him for years."

Our time is running short. I know something else that you must hear.

I sigh. "What's that?"

You will be betrayed tomorrow by someone you love.

The floor rips from below my feet, and I feel like I'm falling even though I was never standing to begin with. "How do you know that? By who? How?"

Goodbye, Ember. Just remember that I will be here should you ever need me.

"By who?" I demand again. "Tell me who will betray me!"

We are out of time. I'm sorry...

I jerk awake and bolt up in bed, breathing in lungfuls of air as if I had been submerged to the point of drowning.

"Ember?"

The sound of his voice brings me back. Despite the worried tone he used, my panic immediately begins to ebb.

"Bad dream," I explain with a sheepish smile. "I'm okay."

The furrow between his brows remains, and I reach out to run a finger over it. "I'm okay."

Lucien begins to relax. "You were talking in your sleep."

Great. Just great.

"Oh? Did I say anything interesting?" Feigning nonchalance has never been one of my strong points.

He shakes his head. "I couldn't catch anything really—you were mumbling more than talking, but it sounded like you were having a conversation with someone. What were you dreaming about?"

I should tell him the truth. I should tell him about these recurring dreams and the Darkness and his warning. I should...but I don't. "I was dreaming about...Mrs. Saldana."

"Your Spanish teacher?"

"Yeah," I say with a nervous laugh. "I was late to an oral exam and she was yelling at me in Spanish. Scary stuff."

He eyes me skeptically for a moment before cracking a smile. "Well, if you're really nervous about it, you could always ask Khalil to tutor you. Your teacher has emailed me several times with praise for Khalil's progress, especially since this is his third language."

I hit him with my pillow.

"Ow! What was that for?"

I hit him again. "For being an ass."

He grins and sets his book on the nightstand. I pull back my pillow to give him another good whack, but he pulls it from my grasp. I laugh and go for the pillow behind him, but he pushes me onto my back, pinning me against the mattress with his hands and his body. The laughter and the smiles melt away into something more primal. I run my hands up his muscled forearms and over the crisp fabric of his dress shirt to his equally powerful biceps. Lucien lowers his head to my neck. Each warm breath against the delicate skin there makes me tremble with want and anticipation.

My hands find his face, and I explore each smooth plane there with light fingers. His brow, furrowed once more, his sharp cheekbones, his strong nose...his soft, full lips.

I want him more than ever, yet the echo of the prophecy sounds in my thoughts, pulling me back. So, before I can do anything rash, I place a hand on his chest and push him away.

"I'm sorry," Lucien says, voice low and husky. He rolls back to his side of the bed. "I didn't mean to—"

"No." I turn on my side, finding his hand and wrapping it in mine. "Don't be sorry. Just think, in two more days we won't have to stop."

His dark eyes shine bright in the low light of the night. "Two days seems like such a long time."

I chuckle. "It is and it isn't."

Lucien nods and settles back down with a sigh I feel in my soul. He picks his book back up and goes to the page he left off on.

"Will you read to me?" I ask as I grab my pillow and fluff it up under my head.

"You won't know what is happening."

I yawn. "I told you—that doesn't matter. I just like the sound of your voice."

Luce smooths the hair away from my face. "Of course."

And he begins to read.

24

Maybe it's because of my little visit from the Darkness, or maybe it's because I stayed up far too late listening to Lucien read, or maybe it's the warning about my imminent betrayal...however you slice it, I am *not* in a good mood the next day.

Even Khalil seems affected by my grouchiness. He's even more pissy than me as we get up, get ready, and go to school. He barely says anything all day long, which is quite unlike him, but it's totally fine by me. I don't feel like listening to his whiny, smart aleck remarks anyway.

Hannah tries to be supportive and helpful as she offers me encouragement—bless her—but I'm really in the mood to listen to her positive, uplifting quotes from famous leaders either.

It's only when the school day ends and I see Lucien once again that my dour mood begins to lift. I crush him in a hug as a greeting.

"You're going to break my ribs," he gasps.

"Sorry," I mumble back after releasing him. "It's been a day."

"You're worried about the final Task?"

"Worried isn't a strong enough word for how I feel right now." Not only do I have to beat my sister tomorrow to save my life and the lives of practically everyone on the Surface, but now I can't lose so that I can be queen and be with Lucien. He says it's the only way we can be together, and if that's the truth then there's no way in hell I'm going to let my sister win.

"What if I told you I had something planned that might take your mind off of things for a while?"

He smiles down at me, dark eyes crinkled in barely suppressed delight. I could think of several things that could take my mind off of the Task for a while, but it's probably not what Luce is thinking of. "I'm listening."

"I can't tell you what it is. That would ruin the surprise, wouldn't it?"

Khalil finally gets to the car, wrenches open the door and throws himself and his book bag into the backseat.

I roll my eyes. "If it can get me away from this curmudgeon for a few hours, count me in."

"Curmudgeon, huh? I read to you for a few nights and you start talking like a scholar. Maybe the next book I read should be in Spanish."

I swat at him, but he's too quick. "You're in an awfully good mood."

He smiles and traps me in his embrace. My arms lock behind him, the hard lines of the gun holstered at his sides under his waistcoat digging into my skin. Lucien—always prepared. "Why wouldn't I be? Tomorrow you will win the last Task and be crowned queen, which means we can finally be together. What could I possibly be upset about?"

I start ticking things off on my fingers. "Well, I could lose, first of all, which is a really depressing thought. Although, if the so-called Oracle is never wrong, I'm going to win and then something awful is going to happen. There's a chance I could *die* during the Task. Equally depressing, if you ask me. I might—"

"Ember." Luce takes me by the shoulders. "I want you to forget about tomorrow. Forget about the Task and Zilah and being queen for tonight and just be with me."

I'd follow Lucien to the moon if he asked me to. "Okay, but where are we going?"

He grins and my knees go weak. "You'll see."

After changing outfits a handful of times, I finally settle on a long-sleeved, burgundy dress with a scoop neck and a hem that hits a couple of inches above my knees. It's definitely not something I would usually wear, but I want to look nice for Lucien tonight since he planned something special—just for me. That thought alone reignites the nervous excitement that has filled every inch of my soul since this afternoon.

The dress isn't a fancy piece of clothing by any means. In fact, I've had it in the back of my closet for ages after buying it on a whim a year ago. It still has the tags on it. But after exhausting all the other options in my closet, I put it on and leave my dark hair down instead of putting it in a ponytail or a braid like I typically do. I coat my lips in a shimmery gloss and even apply a little eyeshadow and blush. I glance in the mirror for a good minute. I look like me, but different. Older, maybe. With a deep breath, I decide to own it and go to meet my Guardian.

The way his eyes rove over me as I walk toward him makes a not unpleasant heat course through my core and bloom in my cheeks. I pluck at the hem of my dress. "Sorry I took so long. I couldn't decide what to wear."

He takes my hand and squeezes my fingers. "You look beautiful. Where's the djinn?"

I pat the tiny purse hanging on my shoulder. "He was in his stone when I got out of the shower. I'll let him out when we get back. I don't know what's been eating him lately, but he was in an awful mood today. Maybe a little time away will get him out of his funk."

With my free hand, I run a finger over the elegant embroidery of Lucien's dress shirt, all thoughts of Khalil and his strange behavior vanishing into the air. Lucien looks dashing as always, but this is a vest I've never seen before. My heart swells to think that he dressed even nicer than normal for our little adventure.

"Do I get to find out where we're going now?"

His lips quirk up. "Not quite yet. Here, put this on."

I laugh as I take the silk cloth from his hands. "A blindfold, really?"

"Just trust me. Here, I'll help you tie it."

My pulse jumps as he steps behind me and covers my eyes. When his fingers are done tying the knot, they slide down the line of my neck and the curve of my shoulders, leaving a trail of goosebumps in their wake.

"Take my hand and hold tight," he whispers in my ear.

"Okay."

He leads me down the hall into the kitchen. The glow of light beneath the edge of the blindfold tells me that he has the portal open. I know when we pass through as the smell of sulfur assaults my nose. Lucien guides me off the ledge and down the steps. It's only when we reach the bottom that I lose my bearings.

After walking for about five minutes, we reach another portal and step through.

"We're here."

I smile a bit nervously. "And where is here, exactly?"

Lucien takes off the blindfold, and I discover that *here* is actually a narrow alley between two tall buildings. Strings of lights crisscross between the railings of the balcony, coating the space in a warm glow.

I glance at the dumpster just to the right of where we stand. "Where are we, Luce? Not that I don't *love* back alleys and garbage receptacles, but I'm kind of hoping there's more."

He laughs, and the sound is sweeter than any music my ears have ever heard. His face practically radiates with happiness. I don't think I've ever seen him smile a more genuine smile. I never thought we'd be here—wherever here is—together. Just standing here next to one another, hand-in-hand, the music of his joy fading into the night, is hard to believe. I reach out and touch his face, half sure that he will vanish and all of this will prove to be a dream.

His hand covers mine as he leans into my palm. He doesn't vanish. His skin is warm and soft, with the barest hint of stubble beneath the sensitive skin of my fingers. This isn't a dream.

"There is more," he assures me, leading me toward the opening at the end of the alley. "Come, and I'll show you."

I squeeze his hand and follow him out of the alley. A gasp bursts from my lips when we reach the end and I finally figure out our destination.

Instead of a road and cars, before us is a thin channel of blue-green water that glitters like melted gemstones. The lights from the lanterns hanging over the doors of the buildings lining the canal cast golden sparkles across the gently rippling water, almost as if it's full of fallen stars. Somewhere, someone is playing an accordion. The music bounces off the walls and echoes against the water. However, the city is quieter than I expected, as if everyone is tucked into bed and already sleeping. And if we are where I think we are, that may very well be true.

"Are we in Venice?" I ask breathlessly, my free hand grabbing his sleeve.

His thumb pushes the opal ring he gave me back and forth on my finger as he watches me take in our surroundings. "We are."

Venice has been on my bucket list for years. Dad allowed me a trip to Rome once when I was fifteen. He actually took a couple of days off of work and went with me. It was just me and him for two glorious days. I fell in love with Italy and its rich history. Every Christmas, Dad gets me a calendar full of images of Italy with the promise that someday we'd go back. And now I'm here, in the Floating City with the person I love most in the universe.

"What are you thinking?" Lucien asks, his voice low and deep. The same golden light reflected on the surface of the water shimmers in the infinite darkness of his gaze.

I swallow and push away the intense, burning need to kiss him. "I'm thinking that I really wish I had my camera right now."

Luce lets out a breath and gives me a sheepish grin. "I knew I was forgetting something. Next time, we'll make sure we bring it."

A man in a striped shirt calls out from down the canal. He waves and rows up to greet us in Italian. Lucien responds and steps into the gondola to shake his hand.

My eyebrows rise. "You speak Italian?"

Lucien offers his hand to help me into the small boat. "Italian, French, Latin, and several other languages. When you're as old as me, you have to do something to occupy your time."

"Well, you are just full of surprises tonight, aren't you?"

He grins and sits with me on the bench. The gondolier takes my free hand and gives my knuckles a chaste kiss before introducing himself to me as Alessandro and calling me *bella ragazza.*

"That means 'beautiful girl' in case you were wondering," Luce says into my ear, his warm breath tickling my neck.

"That's sweet. How much did you pay him to say that?"

My Guardian rolls his eyes but catches my fingers in his again.

Alessandro sings softly as he navigates the canals of Venice. I take in everything with wide eyes—the vibrant colors of the stucco buildings, the balconies draped in crawling vines like something out of a Shakespearian play, the dark storefronts with wide windows giving us a brief glimpse at the wares slumbering inside.

When I turn to Lucien to point out a pair of giant sculpted hands reaching out of the water to brace their fingertips against the facade of a nearby building, I find that his eyes have been watching me the entire trip, a small smile curving his lips.

"Thank you. For all of this, I mean. I've been so nervous and excited that I haven't even had time to think about tomorrow."

He places his hand on my lower back and pulls me close. "That's exactly what I hoped would happen. Are you hungry?"

"Starving. Please tell me there is some fettuccine al burro in my future."

"Of course. We can't come to Italy and not have your favorite Italian dish."

A few minutes later, Alessandro steers us to a tiny restaurant called *Il Palagio* that's nestled between a dark and quiet leather shop and secondhand bookstore. *Il Palagio* is not dark and quiet, though. The warm lights from within flood through the arched windows into the night, washing the canal with a romantic glow fit for a dream.

Lucien once again assists me as we exit the gondola and enter the restaurant. A rich scent of garlic settles over us as we cross under the red and white outdoor awning and step inside. We are the only customers, which isn't surprising considering the time, but the quiet is peaceful and somehow makes the scene more intimate. I wonder what strings Lucien had to pull to make this happen.

We eat a delicious dinner of four courses. The first entree is topped with freshly grated parmesan cheese and dripping in sauce so delicious that I want to lick the bottom of the bowl. When we finish, Luce speaks with the restaurant owner who smiles knowingly and disappears into the back. When he returns, he carries a violin and a bow with him.

"May I?" Lucien rises and offers me his hand.

I stare at him for a moment, just trying to let everything about tonight sink in.

Tomorrow, I will face my sister and hopefully be crowned Queen of Monsters and Beasties. Part of me knows I should be more concerned about what that title means and the responsibilities it holds instead of fixating on the fact that after tomorrow, I will no longer have to hold myself back from what my heart most desires.

But that is tomorrow.

Tonight is all about us.

I take his hand and follow him to the empty area of the restaurant where a large fountain bubbles merrily. Lucien's large hand envelopes mine as his other hand goes to my waist. My free hand rests on the muscled curve of his shoulder as I step close and press my body into his.

We sway back and forth—more so enjoying the closeness of our bodies rather than actually dancing—as the owner makes his violin sing in the corner. I rest my head against Lucien's chest and delight in the steady thunder of his heartbeat.

How did all of this happen? If you had told me just weeks ago that I would be in the City of Masks dancing with Lucien in an empty restaurant in the middle of the night—I would have laughed in your face. But it's not a joke. It's real. It's actually happening. Tears prick at my eyes, making me sniff.

Luce glances down and takes a step back, alarmed. "Ember, what's wrong?"

"Calm down, Lucy. I'm fine."

His concern drops a few notches. "Then why are you crying?"

"Because," I say, reaching up to grab his face. "I am so damn happy right now that my heart could explode."

I stare into his dark eyes, and I know that this is the perfect moment to kiss him. Before I know what I'm doing or he can pull away, I rise on my toes and close the distance between us. My eyes flutter shut as my lips touch his, so soft and open in surprise.

He freezes at first, but after only a heartbeat, he relaxes against me as his lips press firmly to mine. His fingers wipe away my tears before his arms wind around my waist to pull me closer. My hands find his curls and run through them, ruining his neat and styled look with wild abandon. I melt into his frame and realize that I would never be able to have enough of this—enough of his hungry lips pressed against mine or his arms locked around me or his breath filling my lungs. My heart gallops victoriously in my chest, begging for more and more and more.

When we finally break apart, I let out a shaky breath as we go back to swaying along to the soft melody of the violin. Luce rests his head against mine with a sigh. "The Oracle never lies."

"It was just a kiss, Luce. I've felt this way for ages now."

He shakes his head, a gentle sadness shadowing his features. "As simple as it is, a kiss can hold power. Magic, even. There's a reason why all fairy tales include a kiss."

"I'm sorry," I whisper, feeling slightly guilty. "I just couldn't wait for a moment longer. You have no idea how long I've been dying to do that."

He lets out a breath and kisses me again. Once, twice, three times. "Don't be sorry, Ember. Never be sorry for that. I was foolish to think we could trick Fate."

My fingers brush back one of his curls. "I could be wrong, but I don't hear any screams of terror indicating the end of life as we know it. The sky isn't falling. Everything is the same as it was two minutes ago. I wouldn't put too much stock into what some mysterious woman said almost eighteen years ago."

Luce catches my hand and kisses the center of my palm. "You're right. But we should probably keep what happened between you and me for now. At least until tomorrow is over and done with."

"Oh, definitely," I agree. "But it's going to be difficult not to kiss you more now that I know what it's like."

The fingers of his other hand glide up and down my back, and I know he feels the same. Whatever walls we built between us came tumbling down as soon as his lips met mine. There is no going back to before.

After several more lovely melodies from the restaurant owner, Lucien stops swaying but doesn't let me go. "We should get back. You have a big day tomorrow after all."

"We can't stay here forever?"

"If only we could."

"If only."

We leave the restaurant after thanking the owner for a delicious dinner and his wonderful music and clamber back into Alessandro's gondola. We recline back on the cushions and watch the night sky over us as Alessandro steers us back to the alley where the portal awaits. I snuggle into the crook between Lucien's jaw and his shoulder. We don't talk much on the trip back. Instead, we choose to punctuate the comfortable silence with short, gentle kisses that promise so much more in the future. I relish the feeling of Lucien's fingers tracing lazy circles along the curve of my waist, and find an almost overwhelming sadness weighing on my shoulders now that the night is almost over.

Lucien pays Alessandro his fee plus a hefty tip and shakes his hand once again. I call out my thanks to the gondolier as he pushes away from us. Alessandro tips his beret to me and then floats away, singing to himself all the way out of sight.

Luce takes my hand and we amble toward the portal, neither of us in a rush to get back to real life.

"Tonight has been..." Lucien begins and trails off as he searches for the right word.

"Amazing? Wonderful? Magical?"

He laughs and places his hands on my waist to lift me up as he spins in a tight circle. I squeal in delight and surprise until he sets me back down. This time, it's him who kisses me.

This kiss is different from the first one. More urgent, almost as if time is running out. And in a way, I suppose it is. How will we ever be able to pretend that nothing happened between us when every beat of my heart begs me for more of Lucien? I respond to his kiss with equal fervor, afraid that once we get home everything that happened between us tonight will vanish as if it never happened at all.

When he pulls back, it's with a deep breath. "Ember."

"Luce?"

"I just want you to know before we go back that I never thought I'd find myself in a situation like this. I never thought about or even *wanted* to find love, not for all the thousands of years that I have lived. But then you happened. To be honest, I didn't feel anything toward you except exasperation for the longest time."

I snort. "Gee, thanks."

"But that all changed," he continues, ignoring my sarcasm, "about a year ago. When you gave me the socks. Did you know that I had never been given a gift before?"

I shake my head, my heart clenching painfully in my chest. "Never?"

"Never," he repeats. "I think that was the first moment I actually felt something. All these centuries, I've just been existing. Floating from one place to another without any idea of my purpose in this life. And then you gave me purpose. And once you gave me that gift, I realized that there is more to living than just being alive. I think my heart began to thaw at that moment, and with each day, you helped melt it a little bit more. Every smile you gave me, every laugh, every overly dramatic sigh. You made me realize that I am capable of love."

My breath catches in my throat. His words make me feel weightless, as if I'll float away if not for his arms around me, anchoring me to the earth. All this time, he felt this way and I never knew. I smile and put my hand on his cheek. "What are you trying to say, Luce?"

"I love you, Ember. Prophecy be damned."

"I love y—"

A sound like the crack of lightning cuts me off, splitting the night into two parts: the before and the after.

25

Lucien's smile fades as he looks down in confusion. I follow his gaze to a circle of red blooming like a rose on his shirt, just over his heart and the tattoo that's inked there.

"Lucien?" My voice sounds far away, as if I'm yelling down a tunnel. With shaking fingers, I touch the growing stain on his shirt. My fingers come away sticky with warm blood. Overhead, several lights turn on as panicked voices begin to filter through the air.

Lucien's legs buckle, and his hands grip my upper arms in an effort to stay standing. But he's too heavy and I'm too weak. I help ease him to the ground as I struggle to piece together what has happened. It's only then that I see the two bodies lurking in the shadows that veil the end of the alley. They must have followed us here from the canal.

Lucien's hand goes to the back of his waistband, for the gun holstered there, but his hands are shaking and he can't roll over enough to pull the gun free. He coughs and blood splatters my face. I blink in surprise and try to wipe away the wetness on my cheeks, but Lucien grabs my hand. "Ember—run. Go."

"What's happening?" None of this makes any sense. One minute, we're kissing and spinning, obliviously in love. And the next—

The prophecy.

The thought settles in my gut like a leaden anchor sinking to the bottom of the ocean. Could it really be the Oracle's prophecy coming true?

The steadily growing pool of blood puddling beneath Lucien's body soaks into the hem of my dress. "No, no, *no.* It's just a stupid prophecy. I can fix this."

I pull out of his grasp, wad up the end of my dress, and apply pressure to the wound in his chest. He groans, eyelids flickering in pain as I press the fabric down harder.

Lucien takes a shuddering breath. "Leave me. Go find your father."

"I'm *not* leaving you," I grit out between my clenched teeth. "This isn't happening. It *can't* be happening."

"Ember," he whispers, his voice barely audible even though I kneel right next to him. A single tear leaks from the corner of his eye. "I'm sorry."

"Stop. You're *fine.* You're going to be fine."

"I'm afraid he's anything but fine, dear sister."

My head whips up to find Zilah staring down at us with a wicked smile on her painted lips. It takes me several seconds to find my voice. "What have you done?"

She feigns shock. "Me? Why, nothing. Your little djinn, on the other hand... Well, that is a completely different matter."

Her words don't make any sense. Zilah must see the confusion on my face because she steps aside and motions at the other person still standing at the opening of the alley. Khalil reluctantly steps out of the shadows into the glow of the string lights glowing above us. In his hand is a familiar revolver—the same one from the second Task. The djinn refuses to look at me, choosing instead to keep his head turned to the side as a scowl claws at his features.

"Khalil?" My voice breaks in disbelief. "What is she talking about?"

None of this is possible. It must be some horrible nightmare my sick, twisted mind has thought up. It's not possible. Not tonight. Not now.

I face Lucien once again, alarmed to find more blood trickling between his lips, the same lips I kissed just minutes ago. I wipe them away with the pad of my thumb. "Stay with me, Luce. We'll get you back to Dad, and he'll fix you up, okay? You'll be as good as new, I promise." My voice rises as his dark eyes drift off.

"Like I said," Zilah interrupts, "I seriously doubt that. There's no way he'll make it back to the Underworld in time. The bullet Khalil used was specially made—one fourth iron, one fourth wood, one fourth frozen holy water, and one fourth silver. Whatever your precious Lucien is, that bullet is bound to kill him one way or another. Especially since Khalil seems to have truly remarkable aim."

My mind spins in dizzying circles. I'm still applying pressure to his chest to staunch the blood, but it has soaked the fabric through and flows through the cracks in my fingers. Lucien's blood seeps in between the fastenings on the ring he gave me just days ago. The opal glints scarlet in the night.

Fierce tears burn my eyes. I blink them back as a white-hot anger burns through me, filling me with a rage like nothing I've ever felt before. Khalil's betrayal has set my heart on fire, and now the inferno threatens to consume me. I turn to my betrayer. My voice is quiet and dangerous, as brittle as the edges of my broken heart. "How could you? I thought you were my friend."

Zilah giggles. Everything is a game to her. Somewhere in the distance, sirens wail. She answers for Khalil. "It's really all so simple if you think about it, sister. I paid the guards to tell me what the first Task would be. They were responsible for releasing the Underworlders that night, so of course they knew what was going to happen. So, I thought to myself, why not use this opportunity for personal gain?"

Zi stepped closer, careful to keep her heels out of the blood cooling on the asphalt. "I broke into the Pen and found Zaahir first. I promised that fat idiot that I would release him too if he gave me the binding jewelry for Khalil. He gave me a necklace to put on Khalil and a fake bracelet to give to you. Then I bound the djinn to me before I released him. Khalil was *never* bound to you. I commanded him to obey all of your commands, and none of you were ever the wiser—not you, not Father, no one."

"No," I say, shaking my head after glancing at the necklace Khalil always wore. I always thought that Zilah might have played a part in Khalil's release, but I never knew for certain. "Khalil, tell me she's lying. What about the vision I had when I bound you to me?"

The djinn's head droops, shame practically radiating off him in waves. "It was a hallucination. She ordered me to give you one as soon as you put the bracelet on."

My twin blocks Khalil from my sight as she lifts the thin gold chain circling her neck. At the end of it is a round aqua stone, no bigger than a pearl. "My original plan was to just have him wreak a little bit of havoc in your life—maybe kill your mortal best friend or something equally nasty to keep you preoccupied during the Tasks—but it was his idea to sabotage the second and third Tasks. Khalil told me that he would befriend you, learn your secrets, and report back to me if I swore to release him once I'm queen. He's been spying on you for months, feeding me everything I needed to know. And he was happy to do it."

A sob tears through me, ripping at my throat. "No! You're lying. Khalil wouldn't do that. I know he wouldn't."

"Khalil informed me of your plans to talk to Zaahir, so I got rid of him before he could reveal my secrets. It wasn't my neatest work, but I still managed to take care of things without anyone becoming suspicious. Then your little djinn told me about your fear of werewolves, so I made sure you had to pass judgment on one at the second Task."

"But you saved me!" I protest. "If all this is true, why save me? You could have had the throne right then."

Zilah sneers down at me, her normally beautiful face ruined with hatred. "I told you, Ember. I will *win* the Tasks. Father will bequeath the Obsidian Throne to *me.* I am the rightful queen, and I will *not* have you die before you see that day. I wish to look you in the eye as I kill you. I will drink your pathetic human body dry, and then I will take my seat on the throne. There can be no other way."

"But why kill Lucien? Why make me suffer if you just plan on killing me?"

"Because you're the reason the only person who ever loved me is dead!"

I suck in a breath. "I didn't kill Mom, Zi! I had nothing to do with it."

"You were such a sniveling child—always crying and whining. If you had just gone to sleep like you were supposed to, she never would have been in your room. She would have been near Dad and safe. But you pouted and pleaded until she agreed to come sit with you, and that's when the werewolf found her."

Zilah crosses her arms over her stomach, her shoulders curving inward as if it physically hurt her to explain. "Mom was the only person who ever showed me love and affection. And because you took her away from me, I will *never* forgive you. I will spend every waking minute of my life searching for ways to destroy you. Perhaps now you feel a fraction of the pain I felt when Mom died."

"Zilah—"

"But wait, there's more. You haven't even heard the best part yet." Zilah's lips lift in a smile so cold that I can feel it in my bones. Her eyes flash black, shining in the dim light of the alley like black holes. "When Khalil told me that you were in love with Lucien, I thought he was kidding. But I confirmed it myself that day outside of Father's study. You should have seen your face when I kissed him. Priceless." My sister stoops down, putting her face close to mine. "We planned all of this together—the bullet, the gun, *everything.*"

She can't be telling the truth. I remember the stone, tucked safely away in my purse. My hand goes to it, staining the velvet with Lucien's blood as I frantically look for the one thing that would prove everything she just told me as false.

Zilah laughs as she straightens. "The stone you slipped into your purse this evening was a fake, Ember. Khalil has been by my side the entire time."

Lucien tries to say something, but he can't quite seem to form the words.

I've heard enough. Zilah is wasting precious seconds. I need to get Lucien to my dad or a hospital before it really is too late. I get to my feet and start to pull him toward the portal, but he's so heavy that I only make it a few steps. And judging by the amount of blood on the ground, he must have even less time than I thought.

I glare at Khalil through a blur of tears. "Why?"

The djinn has the grace to look ashamed at what he has done. He almost looks as if he's going to be sick as he watches me struggle with Lucien's heavy frame. His hand goes to the collar at his throat. "I told you once, Ember, that I would do anything to be free. I meant it. Zilah has sworn to release me once she is queen."

My shoes slip on the gritty surface of the alley. I tuck my hands once more under Lucien's arms and pull with all my might, and still, he barely budges.

Although it kills me to say it, I realize I don't have any other option. "Please help me," I beg the two people who have destroyed everything. "I'll forfeit the crown to you, Zi, if you promise to help me get Lucien to Dad."

The corners of Zilah's lips pull up. "Khalil, go to them."

Khalil takes a step forward, his movements rigid as if he's fighting the magic binding him to Zilah. He freezes when he reaches us, waiting for the next command.

Lucien reaches up and touches my cheek with trembling fingers, leaving a smear of red behind. I crane my neck to look up into the face of a person I thought was my friend. "Please help me. There isn't much time."

"Khalil," Zilah orders from behind the djinn. "Raise the hand holding the gun and point it at Ember."

The muscle in Khalil's jaw clenches, but he does as Zilah says. He aims the barrel at my forehead, his knuckles turning white from how hard he's squeezing the grip. I close my eyes and wait for my sister's instructions to end me, but it never comes.

"You know what? Let's not be hasty. We are so close to the finish line after all," Zilah says, her voice almost bored. "Khalil, shoot the Guardian instead."

My heart stops. "No—Zilah please, no! Don't do this!"

"I'm sorry, Ember," Khalil whispers. He lowers the gun and fires a second bullet into Lucien's chest.

"NO!"

Lucien's body jerks as the bullet pierces his skin, and then lies still. His eyes, finally having found my face again, drift off into the space over my shoulder as one last breath rushes out of his lungs.

"How does it feel to have the person you love most ripped away from you?" Zilah asks, her voice a whisper. "Maybe now you'll understand the emptiness inside of me."

I wipe the blood from his lips and kiss him again in the vain hope that it will bring him back to me. If kisses had power, maybe mine would be enough to undo what Zilah had done.

My tears fall on his face, but he doesn't stir. Lucien—my Lucien—is gone.

Someone is screaming, and it takes me a moment to realize it's me. Thunder rumbles overhead as the clouds above Venice darken. Lightning shoots across the sky, and a cold wind picks up. My hands curl into claws, and I notice a white glow surrounding my fingers.

I don't think. I don't feel. I just act.

I direct my palms at Zilah and Khalil and watch in amazement as a white energy explodes out of my hands toward my enemies. I want to kill them for what they've done. I want them to suffer, to break, to feel the same agony that grips my heart. The white light knocks both of them into the wall on the far side of the canal. They fall into the water with a splash and disappear, stunned. I can only hope that they both drown.

Lucien's head lies cradled in my lap, his dark hair plastered to his skin by sweat and tears. I kiss his forehead, his nose, the space between his eyebrows that is as smooth as the rest of his skin now that he isn't alive to furrow them in worry for me.

Beneath my hands, his form begins to shift. I watch for the last time as he transforms into a crow. His fingers fade away into blue-black feathers as his face narrows into a beak. The only thing that remains the same are his dark eyes, empty of the light that once filled them with warmth.

I pull his tiny bird form into my arms and sob into his feathers, losing myself in grief, in shock, in pain. How could a night so wonderful become so dark and terrible?

"What do I do now?" I wonder aloud. The sirens that were once so far away sound as if they are just around the corner, and here I am kneeling in an alleyway, completely saturated in blood, cradling a dead bird in my arms.

A voice, rich and deep and ageless, echoes in my head with the answer. *Just remember that I will be here should you ever need me.*

In a daze, I somehow manage to go through the portal. I stumble across the length of the Underworld to the cave on the far side, all the while clutching Lucien to my chest. No guards try to stop me, but I can't bring myself to even care why that is.

I reach the forbidden door and wave my hand at the fence surrounding it. Once again, the white light flares out from the center of my palms. When the light fades away, the fence has melted to a low wall of smoldering metal points. I easily step over the remains and approach the door. The spells and runes carved into iron flash at me almost in warning, as if the magic put there to keep the Darkness inside knows what I'm about to do.

I pound my fist into the metal and rake my nails over the markings. Someway, somehow, the power flowing through me allows me to carve through the protective barriers so that when I reach for the handle and pull, the door cracks open with ease.

A cold wind whispers out of the opening as I pause.

I stare into the pitch black darkness awaiting me on the other side. What if this is a mistake? I have no idea who the Darkness really is. I glance over my shoulder at Dad's estate. Even with all of his power, Dad can't bring the dead back to life. Otherwise he would have brought Mom back to us.

Lucien's head tilts to the side to bump against my arm. For a split second, my heart leaps as the movement fills me with an insane hope. I quickly realize, though, that the movement was just a trick of gravity. Lucien is still dead—murdered by someone who I thought was my friend, someone who I thought I loved.

Just as the Darkness warned me.

There is only one person who can help me now.

Holding on tight to Lucien, I step into the dark and fall into nothingness.

26

Ember...

Everywhere is darkness, so deep and dark and ancient and cold that I can't remember where I end and it begins.

Ember...

It surrounds me, soft as velvet.

I sink into the darkness, down ever further, ever deeper. Just as I'm about to lose all sense of myself, it happens.

A tremor shudders through the nothingness, and a sensation of coldness rolls over me, lifting the hairs on my arms and neck and covering my skin in goosebumps. The cold dissipates as a reassuring presence cradles me under my knees and around my back. Whatever is lifting me reassures and calms me with its presence.

Ember...

A warm embrace, the barest touch of lips on mine.

"Lucien?"

A blanket of comfort darker than the space between the stars settles over me.

Although I cannot see where I am in the darkness, I know I'm falling up. The raw power here in the black is unfathomable. So much power—too much. It has built for so many years, and now the time has come for it—for him—to be free.

Ember... wake up.

I jolt awake—heart slamming into my ribs, screaming and thrashing before I realize I'm no longer falling. It takes a moment for my breathing to return to normal. And when it finally does, I push myself up on my elbows and look around.

I'm in a shallow cavern, lying on my back with my feet facing the door I stepped through earlier. While it's certainly dark in here, it's not an otherworldly dark like the strange dream I just had. That dark was almost *alive*. That dark had so much power that I nearly suffocated on it.

This is just regular, run-of-the-mill darkness.

"Luce?" I call out, but the only reply is the echo of my voice off the cave wall a few feet in the distance. Tears once more spring to my eyes as my throat swells shut in a painful knot. I scramble to my knees and search the floor with my hands. I must have slipped and hit my head when I stepped through the cave door, dropping his body as I fell.

How stupid can I be? Did I really think the thing that talked to me in my dreams would actually be a real being capable of helping me?

Obviously so.

And now look at me, crawling around in the dark on my hands and knees looking for a dead bird.

I stop and rest my head on my arms as a sob of frustration and hopelessness hits me square in the chest. So, *so* stupid.

Carefully, I get to my feet and make my way to the cavern door. A thin crack of light edges the frame. Perhaps if I open the door, enough light will flood in so I can find Lucien's body.

I hesitate as my fingers find the cold steel. What would I do once I found his body? Take it back to the Surface and bury him in the backyard like some kind of family pet that met an unfortunate end? Take it to Dad as proof of Zilah's misdeeds?

Would I even be able to handle seeing his poor, lifeless body once more?

Before I can compose myself enough to pull open the door, a shadow flits over the crack of light as if someone just walked by the exterior of the cave.

I pull open the door and peer outside. "Who's there?"

At first, I see nothing—the Underworld appears exactly how I left it when I entered the cave. Upon closer examination, though, there is something a bit different. A shadow, darker than the rest of the space around it, hovers just outside of the door. As soon as I notice the shadow, it fades, only to reappear a few feet further away.

I step out of the cave and take a deep breath. I glance back into the now illuminated space, mentally prepared for what I will find. Instead...disappointment, confusion, and relief cleave my heart into thirds when I find the cave completely empty. The furthest wall is less than ten feet from the doorway. The entire space is no bigger than my bedroom up on the Surface.

None of this makes sense.

Where is Lucien's body? Why do I remember falling if there isn't even a drop off? Why is the door so heavily spelled if there isn't anything in the cave?

I put a hand to my aching head. I don't know if I really did knock my head when I fell or if it's all the questions swimming around my brain, but I have one hell of a headache. I need to find Lucien's body so we can do *something* to put him to rest.

But that's kind of hard to do considering his body is nowhere to be found.

I turn back to the dark orb. It bobs in the air as if to make sure I'm paying attention before fading away and reappearing a bit further away. It reminds me of a will o' the wisp, but instead of light, it's made of shadows. It wants me to follow it, that much is sure. But where will it take me?

Because I don't know what else to do, I follow the wisp across the Underworld where it leads through Dad's gardens. Black and scarlet roses fill the space with an almost spicy fragrance, making my nose itch. The wisp leads me along the gravel-lined paths, around a fountain, to the stairs leading up to the back door of the chateau.

As I ascend the back steps, I realize for the first time how quiet it is. Usually there are sounds of Underworlders working in the ground floor offices or raised voices from the Pen. It's now eerily silent, like the whole Underworld is holding its breath.

"Where are you taking me?"

The wisp doesn't answer, of course. It just continues to appear, disappear, and reappear as it leads me through Dad's estate. I follow the shadowy being through the hallways, every open door revealing rooms as empty and silent as tombs. After some time, we end up in Dad's study—the same study where Zilah and I sat down and listened as Dad told us about the Tasks.

The wisp glides over to Dad's desk and hovers over something resting on top of the papers scattered there.

"Anyone home?" Someone has to be around here somewhere. I've never seen this place so empty before. "Dad?"

No one answers, so I slowly cross to the desk where the orb still silently levitates.

In the center of the desk is a dagger carved from white wood. I've never seen a weapon quite like it before. Carefully, I lift the knife with steady fingers. It's light but sharp enough that I know it'd draw blood if I slid my finger along the edge.

It's clear by the detailed carvings of roses and thorny vines along the guard that this dagger was craftily made, but why would anyone carve a knife out of wood?

The answer hits me like a slap to the face.

It's a wooden knife—wood can kill vampires.

My fingers curl around the hilt as the same white hot anger from before bubbles up in my chest. Zilah took everything away from me. She laughed as Khalil fired into Lucien's chest. She enjoyed ordering the death of my Guardian and seeing me helpless at her feet.

She murdered Lucien.

I stare into the flickering darkness of the wisp, revenge raging through me like a wildfire. "Take me to my sister."

Seemingly content with my decision to take the dagger, the wisp takes me to the back entrance into the Hall. Father has a secret passage built in his study that leads directly to the Hall—for emergency purposes. I step up to the bookshelves lining the far wall of the study and pull down the second book to the right on the third shelf down. The shelf swings out with ease, admitting us into a passageway that leads straight to the Hall. The passageway is dark and silent, just like the rest of the Underworld.

I follow the wisp, just a spot of darker darkness in the pitch black of the passage. I grip the dagger even tighter, adjusting my fingers to accommodate how sweaty my palms have become. As I gingerly make my way through the passage, something in the dark reaches out and touches my cheek.

I gasp and stagger back, the dagger a reassuring weight in my hand. "Who's there?"

No one answers, although I still feel something besides the wisp in the passageway with me.

I don't have time to waste figuring out what's in the shadowy passage with me. I'm in the Underworld—it could be any number of beasties. Instinctively, I turn to ask Lucien if he felt anything. A sharp pain claws at my heart as soon as I remember. I never realized how reassuring his presence by my side was until it was gone.

His overprotective shadow will never loom over me again. I'll never see him through a classroom window, perched outside in a tree as he keeps watch over me. I'll never see that sweet smile of his or feel his fingers lace through mine. I swallow the anguish that attempts to suffocate me and sidle along the wall for a few steps—just to be safe—and hurry after the wisp trailing ahead of me. We finally reach the door, and as my hand brushes the latch, I lose sight of the wisp. Spinning around, I stare down the dim passage, but the wisp is gone.

I breathe in deeply through my nose. "It looks like it's just me, then."

With the hand not holding the dagger, I pull the latch, and the door swings open—blinding me in the sudden burst of light from the other side. Just like with the second Task, the Hall is packed with Underworld citizens—maybe even more so than the second Task. Dad sits at the Obsidian Throne, glowering out into the crowd as he searches the faces there for me.

Zilah, looking resplendent in a gown composed entirely of gemstones, once again stands behind her chair on the floor beneath the HTF and our Dad. She doesn't look any worse for wear after I knocked her into the canal. Instead of gazing into the throng of onlookers, she only has eyes for the large clock on the opposite wall of the Hall. A smile graces her lips as the minute hand shifts, signally the beginning of the hour. It's only then as the clock's gears click into place that I realize how eerily quiet the cavern of monsters is.

"She isn't here, Father," Zilah announces, voice full of victory, as an ominous tolling fills the room. Her words sound like a shout through the silence of the Hall even though her voice isn't raised at all.

Dad lets out a breath and hangs his head, his hands curling into fists at his sides.

In any other situation, I might have cared what my father thought of me. But now my only thoughts are the wooden blade in my hand and the black, shriveled excuse for a heart my twin has in her chest. I shoulder past a centaur and a leprechaun, eyes trained on Lucien's murderer.

Zilch's cocky smiles drips right off her face as she spies me.

The din of several hundred voices rises as the Underworlders whisper to one another. My name echoes in the cavernous room as Dad stands up and addresses me. "Ember, your tardiness has almost cost you the throne. What is your excuse this time?"

I ignore him. Lucien's familiar face, those asymmetrical lips, that scarred eyebrow, those dark curls, and those bottomless eyes fill my thoughts as I take a step forward.

"Ember," Dad says, a dangerous tone undercutting his voice. "What is the meaning of this?"

I take another step toward Zilah.

"Ember!" Dad yells over the cacophony, and the voices cease as quickly as they began.

"Why don't you ask Zilah, Dad?"

I don't bother looking at him or any other members of the HTF. My eyes never leave Zilah's face as she stares down her elegant nose at me.

"She's the one who murdered Zaahir and sabotaged the second Task, after all. She's also the one that ordered the death of my Guardian just last night in an attempt to keep me from the third Task."

Dad's face blanches. "Zilah, is this true?"

"Of course not," my twin spits. "Ember is obviously unhinged."

"Don't you dare lie to him, Zilah!" I take a step up the stairs toward her. "Don't you *dare* lie to him."

Her ice-gray eyes narrow. "I have no idea what you're talking about."

I give up on hoping that she will change her ways and admit the horrible things she's done. The truth spills from my lips as fast as the words can form. "She used the djinn to spy on me.

This whole time she used him as an informant. This whole time, she's been scheming against me. I was never bound to the djinn—she was. She ordered him to obey me so I would never suspect anything. Then last night, she forced the djinn to murder Lucien. She commanded him to *kill* Lucien. All to keep me distracted from the Tasks."

The silence in the Hall is deafening. I'm almost positive everyone present can hear the pounding of my broken heart.

My voice cracks. "And then—and then when he was gone, I brought him back to the Underworld in his bird form. I didn't know what to do...so, I went to the only person I thought was powerful enough to help me bring him back."

"Oh, Ember." Dad shakes his head, slowly, sadly. "No one is that powerful."

"One person is," I argue, swallowing another sob.

"No one wields that kind of power."

I pause. "The Darkness does."

Once again, the silence of the Hall is so loud that my ears ache with it.

"Ember, what did you do?" Dad finally asks, his voice wavering.

"I did what I had to do!" I look down at my hands and notice that they're clean, any evidence of last night somehow washed away. I'm surprised to see that the bloodied dress I had worn in Venice was gone. The dress I wear now is as black as midnight with a hem that hits me just above the knees and skintight sleeves.

I have no explanation for this new outfit, but I can still vividly recall being covered in Lucien's blood. "I didn't know what else to do. I took Lucien's body to the cave. I broke the spells keeping the door shut and went in. I thought he could help me, but I guess I was wrong. Now it's up to me to set things right." I find Zilah's ice-gray gaze. "I hope this hurts."

I rush the last few steps and raise the dagger over my head, ready to plunge it into the porcelain pale flesh of my sister's chest. A scream explodes out of my throat. All of my grief, my rage, my pain flows through me and out of my mouth as I lunge at Zilah.

"Ember—no!"

Before I have a chance to stab the traitorous bitch in her icy heart, a wave of blue magic knocks into me and tosses me down the dais steps. I roll to a stop in the middle of the Hall floor and attempt to force air into my winded lungs. My side aches like someone is shoving a hot poker into my lungs with each breath, and I wonder if one of my ribs is broken. I ignore the pain and push myself to my feet. My whole body trembles, but I'm steady as I turn to face the dais again. It's only then that I realize I've dropped the dagger. My eyes scan the floor for my weapon. I have to finish the job. Zilah cannot live while Lucien is dead.

The twelve foot oaken doors at the other end of the Hall abruptly crash open, letting in a cold wind that sends chills across my skin.

I brush back the strands of my windswept hair and finally get a glimpse of who the latecomer is, and my heart skips a beat.

There, framed by the towering door, is Lucien.

27

My Guardian.

Alive and breathing.

Impossible.

I'm not even aware that I'm running toward him until I barrel into him and wrap my arms around his neck. A sound bursts from me—something between a sob and a laugh.

"You're alive!" I weep into his shoulder. His neck is warm as I press my face against his skin, and his arms feel so solid as they lock behind me. He doesn't quite smell the same as he usually does—instead of leather and detergent, he smells like a spice I can't quite put my finger on—but I don't care. "I thought I lost you," I whisper, gripping him tighter. I don't think I'll ever let go of him.

Just as that thought crosses my mind, I'm pulled out of his embrace—jerked back into the present quicker than waking from a dream by a vice-like grip on my arm. Dad tightens his hold on me and pulls me back another step. Fear and anger battle it out on his face as he puts himself in front of me. "Stay back," Dad growls at Lucien, his voice deadly soft. "Keep away from my daughter."

"Dad! What in the hell are you doing? Let go of me!"

I'm struggling to break free when Lucien starts to laugh, the sound of which is like nothing Lucien has ever made before. I stop trying to escape Dad's clutches and for the first time, I really look at my Guardian.

The man wears Lucien's face, Lucien's hair, and Lucien's dark eyes. He wears the same dark pants and charcoal gray dress shirt that Luce puts on everyday, and the sleeves are rolled up to his elbows like he does at home as well. His lips pull up at the corners exactly like I know them to do, and the laughter sounds just like Lucien's—but at the same time, it doesn't.

Everything is him, and yet, nothing is.

"Luce?"

The man smiles. It's the same smile I have cherished for so long, but it's not *my* Lucien's smile. "Ember."

I know that voice even though I've only ever heard it in my dreams. "You're not Lucien."

The man spreads out his arms, gesturing at his tall form. "Oh, but I am! I am Lucien, and Lucien is me. We are two sides of the same coin, after all."

I turn to my father, but he keeps his eyes trained on the man before us. "Dad, what is he talking about? Who is this person? Where's Lucien?"

"You know who I am, Ember." The stranger takes a step forward, his hand stretched out toward me as if he wishes me to take it. Dad edges us backward out of reach, and the man sighs. "Really, John? Are the theatrics really necessary? You do know I could take her if I wanted to, yes?"

"Over my dead body," Dad snarls.

"Enough of this!" I wrench my arm free and sidestep my father to face the stranger. I stare up into the face I've looked at a million times before, but the Lucien I know doesn't stare back. I ask the question that I think I already know the answer to. "Who are you *really*?"

The man raises his hand and brushes the back of his fingers across my cheek. "It's wonderful to finally meet you."

The last piece of the puzzle slips into place. My eyes widen in understanding. "The Darkness."

The man's mouth quirks up in a pleased grin, and he bows at the waist with a flourish of his hand. "In the flesh. Thanks to you, Princess."

"How?"

He adjusts the cuffs of his rolled up sleeves, seeming uncomfortable with the way it feels against his skin. "You've been so patient all these years. Could you wait a few more moments? I believe you have more pressing matters at hand."

"Years?" Dad interrupts, his voice harsh and full of denial. "That's not possible."

The Darkness ignores him. From nowhere, he procures the wooden dagger and offers it to me on upturned palms. "Your revenge awaits."

My eyes dart to the dagger, then back to his dark stare. "Tell me who you are. No more riddles."

"He is the very first Underworlder," Dad's voice says from behind me. "He's the oldest and most powerful of all the Underworlders to walk this earth."

The Darkness flashes a grin. "Oh, John. You're so kind to say so."

Dad's hand finds my arm again. "He is evil, Ember, *true* evil. Please listen to me. This *thing* is more dangerous than you know."

My brow furrows, as I recall my father's lesson outside the wendigo's cell all those years before. "There is no such thing as true evil. You taught me that."

Dad vehemently shakes his head. "He's different, Ember. He came before everything, even humans. He created each Underworlder and filled them with hate and corruption. His touch can turn even the most peaceful Underworlder into the most primal of beasts—like the chupacabra, like Bryce. He cannot be trusted."

"Now, Your Highness, why don't we let Ember decide that for herself? Now, if you'll excuse us—Ember, I believe this is yours." The Darkness offers me the knife once more.

My hand twitches towards him out of instinct. It's the hand I've held so often of late. I've traced every scar and line on that hand multiple times in the past week alone. I know it almost better than I know my own. My heart so desperately wants to go to him, but my head reminds me that he isn't my Lucien anymore.

"Don't do it, Ember," Dad warns. He, too, holds out his hand for me to take. "You have no idea how big of a mistake you've made this time."

My heart twinges at his words. "I guess that's all I'm good at, huh, Dad? Classic Ember—making another mistake yet again."

Dismay softens his features. "I didn't mean it like that, Ember. This man...he's—"

"This man has always believed in me. *He* has always been there, especially when you weren't. When you were too busy being a king to be a dad."

I've drawn my line in the sand. Aware of the hundreds of eyes on me, I step away from my father and take the dagger from the Darkness. It's warm against my palm as he gently wraps my fingers around the hilt of the blade.

He leans down to whisper in my ear. "Kill her, Ember. I can feel the hate in your veins. You want revenge for what she's done to you. You *deserve* revenge. She *deserves* to be punished."

He's right. I can feel it too, like a hundred thousand ants biting me from inside my body. I want to kill Zilah, to watch as her beautiful dress soaks up her life's blood. I want to be the one to make it happen, to stand over her as she takes her last breath.

Instead, I raise the dagger and level its point at the base of the Darkness' throat. "Where is Lucien?"

The man smiles again. "You've always surprised me, my little queen. That much will never change."

"Where is he?" The blade nicks his skin as I become more frantic. A single droplet of black blood wells under the dagger's tip.

The Darkness does not seem afraid. "I wasn't lying. He truly is a part of me. He's here within me. Or perhaps I am within him. Either way, we are one and the same."

"I—I don't understand."

"The king knows that I speak the truth. Ask him if you don't believe me."

I glance at my dad but keep the knife trained on the Darkness' throat. "What's he talking about?"

Dad's hazel eyes harden. I can tell that he's weighing just how much to tell me and what information will bring me back to his side. "He is the first and most powerful Underworlder to ever exist."

"So you said." I turn back to the man in front of me. My eyes rove over his smooth skin and young appearance, not quite believing what my Dad just revealed.

"The very first," the Darkness grins. He gestures to the space around us. "All of this? My creation. This 'Underworld' as you call it, was created by my hands, my magic."

Dad nods, confirming this information.

"But why create other Underworlders?" I ask, still not understanding what any of this has to do with Lucien. "Why bring them to the Surface?"

For the first time, the smile on the Darkness's borrowed face wavers. He regains control of his features quickly, though, using the pause to run a hand through his hair—a gesture so Lucien-like that I nearly fall to my knees. "It's really quite simple, Ember. Humanity had something I did not, so I decided that it would be best to just start fresh—a clean slate, if you will. A world of my own where I could rule supreme over all."

"What could humanity possibly have that you do not?"

His calm demeanor cracks, and he swats the knife out of my hands. It skids across the floor out of reach. "Love," the Darkness snarls, spitting out the word as if it was the most vile of curses. His lips lift to show his pointed canines. "They have *love*, Ember—something that I was seemingly incapable of possessing, as hard as I tried. So, I decided to kill them all. Every last one."

"He nearly succeeded at it, too," Dad says, face grim. "If it hadn't been for the first Lord of the Underworld—Ulrik was his name—it's very likely that he would have wiped humanity off of the face of the earth. But Ulrik gathered twelve brave souls to fight at his side against the Darkness that was tearing our world apart. The Darkness is truly immortal, for evil cannot die—but he could be imprisoned."

The Darkness regained his calm and devilish disposition once more while Dad spoke. "Little did they know that I had a trick up my sleeve. Did you know that it's possible to sever a soul in half? It's excruciating, but quite advantageous in the long run."

Dad's hand finds my shoulder and pulls me back. "It's only possible because of his immortality. Any other being would be killed if they tried. But he's right—Ulrik and his huntsmen didn't know soul-splitting was possible. Just before Ulrik was able to confine him, the Darkness broke his soul in two and sent part of it out into the world."

The Darkness scoffs. "Out of all of the Underworlders for my soul to latch onto, it attached to a simple crow. Talk about disappointing."

My heart leaps into my throat. "It was Lucien?"

"Well, like I said, it was just a simple crow at the time. My soul made him into the shapeshifting human form of Lucien you so dearly cherish."

Dad nods, once again establishing the Darkness's story as truth.

"Don't forget to tell her what you did to him, John," the Darkness adds, shaking a finger at him. "She should know the whole truth, after all."

"What do you mean?" I wonder aloud.

"They kept the poor thing locked up for centuries to be sure he wasn't still in cahoots with me," the Darkness explains. "They tortured him every which way to ensure that their big, bad villain was truly put away."

My heart squeezes tight. My poor Lucien.

Gentle fingers touch the back of my arm. "Ember, you don't understand what it was like. The death and the despair and the hopelessness and the carnage. We *had* to be sure."

"Fine. I get it. Sort of. But how did Lucien come to be my Guardian?"

"Lucien was free to go wherever he pleased after we ascertained that he was in no way connected to the other half of the Darkness's soul. As long as his physical form never rejoined the Darkness's soul and as long as you never fell for an Underworlder, the world would be safe." Dad takes a deep breath and shakes his head ever so slightly. "It has been almost six thousand years. I thought the threat of the Darkness's return was over. I thought he was finished, and I *never* thought the prophecy would have anything to do with his release."

The Darkness waves his hand, and every shadow in the room shudders. "Enough of this history lesson. All that matters is that I'm out, and I do think it's past time for me to take back my throne."

Before I even get a chance to open my mouth, he vanishes into the shadows at our feet and reappears before the Obsidian

Throne. He no longer wears Lucien's clothes. Now, the Darkness is dressed in an outfit woven from the shadows themselves. Tight-fitting dark pants lead into shiny black boots. The barest hint of silver embroiders the cuffs and neckline of his equally black shirt. His hands lift to adjust a crown of obsidian sitting atop his curls. The tips of his fingers are as black as his eyes, as if he dipped them in ink. He dusts off his immaculate shirt and seats himself on the throne. I watch in awe and horror as he curls his fingers around the arms of the throne and it begins to change.

The petals of Dad's obsidian roses sharpen into snarling faces and slashing claws. It becomes a monstrosity composed of hundreds of vicious Underworlders almost too terrible to behold.

"Ah, so much better," he says with a sigh as he lounges back in his seat. "Now, it's time to finish what I started all those years ago."

28

Armenius, just one chair to the right of the throne, seems to finally recover from his shock. He unsheathes his broadsword and raises it with a warrior's battle cry.

The Darkness vanishes into a wisp of shadow before Armenius can even begin to bring the sword down. The steel connects with the back of the throne—right where the Darkness' skull had been half a second earlier—and shatters into hundreds of shards.

Without so much as a pause, Armenius tosses the broken weapon away and turns to find the Darkness again. A low laugh reverberates through the Hall, seemingly coming from everywhere and nowhere at once.

"Now, now, now," the Darkness says as he reappears before a Jorogumo. "This certainly will not do. You are in my domain now, Huntsman."

He reaches out and presses one black-stained fingertip to the Jorogumo's forehead. I don't know this particular spider lady well, though I've seen her around the Underworld every now and again. She has always been polite and quiet when we've crossed paths. Dad told me once that she preferred the Surface, but came to Katja for spells to keep humans away from her cherry tree grove in the rural mountains of Japan.

But as soon as the Darkness' finger touches her skin, her entire demeanor changes. Her shocked expression morphs into one of horror as she scuttles back on the thin points of her spider legs. Glossy black hair falls into her face as she drops onto her abdomen and shrieks. The hard exoskeleton of her thorax skids across the black tiles as she struggles against her phantom attacker.

All of this takes only seconds, and then it's over. The Jorogumo gets back to her feet and lifts her head. Any humanity she may have had is gone. The lack of empathy in her face reminds me of the chupacabra in the McDonald's drive thru. My stomach flips over and drops to my feet. This is not going to end well.

The Jorogumo opens her mouth to reveal two rows of dagger sharp teeth in a mouth much too wide for her pale face and eyes black as pitch. She whips her head to where the HTF sits.

"No!" Dad cries from beside me. He throws up a hand and releases a flare of blue light from his palm, but the spider woman is too quick. She charges the HTF with yet another spine-tingling scream. Her long legs effortlessly carry her up the wall to the ceiling over where the HTF sits.

Cielo, the Italian who was erroneously blamed for Khalil's escape, doesn't move fast enough. The Jorogumo stabs through his stomach with one of her front legs. He yells and falls to his knees as Wil steps in to help him.

The Underworlders begin to panic. They surge toward the exits in an effort to escape the Darkness' poisonous touch. Even Zilah looks scared as she gathers up her skirts and makes her way to the secret passageway I entered through. They might be monsters, but the majority of them are not dangerous or even want to be.

But that doesn't even seem to matter once the Darkness touches them.

He vanishes and reappears beside a basilisk. The Darkness runs his fingers over the basilisk's wings and sends him to help the Jorogumo.

The Darkness disappears from that spot and appears at the back of the Hall where the main exit has bottlenecked in the frenzy to escape the room. He walks through the crowd with all the nonchalance of a man strolling through a city park, touching and turning every Underworld he passes by. He whistles as his hand alights on the shoulder of a patupaiarehe. As the normally docile forest spirit descends into madness, the Darkness catches my eye and winks.

Soon the Hall is in utter chaos. The HTF members are overwhelmed by the sheer number of black-eyed Under-worlders attacking them. Dad is yelling orders over the cacophony of screams and cries and other panicked noises, but they go unheard in the mayhem.

A crowd of fleeing Underworlders crashes into us, creating a wedge between me and my father.

"Dad!" I scan the masses for any sign of his salt and pepper hair or broad shoulders. Finally, I see him, but he's been pushed to the other side of the Hall.

"Ember!" He struggles against the horde, but it's impassable. I'm all alone in this mayhem. A yeti bumps into me, and I stumble. When I right myself, I'm almost to the dais again. I lift my head and watch with bone chilling dread as a tatzelwurm crawls up the wall, its six-inch talons digging into the rock wall like knives through warm butter.

Elowen, with Benny perched on her shoulder, is squaring off against a vampire named Maximillian, so she doesn't see the tatzelwurm coming up behind her. The tatzelwurm—a seven foot long creature with the body of a snake and the head of a cat that has a fatal bite and breathes poisonous fumes—sets its black eyes on her and roars.

"Elowen! Look out!"

I think I'm too late or that my voice is lost in the bedlam, but she knocks the vampire she's battling over the desk and turns just in time to prevent the tatzelwurm from pouncing on her back.

"Isn't it glorious?" The Darkness watches the chaos with a look of pure wonder on his face, as if he were a child at a circus show instead of a villain in a room full of deranged monsters.

He reaches out to touch my face again, but I jerk away. "Don't touch me."

"You don't have to worry, Princess. I wouldn't let any of these beasties hurt you. You are safe from everything in this room, including me."

I narrow my eyes. "What do you mean?"

He smiles. "My touch does not affect you. I do not know why, for I have corrupted many men and women before. But for some reason, my touch does not work on you."

"Please, you have to stop this."

His dark eyes glimmer darkly. "Stop what?"

I gesture at the insanity around us. "This! You have to stop it before anyone else gets hurt."

"Oh, Ember. Don't you see? This is what these monsters were *meant* to be. I've only just returned them to their natural state."

"Please," I beg.

The Darkness snaps his fingers, and every single Underworlder in the room goes completely still. The sound of heavy breathing from the HTF and Dad are the only noises in the whole Hall.

The Darkness takes my hand, his black-tipped fingers folding over mine. "For you, Ember, I'd do anything."

"Why? If you are incapable of love, why would you say that?"

"Don't you see, Princess? Lucien loves you and because he's once again part of me, I can feel it too. It's faint, but it's there. I severed my soul knowing the other half would someday find its way back to me, allowing me to be free once more. You just happened to be a pleasant surprise along the way. Thanks to you and Lucien, I will now have everything I've ever wanted."

"Then you don't have to do this! You don't have to kill anyone else now that you've gotten what you wanted."

The Darkness chuckles. "How innocent you are. You are the *only* one I feel anything for, Princess. The rest of the world will burn just as I've always planned."

"I don't want that," I say, my voice trembling. "I just want Lucien back."

"He's right here," the Darkness whispers. He puts my palm over his heart, and I can feel the steady beat of it against my hand. "I *am* Lucien."

I pull away. "No, you're not."

The Darkness sighs and crosses his arms. "You're right. I'm not him, but he is a part of me. I can hear his thoughts in my mind even now. It's really quite irksome to be completely honest."

My heart leaps up into my throat. If he can hear Lucien, if he can feel him...is it possible that Lucien could overpower him? If he could push back the Darkness and control their physical form—maybe, just maybe, we could separate them once more.

"Can I speak to him? Please, just for a moment."

His eyes flicker, and for the second time tonight, his lips pull down in a frown. The moment is fleeting, and soon the confident smirk returns. "Let's make a deal. You do something for me, and I'll let you talk to your crow."

"Ember," Dad's voice interrupts. He stands on the dais, making him visible over the crowd of frozen Underworlders. He has a cut on his cheek and above his eye, and he swipes away at the blood trickling down into his eyelashes. "Don't listen to him. He's lying about Lucien. I'm sorry, but Lucien is gone, and he isn't coming back."

"Ember?"

I know that voice.

I look up into eyes that are now the darkest brown instead of pure black. Lucien's eyes.

"Luce?"

"Ember, listen to me. I don't have much time before he forces me back. You cannot trust him. Don't listen to him. Just forget about me and save yourself."

Tears burn lines down my cheeks. "You know I can't do that."

"You must," Lucien tells me as he takes my face in his hands. "You must if you love me."

He presses a kiss to my forehead. Then my nose. Then my lips.

And I know in my heart that it's Lucien who kisses me at that moment. And I know that he means it as a goodbye.

When I open my eyes, Lucien is gone. The Darkness is back, and he smiles at me once again. "I told you that he's in here. And you can have him, every minute of every day. All I ask of you are two simple things."

"Tell me."

The Darkness drops to one knee on the black stone tiles. He takes one of my hands in his. "I will have no other but you, Ember. Marry me and become my queen as you were always meant to be."

"No!" Dad howls.

Now that I know Lucien is really in the Darkness' body, I feel even more certain about my plan. I believe in the love I have for my Guardian and his love for me. I believe that Lucien can overtake the body where his soul is locked away. I believe that together we can fight the Darkness. Together, we can accomplish anything. And if I have to become the Darkness' queen to save him, then so be it.

I raise my chin and straighten my shoulders. "I will."

The Darkness' smile stretches the widest it's been all night as he gets to his feet and looks around at the frozen Underworlders surrounding us. "She said yes, you fools. I think some celebration is due."

And just like that, the Hall breaks into applause. It just as suddenly ceases as the Underworlders revert back to their unmoving states. Chills crawl across my arms and down my back. He holds such power over the Underworlders. Far more than I've ever seen Dad have. "What's the second thing?"

"We'll have to plan the ceremony, of course, so that will take some time. I've also got quite a bit of your father's work to undo before the wedding. However, the second thing I ask of you, you can actually do right here, right now."

I clench my fists. "What is it?"

He gestures to the crowd of monsters, drawing my attention to a singular body weaving between the rigid Underworlders surrounding us.

My heart begins to hammer as I see what is coming toward us.

Or rather, *who* is.

Zilah shoulders through the last few Underworlders and out into the open space where the Darkness and I stand. Her movements are mechanical and stiff as she comes to a stop a few feet away.

"Zilah?"

The Darkness nods. "It's time to finish what you started."

"Wha—what do you mean?"

"I just want you to fulfill your heart's deepest desires." The shadows in the corners of the room stretch and shiver. The Darkness walks behind me and encircles me with his arms.

There in his hands is the wooden dagger. "If you want to talk to Lucien again, you have to kill your sister."

29

The Darkness makes it sound so easy.

And it *should* be easy. She murdered Lucien, after all. And even though we shared a womb, we have never been close to each other. It should be a piece of cake to just go up to her and stab the wooden dagger into her chest, especially since she can't fight back. It should be easy, yet I feel like the Darkness places Aremenius' five-pound broadsword in my hands instead of a piece of wood.

I just keep telling myself that she killed Lucien. If she hadn't done that, we wouldn't even be in this predicament to start with. She turned Khalil into a backstabbing informant. She nearly got me killed during the second Task. She's also tried to kill me a handful of times in the past. There's no denying she's an evil bitch. And if I kill her—I can get Luce back. Trading her life for his should be the easiest thing I do tonight.

In theory, that is.

The rancor from before is still there, bubbling just beneath the surface of my skin. Just minutes ago, I had rushed the steps with the intention of doing exactly what the Darkness just asked. But now that the Darkness is the one urging me forward, I'm starting to have doubts. Could I really kill my own sister? Is it really the right thing to do?

I adjust my right hand around the hilt of the dagger. It's been sanded and resined, so the grip is as smooth as glass.

"Ember, no! Don't listen to him—don't do it!" Dad shouts from where he stands. I'm honestly surprised he hasn't jumped down to physically stop me yet, but I see why when I look up at him. Two Underworlders—a yeti and a cyclops—are posted beside him, holding him back. He struggles between them, blue light flaring from his hands, but they hold fast.

My eyes blur as I make eye contact with my father. "I'm sorry, but I have to do this."

"No—Ember, no! She's your sister. You can't do this!"

I turn away from him and go to my twin. Zilah stands riveted to her spot, unable to move under the Darkness' hold on her. However, unlike nearly every other Underworlder in the Hall, her face doesn't appear as a blank slate. As I approach, one of her eyes twitches and the corner of her perfectly lipsticked mouth trembles. Her whole body appears stiff with tension as she watches me stride toward her.

I stop in front of her and glare into those cool gray eyes that have taunted and tortured me for so many years. "You brought this on yourself," I say, tightening my grip on the dagger. I place the point over her heart and prepare myself.

"I—didn't kill—Lucien."

My head jerks up. Her whisper was barely audible although I'm inches away and the Hall is quiet as a tomb. "What?"

"I didn't *want*—to kill him," Zilah hisses around her clenched teeth. "He—made me. The Darkness—corrupted me."

I don't believe her. For all I know, this is some last ditch effort to save her own skin. "How?"

"I followed you one night—you went to his cell in your sleep. He—tried to force me to open it after you left, but I couldn't. He still—somehow infected me."

I shake my head. "If that's true, then why did you try to sabotage the Tasks? I thought you wanted to win by the book?"

Zi grits her teeth, and I know that the answer is costing her. A tear squeezes out of the corner of her eye and down her porcelain white cheeks. "I was—afraid that you would win—without even trying. "

Her answer shocks me so much that I take a step back. My immortal, magical, merciless sister was afraid that I—an unremarkable, mortal human—would actually have beaten her at the Tasks had there been no interference. At first the thought seems crazy. Until a moment ago, I would have said Zilah didn't know what fear was. But the more I think about it, the more I think her fears might have been justified. Without the djinn side tracking me in the first Task and the disaster Bryce made of the second Task...I really might have won both.

The sound of her cruel laugh as Lucien lay dying in my arms echoes in my ears, reminding me of just how ruthless Zilah could be. Zilah didn't seem to fight the Darkness much if he really did have a hold on her. Even if she didn't want to kill Lucien, she still did it. An image of her silver eyes flashing black in the alleyway flashes through my mind. Just like Bryce's before he attacked. Just like the chupacabra.

The Darkness' voice rings out across the Hall, imploring me. "Come, Ember. We haven't got all night, darling."

"How are you resisting him now?" I ask, my voice hushed so that only Zilah can hear.

"I'm—part human—you idiot."

Well, that is certainly Zilah speaking, no doubt about that. Now I know for certain that this isn't some elaborate ruse the Darkness is trying to pull on me.

And that would also explain why she's able to fight against the Darkness' hold on Underworlders. The Darkness said he has corrupted humans in the past, but he can't control them—not like he can with Underworlders, anyway. And Zilah is only *half*-vampire.

"Tell me the truth—did you plan on killing Lucien in order to win the third Task?"

She blinks, squeezing her eyes shut. "No."

"What happened?"

"The Darkness gave me the bullet—he made me find the revolver. I never wanted to kill Lucien—but he made me *want* to. I could feel his corruption—eating at me. The Darkness ordered me to command Khalil to kill him. I'm sorry."

My eyes widen. In all of my seventeen years, I have *never* heard Zilah apologize to anyone about anything.

"Ember, please! Don't let him control you. You are better than this," Dad yells from where he's still being held captive. I bite the inside of my cheek hard enough to taste blood in my mouth.

"Silence him!" the Darkness snaps, his patience clearly fraying. The yeti obliges and covers Dad's mouth with a hand covered with white fur, but I can still hear Dad's muffled shouts.

A hand wraps around my arm and yanks me around. The black fingertips dig into my skin. "Why are you hesitating, darling?" the Darkness needles. The term of endearment makes my skin crawl. "Everything you want is at your feet—the sister who betrayed you, your lover, a chance to rule the world at my side. You need only do what your heart already desires."

"I don't know if I can."

"Of course you can! I sense *so* much power and potential in you, Ember. We will rule together over everything—the Underworld and the Surface. Together, we will be unstoppable! All you have to do is prove your worth."

I reach up and run my left thumb along Lucien's—the Darkness's cheek. My fingers continue up along his temple to push a stray curl out of his face. Those midnight sky eyes glint at me with amusement and curiosity, and while I know it isn't him, I know Lucien is watching, waiting to see what I will do.

"Only for always, Luce." I whisper, kissing him one last time. I can almost trick myself into believing that it's Lucien who's returning the kiss. Almost.

I break away first. With a triumphant smile, the Darkness turns me to face my sister once again. He adjusts the dagger in my hand and places it back where I had it before. Zi sucks in a deep breath as the point of the knife disappears into the fabric of her dress. She doesn't move, but Zi's gray eyes meet mine and hold on. She glances down, and I follow her line of sight to the small aqua-colored stone hanging from the silver chain elegantly circling her neck. I meet her eyes again, giving her the smallest of nods.

"This is for Lucien," I say before thrusting the dagger forward, burying it hilt-deep into Zilah's body.

Zilah grunts and hunches over, one hand going to the knife sheathed in her torso and the other going to her right pocket.

The Darkness claps ecstatically. "Well done, Ember! Well done! I always had faith in you."

His elation is quickly dashed as I step beside Zilah and reveal that the knife didn't go where he thought. I yank the knife out of Zilah's abdomen as she procures Khalil's stone out of her dress pocket. She drops his stone onto the floor, and a cloud of aqua smoke envelopes us.

"Khalil, take us to someplace safe," she orders. Her lips glisten with blood. The djinn appears behind us and takes hold of both of our shoulders.

As Khalil's mist swirls around us, I find Dad across the room. *I'll come back for you,* I mouth.

He nods. *I love you, kiddo.*

"No!" the Darkness howls. The lights in the room flicker as he lunges for us, but he's not quite quick enough to catch hold of us or to command Khalil to stop.

With a sensation like the floor being dropped out from beneath us, the djinn transports us away from the Hall, Dad, the Darkness, and Lucien.

30

I land hard in the hot sand and stagger forward onto my hands and knees. Zilah appears next to me in a less-than-graceful pile of skirts and limbs. An uncanny sense of deja vu hits me as I squint into the fierce sunlight. Khalil has brought us to the middle of the desert. Golden dunes stretch as far as the eye can see across the barren landscape.

Zilah gets to her feet with a colorful curse and sets about righting her dress. It's a lucky thing that vampires don't burn in the sunlight, otherwise there would be a Zilah-shaped ball of fire standing next to me right now.

"Ugh!" Zilah examines the slit in her dress where the knife plunged into her stomach. The skin there has already knitted back together, but the dress is completely ruined by the large bloodstain spreading out from the place where I stabbed her in the gut. "I didn't actually think you were going to stab me, Ember."

I get to my feet. "I had to make it look real, didn't I?"

"You ever hear of *acting*, you halfwit?"

I glare at her. In the light of the high sun, her silver hair looks almost gold. "Plus, you deserve at least that much."

She sniffs and crosses her arms over her chest.

"And you," I say, turning to the djinn. "If I had some iron right now, I just might do the same to you."

Khalil can't seem to meet my eyes. "I am so sorry, Princess."

"Why didn't you tell me?"

"You don't think I wanted to? I wanted so badly to say something, but Zilah forbade me from telling you anything about her plans. It killed me not to tell you."

I turn away from him as my arms wrap around my waist. My ribs throb from where I injured them falling down the steps in the Hall, but it's nothing compared to the ache in my chest. My heart hurts so much that it's hard to breathe. Twenty-four hours ago, I was the happiest person on the planet. I had it all. Everything was falling into place.

And now?

Lucien is trapped in a prison inside the Darkness' mind. We left Dad behind with the most dangerous Underworlder to ever exist, and the members of the HTF are either dead or trapped in the Underworld as well. We tricked the Darkness and escaped, which means he will most definitely be coming after us. With every Underworlder at his beck and call, how would we ever be safe from his clutches?

The world is about to get a whole lot scarier and darker, that much is sure. I face my unlikely companions again—a human, a half-vampire, and a djinn against the most powerful force to ever walk the earth.

Khalil shoves his hands in his pockets and breaks the awkward silence. "At least we have each other, right?"

I throw my head back and laugh.

I laugh so hard I fall into the sand as delirious giggles continue to spill out of me.

"She's completely cracked," Zilah mutters. Her tone tells me she actually expected this to happen sooner or later.

"I'm just trying to stay positive," Khalil grumbles.

"This is just great!" I wipe the tears that leaked from the corners of my eyes. "You two really are the cherry on top of this heaping pile of crap that is my life."

"Quit being so dramatic," Zilah snaps. "Get up. We need to come up with a plan to fix this."

I sit up. "Dramatic? You think I'm being *dramatic*, Zilah? It's your fault that any of this happened in the first place. It's your fault too, Khalil. Both of you did this! If you would have never tried to cheat during the first Task, none of this would have ever happened."

"Well, you're the one who made the prophecy come true, Ember," Zilah spits. "You couldn't keep it in your pants for one more day until the Tasks were over?"

The anger that ignites in my chest is so great that it explodes from my mouth as a scream and from my palms as a blaze of blinding white light. The light hits both Zilah and Khalil and knocks them ten feet into the air. They soar over the crest of the dune to land in a heap of limbs at the bottom.

I come back to my senses and stare at my hands as if they're grenades rather than just normal human appendages. "Holy cow."

Crawling to the crest of the dune, I peer down at the two Underworlders at the bottom, half expecting to find them burned to the crisp. That's not the case, thankfully, but they do look a little singed around the edges. "You guys okay?"

Khalil groans and flips over to check on his vampire master. "Yep. Just grand, thanks."

I slide down the dark side of the dune. "Why does that keep happening?"

Zilah coughs and bats aside Khalil's hand as he goes to help her up. "Your Affinity is manifesting, you dullard. Father thought you would've started showing it years ago, but I'm honestly not surprised it took you so long."

I ignore her insult and scrutinize the fronts and backs of my hands. The ring Lucien gave me glints in the light. "Affinity?"

Zilah rolls her eyes. "For the love of—Khalil, please explain it to her before my own head implodes from her overwhelming stupidity."

"As Lord of the Underworld, your father has the power to distribute Affinities to anyone he sees fit," Khalil explains. "I'm sure you know his Huntsmen were all imbued with Affinities to better help them against any Underworlder that they might face. Armenius' strength. Elowen's purple electricity. Your father gave you one too. It appears to be some sort of white light with telekinetic properties."

"When did Dad give this to me?"

Khalil shrugs and looks to Zilah for an answer. She rolls her eyes. "He gave it to you on our first birthday. I'm assuming that you were such a pathetic excuse for a mortal that he deemed it necessary to give you an Affinity to help keep you alive."

"It takes seventeen years to manifest?" I ask, taken aback. "That seems a bit inefficient."

Khalil clears his throat as Zilah laughs. "It's usually instantaneous," she says, voice heavy with disdain. "But as usual, you proved to be quite the disappointment."

I wave my hand at her, hoping I can blast her back up the dune, but nothing happens.

"It takes practice," Khalil says helpfully.

I glare at him. "Don't be nice to me, djinn. I haven't forgotten what you did."

His face falls, but he nods in understanding.

"But I don't hate you."

Khalil's face transforms, glowing with hope. I bite the inside of my cheek. "I get that you were forced to do the things you did. Both you and Zilah. But that doesn't make it any easier to get over the fact that you both betrayed me."

"I know."

"Seeing as how we are currently on the run, can we agree to pick this topic back up when we aren't in a scorching wasteland?"

"Agreed," Khalil says. "So, what do we do next?"

Zilah stands and brushes off her dress. The gemstones sewn into the fabric catch the sun's death rays and reflect them straight into my corneas. "Well, first we need to get out of this godforsaken desert. I'm getting sunburned."

Khalil gets to his feet as well and adjusts his cream-colored turban. "And then?"

I stretch my fingers out before clenching my hands into fists. Now that Zilah and Khalil have told me about my Affinity and its manifestation, I can feel the power building up inside of me, ready to be used again. My palms tingle, as if my hands are submerged in buckets of champagne.

I think my first hint of it was when I first met Khalil in the hospital when my hands tingled right before I socked him. I felt it again when he went berserk in front of the Huntsmen during the first Task, and it finally showed its true potential in Venice and again just now. I can practice it—hone it until I can use it at will. And when I have it perfected, we can go up against the Darkness. But we won't be able to do it alone.

"We need to forge our own HTF. We have to find people to help us fight the Darkness. He's too strong," I answer. "We'll need twelve people—humans with no hint of Underworlder blood. They're the only ones that can resist the Darkness's compulsion. Then we'll break into the Underworld and save Dad. Once we do that, he can bestow Affinities on our new HTF so that we actually have a chance when we face the Darkness again. We will break his soul in half once more, trap him in his hole, and make it so he can't ever get out again."

"Ember," Zilah begins, her voice tight. "There's no guarantee that we will be able to get Lucien back. You know that, right?"

I swallow the lump in my throat. "I know. But as long as there's a chance then that's good enough for me."

Zi nods. "I can't believe I'm saying this, but I agree with this plan of yours. It's a crapshoot, but I don't see any other way for us to save ourselves."

"Not to mention the whole world," Khalil adds. "You can guarantee that the Darkness will go after the Surface as soon as he can."

"And since we are the harbingers of the apocalypse, I do feel sort of morally obligated to save the world," I say, echoing what I told Khalil weeks ago. It rings truer now more than ever. He glances at me and gives me the barest hint of a smile.

I'm surprised to find myself smiling back.

The world as we know it may be coming to an end, my boyfriend may be trapped in the mind of the greatest psychopath to ever exist, and I may be stuck with the two people who helped make both of those things happen, but at least we have a plan.

And that's far more than I usually have when I walk into trouble.

The End of Book One

Acknowledgments

You made it this far, did you? If so, the first person I need to thank is YOU. Thank you to the farthest reaches of the Surface and the darkest depths of the Underworld. Thank you for choosing to join Ember on her journey, and it is my truest hope that you will want to jump onboard the second part of her story.

This book would not have been possible without the army of supporters that has cheered me on for the last six years. There are so many that I owe my thanks to. I just hope I don't leave anyone out.

To Wesley and Lorrin: you both have been with me since the very beginning. You've been there for every idea, every twist and turn, and every stubborn plot hole. Thank you for allowing me to pester you incessantly with questions and ideas. I love you, sibs.

To Cassidy: if not for you, I would have never found Bookstagram and the community of writers that have helped me shape this story into a book. Thank you for reading every single draft of OT and for always being willing to do it. And for talking me off the edge when I wanted to give up.

To my beta readers and my critique partners: Keira, Lina, Celia, Mary, Megan, Selina, Kirsten, and Laura...Thank you for all the hours and days you spent reading OT and for all of the ideas and critiques you have gifted me along the way. Your unwavering encouragement and never-ending kindness are what allowed me to get to where I am today.

To my editor: there are truly not enough words in existence to express how thankful I am for Camilla at Worlds of Whimsy. Your sharp eye, stalwart line editing, and proofreading skills are phenomenal. I thought that OT was done when I sent it to you (silly me), but your suggestions and edits have made this story a thousand times stronger than it once was. Thank you for every hour of hard work you invested in this story. The evidence of your excellence is seen in every line.

To my formatter: Selina, I'm so thankful for your guidance and your expertise every step of the way on this publishing journey. You answered all of my questions (all three thousand of them), and you always took time out of your day to make sure I understood the answer. My words look amazing thanks to you.

To my cover designer, Maria Spada: I am just so blown away by how stunning the cover is. You took the vague idea I had in mind and created something so beautiful out of it. Thank you so much for bringing OT to life!

To my Bookstagram tribe: there are too many of you wonderful humans to thank by name on these last few pages. There were so many days when I felt unworthy or unmotivated. There were several points along the way when I just wanted to burn the whole thing. But every like, every comment, every DM that I received convinced and encouraged me to keep going. I am continuously in awe of how amazing and supportive this tribe is.

To my family: thank you, mom and dad, for instilling a love for reading in me as a child and for always believing in me. Thank you to my grandparents for going out and buying my first ever laptop that I used to write the cringiest vampire love-triangle story that has ever existed. I've come a long way since then, and it's all thanks to that first brick of a laptop. Thank you to my beautiful, wonderful, darling children...who probably added a couple of years apiece to this book. I wouldn't trade either of you for anything.

To my husband, James: this is probably the only part of this book you will read. Thank you for telling me, "Just publish it already!" when I sat on the fence about it for weeks. I love you more than Galileo loved his stars.

About the Author

Rowan Wright is a Texan native who dreams of someday living in a place with all four seasons. When she's not writing (or procrastinating writing), Rowan teaches high school English and theatre in a rural town with more cows than people. She enjoys traveling, coffee, and true crime podcasts. Rowan currently lives in central Texas with her husband, two children, and her two black cats. You can find Rowan on Instagram: @authorrowanwright

www.ingramcontent.com/pod-product-compliance
Lightning Source LLC
LaVergne TN
LVHW041059080826
845145LV00007B/1633